ROTTERDAM

Fernsby's War Book 4

J.C. JARVIS

WHERRY ROAD PRESS

Get a FREE Book!

Before John Howard found sanctuary on the streets of Henry VIII's London, Andrew Cullane formed a small band of outlawed survivors called the Underlings. Discover their fight for life for free when you join J.C. Jarvis's newsletter at jcjarvis.com/cullane

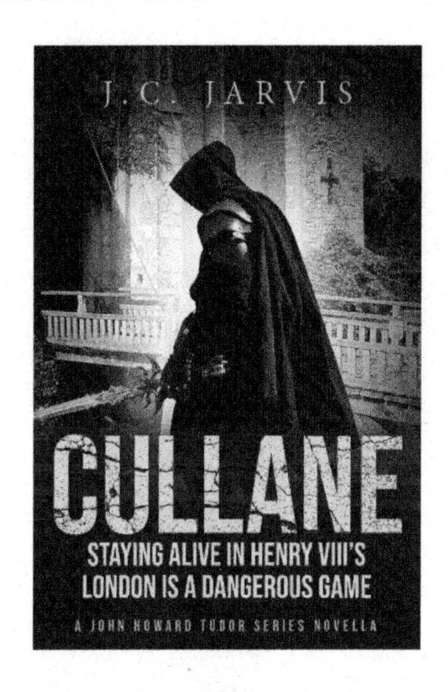

To my wife, Glenda, who is my biggest supporter and my bedrock. Without her support and encouragement none of this would ever have happened.

My editor, Melanie Underwood, who patiently and expertly wove her magic through the pages of the manuscript and turned it into the thrilling book you see today. The deft touch and the care she poured into each page has made the book far better than it could have ever been on its own.

My cover designer, Jane Dixon-Smith, who far exceeds my expectations with the masterpieces she creates every time we work together. Jane is a true master of her art, and I am extremely grateful to be able to work with her.

To our beloved daughter, Tiffany Lattimore, whose memory inspires us every day. Though she is no longer with us, her spirit and love continue to guide and uplift us. Tiffany's bright light and boundless joy remain in our hearts, providing the strength to carry on and find hope in every moment. This book is a testament to her enduring presence in our lives, and we dedicate it to her memory with all our love.

WHERRY ROAD PRESS

Rotterdam

ISBN: 979-8-9883912-6-5

Fernsby's War Series Book 4

Edited by https://melanieunderwood.co.uk/

Cover Design by http://www.jdsmith-design.com/

Foreword

Welcome to the fourth novel in the Fernsby's War Series, which continues to chart the harrowing yet heroic journey of Michael Fernsby through the tumultuous years of World War II.

Rotterdam delves into the intricacies of espionage and survival in a city on the brink of devastation. Michael's journey takes him into the heart of the Netherlands, where the shadow of the Nazi occupation looms large, and every step he takes could be his last.

As always, my commitment to historical accuracy remains unwavering. The events depicted in this novel, from the daily struggles of Rotterdam's citizens to the broader military operations, are rooted in thorough research. I aim to bring the era to life, not just through the grand events but also through the intimate, often painful experiences of those who lived through these trying times.

In keeping with the series' tradition, Rotterdam is written in British English, reflecting both the setting and the perspectives of the characters. This choice ensures consistency and authenticity in the language and idioms used by Michael and his compatriots.

Michael Fernsby's evolution from a naïve youth in Ryskamp to a seasoned agent is a testament to the resilience of the human spirit. His experiences in Rotterdam push him to new limits, both physically and emotionally. His memories and descriptions are intentionally personal and sometimes fragmented, mirroring the chaotic reality of war.

For instance, he frequently encounters vehicles and equipment that he describes based on his limited understanding and immediate impressions. One such vehicle, often referred to in his narrative, is the VW Kübelwagen. I've chosen to keep his descriptions true to his viewpoint, adding explanations where necessary to aid readers' understanding.

Real historical figures and events are portrayed with as much accuracy as possible. Any deviations are in service of the narrative and are minimal to preserve the integrity of the historical record.

I hope you find Michael Fernsby's experiences in Rotterdam as compelling and immersive as the previous books in the series. His journey is far from over, and each step he takes brings him closer to understanding the complexities of courage, loyalty, sacrifice, and love.

Enjoy the journey.

J.C. Jarvis

Rotterdam

By J.C. Jarvis

Chapter 1

Vucht, Belgium, January 10, 1940

Twenty-six-year-old Louise Desmet turned her face away from the icy winds ripping through the open fields as she trudged home from the marketplace. Her cheeks stung and her eyes watered against the icy assault, her head bowed as she clutched heavy sacks of produce tight against her body.

The coarse fabric bit into her numb fingers, and she cursed every step as she made her way down Vrankenstraat.

Her mind drifted to the tiny cottage at the end of the street that had sheltered her family for generations. Her husband, Georges, would have a roaring fire ready for her when she got home, and she thought longingly about the cosy evening they would spend together by the fireside.

This would be their last night together, at least for a while, because Georges had answered King Leopold III's call to arms, and enlisted in the Belgian army. He was leaving in the morning for who knows where, and the thought of never seeing him again tore her heart to shreds.

It was so cold that her breath felt like it froze in her chest. It hurt to breathe, so Louise pulled her scarf higher, the rough wool chafing her reddened skin as she tried in vain to shield her face. Her nose was running, and she could feel the snot smearing and freezing on her cheeks in the frigid morning air.

Vrankenstraat was deserted, which was no surprise, given the brutal winter they were experiencing. Nobody in their right mind would be out and about on a day like this.

What does that say about me, then?

Louise scoffed at herself. If this was to be her last night with her husband, then she was going to make it a memorable one, and at least make a dinner worth eating for once.

As she reached the cottage, she heard a muffled whine, faint at first, but growing louder by the second. With the early morning fog now lifted, she looked out towards the empty farmer's fields that stretched over a kilometre to the River Meuse and the border with Holland.

What is it?

Louise scanned the skies with rising panic. The pulsing, rhythmic sound of an aircraft engine filled her ears, and her heart hammered in her chest as the ugly rumours of German bombs and bloodshed flooded her mind.

Something wasn't right with the sound. The aircraft's engine sounded as if it was struggling, and as she searched the skies, she knew something was wrong.

There it is!

The plane looked like a fly buzzing around a bedroom, but as it got closer, the noise grew louder and the aircraft came into focus.

Louise was no expert, but she could tell that whatever it was, it was in trouble. The single-engine spluttered and struggled, and every time it cut out, the shape of the aircraft came further into focus as it dropped out of the sky at an alarming rate.

The engine spluttered one last time, and then it cut out completely. Louise watched in morbid fascination as the plane dropped like a stone, gravity's vicious grip snatching it from the sky.

The single-engine plane circled overhead as it dropped, the black swastika clearly visible on the rear tailpiece of what looked to Louise like a fighter plane of some kind.

Scared, she looked up to see if other planes were approaching, but the sky was still and silent. Whatever this aircraft was, it was here alone.

The German plane scraped the tops of the trees as it came down in the field at the end of Vrankenstraat. She watched in horror as the wheels hit the rough ground, and the plane bounced uncontrollably towards her.

Her jaw dropped open, all thoughts of the freezing weather now gone as the German plane veered between two Canadian poplar trees at speed.

The gap between the trees was not wide enough for the aircraft to go through, and Louise watched in fascination as both wings broke off as they smashed into the trees.

The grating sound of twisted, crumpled metal filled her ears with a melancholy sound she would never forget. The engine and propeller at the front tore away from the nose section, coming to a halt several feet away at the base of another tree.

What was left of the German aircraft came to a stop less than a hundred metres from where Louise stood. The sudden silence was deafening, and she was sure that whoever was inside must be dead.

She watched aghast as the top opened and a man, obviously the pilot, clambered out and jumped to the ground. Another man climbed down, but he took his time and looked awkward, as though perhaps injured.

Foregoing all thoughts of Nazi invasion, Louise dropped her sacks of produce and ran towards the injured man. Slipping and stumbling, she reached the two airmen, her chest heaving as she tried to make sense of what she'd just witnessed.

Words of comfort and aid froze on her numb lips as she stared into the haunted, wild-eyed face of the pilot, his features streaked with soot and blood. His mouth worked, soundless for a few terrifying heartbeats before he finally found his voice.

"Guten morgen, Fräulein," he began, his words an incongruous pleasantry amidst the smouldering wreck. "We've had a bit of trouble, it seems."

Chapter 2

Louise gaped at the two German airmen, momentarily frozen in place as her mind struggled to process the impossible scene before her. The pilot kept talking, but his rushed words washed over her head.

It wasn't the language barrier – as a language teacher, Louise understood every alarming word.

No, it was because two of the feared enemy that dominated the newspapers and radio broadcasts were standing right in front of her, speaking to her as though it was an everyday occurrence that an enemy aircraft fell out of the skies and landed in a neighbouring country's field.

The hairs on Louise's neck prickled. *Dear God, what was happening?*

"Are you deaf, woman?" The pilot's flushed face showed his rising agitation. "I need a telephone and directions to Cologne."

Louise opened her mouth, but before she could gather herself to reply, the other airman cut in. He was younger, taller, with an ugly, oozing gash above his hairline. He carried a bright yellow pigskin briefcase in his right hand, which stood out in the mid-morning gloom like a spotlight in a darkened room.

"Are you sure we're still in Germany?" The passenger rounded on his companion with a snarl. "You said yourself that you were lost. We could be anywhere."

The pilot jabbed a finger eastward. "The Rhine's right over there! We're in Holland, you imbecile, just over the border. Do not insult me, Major Reinberger."

"She clearly doesn't understand German," Reinberger snapped. "You don't have a clue where we are, do you?"

The major looked to be nearing forty, but it was difficult to read his expression beyond the pain and... fear? Anger?

Perhaps a bit of both, she thought.

Reinberger turned to Louise, enunciating each English word carefully as if she were deaf or dull-witted. "You. Speak. English?"

Louise gave a slow nod. *Better to play ignorant with the Germans for now.* "Yes, I speak English." She gestured to his head. "And you need medical attention. That wound—"

"Never mind that," Reinberger snapped. "Just tell us. Where are we?"

"Vucht. It's a village in Belgium."

The colour drained from the major's face, only to rush back in a mottled tide of crimson. "Belgium?" He whirled on the pilot. "You idiot, Hoenmanns. We're in Belgium!"

"I heard that," the pilot snapped back. "That's impossible. The Rhine is right there, and I know I wasn't that far off course."

"What's that river called?" Reinberger demanded of Louise in his broken English. "The one there, just to the east?"

"It's not the Rhine. It's the Meuse." Louise hesitated, then added, "Holland's on the far bank."

Let them think she was a simple village girl, barely able to mumble a few words of English. Best not to reveal her fluency.

Not yet.

If looks could kill, Reinberger's glare would have struck Hoenmanns dead on the spot. "The Meuse, you trottel! It's not the Rhine. It's a wonder you can find your way to the toilet, never mind navigate a plane!"

Hoenmanns blustered and harrumphed, but Louise could see the truth dawning in his eyes. He knew how badly he'd blundered.

"That's impossible," the pilot answered, but the look on his face told a different story.

The two Germans descended into a barrage of furious argument, seemingly forgetting Louise was even there. She used the chance to study them; Hoenmanns looked to be at least fifty, his craggy face streaked with blood but otherwise unscathed. And Reinberger... What was he trying to hide in that ridiculous yellow briefcase?

"Please," Louise spoke up during a lull in their arguments. "You have a nasty gash on your head that needs attention. I need to get you to a doctor so he can look at it."

"No." Reinberger's refusal was flat and final. He clutched the case tighter. "I have to get back to Germany. Now."

Clearly, Louise's help was neither needed nor wanted. She took a tentative step back, grasping for an excuse to slip away and summon the authorities. She'd let them deal with these arrogant Nazis.

The two Germans continued arguing as Louise backed away. The sound of an approaching vehicle made them stop, and she was glad someone was coming to help.

Two men in border guard uniforms ran over the field

towards the shattered aircraft and the two German airmen.

"Distract them, Hoenmanns!" Reinberger clutched his briefcase and ran towards a copse of trees.

Hoenmanns flew at the border guards, windmilling his arms and spewing rapid-fire German. He was putting on quite the show.

Louise watched the drama unfold, and her stomach clenched as she watched Reinberger pull a wad of papers from the briefcase and attempt to set them alight with his lighter.

"Stop him." She grabbed the arm of one of the border guards. "He's got some kind of invasion plans. For Belgium! He's going to burn them, so they don't get into enemy hands."

Louise looked at the two stunned border guards. "We're the enemy, so stop him!"

Louise turned to Hoenmanns and spoke to him in flawless German. "I understood every word you said."

The pilot goggled at her, his mouth opening and closing like a landed trout. Shouts and crashes broke out in the copse as a border guard tackled Reinberger to the ground.

Louise stood rooted to the spot, her heart hammering wildly. What in God's name was about to happen to her beautiful homeland? And her beloved Georges?

Whatever the full truth of Reinberger's ominous papers, one thing was terribly, irrevocably clear. The German invasion was coming, and all of Belgium would soon be plunged into the flames of war.

Chapter 3

Louise watched with her heart in her throat as one guard stayed with Hoenmanns while the other fought with Reinberger. Acrid smoke stung her nostrils, the crackle of burning paper unnaturally loud in the frigid morning air.

After a brief, violent scuffle punctuated by shouting and the unmistakable thud of fists on flesh, the guard emerged from the trees, hauling a struggling Reinberger with him. He thrust the yellow case at his comrade and shoved his prisoner roughly towards the waiting vehicle.

"You're to come with us, miss." The guard's tone demanded no argument. "What you overheard could prove vital to the security of Belgium."

Numb, Louise clambered into the front seat. As the vehicle bumped and bounced over the uneven road, the Germans spat curses from the rear.

Her mind whirled from the things she'd heard. If they were true, if war really was imminent, what would become of her beloved homeland? Of all the brave Belgian men like Georges?

The drive to the tiny, nondescript border post took

mere minutes, but each one felt like a small eternity. Louise soon found herself ensconced in a cramped, dingy interview room, clutching a mug of tea as she perched on a hard wooden chair. She strained to make out the voices filtering in from nearby.

Raised German voices, the scrape of furniture, a sharply barked order. What in heaven's name was going on out there?

Propelled by nerves and morbid curiosity, Louise set down her mug and crept to the door, easing it open. Barely controlled chaos greeted her in the narrow corridor. Two stony-faced guards were manhandling a red-faced, furiously blustering Hoenmanns into the adjacent room, deaf to his protests.

"Try that again, and you'll be pissing in a chamber pot," one of the guards snarled. "No more clever escape attempts!"

Hoenmanns shot Louise a look of pure venom as he disappeared from view. She ignored the Nazi, turned away – and froze. There, through the doorway opposite, Reinberger knelt on the floor, cradling his right hand against his chest as he rocked back and forth.

Two guards were gingerly extracting charred scraps of paper from the potbellied stove with the aid of a poker and fire tongs. One swore colourfully as an edge crumbled away to ash at his touch.

Reinberger must have burned himself trying to destroy his documents, Louise realised with a surge of bile. The mad fool...

And then Reinberger surged to his feet with a strangled roar and lunged at the captain, scrabbling for his holstered revolver with his one good hand. Louise gasped, certain she was about to see him shot dead before her eyes, but the captain knocked him to the ground with a single blow to the head.

"Have you lost your mind?" he bellowed down at the sobbing major, colour high in his cheeks. "Do that again, and I will shoot you myself."

"Then do it!" Reinberger's voice cracked. "Please, I beg you, let me die now, by my own hand. If I go back..." He trailed off into hitching, wretched gulps for air. "They'll execute me for this failure."

Visibly rattled, the captain snatched up the pile of half-burned documents. "Come with me, please, miss," he said as he strode past Louise. His tone was harsh as he battled to regain his composure.

She scurried after him on legs that trembled beneath her, but he paused on the threshold, calling back to his men. "Get them separated and secured. Intelligence will be here within the hour, and I want them in one piece when they arrive."

He led Louise to a small break room containing a few dented filing cabinets and a scarred wooden table. Someone pressed a fresh mug of tea into her hands and a tin of biscuits.

"Half the town saw that plane go down," the captain said as he settled opposite her, looking nearly as wrung out as she was. "I sent a man to find your husband. It seems he was out looking for you because they found him at the wreckage asking everyone who was there if they'd seen you."

A half smile touched the captain's careworn face. "He's waiting for you at home. He knows you're safe."

"Thank you," Louise croaked, the lump in her throat restricting her breathing. The biscuit crumbs turned to ashes on her tongue.

It felt like hours before a well-dressed, intense man in a

dark suit arrived and introduced himself as Captain Rodrique of Belgian Intelligence. He set a pad of paper and a pen on the table between them and looked her in the eyes.

"I'm told you speak German, miss? That you understood everything those two in there were saying?"

"Yes, I'm a language teacher."

"Good. That's good." He tapped the pad with his index finger. "I need you to write it all down for me. Every word you can remember."

Louise picked up the pen with a hand that she willed not to shake. Slowly, painstakingly, she began to write, the horror of it hitting her afresh as she relived those snatched exchanges.

The men were flying from Munster to Cologne. The pilot was visiting his wife and the passenger, Major Reinberger, was headed to a meeting to discuss the invasion of Holland and Belgium, which, according to Reinberger, was set to happen a few days from now.

Reinberger was carrying the plans for the invasion, or at least his part of it, which was to land paratroopers in Belgium ahead of the invading German army.

The fog was thick and heavy, and the pilot lost his way. He mistook the Meuse for the Rhine, and when they ran out of fuel, he landed in Vucht, Belgium.

The two men argued over the documents, with the pilot stating that he wouldn't have agreed to fly him if he'd known what he was carrying. Reinberger retorted that he wouldn't have agreed to the flight had he known how incompetent the pilot was.

The two men almost came to blows, and it was only the arrival of the border guards that prevented it from happening.

Louise Desmet

January 10, 1940

Louise pushed the pad to Captain Rodrique, who read it carefully.

Rodrique scanned the page, his face like stone. After a long moment, he looked up, meeting her gaze.

"This tracks what we found in the passenger's briefcase. The invasion is coming. Soon."

He reached across and covered her hand with his. "You may well have just saved countless Belgian lives, Miss Desmet. This information... His Majesty will hear of what you've done today."

Louise blushed. "Thank you, Captain, but I didn't do anything other than listen to two men arguing. It's hardly a gallant act, especially when you consider what our brave soldiers are going to be facing in the coming days."

"You stood up to the Nazi menace. You kept your head and used your gifts to gather vital intelligence for Belgium. For all the Low Countries." Rodrique's eyes blazed with conviction. "Never doubt your courage, Miss Desmet. I pray that you and your family remain safe."

With tears in her eyes, Louise rose to her feet. "And the same to you and all your men. May God bless Belgium, Holland, France, and all their people in the coming days."

Louise ran from the guardhouse to her husband with a renewed sense of imminent loss.

Chapter 4

Major Tony Sanders swung his legs over the side of the bed, rubbed his eyes, and sat up. The luminous dial on his watch told him it was 3.45 am, which was way too early to be getting up.

He briefly considered lying down again, but the sickness in his gut about what lay ahead kept him from sleeping.

As the head of Unit 317, the operational division of Britain's Secret Intelligence Service that carried out clandestine missions behind enemy lines, Tony had a lot to worry about.

Nothing bothered him more than the guilt he felt every time he sent one of his agents on what was, essentially, a suicide mission. It was only because of their courage and resourcefulness that any of them ever made it back, which, surprisingly, a great many did.

The phony war had kept 317's missions to a minimum, but ever since the invasion of Poland four months earlier, Sanders had managed to keep most of his agents out of harm's way.

Some of them not on active duties were in the Scottish Highlands, training in all manners of covert skills designed to enhance their chances of success behind enemy lines.

Led by 317's senior agent, Captain Richard Keene, a stately home tucked away from prying eyes had been requisitioned to train intelligence operatives in the art of clandestine warfare.

Every branch of the services sent attendees, and from the feedback Tony had received, the training had proven to be popular with everyone who attended.

He poured himself a cup of hot tea and wondered how the youngest and most resilient agent of them all, Michael Fernsby, was doing in the bleak Scottish winter.

Fernsby had not long returned from the most important and successful mission the unit had ever undertaken, and how he'd pulled it off, Sanders would never know.

Fernsby had somehow entered Berlin, and with the help of a German resistance unit, had stolen highly secretive U-boat strategy plans from under the noses of the Kriegsmarine's hierarchy.

On his return at the end of November, the U-boat plans had been passed to the admiralty and the Government Code and Cypher School, or GC&CS, an ultra-secret facility working out of Bletchley Park, whose job was to monitor and decipher enemy transmissions amongst other things unknown to Sanders.

Fernsby suffered painful but superficial injuries on the mission, and he'd been sent to Scotland primarily for some R&R, but Fernsby being Fernsby, it hadn't taken long before he'd become actively engaged in the training.

Tony marvelled at Fernsby's dedication and resilience. Despite the harrowing nature of his missions, the young captain always managed to bounce back, ready to serve his country once more.

Sanders couldn't help but feel a sense of pride in the man Fernsby had become, even as he worried about the toll these missions might take on him in the long run.

Sitting at his rickety kitchen table, Tony's eyes settled on a framed photograph of his beloved Martha and himself in happier times. The memory of the image tore at his heartstrings.

His breath hitched as the memory of the image once again threatened to break him. It had been taken just a few days before they were due to visit Martha's parents in Surrey, where he'd planned to ask for their daughter's hand in marriage.

They never made the trip because a delivery truck didn't see her crossing the road. Martha died instantly, taking a large part of Tony's soul with her.

Since then, he'd dedicated himself to his career, and at thirty-eight years of age, he'd done well for himself. Most people assumed he was younger than he was, but his youthful looks were fading from the sleepless nights and countless nightmares he suffered as the casualties grew.

He stared at his reflection in the mirror as he shaved, baulking at the deep black lines underneath his eyes. His mother's favourite saying popped into his mind: You've got bags under your eyes like travelling trunks!

He smiled at the memory of his beloved mother, who passed away from cancer just two weeks after Martha died. The loss of the two most important women in his life had left an indelible scar, and it was a wound that time had yet to heal.

Glancing at his watch, Tony pulled himself together. He had a train to catch, and Dansey's telephone call the day before had left him both nervous and intrigued.

For one, today was a Saturday, and unless it was incredibly urgent, no meetings were ever scheduled over a week-end. Further, the meeting was to be held at Bletchley Park.

The last time he'd been there was for a meeting with Winston Churchill, when he'd been directed to send one of his operatives, Michael Fernsby, on the suicide mission to steal the German navy's U-boat secrets.

He dressed and checked himself one last time before locking the flat behind him. He had a train to catch for what was sure to be a meeting of major importance to the security of Great Britain.

As he stepped out into the crisp morning air, Tony couldn't shake the feeling that this meeting would change the course of the war, and the lives of his agents, forever.

The fate of the nation, and perhaps the world, rested on the decisions that would be made at Bletchley Park this day. With a deep breath, he set off towards the train station, his mind racing with the possibilities of what lay ahead.

Chapter 5

The security at Bletchley Park was intense. Even at the weekend, people in and out of uniform scurried around looking like the weight of the world was on their shoulders.

Tony Sanders shrugged. *Perhaps it is for all I know.*

Men with clipboards checked his ID against their rosters at several different checkpoints. Sanders was convinced that Bletchley Park was the most secure location in Britain, even more so than the War Rooms and other sensitive places he'd visited recently.

After waiting for his clearance, Sanders was escorted to the same hut where he'd famously met Winston Churchill back in September.

He felt a twinge of disappointment upon realising that Churchill wasn't present at this meeting, but as he was introduced to the men impatiently waiting for him, his eyes fell on the one man he hadn't met before.

"Tony, glad you could join us," Claude Dansey said sarcastically as he entered.

Dansey, or Colonel Z, as he preferred to be known, was the deputy chief of SIS, and as Unit 317 fell under the auspices of Section V, SIS, he was the man Sanders reported to.

"Sorry I'm late, sir. I was held up at the gate while they checked my clearance."

Sanders headed for the only empty chair around the circular table. Dansey sat to his right, while to his left sat Alastair Denniston, the Scottish head of GC&CS.

"Major Sanders," Denniston nodded as he sat down. "May I introduce Sir James Baker? He's the Permanent Under-Secretary of State for Foreign Affairs, and as such, he is here on behalf of the government."

Sanders reached forward to shake hands with the under-secretary, who appeared to be in his fifties and was dressed as though he'd just walked out of Savile Row.

Somewhere in his forties, Sir James Baker sat ramrod straight, and it appeared to Tony as if he was trying to assert his authority on the men gathered around the table. With Dansey and Denniston, he knew that wasn't going to work.

Baker's dark hair had a few silver threads showing through, and he held Tony's gaze with his dark brown eyes and a look that demonstrated his sense of aristocratic superiority.

"Good morning, Major. I've heard lots of stories about Unit 317, and I'm glad to have you on our side."

Baker's voice confirmed Tony's suspicions. This man came from an aristocratic family, and he was probably titled in some way. Positions like the one he held were normally occupied by the Old Boys Club, so it was no surprise.

"Good morning, Sir James. I'm glad to be of help."

Neither Dansey nor Denniston looked impressed, and Dansey cleared his throat. "Let's get on with it, shall we?"

The secretary sitting at the back of the room to take notes indicated she was ready.

Alastair Denniston passed copies of a document around to everyone present. "Colonel Z knows about this, but you two don't. Read it and get up to speed on the current situation."

TOP SECRET – EYES ONLY

From: GC&CS, Bletchley Park

CC: Sir James Baker, Tony Sanders, Claude Dansey

Subject: German Aircraft Crash in Belgium – Intelligence Update

Date: 20 January 1940

Summary:

On the morning of 10 January 1940, a German Messerschmitt Bf 108 crash landed near the village of Vucht, Belgium, close to the Dutch border. The plane contained a Luftwaffe pilot and a passenger, Major Helmuth Reinberger, who was carrying sensitive documents related to the impending German invasion of the Low Countries.

The plane left Munster and was headed for Cologne, where Major Reinberger was to present his plans for the use of paratroopers in advance of the main invasion force.

The pilot lost his way in dense fog, and after mistaking the Meuse for the Rhine, crash landed in a field after running out of fuel.

Key Points:

Louise Desmet, a local Belgian woman fluent in German, was present at the crash site. She overheard the two Germans arguing, with Major Reinberger berating the pilot for landing them in Belgium instead of Germany and revealing that the documents contained invasion plans. Miss Desmet's account corroborates the physical evidence retrieved.

Reinberger attempted to destroy the documents before being apprehended by Belgian border guards. However, enough material survived for Belgian intelligence to piece together the outline of the German plan.

Analysis indicates the German attack was meant to commence on

January 17. As of today, January 20, no offensive has begun. The delay may be attributable to poor weather, but a more likely explanation is that the German High Command postponed the invasion after realising their plans had been compromised by the plane crash and Reinberger's capture.

Miss Desmet's eyewitness testimony, combined with the partial documents retrieved from the crash site, paint an alarming picture of advanced German preparations for an attack through Belgium and Holland. The information she provided may have bought the Allies precious time to bolster our defences.

Conclusion:

While a German invasion of the Low Countries still appears imminent, the plane crash near Vucht and the subsequent intelligence windfall it provided have likely delayed the German timetable and afforded us a vital window to prepare.

We should move quickly to exploit this opportunity and ensure that any German thrust into Belgium and Holland meets fierce Allied resistance from the outset. Miss Desmet's courage under pressure and her clever handling of the situation should be commended.

Sanders quickly digested the contents of the memo. Although not surprised, as the invasion of the Western countries had been expected for a while, his entire being groaned as he realised that Britain's real war was about to start.

Millions would die, and for what? The thought weighed heavily on his mind as he considered the immense responsibility that lay ahead for him and his team.

"I knew most of this," Sir James Baker announced in his well-heeled, upper-class accent. "The PM has been pushing King Leopold to allow the BEF into Belgium along with French forces so we can stop the German advance before it gets very far."

"What is the likelihood of that happening?" Denniston asked.

"Not much," Baker answered. "The Belgians are keen to remain neutral as long as possible, and who can blame them? If they allowed the British Expeditionary Force and French troops to enter their territory, it would signal to the Germans that they're willing to fight. That's the last thing they want to happen."

"There's been a lot of radio chatter since the incident," Denniston said. "So far, we've been unable to decipher what they're saying, but there has been a noticeable uptick in communications to the German troops massed on the Western Front."

"Are there any indications they are about to attack?" Baker asked.

Denniston shook his head. "Not from what we can see. We need more information from the ground, and that's why we're having this meeting this morning."

"Most of us, anyway," Dansey muttered, aiming his ire at the bureaucrat, the likes of which he despised.

"What do you require from Unit 317?" Tony Sanders asked, speaking for the first time.

"We need information, and we need it fast," Dansey said. "I intend to use the SIS assets we have in Holland to set up a meeting with a well-connected minister who has close relations with SIS, as well as high-level interactions with Dutch intelligence and the growing resistance movement."

"Who might that be?" Baker asked.

"Wilhelm Zobart, the Dutch Minister for Maritime Affairs. He has diplomatic cover, so he is free to move around as much as he likes without raising any alarms. As I said, he is well connected with both our and Dutch intelligence, and he has contact with the Germans. If anyone can tell us what's going on, it's Zobart."

"Are we sure he's not a double agent?" Denniston asked.

"As sure as we can be," Dansey answered. "He's never given any indication of being a double agent, and we have no reason to believe he's about to be turned."

"That sounds like a good plan," Sanders said. "Where does my unit come into this? This sounds more like a job for MI6 and the people already in position over there, not Unit 317."

"Normally I would agree," Dansey said. "But the position in the Netherlands is unstable, as you can imagine. I want you there in case something goes wrong, and my people need immediate evacuation. Getting people out is your speciality so, while your men won't be directly involved in the meeting, I want them on standby in case it goes pear-shaped."

Sanders nodded. "Consider it done."

Dansey leant forward in his chair. "We know that members of the German Abwehr have been infiltrating Dutch and Belgian cities, posing as travellers, salesmen, diplomats and the like to get a feel of the political landscape, as well as detailed plans of military and naval installations."

Finally, something his department could get their teeth into. The prospect of countering German intelligence operatives on foreign soil was exactly the kind of challenge he and his team thrived on.

"They're attempting to set up networks of collaborators and spies, as well as establishing lines of communication with Germany," Dansey continued. "We need you to find out who they are, where they are, and be ready to stop them when the moment arrives. This operation gives you the perfect cover to scope that out while my people set up the meeting with Zobart."

"When is all this going to take place?" Baker asked.

"As soon as possible," Dansey replied. "I'll get my people on it right away, and I'll let you know. It shouldn't take long, and we could get it done before next weekend if we move quickly."

"I'll make sure we monitor the radio frequencies, especially as it pertains to the Low Countries," Denniston said. "I'll let you know if we come up with anything."

"Where will this meeting take place?" Baker asked.

Dansey looked over his glasses at Baker.

"Rotterdam."

Sanders felt a sense of anticipation mixed with apprehension. The stakes were higher than ever, and the fate of nations hung in the balance.

As he left the meeting, his mind raced with the preparations he'd need to make to ensure his team was ready for whatever lay ahead. The clock was ticking, and there was no room for error.

He mentally ran through the list of his best agents, considering who would be most suited for this delicate operation. Captain Fernsby, fresh from his successful mission in Berlin, would undoubtedly be eager to get back into the field.

But Sanders worried about pushing the young man too hard, too soon. He'd need to carefully assess Fernsby's readiness before making a final decision.

Chapter 6

The freezing sea air seared Michael Fernsby's lungs as he pushed himself to the limit, his feet pounding the ice-covered, rock-hard ground. At nineteen, he was no stranger to the gruelling ten-mile race known as the Gaelic Grind at the culmination of the three-week covert warfare training course in the remote Scottish Highlands.

Not officially a part of the training intake, which accepted both officers and other ranks from all branches of the services, Michael had nevertheless joined in with as many of the training sessions as possible.

The brainchild of Tony Sanders, the young enigmatic boss of Unit 317, the EET training course - short for Endurance Escape Training - had been given the all-clear by the PM himself.

After searching for a suitable location, the remote locale of Mallaig, a rugged jewel nestled along the Sea of Hebrides, had been handpicked for its remoteness and breathtaking beauty along Scotland's west coast.

Captain Richard Keene, Unit 317's senior and most experienced agent, took over the training at the beginning of December 1939, and since then, the courses had proven to be very popular with the participants.

The three-week programme began with a baptism of fire – intense physical conditioning that left even the fittest gasping for air. Once the men were in peak form, the real challenge commenced. The goal was to forge them into survivors, capable of not just enduring, but thriving behind enemy lines.

Weapons training was provided for all kinds of arms found in continental Europe, including rifles and revolvers from Germany, Belgium, Holland, and France. This practice ensured the attendees were comfortable with any weapon they could get their hands on.

Self-defence training was the next thing to be taught. Deadly techniques that didn't depend on size and strength were emphasised, and once proficient in that, the training moved onto escape and evasion techniques that gave the best chance of surviving long enough to reach the coast and find a ship back to Britain.

The culmination of the training was a ten-mile race on the final day, where the victor would claim a bottle of the finest Scotch whisky and the bragging rights of being King of the Hill.

The Gaelic Grind, as it was known, was the toughest part of the entire three weeks, and those who didn't complete it failed the course.

Michael Fernsby, an operational member of Unit 317, was the exception. Sent to Glenhaven Manor in early December after a daring mission in Berlin, he was supposed to be recuperating from the superficial injuries sustained during his now legendary three-hundred-mile bicycle ride from the heart of the enemy's fortress to Denmark.

Though his physical wounds would heal, the psychological scars ran deep. At first, he had resisted, hating the isolation, but his respect for Tony Sanders and Richard Keene had won out, and he soon found solace in the solitude.

Despite being barred from official training because he was supposed to be enjoying some rest and recuperation, Michael couldn't resist the call of the wild. Within days, he was tagging along, his competitive spirit reignited.

As an avid runner, he revelled in the physical challenges, quickly establishing himself as the undisputed champion of Heartbreak Hill, a steep, unforgiving incline that reduced grown men to tears.

Heartbreak Hill was around the three-quarter mark of the race, and it separated the men from the boys. Participants physically threw up, such was the exertion required to run up the exceptionally steep hill. Very few made it, and most of those that did, had to walk the rest of the way, or at least a significant part of it.

Now, as he approached the dreaded hill, Michael steeled himself, his determination as unyielding as the icy terrain. He attacked the incline head-on, refusing to yield to the burning in his legs and lungs. With each step, he pushed harder, leaving all but the very best in his wake.

The biting wind whipped at his face, numbing his cheeks and nose, but Michael barely felt it. His focus was singular, his mind locked on the task at hand. He thought of the men he'd left behind in Berlin, the ones who hadn't made it out.

Their faces flashed before him, urging him onward, reminding him of the sacrifices they'd made so he could be here, in this moment, fighting for something greater than himself.

Heartbreak Hill had broken the resistance of all but the most hardy, and now only three men remained at the front of the race. One of them, a gangly-legged pilot from the RAF, briefly hit the front, but he lost his footing on the slippery ice and fell flat on his face.

At the summit, Michael allowed himself a fleeting moment of triumph before plunging down the other side, his stride never faltering. Behind him, Benjamin Townshend, a young army lieutenant and newfound friend, fought to keep pace.

The two had bonded over the course of the three weeks, their shared experiences forging a deep camaraderie. Ben was one of the few who could match Michael's intensity, his wiry frame and cheerful demeanour belying a fierce determination that rivalled Michael's own.

As they raced down the hill, the pale winter sun danced off the snow-covered trees, painting a breathtaking canvas that stood in stark contrast to the hell they'd just endured. For a moment, Michael felt a surge of something akin to joy, a fleeting reminder of the beauty that still existed in the world, despite the horrors of war.

But the moment was short-lived, shattered by the sound of Ben's laboured breathing behind him. Michael glanced over his shoulder, a flicker of concern crossing his face as he saw his friend struggling to keep up.

"Come on, Ben!" he shouted, his voice barely audible over the pounding of their feet. "We're almost there!"

Ben nodded, his jaw clenched tight as he dug deep, summoning the last of his reserves. Together, they pushed on, the finish line at Glenhaven Manor's front door beckoning like a beacon in the distance.

As they hit the final stretch, Michael found his second wind. With a burst of speed, he left Ben behind, his lean, athletic frame built for moments like this. His thick, dark hair, now shorter and tamed with Brylcreem, remained unmoved by the biting wind.

He crossed the threshold, once again the undefeated champion of the Gaelic Grind. Panting, he wrapped himself in a thick blanket, waiting for Ben to emerge from the tree line.

As his friend approached, Michael held out a second blanket, a grin spreading across his face.

"You're a bloody gazelle," Ben gasped, sweat glistening on his brow despite the sub-zero temperatures. "No one should be able to run like that!"

Michael laughed, his breath misting in the frigid air. "It's my misspent youth. Running kept me out of trouble."

"What were you running from?" Ben asked, curiosity mingling with exhaustion.

"My brother and father, usually," Michael replied, a flicker of mischief passing behind his eyes.

As they stepped into the warmth of the grand old house, a familiar voice rang out from the administration office.

"Well done, Michael!" Richard Keene emerged from behind the desk, his smooth Lancashire accent unmistakable. "Still undefeated, I see. You should consider running in the Olympics once this infernal war is over."

Michael grinned, taking in the sight of his fellow Unit 317 agent. Like himself, Richard was a legend in SIS circles, his exploits the stuff of whispered tales. With collar-length brown hair and piercing blue eyes that hinted at the horrors they'd witnessed, Richard cut an impressive figure.

"You must have quite the collection of Scotch by now," Keene continued, a knowing smile playing on his lips. "You'll get your prize at tonight's dinner ceremony."

Michael had been expecting that. It had become customary for the winner of the Gaelic Grind to receive the applause of his fellow competitors at the after-dinner ceremony, which was attended by both the graduating participants and the new attendees who were about to take their place.

The new intake stayed in one of the cottages on the grounds of Glenhaven until the next day, when they would officially move into the big house and begin the rigorous training programme.

"I'll do what I always do and share it with the guys," Michael said.

One by one, the remaining runners stumbled into the foyer, their faces flushed with exertion and cold. They grabbed blankets and hot drinks, most too spent to speak after the gruelling finale to their training.

"How was it?" Richard asked as they filed past.

"Brutal," one officer grunted, heading for the stairs. "I'm off for a hot bath. See you at dinner."

Ben clapped Michael on the shoulder. "See you later, mate. Hell of a performance out there."

Michael nodded, a sense of camaraderie warming him from within. He climbed the grand staircase to his room, his muscles crying out for relief. As he sank into the steaming bath, he let the peace of the Scottish retreat wash over him, the horrors of the past year momentarily forgotten in the stillness of the moment.

But even as he lay there, the weight of what was to come pressed down on him. Britain was at war, and Michael knew that his respite at Glenhaven was fleeting. Soon, he would be called upon again, and his skills and courage would be put to the test in the face of unimaginable danger.

For now, though, he would savour this moment of tranquillity, drawing strength from the rugged beauty that surrounded him. He would carry this with him, a talisman against the darkness that lay ahead.

His thoughts drifted to the men he'd trained with over

the past three weeks, the ones who would soon be scattered across Europe, fighting against the dark shadow cast by Hitler's swastika. They were a diverse bunch, officers and enlisted men from all corners of Britain, but they shared a common purpose, a burning desire to do their part in the face of tyranny.

Michael knew that some of them wouldn't make it back, that the odds were stacked against them in this brutal war. But he also knew they would fight with everything they had. They would never surrender or give in to despair.

As he lay there with the hot water soothing his aching muscles, Michael made a silent vow. He would honour the memory of those who had given their lives for him and for those who had sacrificed everything for the cause. He would fight on, no matter the cost, until the day when peace reigned once more.

Because in the end, that was what they were all fighting for, the chance to find peace, to come home to a world where the nightmares were nothing more than distant memories. And as long as men like Michael Fernsby and Richard Keene stood tall, there was hope that one day, that dream might become a reality.

With a sigh, Michael looked at his watch. He still had plenty of time before dinner at eight.

Chapter 7

Michael lay motionless in the tub, his eyes closed, as the once steaming bathwater slowly cooled around him. The warmth seeped from his skin, replaced by a prickling chill that crept up his spine, but he barely noticed. His mind was far away, lost in a whirlwind of memories and emotions that threatened to consume him.

With a sigh, he pulled his pruned hand from the water, squinting at his watch through the dissipating steam. As dinner wasn't until eight, he had plenty of time to relax before the farewell party began.

A vital part of the EET course, attendees were trained in the use of shortwave radio techniques, as it was the best way of listening to broadcasts from all over Europe.

The British and French governments were already broadcasting coded messages on certain frequencies to the intelligence and resistance groups spread throughout Europe, and there were plans for the BBC to send seemingly innocuous messages in the event of a Nazi invasion.

The purpose of these messages would, amongst other things, be directed at Allied personnel trapped behind enemy lines. If they could find a shortwave radio, they would be able to receive coded messages informing them where to go and what to do in the event of being separated from their parent units.

In his downtime, Michael had permission from Keene to use the radio room and tune in to the broadcasts from mainland Europe. Ever since he'd heard Elise broadcasting in Berlin during his last mission about what had happened to her and her family before she fled Germany, he'd obsessed with finding her again.

He knew Elise was Mina, and he spent every waking moment thinking about her, worrying about her, and wondering where she was.

The memory of her voice filled his heart as he dressed, her words echoing in his mind like a mournful refrain. She'd described the horror of her father being killed, her mother arrested, and she and her sister Senta, forced to flee from their idyllic home.

Michael knew the home she referred to was their Bavarian farm, Ryskamp, and her broadcasts sent shock-waves through his already battered soul.

He'd had little success locating the broadcasts at his home in Sandwich, Kent, and it wasn't until he arrived in Scotland and gained access to a radio with a wider range of frequencies that he was able to tune in with any accuracy.

Driven by a desperate need to find her, to know she was safe, Michael spent every spare moment in the radio room fine-tuning the dials of the powerful HRO receiver.

He'd scour the airwaves for hours on end, his eyes straining in the dim red glow of the radio's light, hoping to catch even the faintest whisper of her voice amidst the crackle of static and the coded messages that drifted between the frequencies.

As he made his way down the hallway, his mind wandered back to his childhood, to the countless hours spent at his grandmother Gigi's side, learning the intricacies of the German language.

Little did he know then how vital those lessons would become, and how they would one day be the key to unlocking the secrets that might lead him back to Mina.

He glanced at his watch, his heart skipping a beat as he realised it was nearly time for Molly Parker's predictable departure. Like clockwork, she would leave the radio room at 17:02 pm, leaving Michael to his solitary vigil. He quickened his pace, the key to the room burning a hole in his pocket.

He sat in front of the heavy, black painted rectangular radio set that was about two feet by one, and just short of a foot in height. He checked to see which coil pack was inserted and made sure it was the right one for Elise's broadcasts. Then he turned it on and watched the light on the front to make sure it turned bright red.

Once it turned red, the receiver was ready. He donned the headphones and turned the huge dial that dominated the front of the receiver.

Sometimes he would discover an interesting broadcast that was obviously German intelligence sending coded messages, and he'd write it down to pass on to the boffins at GC&CS, but that was only if he couldn't find Elise on the airwaves that evening.

As he listened, his mind turned to Mina and the constant pain in his chest that reminded him just how much he worried about her.

What had happened to her? The last time I saw her, she was safe at Ryskamp, and yet here I am, searching the airways for the sound of her voice in the wilderness.

She'd told him herself that her family was helping Jews

escape Germany, so it wasn't a stretch to assume they had been caught in the act. Somehow, Mina and her sister, Senta, had escaped, but her parents hadn't been so lucky.

He turned the dial for over an hour, but there was no sign of Mina's heavenly voice calling to him. Finally, after a lot of frustration, he turned it off and left the radio room. He'd try again later.

He still had a couple of hours to kill, so he went to his room and lay down for a nap. Sleep came quickly, but it brought no respite. The nightmares were waiting for him, their claws sinking deep into his subconscious, tearing at the fragile fabric of his sanity.

David's agonised screams tore through the darkness, the makeshift grave Michael had dug for his brother serving as a stark reminder of all those who had sacrificed their lives for him.

He awoke and sat bolt upright, soaked in sweat. It was always the same every time he fell asleep. First David, and then the woman he'd known by her codename of Mother.

She'd died in another hail of bullets from the Gestapo at the railway station in Ravensburg. He now knew her name was Eva Heinze, as her husband had also worked for the German resistance.

Martin Heinze, her husband, was killed during Michael's last mission in Berlin, along with his entire cell of resistance members. Michael put on a brave face, but inside he was broken by all the people he loved and cared about dying for him.

"Go home, Michael. Go home and forget this stupid war." David's voice reached out from beyond the grave as it often did. Michael's frequent conversations with his dead brother would be a cause for alarm if anyone ever heard him.

"Go home and do what?" Michael spat the words out.

"Too many people have died already, and millions more are going to die. I have to do my bit, David. All those people can't die for nothing."

"What about Mum and Dad? And Judith?" David asked.

"I know, but what can I do about it? Dad's health is already failing, and I don't know what to do."

"Either go home and wallow in your self-pity, or stand up for all you believe in, including me, Gerda Yung, and everyone else you care about. Stand up and fight."

"Make your mind up," Michael said. "One minute you're telling me to go home and the next you're telling me to fight. Which one is it?"

David never answered.

Like a spectre from his darkest nightmares, Albert Kreise's face emerged before his eyes – the man responsible for so much of Michael's pain, the one he'd vowed to destroy.

A tall, wiry man in his early forties, and with a faint scar on the bridge of his nose, Kreise was the embodiment of everything Michael despised about the Third Reich, and he knew that as long as men like Kreise existed, he could never rest.

"That's why I fight," Michael declared, rising to his feet. "Kreise and his ilk are the reason I'll go to my grave fighting. I won't stop until one of us is dead."

He checked his watch and headed back to the radio room. He still had over an hour before dinner.

Chapter 8

The worn leather chair creaked beneath Michael's weight as he faced the imposing HRO radio receiver. His fingers trembled slightly as he checked the coil packs, ensuring they were properly installed for the frequencies he so desperately sought.

As he donned the headphones, the world around him faded away, replaced by a cacophony of static and distant voices. He closed his eyes, allowing the memories of Mina to flood his mind, enveloping him in a warm, comforting embrace.

Her gentle smile, the way her eyes sparkled when she laughed; these images danced behind his eyelids, urging him onward in his quest to find her voice in the wilderness.

With a steady hand, Michael reached for the dial, his heart pounding in anticipation. The shortwave radio crackled and hissed as he turned, each frequency bringing forth a new world of sound.

French, Dutch, and Flemish voices drifted in and out, their words unintelligible to his ears. And then, a familiar tune caught his attention: Erika, the Nazi marching song that haunted his nightmares.

Images of the Wehrmacht marching through the streets of Poland and Western Europe flooded his mind, their boots trampling over the remnants of freedom and hope. He could almost hear the song echoing through the ruins of London, a twisted victory cry for the Nazi regime.

With a shudder, Michael twisted the dial, desperate to escape the oppressive melody.

As he continued his search, another familiar voice filled his ears: Klaus Becker, the Nazi propagandist whose popular radio show, Deutschland Aktuell had once featured Albert Kreise announcing Michael's own death to the world.

The memory of that moment, hearing his own demise celebrated by the enemy, sent a chill down his spine.

Everything Michael had ever heard Becker say was nothing more than a load of old bollocks, so he turned the dial and kept listening.

It was always hit and miss trying to find Mina's broadcasts. For one, she had to be broadcasting at the very moment he tuned in, but also, she constantly changed frequencies so the Nazis couldn't pinpoint her location.

Although she was somewhere in neutral territory, the broadcasts she made were aimed directly at exposing Nazi lies, and Michael was sure Goebbels and his Nazi cohorts hated her for it.

She may have changed frequencies, but they were almost always in the 6 MHz to 9 MHz range, so at least he had a reasonable chance of finding her.

So too did the Nazis, and although Michael didn't think they would send a hit squad to silence her, the invasion of Europe was imminent, and if they entered the town where she broadcast from, Mina would be in serious danger.

And that kept Michael awake at night. As much as he loved hearing her voice over the airways, he feared for her safety, and there was nothing he could do to help her.

He twisted and turned the dial for another twenty minutes, and was about to give up when he tuned to a crackling, barely discernible female voice talking in German.

He fine-tuned the dial, and as he did, the broadcast became clearer and louder. He would recognise her sultry tones anywhere.

It was her! It was his Mina! His Elise!

Michael held his breath and listened as Mina's voice melted his heart once again.

Good evening, my fellow Germans. This is Elise, your voice of hope amidst the despair, bringing you truths from a land where freedom still breathes, albeit through whispers.

Tonight, I come before you not just as a broadcaster, but as a fellow German in the fight against darkness, a darkness that seeks to engulf our very souls within its tyrannical shadow.

We stand at a crossroads in time. The fabric of Europe is being torn apart by the insidious hands of hatred and oppression. The Nazi regime, under Adolf Hitler, weaves a tapestry of lies, painting a picture of unity and strength. But, beneath its surface lurks a truth of hate, of communities shattered, families torn apart, and innocence lost in the fires of unwarranted aggression.

It is time for us to rise, to unite the fragmented pieces of our resistance across the Fatherland. From the bustling port cities of Bremen and Hamburg in the north to the vibrant streets of Munich and the majestic gateway to the Alps in the south, let our voices merge into a thunderous call for freedom.

As she called for unity and resistance, Michael felt a surge of pride course through his veins. In the face of adversity, Mina was brave and passionate and unwavering in her commitment to justice. He could almost see her face, illuminated by the glow of radio equipment, her eyes blazing with the intensity of her convictions.

Together, let us expose the lies that have been fed to us and reveal the ugliness that hides behind the facade of propaganda. Together, we possess the power to overthrow the chains of tyranny, to dismantle the foundations of fear and hatred that Hitler and his Nazis have so meticulously laid.

The Gestapo and the SS, under their evil leaders Himmler and Heydrich, continue to commit atrocities in our name. They arrest and kill men and women for nothing more than their beliefs or their race. How many of us have suffered at their hands, and yet we stand idly by and do nothing out of fear of further reprisals?

Our mission is clear: we must act before the flames of war consume us all; before the whole of Europe is lost to Hitler and his tyrannical Nazis.

Remember, it is not just land or pride at stake, but the very essence of humanity itself. We fight not for conquest, but for liberty, for the right to live in a world where freedom is not just a whispered dream, but a reality for all.

And then, as if she could sense his presence through the airwaves, Mina spoke directly to him. Her words, coded and intimate, transported Michael back to those stolen moments they had shared in the barn at Ryskamp.

And now I speak a personal message, for there is one among you, a soul intertwined with mine, who I hope is listening at this very moment.

To you, I say, remember the nights of endless stars, where the only light that mattered was the one shining in our hearts. A place where time stood still, and the echoes of our laughter filled the air, a secret symphony for only us to hear.

In those stolen moments amongst the broken eggshells and whis-

pered dreams, we found something more powerful than fear, stronger than despair.

We discovered hope, a hope that carries me through each day, through each broadcast. It is a hope that we can survive this war and reunite at the place we first met when it is over.

It is this hope, this unbreakable bond, that I wish to remind you of. Our shared dreams, our plans for a future where love triumphs over hate, where peace is more than just a fleeting thought.

Keep this memory close, as I do, and let it be our guiding star through the darkest of nights. Until we can once again gaze upon the same sky without fear, know that my heart is always with you.

This is Elise, signing off but never saying goodbye. Stand strong, stand together, and believe in the power of our united spirits to usher in a new dawn for Europe and the world. Keep the flame of resistance burning bright, for with its light, we shall find our way home.

The radio crackled as her voice faded into the unknown. Michael's heart swelled with love and longing, the ache in his chest a physical manifestation of the distance that separated them.

He closed his eyes, allowing her words to wash over him, to fill the void that had consumed him since the day they parted.

Wherever she was, whatever she was doing, he would find her. Somehow, some way, if it was the last thing he ever did, he would find Mina and hold her in his arms one again.

Chapter 9

Glenhaven Manor had two dining rooms on the ground floor. The first one was used to seat the twelve attendees of the EET. Staff members took their meals in the second dining room, where they could discuss the participants in private.

As the clock struck eight, Michael entered the dining room, his mind still reeling from the emotional impact of hearing Mina's voice on the radio. He took his seat beside Ben Townshend, his friend's words barely registering as he stared at the table, lost in thought.

"Glad you could join us," Ben said mockingly. "Were you asleep?"

Michael shook his head, his eyes distant. "I was in the radio room."

Ben's expression sobered, his brow furrowing with concern. "Of course you were. Did you get any joy?"

Michael nodded slowly. "I heard her."

Ben leant in closer, his voice lowered. "Is everything alright? You look a little demoralised, which isn't like you at all."

Michael forced a smile, trying to mask the inner turmoil that threatened to consume him. “I’m fine,” he assured his friend, his gaze finally meeting Ben’s.

“Well?” Ben asked. “What did she say?”

“She was rallying the German resistance movements to join together and overthrow Hitler.” Michael’s words were steady, but his heart ached with the memory of Mina’s voice, the ghost of her touch, and the way her smile could melt away the world’s troubles.

Corporal Liam Longdon’s voice cut through the silence that had settled over the room, drawing everyone’s attention.

“That’s what we all want, isn’t it? If the Germans rise up and overthrow Hitler, we won’t have to do it for them. Everybody wins.”

The room was silent, which Michael hadn’t realised. He’d been so entrenched in his thoughts that he hadn’t noticed everyone was watching him, listening in to his conversation with Ben.

“I wish it was that easy,” he answered. “Then we could all go home.”

A Scottish officer from the 5th battalion, Argyll and Sutherland Highlanders, rose to his feet, his glass held high in the air.

“Your girl sounds like a brave woman,” he declared, his voice thick with admiration. “The good Lord knows we need courageous souls like her, so I propose a toast to all the brave men and women around the world who are standing up to the evil knocking on our door. I pray we are as valiant as they are when our time comes to face the enemy head-on.”

“Aye, aye!” The room erupted with shouts and the scraping of chairs as the thirteen men stood, their glasses raised in a toast to Mina and the countless other brave souls facing the malignant evil across the globe.

Michael's vision blurred, and a large lump formed in his throat as he tried to speak. "Thank you," he mumbled, before sitting down and dabbing at his eyes with his serviette.

"That was touching," Ben said, clapping Michael on the shoulder. "After all you've been through, you deserve it."

As dinner was served, the mood in the room lightened, the shared bond of having completed the gruelling Endurance Escape Training course uniting the men, regardless of rank or background.

Conversations flowed freely, contact details were exchanged, and promises to keep in touch were made, even as Michael silently wondered how many of them would survive the war that loomed on the horizon.

However many it was, it had been an honour knowing them.

His gaze drifted to Ben, the young lieutenant from Cornwall who had become his closest friend during his time at Glenhaven Manor. At twenty-two, Ben was a kindred spirit, his enthusiasm and intensity matched only by his athletic prowess.

Michael marvelled at the twists of fate that had brought them together, two young men from different walks of life united in their determination to fight for what was right.

Hailing from Cornwall, Ben had the distinctive Cornish twang that sounded like a fisherman singing to his catch on a misty morning.

His father was a fisherman, and Ben had been studying at the University of Edinburgh before the war started.

He enlisted in the spring of 1939, and although his

father wanted him to follow in his own footsteps and join the navy, Ben went ahead and joined the army.

Now, he was a proud lieutenant in the Grenadier Guards, the most senior infantry regiment in the British Army.

As the dinner drew to a close, Richard Keene entered the dining room, his presence commanding the attention of all present. "We're waiting for you in the reception hall," he announced, his voice crisp and authoritative. "There are drinks all around as we go over the course and hand out the awards. Be there in five."

The men filed out of the dining room, following Richard into the grand reception hall next door. A large table, extended to accommodate twenty-four men, dominated the centre of the room, its polished surface gleaming in the candlelight. The staff took their seats around the edges of the tartan rug that covered the floor, and Michael, as a guest rather than an official participant, joined them.

Richard Keene stood on the stairway at the far end of the hall, his gaze sweeping over the assembled men. The outgoing intake occupied the first six chairs on either side of the table, while the new recruits filled the remaining seats, their faces a mix of anticipation and nervousness.

Eleven of the seats were occupied, which meant that either someone wasn't coming, or he was late. Either way, he'd better have a good excuse, or Richard Keene would write a scathing letter of complaint to his commanding officer.

"Gentlemen, shall we begin?" Keene's voice echoed through the hall, silencing the murmurs of conversation. He cleared his throat, his eyes shining with pride as he addressed the room.

"Gentlemen, distinguished guests, and most importantly, the courageous souls who have just completed the

Endurance Escape Training programme. As we gather here this evening, I find myself reflecting on the past three weeks—a period of intense learning, unyielding determination, and unparalleled camaraderie."

As Keene spoke, Michael's mind drifted to the challenges they had faced, the bonds they had forged, and the skills they had honed. He thought of the countless hours spent pushing their bodies and minds to the limit, learning to survive in the most unforgiving of circumstances.

"The essence of what we've endeavoured to impart goes beyond mere survival; it's about empowerment, about passing on the torch of knowledge so that others may also find their way through the darkest hours," Keene continued, his voice rising with passion.

"I urge you, share what you have learnt and teach others so our collective strength grows, ensuring that if any of us find ourselves isolated behind enemy lines, we are never truly alone. You have the wisdom and the knowledge you take back with you."

Michael's heart swelled with pride, the weight of Keene's words settling upon his shoulders like a mantle of responsibility. He knew the knowledge they had gained, the skills they had mastered, could mean the difference between life and death, not just for themselves, but for the men serving alongside them in the heat of battle.

"Speaking of exceptional individuals," Keene's voice cut through Michael's thoughts, drawing his attention back to the present. "I cannot let this moment pass without acknowledging a young man who, though I have known him but a few months, has shown the kind of strength, integrity, and skill that inspires us all."

Michael felt the eyes of the room upon him, his cheeks flushing with a mixture of embarrassment and gratitude as Keene continued.

"Michael Fernsby, you have not just excelled in every task set before you, you've shown what it means to be a true comrade. Your prowess on the field, your victory in the Gaelic Grind, speaks volumes, not just of your physical capabilities, which I daresay could rival any Olympian under different circumstances, but of your unwavering spirit."

Keene raised his glass, his eyes locked with Michael's. "Your dedication to our cause, your loyalty to your brothers and sisters in arms… I trust you with my life, and I am profoundly proud to have worked beside you."

The room erupted in cheers, glasses clinking as the men toasted Michael's accomplishments. He rose to his feet, his heart pounding as he accepted the bottle of Scotch from Keene, a symbol of their shared victory.

"I may have this in my hands," Michael began, his voice trembling with emotion, "but it is a gift to all of us here this evening. Alone, we are nothing, but together we can stop the tyranny in its tracks."

He raised the bottle high, his voice ringing out through the hall. "To victory!"

"To victory!" The roar of the men echoed back, their voices united in a single, powerful cry.

As the cheers died down, the entrance door swung open, revealing a shadowy figure carrying a large trunk. The man stepped into the light, his upper-class, aristocratic voice cutting through the silence.

"I'm sorry I'm late, gentlemen. I had a meeting with my mother and our lawyers, and it ran later than expected."

Michael's blood ran cold, the smile fading from his face as he recognised the voice. He didn't need to see the man's face to know who it was—Robert Stourcliffe Junior, the son of the traitor Robert Stourcliffe Senior, the shipping magnate who had committed suicide rather than face the damage he'd done to Britain by passing vital shipping information to the Nazis.

The same man who, in a final act of contrition, or perhaps desperation, handed four of his ships back to Michael's father, a gesture that had done little to heal the scars left by his betrayal.

The tension in the room was palpable, the air thick with unspoken questions and lingering doubts. Michael's mind raced, a kaleidoscope of memories and emotions threatening to overwhelm him as he stared at the man before him, the ghost of their shared past hanging heavy between them.

Young Robert was a year or two older than Michael and had never forgiven him for punching him on the nose and stealing his black Labrador while at Cambridge University in what now seemed like another lifetime.

Michael had been expelled from Cambridge for that incident, but nothing he did would ever create better relations between them.

Their eyes locked, a silent battle of wills unfolding between them as the room held its breath, waiting to see how the past would collide with the present. Would the sins of the father be visited upon the son, or would this be a chance for a new beginning, a fresh start in the face of the looming darkness?

"Fernsby!" Robert Stourcliffe Junior roared.

Chapter 10

The room fell silent. Everyone knew of their hatred for each other, as it had been splashed all over the newspapers for weeks on end. After Robert Senior killed himself, the newspapers couldn't get enough of it, and they dug up everything they could on the Stourcliffes, including the hatred they had for the Fernsby's.

Michael looked straight ahead, his body tense. The air crackled with tension, and he stared at Stourcliffe as if he were looking at Medusa herself.

Stourcliffe's words cut through the silence, his voice dripping with disdain as he spoke. "If this leech is on the course, then I demand to be released," he sneered, his accent a relic of a bygone era.

"He's stolen everything from my family. He even stole my dog. Did he ever tell you that?"

His eyes swept the room, challenging anyone to defend the man he so clearly despised.

Michael felt the heat rising within him, a crimson tide of anger that threatened to consume him. He clenched his fists, fighting the urge to lash out, to make Stourcliffe pay for his words. But he knew he couldn't, not here, not now.

"His family are nothing but thieves and liars," Stourcliffe continued, his voice rising with each word. "He should be in jail, not in a place as grand as this."

Michael couldn't hold back any longer. "I would ask if you got here by boat, but you don't have any ships left, do you?" he taunted, the words slipping from his lips before he could stop them.

He knew it was a low blow, but Stourcliffe had a way of getting under his skin like no other.

Stourcliffe's face reddened, his eyes narrowing behind his gold-rimmed glasses. "I have plenty of ships left, thank you, Fernsby. Unless your thieving father is trying to steal those too."

Michael scoffed, shaking his head in disgust. "I see the silver spoon is still stuck firmly down your pampered throat. I'd have thought your father's treachery might have humbled you a little."

Stourcliffe drew himself up to his full height, towering over Michael by a good few inches. He glared at him with a look of thunder.

"I'd be careful if I were you, Fernsby," he warned, his voice low and menacing. "My family has powerful friends, and they don't like you any more than I do."

"You have friends?" Michael asked, feigning surprise. "That's surprising."

"How's your father these days?" Stourcliffe shot back, his face twisted into a sneer. "It's a great pity he didn't die in that wretched accident."

Now it was Michael's turn to feel his face turning deep red. His vision clouded as he stepped forward, ready to strike. But before he could, he felt a hand on his chest, pushing him back. It was Ben, his friend and fellow trainee, stepping between them, his face a mask of concern.

"That's enough," a voice rang out, cutting through the tension like a knife.

It was Richard Keene, his face a thundercloud of anger as he glared at Stourcliffe.

"Lieutenant Stourcliffe, what are you doing here? The manifest made no mention of you. I'd have blocked it if it had."

Stourcliffe turned to face Keene, his posture defiant. "Sir, I assure you that if I'd known Fernsby was here, I would have never agreed to attend."

"So, why are you here, then?" Keene asked again, his voice like steel.

The reception hall was so quiet, you could hear a pin drop. Michael glanced around, taking in the faces of the other officers, some of whom knew Stourcliffe from their family connections.

None of them seemed surprised by his behaviour, and Michael couldn't help but wonder what they really thought of the man.

"I asked my commanding officer if I could attend as it might serve as a distraction from current events," Stourcliffe said, his arrogance shining through. "Whoever was supposed to be here stepped aside, and here I am."

He glanced at Michael. "Now I regret my decision."

"It wasn't your decision to make, Lieutenant Stourcliffe," Keene snapped. His eyes blazed, and Michael had never seen him this angry before.

"Well, I'm here now, Captain. If you have any objections, I suggest you take it up with the PM, because he gave me his personal blessing to be here."

"I'll do just that," Keene answered. "Both of you, to my office, now. And that's an order!"

Michael followed behind Stourcliffe, his hands clenched into fists at his sides. It took every ounce of self-control he had to not reach out and kick the man's pampered arse as they walked.

"Close the door," Keene said after they filed into his sparsely furnished office.

Michael closed the door and stood as far away from Stourcliffe as he could.

"I'm going to call your CO this evening," Keene said, his voice tight with anger. "But for now, you will behave like an officer in the British Army and show respect for your peers. Especially when they outrank you. Do I make myself clear, Lieutenant Stourcliffe?"

Stourcliffe glowered, his face a mask of petulance. It was clear he wasn't used to taking orders, especially from those he considered beneath him.

"I know you think it beneath you to take orders from mere peasants like us," Michael said. "But I'd listen to Captain Keene if I were you."

"That's enough, Michael," Keene snapped.

"Well?" Keene asked, tapping his fingers impatiently against his desk.

"I refuse to be here with that thief." Stourcliffe stood his ground. "Send me home if you have to, but I'm sure the PM will be vexed if you do."

Keene's chair slammed against the wall as he leapt to his feet. "Don't ever threaten me, Stourcliffe. I know all about your arrogant family and your sense of entitlement, but let me tell you. In here, everyone is equal, including you."

"He isn't treated equally," Stourcliffe complained, pointing an accusing finger at Michael. "You think I haven't heard the stories of how the celebrated arsehole

Fernsby is paraded around like he's some kind of hero? It's pathetic, and I'll have no part in it."

Keene opened his mouth to say something, but Michael cut him off. "I've been here long enough. I'm fully healed, and I'm fit. There's a war to be won, and I'm ready to get back to work. I'll leave first thing in the morning and leave his pampered arse with you. Good luck."

"Michael, there's no nee—"

"I'm ready, Richard. It doesn't matter what Tony Sanders says, I'm going back to London first thing tomorrow morning."

Keene bowed his head. "You're right. I'll let Tony know."

He looked up at Stourcliffe, his eyes filled with a cold fury that made even Michael step back. "Even you have superiors, Stourcliffe, and I'll be speaking to them this evening. I want you gone, but if you must stay, be warned. Put one step out of line, and I'll be all over you."

"As long as he isn't here, everything should be fine, Captain," Stourcliffe said, a smirk spreading across his face as he looked at Michael.

Michael felt the anger rising within him once more and knew he had to leave before he did something he would regret. He stepped out of the office, closing the door behind him with a snap. He closed his eyes, mumbling to himself as he made his way back to his room, his mind a whirlwind of emotions.

Twenty minutes later, a knock on the door pulled him from his thoughts. He opened it, expecting to see Ben standing there, ready to offer his support and understanding.

It wasn't Ben. It was Richard Keene.

"May I come in?" he asked.

Michael stepped aside, letting him enter. His clothes

were strewn all over the bed, a testament to the anger that had consumed him as he packed.

"I see what you mean about Stourcliffe's arrogant entitlement," Keene said. "I told his CO that I wasn't accepting him into the course and that he was leaving in the morning, as I can't have someone like that here. He would upset everyone, and he'd end up getting filled in by someone. Probably me, if truth be told."

Michael shook his head and smiled. "There would be a queue, I'm sure. If he's leaving, for God's sake, make him wait until the afternoon. The last thing I want is to be on the same train as him. I'd end up throwing him out of a window."

Keene laughed. "I spoke with Tony Sanders. He wanted you to stay for another three weeks, but he understands you are ready. He told me to tell you to go home to see your family and report back to London a week from Monday."

"Thank you, Richard. I appreciate everything you are doing up here."

"I also told Tony that I'm done here. I'm not cut out to babysit pampered babies. It's time to get back out there and do some real work. There's a war to be won, and I don't want to see it out here."

"I bet he was happy to hear that," Michael said. "When do you leave?"

Keene's lips parted in a half smile. "He told me to hang tight through this next three weeks and he'd find a replacement for the next one."

"I'll see you in London then," Michael said, holding out his hand.

Keene took it, his grip firm and reassuring. "Take care of yourself, Michael," he said, his voice filled with genuine concern. "And give my best to your family."

The next morning, Keene stopped Michael before he jumped on the bus taking the twelve participants to the train station in Mallaig.

"We've been overridden, it seems." His facial expression was one of disappointment. "Stourcliffe stays, although his CO read him the riot act last night and told him that if he stepped out of line again with his arrogance, he would personally come up here to kick him out himself and banish him to kitchen duty for the rest of the war."

"I bet that brought a smile to your face," Michael said.

"It did. Normally, I'd object, but as this is my last course, I'll see it through and put up with it. I'll enjoy making the arrogant snob work hard, and that's going to make it worthwhile."

Ben sat with Michael on the train to London, and they parted with promises to stay in touch.

"Don't be a hero," Michael said as they parted. "This is going to be a long war, and we need you to make it through."

"You're the one who needs to remember that," Ben said. "Take care of yourself, Michael. I hope you find Mina after the war is over."

Michael felt strangely alone as Ben headed for the Cornwall-bound train. He rarely took to people like he had with Ben, and he hoped their paths would cross again at some point in the future.

Michael shrugged and climbed aboard the train to Canterbury. With any luck, he'd be home before curfew.

Chapter 11

Giselle Fernsby stood in the living room, staring at the unopened letter as if it was toxic. At sixty-five years old, Gigi, as she was affectionately known, was the matriarch of the Fernsby family, a position bestowed upon her by virtue of her senior status.

Her once vibrant chestnut hair, now elegantly streaked with silver, framed a face etched with worry lines. She'd been there for hours, afraid to open it in case it gave her the news she was afraid to hear.

"Mother, you have been staring at that damned letter for hours," Gerald Fernsby, Michael's father, said. "We're as keen as you are to find out what it says."

"Michael should be here any minute," Gigi answered, glancing at the grandfather clock ticking away in the corner of the room. "He was on the three o'clock train from Colchester according to his telephone call this morning."

"What's it got to do with Michael?" Dorothy Fernsby, Gerald's wife and Michael's mother, asked. "Just open the bloody thing, Gigi, and put us all out of our misery."

Dorothy sat in her favourite armchair, looking as content as Gigi had seen her for a long time. After the tragic loss of her son, David, Dorothy's vibrant presence had withered, along with her ability to enjoy life.

It was only recently, after the passing of time and the turning of their fortunes, that Dorothy had shown any willingness to enjoy life again.

At forty-six, Dorothy's long, wavy brown hair mirrored the fashion trends of the day, and her youthful, wrinkle-free complexion made her look a decade younger than she was.

Gigi allowed a smile to pass over her stern Germanic features. She and Dorothy had experienced their share of differences in recent months, most of them born of Gigi's well-intentioned meddling.

It had been her idea to send David and Michael to Germany in a desperate bid to rescue her Jewish father and son from the clutches of the Nazis.

They failed, and when Michael came back alone, it almost broke the Fernsby family apart. If it wasn't for Michael's interventions, it would have, and Gigi would be forever grateful to her only remaining grandson for his selflessness.

A bang at the door of their house on New Street in Sandwich, Kent, ended the Fernsby family's long wait.

Michael is here!

Warhurst, the silver-haired trusty butler, who'd served the Fernsby family for decades, answered, but before he could allow Michael inside the house, a blur of jet-black fur came bounding down the stairs, barking with unrestrained joy.

Lucy, the Labrador Michael had rescued from the cruel hands of Robert Stourcliffe Junior, skidded across the polished floor, her paws scrabbling for purchase. With a final leap, she crashed into Michael, sending them both tumbling to the ground in a tangle of limbs and paws.

"Lucy!" Michael shouted, enjoying every second of the sort of love only a dog can provide. "Are you glad to see me?"

"Woof!" told Michael everything he needed to know.

After extricating himself from Lucy, Michael made his way to the sitting room, falling over Lucy several times as she ran between his legs and around him in a frenzy of joy.

"Judith!" Gerald thundered. "Get control of this damned dog."

"I'm coming, Dad. Keep your hair on. She's just excited to see Michael, that's all." Judith, Michael's fifteen-year-old sister, shouted back.

Michael watched in loving fascination as Judith, who was the spitting image of their mother in pictures of her younger self, grabbed Lucy by the collar and pretended to admonish her as she dragged her back upstairs.

"Mum, Dad, Gigi." Michael turned his attention to the adults waiting in the sitting room for him. "It's great to see you."

Dorothy and Gigi gave Michael a big hug in the middle of the room, and Judith soon joined them.

"Alright," Michael laughed. "I can't breathe."

He pulled himself away and approached his father, who had just about struggled to his feet. Michael inwardly grimaced at the deterioration in his father's appearance in just the few short weeks since he'd last seen him.

Although Gerald was only forty-two years old, a heart condition and a terrible automobile accident had taken their toll on his appearance. His brittle hair was thin and grey, and he had a growing bald spot on the top of his head.

While he put on a brave face, Gerald struggled with his

injuries. After fracturing his left leg in the accident, he found it hard to walk without a cane. His left shoulder had been shattered, making even the simplest of movements difficult.

His emotional scars were taking a lot longer to heal than his physical ones, and Michael worried he would never fully recover from them.

Both his parents had taken David's death hard, and both lost the will to live. It was only due to Michael's and Judith's insistence that they'd found the fortitude to carry on and rejoin the human race.

Their fortunes had changed dramatically the previous year after Michael discovered a lost family heirloom in Germany. It had belonged to Gigi's father, and once Michael took it back to England, Gerald sold it for a king's ransom. He not only paid off the substantial debts of his struggling brewery business, but also saved their home from repossession and turned around the fortunes of their business with a fresh injection of capital.

In addition, Robert Stourcliffe had returned four of the Fernsby family ships before his death a few months earlier. He'd bought them during the Great Depression when Gerald fell into hard times along with everyone else.

Michael shook his father's hand and helped him into his armchair. Then he took his own seat and faced his family.

"Well, what have I missed?" he asked.

"Gigi got a letter this morning from the government," Dorothy said. "We've been waiting for her to open it all day, but she wanted to wait until you got here."

"What is it?" Michael asked.

"That's what we're about to find out," Gerald said. "For goodness sake, Mother. Open the damned letter."

Gigi grimaced and nodded her head.

Chapter 12

Gigi's hands trembled as she held the envelope, her fingers tracing the edges as if trying to ascertain the contents through touch alone. Her face, usually so full of life and colour, had turned ashen grey, and her eyes were wide with a fear that Michael had rarely seen before.

"Here," she said, her voice barely above a whisper as she thrust the letter towards him. "You open it. I can't do it."

Gerald's brow furrowed, his voice rising in frustration. "Good Lord, Mother! You're acting as though the government is deporting you back to Germany. It's just a letter, so why don't you open the damned thing and put us all out of our misery."

Gigi's lips pressed into a thin line, her expression grave. "That's what I'm worried about."

The room fell silent, the weight of her words settling over them like a shroud. Gerald's face softened, his anger giving way to concern.

"Surely they can't do that?" he asked, his tone gentler

now. "You're not a Nazi spy. For heaven's sake, you've lived in England for decades."

"Be quiet and let Michael open it," Gigi insisted, her eyes never leaving the envelope.

As his grandmother had before him, Michael turned the thick envelope over in his hands, examining the official seal and the typed address, before reaching for his penknife.

With a quick, precise motion, he sliced through the envelope, the sound of tearing paper unnaturally loud in the quiet room.

"There's a card and an accompanying letter," he announced.

Every eye in the room was fixed on him, the tension palpable. Even Lucy, usually so full of energy, sat perfectly still beside Judith, as if sensing the gravity of the moment.

"It's from an internment tribunal." Michael looked up, his cheeks flushed. "What's this about, Gigi?"

Gigi's hands twisted in her lap, her fingers knotting together. "I received a notification when the war started that as a German living in Britain, I was now classed as an enemy alien. I was mortified, especially when the letter told me I was being considered for internment."

"What?" Gerald fumed. "This is an outrage. Why didn't you tell me? I would have spoken to the PM about it immediately."

"That's exactly why I didn't tell you," Gigi replied. "I knew you'd make a fuss, and I didn't want to upset you any more than you already were. Our family has been through enough because of my actions, and I didn't want to add anything else to it."

"This is different, Mother." Gerald shot her a sharp look.

"Maybe," Gigi said. "But there must be thousands of

people just like me who are going through the same emotions right now."

"Well?" Dorothy asked Michael. "What does it say?"

Michael read the card first.

"The headlines are a little ominous." Michael looked up at Gigi. "It's got your name on it, right below where it says you're a female enemy alien."

Blood drained from Gigi's face as she stared at her grandson. Michael could see her hands trembling in her lap, and he felt sorry for her.

"I'll put you out of your misery," he said. "You are in category C, which means that you are not deemed a danger to the state."

"What does that mean?" Gigi's voice was hoarse.

"It means you are exempt from both internment and restrictions. You're free, Gigi!"

Gigi bowed her head as tears of relief streamed down her face. Judith and Dorothy comforted her, and even Lucy placed her head in Gigi's lap. Gerald clapped in his chair, his deep frown finally vanishing with Michael's words.

"I was worried they were going to send me back to Germany," Gigi said. "After all that's happened, Hitler would have had me killed."

"Or held as hostage until Michael gave himself up to them," Gerald said. "The government would never put us in that situation, Mother, so this was never in doubt."

"Well, now that's out of the way, how about you tell me what's been happening here while I've been gone?" Michael asked.

"Judith got herself a boyfriend," Gerald said, playfully teasing his daughter.

Judith's face turned red, and she stuck out her tongue towards her father. "That's not funny," she said.

"You've got a boyfriend?" Michael joined in the fun at

Judith's expense. "It's a good job I'm here then. What's his name?"

"I'm not telling you anything," Judith answered, her embarrassment plainly obvious.

"Leave her alone," Dorothy defended her. "He's a nice boy, and he doesn't need any harassment from you."

"I'm happy for you, Judith," Michael said. "Just make sure he's not a member of Moseley's Blackshirt fascists before you bring him here."

Judith allowed a small smile to cross her lips. "He's not a fascist. That was the first thing I asked, especially after they kidnapped me last year."

"That's good to know," Michael said. "So, Father, how are things with you?"

Gerald sighed. "It's almost dinnertime and I'm starving. We'll talk about it after we've eaten."

"We have food?" Michael joked. "Didn't they just bring back rationing a couple of weeks ago?"

"Indeed, they did," Dorothy answered. "Petrol was first, as we all expected it would be. Then, on January eighth, they told us that bacon, ham, butter, and sugar would be rationed. We've already got our ration books, so it's going to be difficult from now on."

"It's the same for everyone," Michael said. "So, it's only fair. We'll manage, just like those before us did in the last war."

"We're growing our own vegetables in the rear garden," Gerald said. "I can't do it myself, but I hired a few men from the town to help."

"The rear garden is over an acre," Michael said. "You'll produce way more than we'll ever need. What are you doing with the surplus?"

"That's the whole point of it," Gerald announced proudly. "The bulk of what we grow will be handed over to the local people free of charge. We're doing all we can for the war effort, Michael. We might not fight like you are, but we're doing all we can to help."

"I'm proud of you, Dad," Michael said. And he meant it. He knew how important simple things like potatoes and carrots would be in the coming months.

The Fernsby family filed into the dining room. Lucy tried sneaking past Gerald, but he wasn't having any of it. "Take that dog upstairs, Judith!" he roared.

But he smiled. Everyone knew he loved Lucy just as much as everyone else did.

Chapter 13

Although not expecting dinner to be a starvation fest, Michael was pleasantly surprised at how good it turned out to be. Considering the circumstances, it was one of the best meals he'd ever had.

The soup, which his father had been so proud of, was a far cry from the watery gruel Michael had been expecting. Instead, it was a hearty, thick concoction, brimming with chunks of tender carrots, potatoes, onions, and leeks, all plucked fresh from the family's garden.

But it was the main course that truly stole the show. A golden-skinned roast chicken, its meat tender and juicy, sat at the centre of the table, surrounded by a glorious array of roasted potatoes, parsnips, and cabbage, all glistening with butter and seasoning.

As Michael loaded his plate, he couldn't help but marvel at the vibrant colours and earthy scents of the homegrown vegetables. It was a feast for the senses, a testament to the love and care that had gone into every bite.

Between mouthfuls of succulent chicken and perfectly

crisp potatoes, Michael sipped at the steaming cup of English tea his mother had poured for him. It was a rare treat, he knew, one that his mother had been saving for a special occasion just like this.

"That was truly excellent." Michael slumped back in his chair, feeling about as stuffed as he ever had. "It's amazing how good homegrown vegetables can taste. Who was the chef? Whoever it was, I need to thank them for such an outstanding meal."

Judith broke out into a proud smile across the table.

"This was all the work of Judith and myself," Dorothy said with a wide grin on her face. "The cook we employed joined up right after Christmas, so we're managing on our own. We've done a good job, even if I do say so myself."

"This was you and Judith?" Michael was dumbfounded.

"What?" Judith pointed at him from across the table. "What, you didn't think I could cook anything?"

Michael held up his hands in surrender, a chuckle escaping his lips. "I just never knew," he said, shaking his head. "You and Mum have truly outdone yourselves. I might just have to take you back to London with me, so you can cook for me every day."

"Ooh, I'd love to go to London." Judith's eyes lit up.

"Forget it," her father said. "You might have left school at Christmas, but you're needed to help around here."

"I want to do more for the war effort," Judith answered back. "I'm not just sitting here while everyone else gets to do things for the country."

"We've already had this conversation. You're too young, so you are staying here where I know you are safe, at least for another year or two."

"Help me, Michael," Judith pleaded with her brother. "Tell him I'm needed in London, where I can help with the war effort. Other girls my age are going, so why can't I?"

Michael leant back in his chair, scratching at his chin as he mulled over his sister's words. He could see both sides of the argument and could understand Judith's burning desire to contribute, to feel useful. But he also knew the dangers that lurked beyond the safety of their home, the horrors that he himself had witnessed firsthand.

"I know you want to help, Judith, and I admire you for that. However, what would you do? What skills do you have that could be useful for the war effort?"

All eyes fell on Judith, whose face dropped like a stone. "I… I… You know I don't have any. But I can make dinner for someone at least."

"That's not enough," Michael said. "You're intelligent and kind, and I've seen for myself how brave you are. Cooking dinner for someone will not be enough, Judith. I'm sorry."

Judith's eyes filled, and she looked down at the table. "You got to go to Cambridge, and now look what you're doing."

She looked up at Michael. "What *are* you doing, anyway? You never tell us."

Michael smiled at his sister. "I have an idea," he said, avoiding her question. "You might not like it, but I think it's a great way to prepare you for London."

"What?" she asked.

Michael glanced at his father, seeking his approval before he spoke. "I think you should work for Dad," he said, his voice steady. "Learn to be a skilled typist. If you apply yourself, which I know you will, you could be proficient enough to work for the government by the time you're eighteen."

He looked Judith in the eyes. "This war isn't going to

end anytime soon. It'll still be going on when you're old enough to go to London. And with your language skills, you could be in high demand in a lot of different places. Places I can't even talk about right now."

Judith looked at her brother for a long moment. Then she shifted her gaze to her father, who looked approvingly at her pleading expression.

"I'd be honoured to have you work for me. You can start in the typing pool on Monday. I'll pay you well, and I'll make sure you're trained by the best typist we have. Michael's right, we all need to do our bit for Britain, and I can't think of a better way for you to contribute."

"Thank you!" Judith leapt out of her seat and ran to Michael. After hugging him, she kissed her father on the bald spot at the top of his head.

"I won't let you down. Either of you."

"I know you won't," her father said. "I'm very proud of you, Judith."

As Judith ran happily to her room, Michael turned to his father. "Thank you for doing that for her, Dad. She won't disappoint you."

"She's my daughter. I know she won't," Gerald replied proudly.

"How are you doing?" Michael asked. "How's the health these days?"

"Your father might look like he's not going to survive," Dorothy spoke up. "But I haven't seen him this active since before we lost David."

"I'd give it all up for one more day with David," Gerald said.

The atmosphere in the room turned sombre at the mention of David.

"We all miss David," Michael spoke softly. "But the last

thing he'd want for any of us is to stop living. We all need to move on and remember him that way, by living the best life we can."

"I agree," Gerald said. "And I'm doing my best to do just that."

"We all are," Dorothy agreed.

The conversation turned to lighter topics, then to the success of the family brewery and the ships they had regained from the Stourcliffes. But even as they laughed and reminisced, the shadow of David's absence lingered, a constant reminder of the precious fragility of life.

"The brewery business is doing very well," Gerald said. "The injection of capital the sale of the doubloon gave us has breathed new life into it. It's thriving like never before, and it is you I need to thank for it."

Michael shook his head. "I'm glad I found it, but the work is all you, Father. What about the ships we got back from Stourcliffe?"

"I must admit, I was bowled over when that happened," Gerald said. "I thought it might be a sick joke at first, and I wasn't convinced until I received the transfer of ownership papers."

"I thought the same, but after a run-in with Robert Junior, I knew it must be genuine." Michael kept the details to himself.

"I got a threatening letter from his barrister, but when I showed it to our lawyers, they told me it was just bluster on young Robert's part. They dealt with it quietly, and I never heard from them again."

"What have you done with them?" Michael asked, curious as to how his father was running two large companies, especially as his health was poor.

"Its early days yet, and I'm still waiting for all the legal stuff to come through. They are currently at the Port of London."

"What will you do once everything is transferred?" Michael was genuinely interested.

"As much as young Stourcliffe didn't like it, after his father's treachery came to light, several of his father's senior employees wanted no further involvement in his company. They have agreed to work for me, and I currently have them employed in London getting everything ready to transport merchant goods that will serve the war effort as soon as we can."

"I'm happy for you, Father. Just don't overdo it and make yourself even sicker than you already are. We need you here, so please take care of yourself."

"Thank you, Michael," his mother said. "I hope he'll listen to you, because he won't listen to me."

"Nor me," Gigi said. She'd been quiet all evening, reading the letter from the immigration tribunal over and over.

"Promise?" Michael asked his father.

"I promise, son. I'm preparing it for you once this infernal war is over."

"Don't worry about me," Michael said. "Just take care of yourself. We need you to be around long after we beat the Nazis."

"Here, here," Dorothy said. "Listen to your son, Gerald."

Later that night, as Michael lay in his bed, his mind churning with thoughts of the week ahead, he couldn't shake the image of Mina from his mind. Her voice, her smile, the way her eyes had sparkled in the barn, it all came rushing back to him, as vivid and real as if she were lying there beside him.

He knew what he had to do, knew that he wouldn't rest

until he found her, until he heard her voice again, even if only through the crackling static of a radio broadcast. And so, as he drifted off to sleep, his heart full of longing and determination, he repeated his silent promise to himself and to her.

He would find her, no matter where she was.

Chapter 14

Rotterdam, February 6, 1940

Thirty-two-year-old Jamie Hawke crossed the bridge over the canal leading into the historic Delfshaven district of Rotterdam. The tiny strip of land sandwiched between two waterways was as mysterious as it was historic.

He glanced at his watch, the luminous dial casting an eerie green glow in the gloom: 19:40. He had twenty minutes until the meeting was set to begin.

The Delfshaven district had changed little since the seventeen hundreds. Cobbled streets branched off from the not much bigger main thoroughfares that crisscrossed the district in an endless maze of dead ends and cul-de-sacs.

As he walked, Jamie marvelled at the timeless beauty of the district, the gas lamps casting a warm, flickering glow that danced across the weathered facades of the ancient buildings.

It was like stepping back in time, into a world where the modern trappings of the twentieth century had yet to take hold.

But beneath the quaint, picturesque surface, Jamie

knew that danger lurked around every corner. The Delfshaven district was the perfect place for clandestine meetings and nefarious deeds.

The weather suited the occasion, and the dark, misty rain added to the tense atmosphere as Jamie stepped out of a concealed doorway onto the cobbled street, heading for the rendezvous point at Cafe Verhaal, a nondescript backstreet cafe that was easy to miss in the darkness.

The dull green facade and faded letters above the vine-covered entrance whispered of secrets long kept, offering no hint of the warmth and history that lay within its walls.

The scene reminded Jamie of how he imagined Whitechapel would have looked in the days of Jack the Ripper. Cobbled streets, slippery underfoot, led the way to a hundred hiding places where men with bad intentions could go about their work unhindered while the rest of the city continued on, oblivious to the events going on just a few streets away.

The nearby Nieuwe Maas river carried a heavy fog that rolled in off the North Sea. As the second largest city in Holland, Rotterdam was a major seaport, and its many canals linked the different districts to each other in a maze of waterways and narrow streets that only seasoned locals knew how to navigate.

Using the pretence of tying his shoelaces, Jamie glanced around him to make sure nobody was following. It was an impossible task, with deep, dark doorways and alleyways in every direction, so Jamie relied on his instincts that had never failed him before.

Although the atmosphere crackled with anticipation, Jamie put that down to his imagination, which was running wild with images of pirates and spies hiding in every dark corner.

His spine tingled, but not in a manner that warned him

of danger. It was something he could never put into words, but he'd risked his life enough times to know what his instincts were trying to tell him.

And tonight, they were telling him he was safe.

For now, at least.

With a quick glance over his shoulder, Jamie pushed open the door, the tinkling of a bell announcing his arrival. He stepped into Cafe Verhaal's intimate interior and was taken back in time by the scent of aged wood, stale beer, and fresh coffee.

Dark wooden beams stretched across the ceiling, and antique furnishings dotted the space, their worn surfaces telling tales of countless whispered conversations. Low lighting cast deep shadows, adding to the cafe's sense of timelessness and mystery.

Small windows, their thick curtains drawn, ensured privacy from prying eyes, while bookshelves lined with old books and curiosities created a cosy, secretive feel.

Jamie scanned the room, noting its nooks and crannies, each offering a private corner for discreet discussions. It was clear why this place had been chosen for the meeting.

As he entered, he caught the eye of the cafe's owner, a grizzled man in his forties who had seen his share of action in the First World War.

Bram was an active member of the growing Dutch resistance movement, and his cafe was a regular meeting place for men and women who wanted to avoid the growing threat of the Abwehr.

Bram threw a subtle nod in Jamie's direction, telling him that his presence was welcome. Jamie nodded back and headed to a table that overlooked the meeting room at the back of the cafe.

He was early, so wasn't surprised the room was empty. That was how he'd planned it.

Jamie took his seat and ordered a coffee from the waitress who came to take his order. Once settled, he relaxed and studied the patrons in the half full cafe, taking stock of their body language and the way they watched others coming and going.

They must be regulars because Bram would have let him know if there were any strangers in the cafe this evening. Jamie relaxed and waited for the meeting's participants to arrive.

He was used to places such as this. As an expert in reconnaissance and surveillance operations that required stealth, he was one of Unit 317's most experienced operatives.

With the imminent threat of war, Jamie spent more and more time in dark, dank places all over Europe. Resistance movements were growing, and Britain's intelligence services needed to know who they were and what they were doing.

Liaising with them was a big part of Jamie's remit for Unit 317, and he understood the vital importance of his role. He took it seriously, because he knew that if Western Europe had any hope of defeating the Nazis, the resistance movements in the occupied countries would have a critical role to play.

As he waited for the participants, his mind cast back to 317's offices in the War Rooms underneath Whitehall almost two weeks earlier. Tony Sanders had called him to an emergency meeting and stared at him through tired eyes that looked as though they hadn't closed in days.

"This is a big one," Sanders had told him. "Zobart is arranging a meeting between SIS, the Dutch resistance, and Dutch intelligence. We need to know the situation on the ground and when the Germans are likely to attack. Your job, or at least a part of it, is to monitor the meeting and extract the SIS operatives if the shit hits the fan."

"What's the other part of my mission?" Hawke asked. There was always an active element to his missions, and this was what he'd been waiting for.

"The MI6 operatives will pass you a file containing the names of suspected Abwehr agents working in Rotterdam. Your task is to identify them, photograph them, and find out who they are working with. Don't engage, just photograph. Then bring the information to me so we can decide what to do next."

Hawke smiled at Sanders. He loved his job.

The bell tinkled, dragging Jamie back to the present.

The first person to enter was Lucas Van Der Berg, a respected officer from the Dutch military intelligence. Jamie knew him well from previous encounters they'd shared.

Van Der Berg nodded as he strode past and entered the meeting room. As he did, the bell tinkled again, and this time it was the first of the two MI6 operatives, Charles Bennett.

He and Emma Clarke had travelled from Amsterdam for this meeting, and neither was known to Jamie. He only knew them from the photographs supplied to him by Sanders in London.

Bennett slipped a large brown envelope into Jamie's lap as he walked past, their eyes never meeting, and their body language never letting on that they knew each other.

As Bennett entered the room with Van Der Berg, Emma Clark entered the cafe. She was as pretty as her photograph had depicted.

In her mid-twenties, Emma's shoulder-length dark hair demonstrated the soft waves currently in fashion. In different circumstances, she was exactly the type of girl Jamie would ask out for a date.

But not tonight. Not now. He shrugged off his feelings and concentrated on the task at hand.

The only one missing now was Pieter De Jong, the charismatic leader of the Dutch resistance. Jamie had read a lot about him, but this was the first time their paths would cross in person.

As he watched the main door, footsteps from behind took Jamie by surprise. De Jong had entered the cafe from the rear, which Jamie hadn't been expecting.

He kicked himself for focusing too much on Emma and losing track of his mission, which, although expected to be uneventful, nevertheless was potentially dangerous.

Two burly guards stood at the rear door, obviously members of De Jong's resistance unit and his personal guards.

Once they were all present, the door was closed, and the secret meeting got underway. Although not privy to the details, Jamie knew enough of what was going on to understand its importance.

The Dutch players would share critical insights into German communication patterns and potential vulnerabilities, based on the latest decryptions and analysis.

They would also pass on the latest news of German troop movements and their spies, informing SIS what they were up to in these final moments before the expected invasion.

In return, the MI6 operatives would pass on what they knew about the situation, and they would offer promises and guarantees that they would coordinate their work with the Dutch so they could work together to meet the Germans head-on.

Fifteen minutes later, with the meeting in full swing,

Jamie got up to leave. His job inside Cafe Verhaal was over.

He would wait in the shadows until Emma Clark and Charles Bennett exited the cafe, and then he would watch as they left for Amsterdam.

His real mission would begin the next morning.

Chapter 15

A movement at the rear of the cafe caught Jamie's eye as he stepped towards the front door. A flash of steel in the dim light told him something was amiss, so he changed direction and ran towards the meeting room.

One of the guards pointed his weapon at the other. His free hand unlocked the rear doors.

Jamie's hand flew to his pistol, but he was a split second too late. Before he could react, the rear door burst open with a splintering crash, and three more men charged into the cafe, their guns drawn, and their faces twisted with malice.

They moved with the precision of trained killers, their eyes cold and merciless as they turned their weapons on the loyal guard.

The man barely had time to cry out before a hail of bullets tore through him, sending him tumbling to the ground in a heap of blood and shattered bone.

Two attackers kicked open the door to the meeting room while two others charged towards the patrons huddled in terror at their tables.

A machine gun let rip on everyone in the cafe. Nobody had a chance, and within seconds, blood splattered the walls as men and women fell under a hail of bullets.

Bram reached under the counter, but he was mown down before he could reach his weapon. Jamie watched as at least three bullets tore into him.

Jamie hit the ground, rolling to the side as bullets whizzed past his head. He brought his pistol up, sighting down the barrel at the maniac with the machine gun. His finger tightened on the trigger, and the gunman's head snapped back, a spray of blood and brains painting the wall behind him.

One down, but there were still more to go. Jamie spun, searching for his next target, and spotted another assailant crouched behind an overturned table. The man wore the uniform of the Dutch military reserves, but Jamie knew better.

The aggressors shouted at each other in German, and Jamie was in no doubt that they were members of German intelligence, perhaps the Sicherheitsdienst, or the SD, as it was better known.

The SD was the intelligence wing of the SS, and they were notorious in intelligence circles for being fanatical and ruthless.

He inched his way towards the meeting room, his heart pounding in his ears as he prayed that the MI6 operatives were still alive. The sheer amount of gunfire made it seem impossible, but he had to try. He had a mission to complete, and he would see it through to the bitter end.

A flicker of movement caught his eye as an attacker emerged from the meeting room. The man started towards his comrade behind the table, but Jamie was faster. His pistol barked twice, and the man crumpled to the ground, his eyes wide with shock.

Two down, two to go.

A burst of automatic gunfire ripped through the overturned table Jamie was hiding behind. A bullet caught him in the head, sending his world into a white-hot frenzy of agony and confusion.

As everything went dark, pangs of sorrow and regret surged through his brain. He was sorry for all the things he would never do, and he was sorry for all the people he would never see again, especially his parents back home in Wales.

And as the last vestiges of life slipped away, he sent up a final, desperate prayer, a plea for mercy and forgiveness in the face of the unknown.

~

FROM THE SHADOWS of a nearby alleyway, SS Sturmbannführer Albert Kreise's slate grey eyes watched as the carnage unfolded, his thin lips curled into a smile of cruel satisfaction. Each gunshot was a symphony to his ears, a testament to his guile and ruthless efficiency.

Like the phoenix rising from the ashes, Kreise had risen from ignominy and banishment to prove himself once again worthy of Heydrich's praise. And now, as the screams of the dying filled the night air, he knew his redemption was at hand.

Kreise was a patient man, a man who knew the value of biding his time and waiting for the perfect moment to strike. He had endured the sneers and whispers, the sidelong glances, and the mocking laughter of his fellow SD agents as he toiled away at his desk, reduced to little more than a glorified clerk.

One telephone call from Heydrich. That was all it took.

At over six feet tall and in his mid-forties, Kreise was

back where he belonged at the forefront of the SD's operations in Holland. And he would make damned sure that he never let his master down again.

He didn't know what caused Heydrich to make that call, but he didn't care. He'd never liked Bonn, and as for the other SD agents who made fun of him, he would not forget who they were.

He would do whatever it took, no matter how many people had to die, to remain on the good side of Reinhard Heydrich, head of the infamous Reich Security Main Office, or RSHA, for short.

The RSHA controlled the security and intelligence agencies of the SS, including the Gestapo, SD, and the Kripo, the German criminal police department.

This made Heydrich, or the Blond Beast as he was known, an extremely powerful man. He was ruthless, and Kreise knew several men who'd crossed him, never to be seen again.

He knew he didn't have long before the Dutch authorities got there, so he crossed the street and got to work, making sure there was no trace of any German involvement.

As far as the world was concerned, this was a Dutch criminal matter, where one resistance group had a misunderstanding with another, resulting in a bloodbath of epic proportions.

Kreise entered the building and made a beeline for the agent from Unit 317. Using a concealed camera hidden inside a cigarette case, he took several pictures of the dead operative.

His source didn't know who 317 was sending, but he'd been assured that one agent would be there to assist MI6 in case of an emergency.

For the first time, Kreise had outwitted Unit 317. He'd

rather have captured the operative alive because his own particular skills at interrogation would have worked wonders for their knowledge about the secretive British Special Operations Unit.

But the man, whatever his name, was dangerous, and his men did the right thing in killing him before he could ruin the mission.

As it was, he'd taken out two of the SD agents Kreise had sent in, and they were two of his best men. Unit 317 had to be respected, and even Kreise begrudgingly admitted to himself that he admired them.

He kicked at Jamie's body, secretly wishing it was Michael Fernsby lying before him.

He shrugged and barked orders at his two remaining men.

"Get our dead out of here and make sure you don't leave anything behind."

"Yes, Sturmbannführer Kreise," came the reply.

The two remaining men dragged their fallen comrades out of the rear doors to a waiting vehicle. Kreise entered the meeting room and stood over the dead bodies of his sworn enemies.

Two members of MI6, a Dutch Intelligence Officer, and the recognised leader of the Dutch resistance. Not a bad night's work.

He took several photographs of the deceased agents and seized the files they had in their possession, replacing them with leaflets from a rival Dutch resistance unit that was known to have grievances with Pieter De Jong.

On the way out, he photographed the cafe's owner, known only as Bram. He was known to have had dealings with just about every group and intelligence unit that resisted the Germans, so his death would be welcomed in the hallowed halls of the RSHA.

He stopped one last time at the body of Jamie Hawke

and stared at him for a few seconds before whispering a few last words in English.

"You may not be Michael Fernsby, but you'll do for now. One day it will be him lying at my feet, and that will be the best day of my life."

Kreise took the envelope from Jamie's inside pocket and kicked him as he stepped over him, firing one last parting shot of hatred. Then he left, determined to enjoy the look on Heydrich's face when he showed him the photographs and evidence he'd gathered that night.

The Dutch press, orchestrated by the Abwehr agents that had infiltrated them, would make sure Germany wasn't blamed for the incident.

SS Sturmbannführer Albert Kreise was a happy man.

Chapter 16

The shrill ring of the telephone stopped Alison Turnberry in her tracks. It was ten pm, and Unit 317's secretary should have gone home hours ago.

She sighed and let go of the door handle.

With a heavy sigh, Alison turned back, her eyes fixed on the telephone that demanded her attention. The direct line to Tony Sanders rarely rang without good reason, and the urgency of its tone sent a shiver of apprehension down her spine.

"Sanders?" The gruff voice on the other end of the line was immediately recognisable, its tone as sharp and unyielding as the man himself.

"No, sir. This is Alison Turnberry. Major Sanders isn't here."

"Find him. Tell him he needs to be in my office at eleven sharp." The line went dead. Dansey was never big on conversation, but even for him, this was terse.

It must be really important.

With a sense of growing unease, Alison hurried through the labyrinthine corridors of the War Rooms, her footsteps echoing off the damp, shadowed walls. She knew exactly where to find Tony Sanders, the memory of his parting words still fresh in her mind.

He had left the office on time for once, a rarity in itself, to meet with Richard Keene, the man whose stint as head of the Endurance Escape Training course in Scotland had come to an end.

As Alison emerged into the night, the cold, drizzling rain seemed to mirror the sense of foreboding that had settled in her gut. She pulled her coat tighter around her shoulders, the damp fabric clinging to her clothes as she hurried through the deserted streets.

The Red Lion pub, nestled on the corner of Parliament Street and Derby Gate, normally glowed like a beacon in the darkness, its warm light spilling out onto the glistening pavement. But not now. Not with the blackout.

The pub was alive with the raucous laughter and chatter of its patrons, the air thick with the scent of ale and cigarette smoke. Alison pushed her way through the crowd, her eyes scanning the room for the familiar faces of Sanders and Keene. She spotted them by the window, their heads bent together in conversation, and a wave of relief washed over her.

"Alison!" Sanders looked up in surprise, his eyebrows arching as he took in her bedraggled appearance. "What are you doing here? Come and join us."

Keene rose to his feet, a smile tugging at the corners of his mouth as he reached out to shake her hand. "It's good to see you again, Alison," he said, his voice warm with genuine affection. "Did you miss me?"

Despite the gravity of the situation, Alison couldn't help but return his smile, a hint of mischief sparkling in her blue eyes. She knew the effect she had on men, the way they responded to her delicate features and quick wit. But

Keene and Sanders were different, their respect for her running deeper than mere physical attraction.

"Of course I missed you, Richard," she quipped, her tone light and teasing. But as she turned to Sanders, her expression sobered, the urgency of her mission returning in full force.

"May I get you a drink?" Sanders asked, gesturing to an empty chair at their table.

"No, sir. I'm sorry to interrupt your evening." Alison glanced around the pub, her voice lowering to a conspiratorial whisper. "Colonel Z called. He sounded vexed and told me to find you and tell you to be in his office at eleven sharp."

Sanders nodded, his brow furrowing with concern. "Did he give any indication as to what it was about?" He looked at Keene, who had shifted in his seat, his eyes sharp and attentive.

"No, sorry." Alison shook her head, a sense of unease settling in her stomach.

Sanders turned to Keene, his expression grave. "It's probably about your mission. I haven't told you yet because you've only just got back from the north, but we have an important task for you."

Keene nodded. "I was hoping you'd say that. Should I accompany you?"

"No. Go home and get some rest. I'll call if I need you this evening. Otherwise, be in the office tomorrow morning and we'll discuss it then."

The two men shook hands and Sanders left his half-finished pint and turned towards the door. He dashed out of the Red Lion with a sense of dread hanging over him. Keene walked out with Alison.

If Dansey was summoning him at this hour, it must be important.

Chapter 17

Dansey appeared agitated, which signalled that something had either happened or was about to happen. He kept things close to his chest, and the fewer people who knew what was really going through his mind, the better.

He stared at Tony Sanders through round glasses that appeared too small for his head. "Sorry to drag you away from the pub, Sanders, but this can't wait."

"There's no problem, sir. Has something happened in Rotterdam? I got a communication from Jamie Hawke earlier, and I was coming back here later to check the transmissions. I wasn't expecting to hear from him until tomorrow morning, when the main phase of his operation was due to begin."

Dansey picked up the file that sat on his desk. Then, in a rare burst of anger, he threw it forcibly back down again.

"I just got off the telephone with Denniston. Someone set us up." He spat the words out.

Sanders felt his stomach lurch, an icy dread settling in his gut as he leant forward in his chair. "What happened?"

"I don't know the full details yet, but I'm going to meet with Denniston and others at Bletchley Park tomorrow morning."

He fixed Sanders with a stare that pierced straight through him, his eyes blazing with a mixture of grief and rage.

"Hawke is dead," he said, the words falling like hammer blows in the stillness of the room. "So are two MI6 operatives."

Sanders felt the blood drain from his face. "What happened?"

"Like I said, I don't have the full details yet. It appears everyone showed up, and the meeting was going ahead as planned. But someone was waiting for them. They shot up the entire cafe, killing everyone in there."

Fire blazed in Dansey's eyes. "Including all our men and women."

Sanders slumped back in his chair, his mind reeling as he struggled to process the enormity of the loss. "They killed everyone?" he asked, his voice hollow with disbelief. "Including the Dutch?"

"Everyone," Dansey snarled. "We'll know more tomorrow. Be at Euston Station at six tomorrow morning. You're coming with me."

Sanders nodded, his jaw clenching with grim determination as he rose to his feet.

He went to his own office and slammed the door. Jamie had been a long-serving member of 317 and he was very fond of him. Whoever killed him must have been well prepared, because Jamie was no fool and would have seen most ambushes coming from a mile away.

He clenched his fist at the thought of informing his parents in Swansea of the loss of their beloved son.

He left word for Alison to inform Keene of his absence and stumbled out of the War Rooms. He wouldn't get much sleep this night.

Chapter 18

The atmosphere in the room was heavy with a palpable sense of loss and tension as the men took their seats around the circular table at Bletchley Park.

The same people who had gathered for the previous meeting were present once more—Dansey, Denniston, and James Baker, the Permanent Under-Secretary of State for Foreign Affairs. But the air was thick with the weight of recent events, the tragedy in Rotterdam casting a dark shadow over the proceedings.

Tony Sanders sat in stony silence, his eyes bloodshot and his face etched with grief. The loss of Jamie Hawke, one of his first recruits to Unit 317, had hit him hard, a blow to both his professional pride and his personal sense of loyalty.

Hawke had been more than just an excellent operative; he had been a good man, a friend, and his absence left a gaping hole in Sanders' heart.

"Tony?" Dansey shouted. "Are you listening?"

Sanders looked up, blinking as he tried to focus on the

man across the table. "I'm sorry," he said, his voice rough with emotion. "I was thinking about Jamie Hawke."

"A terrible loss," Dansey said. "He was a good man. So, too, were the MI6 operatives we lost. Both Charles Bennett and Emma Clarke were excellent agents who will be badly missed."

"Their loss must not go unavenged," Baker said. "But do we know what happened? Do we even know who killed them?"

Dansey passed around a report that had recently been typed up. "You don't need me to tell you, gentlemen, that the information in this report is not to be discussed outside this hut."

He fixed Baker with a pointed stare, his eyes narrowing as the other man's face flushed with indignation.

"The information will be shared with the PM, and a few others he deems fit to hear it," Baker retorted, his voice rising with barely contained frustration. "If you have any problems with that, Dansey, I suggest you take it up with the PM directly."

Dansey scowled. He hated bureaucrats and their uninformed opinions.

Sanders read the brief, struggling to control his surprise when he reached Dansey's conclusions at the end.

Denniston cleared his throat, breaking the tense silence that had settled over the room. "The Dutch newspapers are reporting that it was an inside job," he said, his voice carefully neutral. "They claim it was a rival resistance group that had issues with Pieter De Jong, the resistance leader."

"Utter rubbish," Dansey replied. "For one, nobody else would have known about it, and for another, the owner of the cafe was well known to all the resistance groups in Rotterdam. A rival group wouldn't have killed *him*, even if it was them that did it, which I don't believe for a second."

"Who was it then?" Baker asked.

"The Dutch government and intelligence services are angry," Dansey ignored the question. "They categorically deny that a rival resistance group carried out the attack."

"What are they saying in regard to who did it?" Sanders asked.

"They didn't say anything," Denniston replied. "Because they don't know. The attackers were dressed in Dutch military reserve uniforms, and they used Dutch military equipment to carry out the attack. That's all they know."

"How did you come to the conclusion that Zobart was behind the attack?" Sanders referenced Dansey's conclusions.

"Because he was the only man in Holland that knew about it outside of the men and women who attended," Dansey said. "He organised the meeting, and he was the only one who knew all the details."

Sanders shrugged. "Apart from those of us here in this hut."

"Which we immediately cleared of any involvement," Dansey cut him off.

Baker glared at Sanders, his face flushed with indignation. "I know you object to my presence here," he said. "But that does not mean I am a German spy. I take great offence at your accusations."

"I'm not accusing you of anything," Sanders said. "I was merely stating a fact."

"You're forgetting that you and I are the only men who knew what Hawke looked like," Dansey said. "So, unless you are suggesting that I was involved, we can safely rule out anyone here."

"Of course not," Sanders said. "But Zobart didn't know what he looked like either."

"I wouldn't be so sure about that," Dansey said. "Zobart is a shrewd operator, and he would have known everyone there except Hawke. It wouldn't take much guesswork to figure out who the stranger in the room was."

The hut fell silent as everyone digested Dansey's words.

"How do we prove it was Zobart?" Denniston asked, breaking the silence. "We have nothing in the way of communications, or we'd have taken him in by now."

"He's too smart for that," Dansey said. "Even now, he's showing the world how distraught he is at the loss of so many great Dutchmen. He does, of course, deny all involvement with the intelligence services and the resistance, but we know better, even if the press doesn't."

The room fell silent again as each man mulled over Dansey's words.

"Let's start with the attack itself," Dansey said. "Whoever did it knew who was there and what it was about. They were waiting for them. At least one member of the resistance was probably involved, and they would have helped the other attackers enter the cafe from the rear."

"We know that's what happened by the way witnesses outside described it," Denniston added. "Whoever did it entered from the rear, and that would have been sealed before the meeting started."

"So, we can agree that at least one member of the Dutch resistance was involved," Dansey said. "No matter how much Zobart and the Dutch government deny it."

"Agreed," Sanders said. "It wouldn't have been possible without some collusion between them."

Dansey leant back in his chair, his eyes distant as he considered his next words. "After that, and this is pure speculation at this point, I believe the German SD carried out the attack. They are well trained, and they are more than capable of carrying out such an operation."

"Again, I agree," Baker said. "But why? There are intelligence meetings all the time. So why now? Why attack this one?"

"Because Hawke was about to find out who the German spies and implants were in Holland," Sanders said, realisation suddenly entering his brain. "Pieter De Jong knew the Germans who were infiltrating their country as reporters, salesmen, and anybody else who could influence and provide information about military installations and the vital ports in Rotterdam."

"Correct," Dansey said. "There's your reason why this happened."

"So," Denniston said. "The question is, what do we do about it?"

"We all agree that Zobart is a likely double agent," Dansey said. He looked at the faces gathered around the table, studying each one as they nodded in agreement.

"We need to catch him in the act," he continued. "Zobart is shrewd and won't be easily cornered. He'll cut off all ties with us at the first hint that we're onto him, so we have to proceed with caution."

"So, what do we do?" Sanders asked.

"I have an idea," Dansey said. "But you won't like it."

"What?" Sanders asked.

"I know a British businessman who does a lot of work in Holland." Dansey pulled another file out of his briefcase and passed it around the table.

"He was photographed in Antwerp meeting with known Abwehr agents. We dug deeper and discovered that he meets regularly with Germans all over Holland."

Denniston's eyes widened with surprise, his brow

furrowing with concern. "Why didn't you arrest him?" he asked.

"We were about to when the Stourcliffe affair blew up in our faces. We needed all our resources to deal with his treachery. This man wasn't a priority, so we didn't follow through with it."

"What kind of information was this man passing?" Denniston asked, his face a picture of incredulity.

"Lower-level information mostly," Dansey replied. "He was tailed taking photographs of naval and military installations around Britain, as well as detailed manifests of shipping lanes he knew of because of his business interests."

"That's hardly lower-level information." Baker spoke up. "That could damage the country in many different ways. He needs to be arrested and removed from society."

"Which is why I am proposing we do it my way," Dansey said.

The hut fell silent again as everyone braced themselves for what Dansey was about to say.

"Like I said, you won't like it. But this is war, and the man's a traitor to our country."

Chapter 19

Albert Kreise felt the weight of fear coiled in his gut like a python as he ascended the steps to the RSHA office at Prinz-Albrecht-Strasse 8 in the heart of Berlin.

The air seemed to grow thicker with each step, the looming presence of the building pressing down on him like a physical force.

As he approached the entrance, Kreise couldn't help but notice the heightened security that had gripped the city since Fernsby's audacious theft of the Kriegsmarine's confidential U-boat plans from Admiral Ludsecke the previous November.

Armed SS guards stood at attention, their eyes scanning the street with a cold, calculating gaze that seemed to pierce through to Kreise's very soul.

Whatever stunt the British had pulled off would never happen again. Himmler and Heydrich had made triple sure of that.

Kreise paused at the threshold, his hand trembling as he reached for the door handle. He knew he should be feeling triumphant, flushed with the success of his mission in Rotterdam, but all he could feel was a sickening sense of dread, a certainty that he was walking into the lion's den.

The RSHA office housed the most feared security apparatus in the world, a labyrinthine network of spies, assassins, and ruthless enforcers, all under the command of the infamous Reinhard Heydrich.

Kreise had seen firsthand the depths of the man's cruelty, the casual ease with which he could order the execution of anyone who dared cross him.

He'd been lucky the last time he'd been at the RSHA. If it wasn't for the good work he'd done with the British businessman, Robert Stourcliffe, and the British MI6 operatives in Venlo, Holland, he'd be as dead as Admiral Ludsecke was.

Banishment to desk duty in Bonn was a picnic compared to what Heydrich had done to others, so even in his rage, Heydrich had seen a quality in him that was worth saving.

Now he'd proven Heydrich right, and he was nervously hoping that the Blond Beast would recognise it and allow him back to full-time operational duties.

The secretary looked him up and down with a look of disdain when he entered the rarified atmosphere of the office on the top floor. She told him to take a seat, and the look on her face when he'd been made to wait for over an hour told him she was enjoying watching his discomfort.

Finally, her telephone rang, and when she replaced the receiver, she pointed towards the door behind her desk.

"He'll see you now."

Kreise rose on unsteady legs, his heart hammering in his chest as he crossed the room with measured steps. He paused outside the door, his eyes drawn to the gleaming brass nameplate that bore the title SS Obergruppenführer Heydrich in stark, unforgiving letters.

This was it, the moment of truth. He drew in a shaky breath, his knuckles white as he rapped on the door, the sound echoing like a gunshot in the stillness of the hallway.

"Enter," came the reply, the voice cold and clipped, devoid of any warmth or humanity.

Kreise stepped into the office, his eyes immediately drawn to the figure seated behind the large, ornately carved desk at the far end of the room.

Reinhard Heydrich, the architect of terror, and master of the RSHA, looked up from his papers, his icy blue eyes locking onto Kreise with a gaze that seemed to strip away all his humanity.

Heydrich was the embodiment of the Nazi ideal. His tall, slender frame and pale blond hair were the perfect representation of Aryan superiority. His features were sharp and angular, his high forehead and straight nose lending him an almost predatory air, while his thin lips were set in a hard, unforgiving line.

But it was his eyes that truly set him apart, those piercing, merciless eyes that seemed to look right through a person, to see the very depths of their fears and weaknesses.

Kreise had seen grown men wither under that gaze, had watched as hardened soldiers and seasoned spies crumbled like dust in the face of Heydrich's relentless scrutiny.

He snapped to attention, his right arm shooting up in the Nazi salute as he bellowed, "Heil Hitler!" with a fervour born of desperation and fear.

Heydrich threw his right hand up in a half-hearted gesture.

"Heil Hitler. Sit down, Kreise."

Kreise gulped for air and did as he was told.

"You did well. Our little operation in Rotterdam went

perfectly. I think congratulations are in order, Sturmbannführer."

"Thank you, Obergruppenführer Heydrich. The operation couldn't have gone better if we'd tried. Not only did we prevent the British from getting their hands on the names of our operatives working in the city, but we also set back their intelligence operations for months. Not to mention that we took out the leader of the Dutch resistance. He would have been a problem for us in the future."

"Are you aware of the recent directive the Führer gave us?" Heydrich eyed Kreise as a cat would eye a mouse.

"I'm sorry, Obergruppenführer Heydrich. I try to keep up with such things, but I must have been travelling, because I didn't read anything from the Führer."

Heydrich sat back in his chair and crossed his hands. "The Führer was – is – furious about the recent British operation in Berlin. The one where you allowed them to get away with the Kriegsmarine's U-boat plans."

Kreise felt the blood drain from his face, his heart pounding in his chest as he realised the true purpose of the meeting. He glanced towards the door, half-expecting a squad of armed SS guards to burst in at any moment and drag him away to his doom.

"I apologise for my failures, Obergruppenführer Heydrich."

Kreise was sick of apologising for it, but he didn't dare say that.

"The Führer read a report about the operative behind the Ludsecke affair, and even he had to begrudgingly acknowledge the resilience and aptitude displayed by the British spy."

"That particular department is of the highest calibre, Obergruppenführer Heydrich. However, I did have success against them in Rotterdam."

Kreise puffed his chest out, proud of his achievements in Holland.

"Unit 317. That was the first time the Führer had heard of them." Heydrich ignored Kreise.

"They are a top-secret organisation," Kreise said.

"Do not interrupt me again," Heydrich snapped.

Kreise blushed and bowed his head.

"Yes, Kreise, they are an ultra-secret British weapon. Blunt, but effective. I think we can allow them that. However, after Hitler heard of what they did, he was furious that we, that is you, weren't able to stop them."

Kreise opened his mouth to say something, but thought better of it.

"He ordered that all members of this Unit 317 are to be executed on the spot whenever we come across them," Heydrich said, his voice cold and pitiless. "They are not to be captured or treated as regular prisoners of war. The Führer wants them to be defeated and eradicated."

Kreise waited for a moment before speaking to make sure he had Heydrich's permission.

"That's exactly what happened, Obergruppenführer Heydrich. I heard on good authority that a member of Unit 317 would be at Cafe Verhaal that evening, so I ordered my men to kill him on sight. I am happy to say we succeeded, and the operative is dead."

"Am I right in assuming that was the first time we have had any success against this Unit 317?" Heydrich asked.

"I can't speak for any other department, Obergruppenführer Heydrich, because I don't know. But as far as I'm aware, it is the second time. I killed another one of their operatives in Denmark last year."

"Ah, Denmark. I'd forgotten about that one. The less we speak of that operation the better it will be for you,

Kreise." Heydrich's cold eyes stared at Kreise, chilling him to his bones.

"Make sure you continue to have success against them," Heydrich continued. "I also hear that none of the Dutch newspapers are reporting any German involvement. They are all saying it was Dutch resistance in-fighting."

"Yes, sir. That's what they are reporting." Kreise raised his head and looked Heydrich in the eye. "However, from what I hear, neither the British nor the Dutch intelligence agencies believe it is anything other than a German operation. They just can't prove it."

"Nor will they be able to. You did well, Kreise. I was right to reinstate you. From now on, you are relieved of your clerical duties. You are to meet with your contact in Holland and set up a network for the SD ahead of the forthcoming occupation."

Kreise stared at Heydrich.

"You are now in charge of SD operations in Holland. Begin in Rotterdam, as the port has strategic importance for us. Crush the resistance, infiltrate the Dutch intelligence, and defeat the British and French intelligence services."

"Am I getting a promotion, Obergruppenführer Heydrich?"

"Prove yourself first, Kreise. Do well, and you will be promoted. Fail me again, and you will regret the day you were born."

"Yes, sir. When do I start?"

"Immediately. I want you in Rotterdam next Monday."

Kreise rose to his feet, threw his hand in the air, and gave the most heartfelt Nazi salute he'd ever given.

Chapter 20

With a reputation for refined elegance, Cafe Loos in the Westplein district of Rotterdam was the perfect place for the dinner meeting that was about to take place.

Alexander Shaw, the fifty-year-old Commercial Attaché to the British Embassy in The Hague, was in Rotterdam to discuss the maritime trade routes between Britain and the Netherlands.

At least that was the official story. Given the rising tensions and the threat of a German invasion, it provided the perfect cover for his evening's meeting with Wilhelm Zobart, especially after his new promotion within the Dutch government that now granted him the esteemed title of the Dutch Minister of Defence and Maritime Affairs.

Although not as sprightly as he once was, Alexander Shaw gave the impression of a successful government official. Silver streaks lined his short cropped dark hair, and his piercing hazel eyes reflected a life of dedicated service.

His fit, commanding presence spoke of rigorous discipline, while his seasoned, yet approachable demeanour hinted at depths of wisdom gained from decades in espionage.

Alexander Shaw was no diplomat. In reality, he was one of the top MI6 operatives in the Netherlands, and his mission today was of the utmost importance.

The restaurant at Cafe Loos was on the second floor, and Shaw was led to his table in a discreet, private room overlooking the busy Hofplein railway line. Known for its Art Nouveau decorations, Cafe Loos was a popular meeting place for diplomats and businessmen alike who needed privacy to discuss important matters.

He was early, as he always was. Shaw took the time to mull over the story given to him by Claude Dansey, the deputy head of Britain's Secret Intelligence Service.

The story was as incredible as it was fictional, and the moral implications of what he was about to do weighed heavily on Shaw's mind.

If Zobart truly was behind the attack on Cafe Verhaal, the sacrifice would be worth it, but only if the man he was about to set up was a traitor. Otherwise, he would be throwing a good friend and patriotic British businessman to the wolves.

Shaw sighed and closed his eyes. He'd worked for MI6 for almost twenty years, and never in all that time had he been asked to do what he was about to do.

It didn't feel right at the time Dansey asked him to do it, and although he'd agreed on the grounds of national security, it didn't feel right now.

Shaw didn't have time to reflect on his decision any longer, because the door opened, and the charismatic figure of Wilhelm Zobart was ushered in.

A few years older than Shaw, Wilhelm Zobart's exuberant personality singled him out from a crowd. Although not loud, Zobart had a knack for attracting attention, which wasn't a bad thing for a man in his position.

Shaw watched as he spoke to the usher as if he'd known him all his life. Whether this man was a traitor to his country or not, it was difficult to dislike Wilhelm Zobart.

Of average height, Wilhelm Zobart's mousy grey hair curled over his ears, but his standout feature was his thick, bushy eyebrows that, in everyone's opinion except Zobart's, needed shaving off.

"Wilhelm, it's good to see you again." Shaw rose to his feet to greet his old friend.

"Likewise, Alex. I must say I was surprised that you wanted to meet with me here, especially after that terrible affair at Cafe Verhaal."

"A terrible matter, for sure." Shaw lowered his head for a moment to show respect for the lives lost in the ambush. "Did you ever get to the bottom of who was behind it?"

Zobart eyed Shaw carefully, and he hesitated with his reply. As he opened his mouth to speak, a knock on the door stilled their conversation.

It was the waiter, and after their orders were taken, Shaw kept the conversation light, and away from any serious matters.

Dining in Cafe Loos was exceptional, and this evening was no exception. A glass of sherry served as an apéritif, followed by oysters on the half shell as a starter.

Both men had poached Dover sole as their main course, which was gently poached to perfection. It was served with hollandaise sauce on the side, adding a rich, buttery complement to the dinner.

Baby carrots, steamed asparagus, and new potatoes filled out the dinner, and both men ate silently as they took their fill of the excellent cuisine on offer.

After dinner, they were left alone with a second bottle of wine. The food inside Shaw's stomach sat heavy as he considered his next words.

"You never answered my question earlier. How is the investigation going into the Cafe Verhaal attack? Do you know who was behind it?"

Zobart dabbed the corner of his mouth with his serviette and looked up at Alexander. "Not yet. We have our suspicions, but we haven't yet found the proof we need."

"Was it a resistance group that was behind it?"

It was obvious that Zobart didn't want to discuss Verhaal, but Shaw wasn't letting him off the hook.

"Is this why you invited me here this evening, to ask how an internal Dutch investigation is proceeding?" Zobart asked.

"We have an interest in it too, Wilhelm. Three members of SIS died in the attack, and we are as keen to find out who was behind it as you are."

Zobart sighed. "You are correct, my friend. Although I fail to see what any of this has to do with the British Commercial Attaché, you are, of course, absolutely right."

Shaw smiled at Zobart. "I think we both know the truth, Wilhelm, so let's not pretend, shall we?"

Zobart's bushy eyebrows rose as he smiled back across the table. "Of course I know, Alex. I make it my job to know who I'm dealing with."

"In that case, tell me how the investigation is going."

Zobart sighed. "As I said, we have our suspicions, but until we can prove it, that is all they are… suspicions."

"Fair enough," Shaw replied. "But are you sure it *was* the Dutch resistance behind it? Are you sure it wasn't the Germans?"

"There is nothing to implicate the Germans." Zobart threw his hands in the air. "We're following the evidence, and so far, it is leading us towards the resistance. That's all I can tell you, Alex. When I know more, I'll let you know."

After a brief silence, Zobart glanced up at his friend. "What's the latest from your side? Is there anything I should know?"

Shaw took a deep breath to stop the bile rising in his throat. "I have some news that you may find interesting, especially after the Stourcliffe saga we just endured."

At the mention of Robert Stourcliffe, Zobart's eyes grew wide. Shaw knew about the bribes he'd taken because Stourcliffe had left detailed notes about his dealings after his suicide.

In Shaw's opinion, and many others in SIS, the fact Zobart had taken bribes from Stourcliffe, an English businessman whose trade agreements with the Dutch were vital to both countries, didn't mean he was a double agent also taking bribes from the SD.

One just proved he was greedy, but the other accusation was much more serious. Shaw, like many others, didn't believe it true for one second.

"Well?" Zobart asked. "What is it?"

Shaw leant forward as if someone might hear outside the closed door.

"I was in London last week when I got a call to meet with Claude Dansey."

"Ah, Dansey," Zobart sneered. "Colonel Z. The man who lost all credibility in the Netherlands after the fiasco in Venlo last November."

"Yes, well, he's a highly valued member of our intelligence committee." Shaw wasn't fond of Dansey either, but he wasn't discussing it with a Dutchman.

"What did he tell you?" Zobart sneered again. "That the German SD was behind the Verhaal attack, and that the Dutch government knew about it all along? Does he really believe that we would have allowed it to happen if we'd known about it?"

Zobart's voice had risen several levels, and his cheeks flushed.

"Calm down, Wilhelm," Shaw said. "We discussed no such thing. In fact, what we discussed is a serious breach of Britain's security, as well as yours."

Zobart leant back in his chair. "I'm listening."

Shaw swallowed again. *This is it.*

"I believe you know Edward Harrington."

"Harrington?" Zobart's eyes shot up. "Of course I know him. He's very important to our maritime trading agreements. Not as much as Stourcliffe was, but he's a big player in the maritime trade between our two countries."

Shaw clenched his fist under the table. "He's not what you think he is."

"What do you mean?" Zobart asked. "Are you insinuating he's spying for the Germans?"

"I'm not only insinuating," Shaw answered. "I'm telling you he is."

Zobart pushed his body back against his chair, his eyes as wide as saucers. "How do you know this?" he asked.

"We photographed him in Antwerp and other locations, including Rotterdam, meeting with known Abwehr operatives. When we discovered his treachery, we monitored his activities both here and in Britain."

"Why wasn't I informed earlier?" Zobart looked angry. "We could have helped each other."

"That's exactly what I'm doing right now," Shaw explained. "We wanted to make sure he was definitely working for them first."

"What information has he been passing?"

"We watched him snooping around military installations all over Britain. We also know he was passing information on regarding our merchant navy, just as Stourcliffe did."

"How long has this been going on?" Zobart asked.

"Too long. He fell under the radar once the Stourcliffe affair broke out. Then we discovered something even more damning about him."

"I'm all ears." Zobart leant forward.

"He was followed to a meeting in The Hague where he met with an SD agent. This operative has ties going all the way back to Heydrich himself, so it's a big deal, to say the least."

Zobart's eyes grew wide again. "All the way to Heydrich? Who is this agent?"

"We only know his alias, but we're working on discovering his true identity." Shaw looked Zobart in the eyes.

This is it. This is the moment.

"Harrington's involvement is deeper than we ever suspected, even more than Stourcliffe's. We want to catch him in the act, meeting with the SD agent. If we can, we can break up the entire German operation in the Netherlands. It's a big deal for both of us."

Zobart stared back at Shaw. "If what you say is true, this could be big news for us both."

"There's more." Shaw was now in the meat of the deception. "Like you, we suspect the Verhaal incident was a Dutch operation. However, unlike you, we believe it was executed with the help of the SD."

Zobart stared, his eyes never leaving Shaw's.

"The operation was too smooth, too professional, for it to be the work of just a rival resistance group. I'm giving you top-secret information here, Wilhelm, so you must keep this to yourself."

A perceptible nod confirmed Zobart's acceptance.

"We believe if we break up Harrington's spy network, it

will lead us to the true perpetrators of this heinous crime. If the SD were involved, then so too were some senior Dutch people, either politicians or intelligence operatives. Either way, we can catch them and break up their operation once and for all."

Shaw sat back, his pre-planned speech over with. He felt like he wanted to vomit, but instead, he locked eyes with his Dutch counterpart and allowed the silence to envelop them as the implications of what he'd just revealed sank in.

"Are you sure of this?" Zobart finally asked.

"Positive."

"Then, on behalf of the Dutch government, I can assure you we want to help. This will be a joint operation, and London must cooperate at the highest levels."

"You know how London is," Shaw answered. "London will do what London wants to do with this. It's out of my hands. All I know is that they are treating it as a top priority, and they want it over with as soon as possible."

Zobart glared at Shaw. "Very well then. I ask that you keep me informed, and I assure you we are at your service to assist as best we can."

The two men shook hands and said their goodbyes. Shaw remained behind for a good half hour after Zobart left, drinking away his guilt and wondering how much truth was in the story he'd just told.

The last thing he wanted to do was set up an innocent British businessman, even if it did prove Zobart's innocence or guilt.

THE HAGUE WAS LESS than an hour's drive from

Rotterdam. Once there, Shaw went immediately to his office and dialled Dansey's private number.

"It's done." His voice was hoarse.

"Did he fall for it?" Dansey asked.

"Time will tell," Shaw answered. "If Harrington shows up dead, we'll know Zobart's guilty. If he doesn't, well, you were wrong, and the mole is someone else."

"Correct," Dansey said. "If Zobart's guilty, he'll be worried that Albert Kreise is the SD agent you referred to. If he's captured, Zobart will be exposed, and he won't want that to happen."

"What do we do now?" Shaw asked.

"We sit and wait."

Chapter 21

Hampshire, England, February 29, 1940

Ever since returning to London from Scotland a month prior, Michael Fernsby had been on standby. Tony Sanders didn't want to see his time wasted, so immediately on his return from family leave at the end of January, he'd sent Michael to the new training facility set up for Unit 317.

Ravenscourt Manor was, to an unsuspecting public, the picture of an idyllic British countryside mansion. Set in the New Forest, Hampshire, Ravenscourt Manor was founded by King John in the early thirteenth century.

Originally a part of the famous abbey, the manor house was built after Henry VIII's reformation in 1538 when he declared himself head of the newly formed Church of England and dissolved the monasteries in England.

Although the manor underwent extensive renovation and expansion during Victorian times, much of the original church and its surrounding lands remained intact.

The New Forest, with its extensive woodlands, provided a perfect location for Unit 317's unique training requirements. Far from the hustle and bustle of the big cities, Ravenscourt Manor was hidden from prying eyes.

The large, deep river leading to the English Channel gave easy access to France and mainland Europe, as well as giving opportunities for any water-based training that other divisions of the military may find useful.

Especially the Royal Navy.

Michael would never forget the day he arrived and saw Ravenscourt Manor for the first time. It took his breath away with its sheer beauty and elegance, and as an avid student of ancient architecture, he was in heaven from day one.

The main house, an imposing structure of renaissance and Victorian architecture, was riddled with sprawling wings and hidden passages.

Its historic charm belied the intensity of the activities within—rooms once dedicated to leisure now hosted sessions on physical fitness, guerrilla tactics, escape and evasion techniques, surveillance tactics, language training, and silent killing.

It was now the central hub for instruction and strategy sessions, and it was the place where he lived and worked.

The grounds of Ravenscourt Manor were equally transformed. The manicured gardens and ornamental lakes of the past now featured obstacle courses, firing ranges, and areas designated for explosives training.

The dense woods surrounding the estate offered a natural obstacle for survival training, teaching operatives how to live off the land and move around unseen.

The training went far beyond anything that was taught in the Endurance Escape Training in Mallaig. That was primarily aimed at regular soldiers and airmen who found themselves cut off behind enemy lines, needing to avoid the enemy while they found a way back home.

It was mainly defensive in nature.

This training was, by its very definition, offensive in nature and was designed to make Unit 317 the most dominant offensive operational unit in the British Armed forces.

It was the most intensive training Michael had ever undergone, and he enjoyed every second of it. It also gave the other operatives who weren't currently on active duty a chance to get to know each other.

It was policy for members of Unit 317 not to know much about the other operatives. They didn't even know how many of them there were, and they certainly weren't privy to what operations they were assigned to.

Clearly, this was all done for operational security. In the case of capture, which members of Unit 317 were more vulnerable to than most, they wouldn't be able to give any straightforward answers to the inevitable questions the enemy interrogators would throw at them.

The eight operatives at Ravenscourt Manor went only by their first names. Surnames and any personal details were expressly forbidden. So too were any conversations about past operations, although some were so legendary that everyone knew about them.

For Michael, that meant everyone knew about his exploits with Gustav Adler and the manner in which he'd twice escaped the grip of the Nazis in their own backyard.

His three-hundred-mile bicycle ride into Denmark was considered especially impressive, and his ingenuity was discussed as part of the escape and evasion training. Although Michael wasn't mentioned by name, everyone present knew who it was about.

Michael enjoyed an environment where he didn't have to explain himself, and where his personal situation was kept private. All he wanted to do was train and learn as much as he could.

The better he got at his job, the more chance he had of surviving the war.

With this thought in mind, he looked at the other seven men gathered around the rectangular dining table in what had once been the great hall. Large portraits of previous owners glowered down at them from the walls, no doubt disapproving of these men invading their grand domain.

Michael wondered how many of those gathered around the dining table would live to see the end of the war. Not many, if any at all. He silently shrugged as he realised he was including himself in his statistical analysis.

As it had been at his home in Sandwich, most of the food was homegrown on the extensive grounds of Ravenscourt Manor. Fresh fish was served with potatoes, carrots, and asparagus.

Conversation was light during dinner. After a hard day's training, everyone was tired and ready to rest.

"Great run today, Michael," one of the older operatives called Thomas said. He was in his mid-thirties, with well-defined muscles and a strength that was unmatched in the group. Michael placed his accent as somewhere close to Norfolk, but that was the extent of what he knew about him.

"Thanks," Michael answered. "It was a tough one, especially with those rucksacks they made us carry."

"Yeah," another named Harry spoke up. "They must have been a hundredweight or more." Harry spoke in a distinctive Liverpool accent. "Me legs are killing me now."

Everyone agreed, and the discussion turned to more mundane topics as several men talked about their aches and pains.

There never had been much serious banter at Ravenscourt. The operatives were allowed out in the evenings and weekends, and many of them frequented the local pub, the Yachtsman's Bar, which was in a nearby village a couple of miles away.

This evening was no exception, and Michael waited until the men piled into the pub before heading to the radio room to listen to the shortwave broadcasts from mainland Europe.

As it was a training facility, the radio room was not manned around the clock and Michael took advantage of this and spent every evening searching the airwaves for his beloved Mina.

He lived for the nights when he'd hear her voice calling to him through the National HRO radio receiver, and his heart melted every time. He studied her words, searching for clues as to where she might be.

All he knew was that she wasn't in Germany. He'd always assumed she was in France because that was the closest country to her home in Bavaria but nothing she'd ever said gave away her location, which was a blessing to Michael's ears.

If he knew where she was, then so too, would the SD and the Gestapo. Her broadcasts were digging at the heart of Nazi lies, and the more she broadcast, the more of a target she would become.

Especially after the expected invasion of Western Europe.

Michael clung to the hope that the French, along with the British, would be able to push the German advance back and defeat them. Belgium and Holland didn't have the military resources to stop them, but with British and French forces combined, he had full confidence that the Germans could be defeated.

And then he would find Mina.

He changed the coil pack to the right frequencies, donned the headphones, and turned the HRO on. Once the light at the front turned bright red, the receiver was ready.

He turned the dial, slowly and carefully, listening for her voice in the wilderness. Several different language broadcasts came and went. Most he couldn't understand, but the German ones came across loud and clear.

Many of them were propaganda, telling whoever was listening how great Hitler was, and how their glorious leader was creating an empire that would last for a thousand years.

Michael scoffed. *If I have anything to do with it, your thousand-year Reich will fall by the summer.*

He turned and turned, and as he was about to give up, he heard her. Faint and crackly at first, but as he fine-tuned the dial, her voice grew louder and clearer.

Michael's heart skipped a beat, and his pulse rate increased as her opening words fell into his ears.

Good evening, my dear listeners. Tonight, it saddens me to speak. Not just from a place of shelter, but from the very heart of our collective struggle.

There's a story untold in any official Nazi narrative, a story that sheds light on the lengths to which some will go to stifle our yearning for freedom.

News has come to me regarding a terrible incident in a quaint cafe in Rotterdam, Holland. In this cafe, known only to a select few as a haven of whispered truths, a grievous act was recently committed.

Under the guise of night, lives dedicated to the cause of liberty and freedom were brutally extinguished. The attackers, Nazi cowards cloaked in the darkness, betrayed not just the brave men and women who resist Nazi tyranny, but the very essence of what it means to be human.

This incident, lost amidst the cacophony of our daily struggles, was a targeted strike not just against those who resist, but against the innocent who found themselves in the wrong place at the wrong time.

And yet, from this darkness, a beacon of resilience emerges. For every voice silenced, a dozen more shall rise, echoing through the alleyways and airwaves, a chorus of defiance against those intent on destroying everything we hold dear.

Unless Europe unites as one, the dark heart of Hitler will continue to threaten us as we have never been threatened before.

All of you who follow me know what the Nazis did to my family, and we are but one. There are many more coming to light, far too many for one person to reveal. This evil will never stop unless we rise together and stop them now, before it's too late.

Michael listened intently, scribbling her words down as fast as he could. She was obviously referring to a recent incident in Rotterdam, but what? Nothing had been reported on the radios or newsreels in Britain, so whatever it was, it had been kept quiet.

Is she in Rotterdam? I thought she was in France, but if she was, then why send a message about an incident that occurred in Rotterdam?

Michael sighed. She was probably just reporting on something she'd heard about. But how had she heard about it when he hadn't?

It was probably something to do with the Dutch resistance, but Michael would make a point of mentioning it to Tony Sanders when he had a chance to find out what event she was referring to.

And now, to my friends across Europe, a simple reminder: The lark sings at dawn, even in the deepest winter. This is not just a call to awaken to the beauty of the morning, but a signal, a directive from the heart of our struggle to yours. Be ready, for the dawn is near.

Michael gasped, the breath catching in his throat. Clearly, this was a call to action, a warning of a pending event that would strike at the heart of the Nazi war machine.

What was she talking about? And why was Mina

broadcasting the message? Was she working for a resistance group?

The thought of Mina working for a resistance group or on behalf of an intelligence agency from whatever country she was hiding in filled Michael with a mixture of dread and pride.

Dread, because actively working against the Nazis put her firmly in the firing line of men like Albert Kreise. The thought of Kreise getting his hands on Mina made him want to retch.

And pride, because even after all she and her family had been through, she was still fighting back, standing up to the evil that was casting a shadow across Europe.

To the one who understands the silent messages carried on the wind, remember the nights when the stars whispered secrets of a future bright with promise. Our dreams, entwined within the roots of the old forest, remain unbroken, a testament to the enduring power of love.

This is Elise, your companion in the darkness, reminding you that though the night may seem endless, the dawn is always within reach. Until we speak again, let the courage of your convictions light the path ahead.

The last part was a clear message to Michael. He closed his eyes and fought back the fear that was tearing at his soul. He felt hopelessly inadequate and insignificant at the sound of her voice talking to him, trying to reassure him that everything would be alright.

I have to find her. I will find her. No matter what I have to do or where I have to go, I will find her.

Chapter 22

April 8, 1940

Somehow, Claude Dansey managed to procure fresh coffee beans, which were about as rare as hen's teeth. Especially now, as rationing fever placed a stranglehold around Britain's grocery stores.

Wherever he got them from, Dansey's secretary made fresh ground coffee every morning, which acted as a searchlight in a dark fog for someone like Tony Sanders, who detested the chicory-laced Camp coffee everyone else had to make do with.

Sanders helped himself to a second cup from Dansey's personal stash while he waited for his boss to arrive at his office for their scheduled meeting. It was unlike Dansey to be late, so whatever the cause, it must be important.

Eventually, forty-five minutes later than scheduled, a weary-looking Colonel Z strode into his office in the War Rooms underneath Whitehall.

"Two coffees, please," he said to his secretary, ignoring the usual morning pleasantries. "And hold all my calls until this meeting is over. Tony, close the door behind you."

Tony pulled a face at the secretary, who smiled back at him. They were used to Dansey's cloak-and-dagger attitude, but this was a little dramatic, even for him.

The outward humour displayed by Sanders hid the inner turmoil that swirled inside him. His shoulders tightened, and as he took his seat in the private office, he wondered which of his men would be sent on their next deadly mission.

"How's the training going at the new facility?" Dansey asked.

"Ravenscourt is proving to be a big success," Sanders answered. "Every operative that is not currently on active service is there, and from the reports I receive, they are thriving and enjoying the training immensely."

"Good. An elite unit requires elite training. This was overdue, so I'm glad it's finally working for you."

Sanders stared at Dansey. He was waiting for the punchline.

Dansey sat back and looked Sanders in the eye. "It's time to put that new training into effect."

Although he'd been expecting it, sending his men to war always made Tony's heart falter, especially after the recent death of Jamie Hawke.

"What's the mission, sir?" he asked.

Dansey leant forward and rested his chin in his hands. "You won't have heard yet, but the newspapers and radio stations will be all over it tomorrow morning. It's the biggest breaking news scandal since the Stourcliffe affair."

Sanders' brow furrowed. "What happened?"

"Sir James Baker was at RAF Biggin Hill yesterday. He was there with several other dignitaries to inspect the new squadron of Spitfires, along with the Hurricane fighters that were already there."

"I knew this, sir. In fact, I would have liked to have

gone myself. I'd love to see a Spitfire close up. I think it's the most graceful fighter plane ever built."

"While I agree, the Spitfire isn't the reason for this meeting." Dansey hated small talk.

Sanders sat in silence, waiting to discover what any of this had to do with Unit 317.

"After the presentation, the politicians made their way back to London and their respective offices. Sir James Baker never made it back."

Sanders shot forward in his chair. "What happened to him?"

"A London police officer found him late last night in a warehouse in East London. He'd been badly beaten and clearly tortured, as there were cuts and burn marks all over his body. And his throat was slit."

"Bloody hell," was all Sanders could think to say. "Why would anyone do that to him? I mean, he was involved in many intelligence briefings, but he wasn't a well-known public figure."

"Clearly, someone knew his importance to the war effort," Dansey said. "No man could withstand what he endured, so we have to assume the worst and accept that he spilled everything he knew from all the intelligence briefings he'd attended, including ours."

Dansey's face turned deep red. "That's why we shouldn't have politicians and bureaucrats involved with our planning and coordination meetings. They're too exposed, and they're easier targets than we are. They should be banned from our meetings, and it's something I've taken up with the brass on several occasions. All to no avail, I'm afraid."

Sanders ignored the callousness of Dansey's comments. He knew deep inside he was as shaken by this news as he himself was.

"A terrible tragedy," Sanders said. "I quite liked Sir James. I bet his family is devastated. Do we have any idea who was responsible?"

Dansey pursed his lips. "Fortunately, the police officer did his job correctly. He sealed off the warehouse and called Special Branch, who called MI5, who in turn called me."

"Did the crime scene reveal anything that we can go on?" Sanders asked. "It sounds to me as if there's an enemy cell operating on British shores."

"I agree, and MI5 is on it. I have a different task for your unit. One that requires special handling."

Here it comes.

"What's that, sir?"

"Edward Harrington."

Sanders cocked his head in surprise. "Harrington?" he asked. "The businessman we set up with Zobart?"

"The one and only." Dansey nodded.

"I thought we'd discounted Zobart?" Sanders asked. "After the British Embassy passed on the false information, we expected Harrington to disappear. Clearly, he hasn't, or you wouldn't be talking about him now."

Dansey paused a moment. "This isn't about Zobart. This is all about Edward Harrington."

"I see," Sanders said. "I just wanted to clear that up, so there is no confusion. What does Edward Harrington have to do with this?"

"I was late this morning because I had a meeting with MI5. They were tasked with tailing Harrington in Britain to see what he was up to. He was regularly seen photographing military installations, and we already know he's passing them on to his contacts in Holland."

"If we know Zobart is not the mole, isn't it time we arrested Harrington?" Sanders asked, confused.

"We were about to. MI5 was collecting evidence to present to the courts that would convict him of treason. Harrington was at Biggin Hill yesterday and was pictured photographing the delegates as they arrived and left the RAF base."

"It proves he was taking pictures of the RAF base," Sanders said. "But it doesn't prove he was involved in Baker's murder."

Dansey threw three photographs onto the desk in front of Sanders. "These were taken by MI5 yesterday. Look at them closely and tell me where Harrington's focus is."

Sanders studied the photos that depicted Edward Harrington taking photographs of the London delegation at the airfield. From the camera angle, it appeared as though Harrington was focusing his attention on the group of men that included Baker, and when Baker broke off on his own, Harrington's body angle moved with him.

"It does appear as though he was focusing on Baker," Sanders said, agreeing with Dansey's assessment. "Why wasn't he arrested yesterday? He was caught red-handed."

"Because we still need to find out who he's working for. If it isn't Zobart, then who is it? Obviously, someone in high authority is directing his actions, and I intend to find out who it is."

"What do you require from us?" Sanders knew it was past time this traitor was apprehended.

"Harrington took the late afternoon ferry from Dover to Calais yesterday and we suspect he is in Holland by now. We want you to go over there, find him, and do whatever needs to be done to discover who his handlers are."

Dansey paused and Sanders could feel the tension in the air.

"If you can't get him back here, we want him eliminated. He's caused this country enough damage by now, and the murder of Sir James Baker is the final straw. He might not have physically killed him, but Sir James's blood is on his hands."

Tony Sanders closed his eyes and took a deep breath. "You want us to take out a British citizen? Do we have authorisation for that?"

"We have the go-ahead from the very top. You are hereby ordered to do whatever it takes to find, interrogate, and silence Edward Harrington."

Sanders rose from his chair, his face ashen from the orders he'd just received. "As always, Unit 317 will do our best, sir."

No matter how many times he was ordered to carry out dirty jobs, Sanders always felt disgusted, as though what he was doing was inhumane and wrong. He sighed as he left Dansey's office.

For king and country, that's how he filed it in a corner of his brain that would be locked away, only to come out in his nightmares.

For king and country.

Chapter 23

Tony Sanders jolted awake, his heart pounding as the telephone's insistent ring pierced the pre-dawn gloom.

The meeting with Dansey the day before hadn't sat well with him, and he'd tossed and turned all night, trying to come to terms with what he was about to do.

He glanced at his watch that told him it was almost five am. Telephone calls this early meant only one thing: something of great importance had happened.

Assuming it was someone from the War Rooms telling him what the radio and newspapers were reporting about the grizzly death of Sir James Baker, Sanders gritted his teeth and shook his head to clear the sleep from his mind.

He'd read the reports and seen the photographs. The last thing he needed at this ungodly hour was another discussion on the horrors of war.

"Sanders," he rasped into the handset. His tongue felt thick and about as dry as cotton wool.

"Sanders, it's Z. Have you heard the radio this morning?"

"Colonel Z?" Sanders was shocked Dansey would call

so early, especially on his private line at home. "No, sir, I haven't. I'm assuming it's wall-to-wall coverage of Sir James Baker's grizzly end?"

All sleep faded as he focused on Dansey's words. The boss wasn't known for early morning calls, especially as they'd held a meeting the day before regarding the same information he assumed was now being reported.

"The Germans invaded Norway and Denmark this morning. There's an emergency meeting at the War Offices at seven am. Don't be late."

An icy chill skittered down Sanders' spine.

Richard Keene.

The invasion wasn't a surprise because they'd been expecting it for some time, but Richard Keene was in Denmark, and that worried Sanders more than the invasion.

I hope he got out in time before the Germans got there.

Clinging to that hope, Tony Sanders quickly dressed and ran out of the door.

The conference room was packed with brass from all departments. Their meeting was ending, and as the generals, brigadiers, and colonels filed out, they were replaced by members of the SIS.

Dansey sat at the head, and Sanders noted senior members of MI6, MI5, as well as Alastair Denniston from Bletchley Park's GC&CS. This was a high-level meeting.

"Gentlemen." Dansey's words silenced the room. "We've all heard the news by now, and except for MI5, we all have a vested interest in what is going on. As much as we feel for the people of Norway and Denmark, our focus must be on our men and women over there and how we can get them out."

Chatter rose around the conference table, and Dansey raised his hand to silence them.

"The last we heard, King Haakon, along with the Norwegian government and the British Ambassador, have left Oslo and are headed north. A combined British, French, and Polish assault force is there, and they are trying to secure the Norwegian ports and send the Nazis back into the sea."

"What is the status?" asked Cunliffe, a man Sanders knew from MI6.

"As you can imagine, there is a lot of confusion, and reports from the ground are hard to come by. We'll update your departments as and when we get any news."

Dansey stared at the men gathered around the room. "You don't need me to tell you that the phony war is over. This action, today, is the beginning of what will become a bloody and lengthy war. The invasion of Western Europe is imminent, and we need to be prepared for whatever happens."

"What are we doing about the men and women stuck in Norway and Denmark?" asked Sir Vernon Kell, the head of MI5, or K as he was known in intelligence circles.

"We're working on that," Dansey said. "We won't be able to get them all out, but those in Norway are trying to get to Narvik. That's their best chance to get out."

"What about those trapped in Denmark?" Tony Sanders asked.

"Norway was always going to be our priority," Dansey replied. "The Norwegian Atlantic coastline is of vital importance. If we control that, we can cut off the iron ore shipments from Sweden that are vital to the German war effort."

Dansey lowered his voice. "Unfortunately, it appears as though Denmark is offering little resistance, and we expect the government to surrender before the day is done."

"Richard Keene is in Denmark," Sanders persisted. "I want to send someone to get him out."

"Absolutely not." Dansey's lips curled into a snarl. "It would be a suicide mission, and we can't afford to lose good men on a wild goose chase. Keene is the best at what he does, and if anyone can get out of Denmark, it's him."

Sanders only half listened to the remainder of the meeting, a question-and-answer session where everyone else asked the questions and Dansey didn't have the answers.

After a further fifteen minutes, Dansey brought the meeting to a close. "Once we know more, your departments will be updated. Until then, gentlemen, remain alert and be prepared for the German offensive to begin in Western Europe, for it is surely coming."

As the men got up to leave, Dansey turned to Sanders. "I need you to stay here. We have other matters to discuss."

Chapter 24

The empty conference room was heavy with a mixture of despair, anticipation, and stale cigarette smoke. Tony Sanders rubbed his eyes, raw from lack of sleep.

"I know you're worried about Richard Keene." Claude Dansey spoke softly. "He's one of our best operatives, and I know how close you are with him. But there's nothing we can do. If we sent in a team of Unit 317's best men to get him out, we risk their lives for nothing. We need your unit now more than ever."

"I'm aware of that," Sanders replied. "My gut reaction was to get him out, but as you said, if there's anyone that can pull off the impossible, it's him."

"And Fernsby." Dansey stared at Sanders. "He's proven repeatedly how resilient he is. He's pulled off the impossible more than once, and I need you to send him to Rotterdam."

Sanders nodded slightly. "I deliberated long and hard last night on who I was going to send on the Harrington mission. As much as I'm loathe to send a young man, he is the perfect candidate for this job."

"Fernsby it is then," Dansey said. He leant forward until his face was inches from Sanders'. "We need to know who Harrington's handler is. We know it isn't Zobart, so it has to be an SD agent. We can't fail with this, Tony."

"Fernsby won't fail us." Sanders clenched his jaw. "He has good reason to despise the SD more than most."

A thin smile creased the corner of Dansey's stern mouth. "Which is exactly why I want you to send him."

He rose to his feet and approached the door before turning one more time to face Sanders. "I've got a team of MI6 operatives searching for Harrington. As soon as they turn something up, I'll let you know. In the meantime, get Fernsby back here so we can prepare him for the mission."

Sanders nodded and followed Dansey out of the conference room. He had work to do.

Chapter 25

Michael Fernsby stared out the window as the train carried him back to London, his mind a whirlwind of conflicting emotions. The rolling hills and picturesque villages of the English countryside passed by in a blur, but he hardly noticed, so consumed was he by the thoughts that raced through his head.

He'd been away for months, first in Scotland and then at Ravenscourt Manor, honing his skills and pushing his body to its limits. The training had been gruelling, but it had also been exhilarating. He'd felt alive in a way that he hadn't in years, his senses sharpened, his reflexes quickened, his mind as sharp as the weapons he wielded with such deadly precision.

But now, as the train drew ever closer to London, he felt a growing sense of unease. He knew he should be eager to get back to active duty, to throw himself into the fight against the Nazis with everything he had. And yet, if he was honest with himself, that wasn't what he truly wanted.

More than anything else, he wanted to find Mina.

She consumed his every waking thought, her voice echoing in his mind like a siren's call. He'd heard her broadcasts, each one a coded message he couldn't decipher.

She was out there somewhere, risking her life to fight the war in her own way, and the thought of her in danger made his heart clench with a fear he couldn't put into words.

As the train pulled into London, Michael gathered himself for what was to come. Sanders had told him on the telephone that he was needed for something important, and Tony wasn't one to exaggerate.

Whatever it was, it was big. He just hoped it gave him the chance to find Mina at the same time.

He stepped onto the platform, his senses immediately assaulted by the sights and sounds of a city preparing for war. Sandbags lined the streets, their dull brown a contrast to the grey concrete of the buildings they protected.

Soldiers in crisp uniforms marched by, their faces set in grim determination. The large anti-aircraft guns remained silent for now, but their presence was a constant reminder of the threat that loomed over the city.

Michael made his way through the crowded streets, his destination the nondescript building that housed the War Rooms. As he approached the checkpoint on Horse Guards Avenue, he couldn't help but notice the increased security measures.

The sandbags were piled higher now, and the guards who checked his identification were armed to the teeth.

Once through, he walked past the War Office and turned right, down the next street until he reached two large doors separated by a smaller door, painted dull green, between them.

Michael stopped and showed his identification for the

fourth time. The young corporal on guard duty gave him a stern look.

"Name?"

"Captain Michael Fernsby," Michael replied, his voice calm and even.

The corporal looked as if he didn't believe what Michael was saying. He ran his finger down the list until it stopped by an entry near the bottom.

"Good morning, Captain," he said, his tone softening slightly as he snapped off a salute. "What's the codeword today?"

In order to use the smaller green entrance to the underground War Rooms, whoever entered was required to give the guards the password of the day. Luckily, Sanders had provided it, along with his orders to return to London that morning.

"The sky over St Paul's looks nice this morning," Michael said.

The corporal nodded, a hint of a smile playing at the corners of his mouth. "Have a good day, Captain Fernsby," he said, stepping aside to let Michael pass.

He hurried through the door, the sudden drop in temperature sending a shiver down his spine. The narrow passageway was damp and musty, the air heavy with the aroma of mould and stale cigarette smoke.

He followed the steep stairs down, down, down, into the bowels of the city, the intermittent lights casting eerie shadows on the rough stone walls.

Eventually, the stairs ended, and Michael walked into a cacophony of activity where senior officers mixed with men and women in civilian attire, all of whom looked as though their world was about to end.

The serious nature of Britain's war effort wasn't lost on anyone down there, and Michael felt the collective responsibility as Britain faced the might of Nazi Germany.

He found the unmarked office used by Unit 317 and entered. The hustle and bustle of activity in the corridors outside the office were mirrored inside as Alison Turnberry, the unit secretary, was listening to the radio and transcribing furiously as she noted the contents of the coded message.

Tony Sanders was in his office, studying a file he held in his hands. A steaming cup of coffee sat on his desk, and Michael resisted the urge to grab it as he approached.

Alison looked up and gave a small wave to acknowledge his presence. She was concentrating hard on the messages she was receiving and didn't have time for small talk.

Sanders, his face lined with exhaustion, smiled as soon as he saw his young protege.

"Ah, Michael. It's good to see you. How was the New Forest?"

"Outstanding," Michael replied as the two men shook hands. "Ravenscourt is the perfect place for our needs. You did a first-class job of finding it, Tony. Everyone loves it, and the training is top-notch."

"I'm glad to hear it." Sanders' expression became serious. "I'm glad you're here, Michael. The shit's hitting the fan and the situation's getting bleaker by the day."

"I heard on the radio." Michael replied. "Is it true that Richard is stuck in Denmark?"

Sanders nodded, his eyes heavy with more than just sleeplessness.

"Is that why I'm here?" Michael pressed him. "Am I going to get him out? After all, he helped me in Denmark last year. Without him and John Palmer, I wouldn't be here today. I owe him one."

Sanders didn't answer for a moment while both men remembered the sacrifice and courage of John Palmer, who'd lost his life by helping Michael escape Kreise in Denmark the previous November.

"Unfortunately, no. That's not why you're here." Sanders looked up from his desk. "We have a very important task for you."

Michael protested, but Sanders waved him silent.

"Sit down, Michael. Don't think for a moment that I haven't argued about sending someone over there to help Richard, but the conflict is hotting up and we need our operatives in active theatres to do what they've been trained to do."

"Search and rescue is a big part of what we do." Michael's voice was caustic. "I can get Richard out of there."

"If anyone other than yourself can evade the Nazis long enough to find a way to safety, it's Richard Keene. He'll be alright. You have something else to do."

Michael was about to speak when Alison knocked on the door and rushed in without waiting for an answer.

"I'm sorry to interrupt, Tony, but I just received a message from Richard in Denmark. I've decoded it, and this is what it says."

She handed Sanders a typed message, which he read out loud so Michael could hear it.

Germany invaded yesterday. Denmark has already fallen. The government surrendered to save the country from a bloodbath. I got out of Copenhagen just in time and am heading for Sweden.

This will be my last message as I'm leaving the radio behind. Will contact again when I'm safe.

RK

Sanders sagged back in his chair, his face awash with

relief. "Thank God for that," he said, his voice barely above a whisper.

Alison beamed, her eyes shining with unshed tears. For a moment, the tense, dark atmosphere of Unit 317's small office lifted.

Alison returned to her desk and Sanders looked at Michael, his facial expression back to what it was earlier.

"You won't like what I'm about to say. The order came from the very top, and they requested you by name. I don't have the authority to override, and honestly, I wouldn't even if I could. As much as I don't like it, it's a vital operation that calls for a man with your particular set of skills."

He slid a file across the desk, the words 'Top Secret' stamped across the front in bold, red letters.

Michael digested the information, his eyes growing darker with every line he read.

"Let me get this straight. Dansey allowed this Harrington to continue his spying activities even though he knew all about them?"

Sanders nodded. "I said you wouldn't like it."

"I read about Baker in the newspapers," Michael said. "Terrible ordeal. Poor chap must have suffered terribly. What I didn't know about was his involvement with SIS."

"You weren't supposed to. We met in secrecy for a reason. What happened to poor old Baker was the direct result of Harrington spying on him."

"Why wasn't he stopped earlier?" Michael asked. "If you knew he was taking photographs and passing information to the SD, then why wait? Baker would still be alive if we'd done our jobs properly."

"I can't argue with that. Colonel Z wanted to find his handler. We believed it was Zobart in Holland, so we set Harrington up as a decoy to flush him out. He's still alive, so Zobart was a red herring. Harrington is handled by someone else, probably SD."

"It could be Kreise." Michael spat the name out. "We know he's operating in Rotterdam because of what happened to Stourcliffe. This is something that fits with him perfectly."

"I agree. We think it *is* Kreise, which is why we're sending you over there. Find out what Harrington is up to. Question him, and get him back here any way you can. That way, you don't have to do what they're asking. That's my advice."

Michael's mind raced, images of Kreise's cruel smile and cold, dead eyes flashing through his thoughts. He'd love nothing more than to put an end to that monster's reign of terror once and for all.

"Don't allow your feelings to impede the mission," Sanders warned. "Kreise is as clever as they come, and if he finds a weakness, he'll exploit it and kill you."

"I know what Kreise is all about," Michael said, his voice hard as steel.

He flipped through the file again, his brow furrowed. "The report made no mention of Harrington's whereabouts," he said. "Where is he, and how do I get to him?"

"How you get to him is down to you. Use whatever situation you find yourself in to get close to him. I don't know where he is. Not yet."

"What do you mean, not yet?"

"He's somewhere in Holland. Probably Rotterdam, but that's all we know so far. Dansey has agents looking for him. Your job starts when they find him."

"What do I do in the meantime? Do you want me to go to Rotterdam and wait for him?"

Sanders shook his head. "No. Your presence will be noticed, and Harrington will never show up. Stay in

London and study the files. Learn everything you can about Harrington, so you'll be ready when they find him. As soon as they do, you're off."

"Consider it done."

Michael didn't like the idea of taking out a British businessman and fervently hoped it wouldn't come to that. If he could get to him, he could somehow get him back to London, even if he had to tie him up and drag him back.

The prospect of spending time in Holland was exactly what he wanted to hear. He was fairly sure Mina was there somewhere, even though it was still possible she might be in France. As long as he found her before the Germans invaded, everything would be alright.

France and Britain would repel the German advance, and Michael would keep Mina and her sister safe until the war was over.

Simple.

Chapter 26

May 4, 1940

The streets below Michael's rented flat above the market stalls and shops on Berwick Street in the heart of London's Soho district were damp and quiet as he unlocked the door to the stairs leading up to his flat.

He'd just returned from a five-mile run around the early morning streets of the city, and he was drenched from the heavy drizzle that Britain was famous for.

As it was a Saturday, he wasn't expected in the office. He'd been in limbo ever since his meeting with Tony Sanders nearly three weeks earlier, and as much as he hated the cramped office underneath Whitehall, he'd kept himself busy by learning everything he could about Edward Harrington.

By now, he knew everything there was to know about the English businessman, including details about his expensive divorce after his wife caught him cheating with the wife of a rival businessman.

The costly divorce was the reason SIS suspected Harrington had begun selling secrets to the Nazis.

Add this to the fact that he beat his wife to a pulp during their separation, and Michael had good reason to despise the man.

Whatever sympathy he'd held for him at the beginning of his brief had long gone. Now all he wanted was for Harrington to get what he deserved, although he still held the belief that he'd somehow get him back to London so he could go on trial as a spy.

Dripping with sweat and rainwater, Michael glanced at the scene below his window as he wiped himself down with a towel. The drenched streets glistened in the dull, early morning half-light as men and women began setting up the market stalls for what they hoped would be a busy Saturday.

Although he'd been in London for weeks, Michael hadn't been allowed to visit his family in Kent. He was on active standby, waiting for MI6 to locate Harrington somewhere in Holland. The moment he was sighted, Michael would be called to action.

There was no time to go home.

He'd just about got himself dry when a heavy bang on the front door startled him. As far as he knew, the only people who had a key to the downstairs door leading to the street were the residents of the flats and the owners of the building, neither of whom Michael had much to do with.

One of the main reasons he'd rented this particular flat was for that very reason. After the deliberate car crash that injured his father so badly, Michael was acutely aware of the threat to his life.

The always-locked door to the street, and the narrow stairs leading to the apartments upstairs, afforded him vital time to prepare and react should the need ever arise, which was why he was so surprised that someone was banging on the door to his flat right now.

As a member of Unit 317, Michael was allowed to carry his weapon at all times. He still favoured the German made Walther PPK over British made guns, and he grabbed it before padding over to the door.

"Who is it?" he shouted, standing to the side in case a series of bullets ripped through the wooden door.

He knew he was acting over the top, but after what had happened to his father, which was supposed to have been him, he was very careful wherever he went.

Much to his father's aggravation, he'd insisted on hiring a team of bodyguards who protected his family around the clock. He'd even had his father build a small cottage at the rear of the house where they could live.

It wasn't much, but the extra peace of mind it brought allowed Michael to concentrate on his work and not worry about the safety of his family, especially after Judith's kidnapping the previous year.

If only I could do the same for Mina.

The thought flashed through his mind as he waited for a response from whoever was behind the door.

"Captain Fernsby, it's Corporal Smith. I'm sorry to bother you, sir, but I have an urgent message for you."

Michael recognised Corporal Smith's voice as they exchanged pleasantries every morning outside the green door at Whitehall.

Excitement and testosterone mixed together, causing the pit of his stomach to churn.

They've found Harrington!

He hid his weapon and opened the door. Corporal Smith stood to attention and saluted as soon as he opened it.

"I'm sorry to bother you at the weekend, sir, but Major Sanders has an important message for you."

Corporal Smith held out a sealed envelope to Michael. "He ordered me to deliver it personally."

Michael took the envelope and stared at the man delivering it. Somewhere in his mid-twenties, Corporal Smith was small and stocky. He looked to be in shape, and Michael detected his accent to be from London's East End.

"Is there something wrong, sir?" Corporal Smith's face turned red.

"No, why?"

"You're staring at me, sir. Is there something you would like me to relay to Major Sanders?"

"Hmm." Michael allowed a faint smile to curl his lips upwards. "How did you get past the door downstairs?"

"The door, sir?" Corporal Smith looked uncomfortable.

"Yes, the front door to the street. We keep it locked at all times, and as far as I know, only the residents have a key for it."

The corporal's face turned beetroot red. "The major told me you might ask me that."

"Well?"

"Major Sanders gave me the key. I didn't know that I wasn't supposed to have it."

Michael shook his head. *Sanders! That sneaky fox had a key made somehow. I bet he's got a key to my flat too.*

"You're not in trouble, Corporal Smith. You were only carrying out orders. I was just curious."

"Is that all, sir?"

"Yes, thank you. I'll take it from here."

Corporal Smith saluted Michael one more time and clomped down the stairs, glad to get away from the young captain in the flat above.

Michael closed the door and eyed the envelope in his hand. The familiar tingling of expectation made the hairs on his arms rise, and he closed his eyes as he prepared himself for the inevitable outpouring of fear and trepidation as the contents revealed themselves.

He sat on the couch, his fingers trembling slightly as he tore open the envelope. He pulled out a handwritten note and held it up to the light so he could read it.

They've found him! We only have a brief window, so report to HQ immediately.

Tony

Michael closed his eyes and jumped up from the couch.

Chapter 27

Michael hurried down the damp corridors to the unmarked office occupied by Unit 317. Although it was a Saturday, Alison Turnberry was sitting at her desk, sending and receiving coded messages from all over Europe.

Tony Sanders sat in his office and waved Michael in as soon as he entered the main office.

"Shut the door," he ordered.

Michael thought he looked tired as he sat in a chair opposite.

"Sorry to break into your weekend, but MI6 sent a message a short time ago informing us they'd found Harrington."

Michael nodded. He knew why he was there.

"Wait right there." Sanders rose and strode purposely out of the office. Michael presumed he was fetching a file from Dansey's office, but he returned a few minutes later carrying three steaming hot cups of coffee from Dansey's private stash.

Alison was delighted, and gave the thumbs up sign as she continued deciphering the messages that were coming in. Michael hoped some of them were from Richard Keene, informing the unit that he was safely out of Denmark.

"Is Richard safe?" he asked as Sanders closed the door and retook his seat opposite Michael.

"We haven't heard from him yet, but you know yourself that it takes a long time to extract oneself from enemy territory. I have no fear for Keene. With all due respect, he's the best we've got. If anyone can do it, he can."

"I still wish you would send me over there to assist," Michael said. "He did it for me, and I would love the chance to return the favour."

"That opportunity may arise one day," Sanders answered. "But not today."

He pulled a file from a drawer beneath his desk and pushed it towards Michael. "In there, you will find your alias and travel documents. Study the file so you know your new identity inside out."

Michael pulled the file towards him but didn't open it.

"Where is he, and what do you want me to do exactly?"

"MI6 photographed him in Rotterdam, meeting with his known Dutch business associates. After some discreet enquiries, they discovered he was due to attend another meeting next week. You will be there to intercept that meeting and bring him home."

"Who is he meeting, and where is it taking place?"

"It's all in the file," Sanders pointed at the file sitting in front of Michael. "He is supposedly meeting with known Dutch business associates of his in the port of Rotterdam, but we think it's a front."

"Why?" Michael would study the file later, but right now he wanted to hear it from Sanders' own mouth.

"Because the meeting is late at night in an abandoned

warehouse. We think he's trying to get safe passage to Germany, and he's meeting his handler to thrash out the details."

"You think he's trying to defect?" Michael asked.

"It makes sense," Sanders answered. "He knows we're onto him, so he can't return to England. The only place he'll be safe is in Germany, so my best guess is that's where he's trying to go."

Sanders leant forward and looked Michael in the eye. "We want you to stop him before he defects. By any means possible."

Michael held his gaze.

"By any means possible?"

"By any means possible. Find out who his handler is. Even though we don't think Zobart is involved, we want to know who he's working with. If we can get hold of them, we can blow a hole right through the German intelligence units operating in Holland. This is big, Michael, and I know you won't let us down."

The ensuing silence was surrounded with an intense atmosphere. They both knew what was at stake, and there was a lot riding on Michael's young shoulders.

"If his handler is who we think it is, we owe it to ourselves to end it right there. Albert Kreise was the man responsible for Jamie Hawke's death, and we all know what he's done to your family."

"I don't need any extra motivation." Michael's jaw was set like stone. "We might be at war with Germany, but in Kreise's case, it's personal."

"Follow your training and don't allow emotions to dictate your actions," Sanders warned. "The mission is too important, and we want you back in one piece."

"Hopefully with Harrington in tow and Kreise dead," he added after a brief pause.

"When do I leave?" Michael asked.

"The meeting is set for May ninth, so you leave on Monday. You will pose as a crew member on a fishing boat leaving Harwich Harbour. It will take you to the Hook of Holland, and MI6 operatives will meet you there."

"How will I get to Rotterdam?"

"Rotterdam is less than twenty miles from the Hook of Holland, and MI6 will get you there and provide shelter until the operation takes place."

Michael stared at Sanders, the tension clear in his facial features. "Assuming I get my hands on Harrington, how do I get him back here?"

"MI6 knows what you're there for. They will drive you to a concealed field outside the city where our Lysander will be waiting for you."

Michael suppressed the bile in his throat as his hatred for Kreise bubbled to the surface.

"Tension is high all along the border," Sanders warned. "The German invasion is expected any day, so at the first hint of any military action, you have to get to the Lysander and out of Holland. Do I make myself clear, Michael? I don't want any heroics over there."

"What if they attack before or during the operation?"

"Then abort and get out. It's going to be a long war and we need you to be safe."

Michael nodded. "Understood."

He grabbed the file and left Sanders to his thoughts, sitting at the desk near Alison to study the file.

It was 9.30 am when he glanced at his watch. He would have the file memorised by dinnertime that evening.

With the possibility of ending Kreise's reign of terror as well as the potential to seek out Mina, wherever she was, he would be ready.

This time, Kreise was not going to get away from him.

Chapter 28

The one-hundred-mile journey northeast to Harwich Harbour was exactly as Michael had wanted it to be, quiet and relaxed, as it gave him time to go over his mission and get everything straight in his head before it began.

More importantly, it gave him time to adjust mentally to where he could find that hidden lever buried deep inside the recesses of his brain and turn off his everyday feelings and emotions.

With each passing mile, he could feel himself retreating inward, the layers of his everyday self fading away to reveal the cold, hard core of the agent beneath.

He'd done this often enough by now to know that the Michael Fernsby everyone knew and loved would not survive in the cruel world of counter-espionage where he operated. He had to park his emotions and bury them, protect them, so he could live again in the normal world once this was all over.

If he survived.

Tony Sanders, as he always did, drove Michael to his destination port in England. He may be Michael's boss, but it was evident from his actions that he cared deeply for the men he was sending into the heart of the enemy.

They left London early to avoid any possibility of driving in the blackout that came with the lowering of the sun every evening. The increase in shambolic road accidents and serious injuries had exploded since the introduction of the blackout, and the last thing either man wanted was to be caught on the open roads after dark.

"It's more dangerous than being on the run in Nazi Germany!" Sanders commented. It was a statement Michael couldn't argue with.

They stopped for an early lunch at a cafe outside Ipswich. Both were delighted to discover they served all day breakfast, but their faces dropped when they saw what was on the menu.

Rationing had severely curbed the availability of bacon and sausages, and eggs were a luxury that many cafes had few of.

Both men ended up with a bowl of porridge, served with a small amount of extra milk.

Michael's eyes lit up when the cafe's owner produced the one luxury neither was expecting. He approached their table carrying a green tin with gold lettering that most people in Britain would recognise instantly.

Given the rationing of sugar, Michael hadn't expected any syrup, but he gladly took the iconic Lyle's Golden Syrup from the outstretched hand and looked longingly at the golden lion on the front of it.

"Just one spoonful each, please," the cafe's owner said in his soft, west country accent. "It's the only one I've got, and I'll probably not see another one for weeks."

Michael dipped his spoon and turned the thick golden syrup over and over as he lifted it towards his porridge. He took special delight in watching it seemingly defy gravity before falling into the bowl in one big blob.

He watched Tony do the same, and they both stirred their porridge to make a big, gooey mess that was delightful on the tongue.

They ate in silence, and for a few minutes, the weight of the mission rose from their shoulders. The syrup somehow lifted their spirits more than it ever would in peacetime, and Michael enjoyed five minutes of tranquillity.

"That was a welcome surprise," he said as they left the cafe. "If it's my last memory of England, then I'll die a happy man."

"Don't say that." Sanders admonished him. "It was good, but I want you back in one piece."

The remaining twenty minutes were driven in silence as Michael once again went over the details of his mission and the alias he would be using.

Sanders pulled up outside a guesthouse on the outskirts of Harwich Harbour and turned to face Michael, who could see the pain lining his exhausted features.

"Remember, Michael. No heroics. Get in, grab Harrington, and get him to the Lysander. I expect you back here late on Thursday night. That gives you four days to get it done."

"I'll do my best," Michael said. "From the sounds of things, it should be straightforward enough, but you know as well as I do that things don't always go as planned."

"The German invasion is expected any day, so be vigilant and get out at the first sign of any activity. You'll be no use to us as a prisoner."

Michael scoffed. "Do you think Kreise would really allow me to be a prisoner if I was captured by the Germans?"

"That's what worries me. We're closer to hostilities than we've ever been. At least since the end of the First World War."

Sanders reached forward and grabbed Michael's hand. "You know what to do, so be careful and get Harrington back here before next weekend."

The two men shook hands. Then Michael stepped out of the vehicle and watched as Sanders drove away. The solitude washed over him, and he stood for a moment on the pavement before turning towards the closed gate of the guest house that would be his refuge on his final night in England.

Chapter 29

The Herring Gull bobbed gently on the inky waters of Harwich Harbour, a silent shadow against the bustling backdrop of the port.

Even at two am, the docks thrummed with life, the clang of machinery and the shouts of dock workers mingling with the mournful cries of gulls soaring overhead.

Michael breathed deeply, the briny tang of the sea air sharp in his nostrils, undercut by the pungent reek of fish and diesel fuel.

He approached the boat cautiously, his footsteps echoing hollowly on the weathered planks on the quieter southern side of the pier. *The Herring Gull* looked much like any other fishing vessel tied up in the harbour, her paint faded and peeling, her nets worn and frayed from countless voyages on the unforgiving North Sea.

A sudden flare of light blinded him, and he threw up a hand to shield his eyes, squinting against the glare of a powerful torch beam.

"Hold it right there." The voice was gruff, laced with

the unmistakable accent of a man who'd spent his life at sea.

Michael swallowed, his mouth suddenly dry. "Julien Mercer," he said, the alias feeling strangely familiar after repeating it hundreds of times over the previous days. "I was told there might be work for me here."

"Who sent you?"

"Someone I met at the Fisherman's Arms last night called Johnson told me."

There was a pause, the torch beam never wavering from Michael's face.

"Keep your hands where I can see them and come aboard."

The torch clicked off, and a dim light flickered to life on the deck of *The Herring Gull*, illuminating the cluttered expanse of rope and tackle along with the gleam of wet wood and rusted metal. Michael picked his way carefully across the gangplank, his heart hammering against his ribs as he stepped onto the gently rocking deck.

He turned and looked at the darkness behind him. "Goodbye, England," he muttered. With sadness in his footsteps, he turned to face the man behind the gruff voice.

The Herring Gull was no ordinary fishing vessel. Manned by four members of Naval Intelligence on secondment to the SIS, it was equipped with state-of-the-art communications equipment, and an array of hidden small arms weapons that could be used in an emergency.

A shortwave radio transmitter capable of sending and receiving messages across the North Sea was hidden underneath a toolbox, and a Morse Code telegraph key was concealed in a hidden drawer underneath the navigation table in the cramped galley.

A heavyset man emerged from the shadows. Even

under a woollen sweater and a set of oilskins, Michael could see that he'd spent much of his life as a mariner.

Like *The Herring Gull* herself, his weatherbeaten complexion showed a patchwork of deep lines and creases that spoke of years squinting against the glare of the sun and bracing against the biting sea winds.

Michael recognised the man's face from the photographs in his mission brief. Sanders was nothing if not meticulous, and he left nothing to chance.

This was Barker, the ship's captain, and the man in charge of the North Sea crossing.

"Go inside and stay out of sight. Don't communicate with my men, and we'll have you on target by mid-afternoon."

Barker turned, beckoning Michael to follow. Clearly, he was a man of few words, but as the brief stated, he was the best at what he did.

The other three crew members ignored Michael as he entered the galley. Although they acted as regular fishermen, Michael knew from the brief that each man was an expert in his field. One was a navigator, another an engineer, and the fourth was a communications specialist.

Together, they formed the best clandestine naval team the Royal Navy had to offer.

"You can get a brew over there." Barker pointed to a tea urn sitting on top of a small stove. "Help yourself."

"Thank you." Michael did just that. At this ungodly hour, he needed a cup of hot tea.

"I hope you're not seasick," Barker sneered. "It's going to be a bit rough out there."

Michael shrugged. "I don't know. I've never crossed the North Sea in a fishing boat before."

Barker pointed to a bucket. "Use that if you have to,

but do not go outside this galley. Discretion is paramount and you cannot be seen on deck."

"I understand."

As *The Herring Gull* nosed out into the open sea, the waves began to rise, causing the deck to pitch and roll beneath his feet. Michael clung grimly to the edge of the table, his knuckles white, his face pale and clammy.

He'd never been prone to seasickness before, but the combination of nerves and the relentless motion of the boat was proving too much for his stomach to handle.

He lunged for the bucket in the corner, retching miserably as the crew looked on in silent amusement. Barker poked his head through the hatch, his face splitting into a wry grin as he took in the scene.

Michael smiled sheepishly at the sea captain, who shook his head before heading back on deck.

Michael had planned on using the time during the crossing to go over his mission and make sure everything was straight in his head, but his guts told him otherwise.

"I've never felt as sick in my whole life," he complained to Barker, who was the only member of the crew he was allowed to speak to.

Barker laughed. "You look a little green, Mercer. Look on the bright side. You only have another eight hours to go."

The other crewmen laughed, and Michael smiled back, putting on a brave face.

Eight hours! My stomach can't take another eight minutes, never mind eight hours.

By mid afternoon, he'd had enough of the fishing boat and the rough seas, and was glad when Barker told him they were approaching the Hook of Holland.

"Stay in here and don't come out, no matter what

happens," Barker ordered. "I'll let you know when it's time to leave."

Michael didn't argue. The mere thought of standing up made him want to heave.

From the window, he could see that the landscape had changed, the rugged coastline of the North Sea now giving way to the flat, low-lying fields and dykes of the Dutch countryside.

He could see the outline of windmills in the distance, their sails turning lazily in the breeze, and the gleaming ribbon of a river winding its way through the lush green landscape ahead in the distance.

They were approaching the Hook of Holland, the bustling port that marked the entrance to the Nieuwe Maas, the great river that flowed through the heart of Rotterdam and deep into the interior of the Netherlands.

Michael watched in fascination as Barker guided the boat through the labyrinth of channels and waterways, *The Herring Gull*, just another anonymous fishing vessel among the dozens that plied these waters.

But as they drew closer to the port, the signs of heightened tension and looming conflict became impossible to ignore. Minesweepers patrolled the harbour, their decks bristling with guns and armed men, while anti-aircraft batteries loomed on the shoreline, their barrels pointed ominously skyward.

Columns of Dutch soldiers marched along the quayside, their uniforms crisp and their faces grim, a tangible reminder of the storm clouds gathering on the horizon.

The diesel engine, so smooth and rhythmic during the crossing, suddenly began banging and clanging, making unnatural noises that sounded as though it was about to give up at any moment.

As *The Herring Gull* slipped away from the industrial

bustle of the Hook of Holland, Barker skilfully navigated the vessel into the congested, narrower sea lanes that gave access to the Nieuwe Maas river.

These waterways, a labyrinthine network from the North Sea to the river's mouth, demanded a navigator's full attention and skill, especially as they were full of naval and fishing vessels.

Michael watched as the crew hoisted different coloured flags on their mast. On top was a blue one, underneath that a white one, and below that they flew a green one.

The flags fluttered heavily in the wind, and although he didn't question Barker, he realised they were a signal to whoever was waiting for them on arrival.

A few other fishing vessels were unloading their catches on the edge of the river, and *The Herring Gull* docked alongside them.

An official-looking man spoke in rapid-fire with Barker, who gestured at his boat with wild arm movements. The sound of the engines alone was enough to convince the official they needed help, and he pointed to a covered dock where, hopefully, *The Herring Gull* could get the repairs it needed to get back across the North Sea.

"The crew is to get off here while I take her in for repairs," Barker said as soon as he re-entered the cabin. "Get off with them and follow them into the port. Watch for a man carrying an orange basket. That's your cue, and the rest of it is up to you."

"Thank you, Captain." Michael, still feeling horribly sick, rose unsteadily to his feet.

"I don't know what you're here for, but I wish you all the best. Be quick, because I fear that war in Europe is imminent."

Michael nodded. "I will."

He grabbed his trusty rucksack that had been on almost every mission with him and wobbled onto the deck.

Chapter 30

Michael stayed with the other crew members until they were inside a large warehouse of sorts, where men and equipment mingled in a cacophony of noise.

Conversations in several languages could be heard as Michael split off on his own. French, Dutch, Italian, English, and even some German were evident. Michael ignored them all and focused on finding his contact.

An older man with silver streaks in his short cropped dark hair caught his eye. He was carrying a bright orange basket, which Michael presumed was full of fish.

He approached the man casually so he wouldn't draw attention to himself. The contact was examining his basket as if he was checking the quality of the fish.

Michael spoke in his native English, using low tones so as not to be overheard. "I was told the herring here was particularly good this season. Would you recommend it?"

The middle-aged man looked up in surprise at the young man standing next to him. Michael knew by the look on his face that he'd been expecting someone older and more seasoned than he was.

If he was correct, the codeword 'herring' would let the man know who he was.

"Ah," the man replied in a cultured English accent. "The herring is decent, but if you're looking for something truly exceptional, the mackerel's where it's at this time of year."

With the use of the word 'mackerel', Michael knew he'd found the right person.

"Follow me." The contact looked away, avoiding eye contact and keeping his voice low.

He strode towards the entrance doors, and Michael followed a safe distance behind. His stomach, empty from the rough North Sea crossing, churned and groaned as he walked, and for a moment he thought he was going to throw up over the floor in front of everyone.

A great way not to stand out. Michael berated himself and took deep breaths to try and control the heaving sensations in his stomach.

At the vehicle, the contact placed the basket in the rear and waited until Michael climbed into the passenger seat. He spoke rapidly as they drove off.

"Alexander Shaw, Commercial Attaché to the British Embassy." He reached over and shook hands with Michael.

"Julien Mercer." It was better for both if he didn't reveal his real name.

"Colonel Z filled me in on the details. I have sorted out a place for you to stay, and once you've grabbed Harrington, I'll take you to rendezvous with the plane that will take us all back to England."

"You're coming too?" Michael was surprised. "That wasn't in the brief."

"A late change of plans, I'm afraid," Shaw said. "The tension along the border is as high as I've ever known.

We're expecting the Germans to invade any day now, so I've been ordered to return to London with you. This will be my last mission in Holland."

Shaw talked for the rest of the drive to Rotterdam, but Michael was barely listening. The sickening feeling in the pit of his stomach wasn't because of the sea crossing; it was because the thought of Mina and her sister trapped and alone in the path of the marauding Nazis filled him with dread.

"Are you listening, Mercer?" Shaw's words pulled him back to reality.

"I'm sorry. I was contemplating the ramifications of the Nazis invading Western Europe. What did you say?"

Shaw nodded, acknowledging the dire situation the Netherlands and the other countries west of the Rhine faced. "The situation is serious, but I have every confidence that France and Britain will send them back across the border with their tails between their legs."

"I hope so." Michael meant it.

An hour later, Shaw pulled up outside a dilapidated house sitting back from a road that Michael couldn't pronounce. It was on the corner of two streets with one of the city's many waterways in front of it.

A copse of trees surrounded the isolated house, and Michael congratulated the MI6 agent for finding the perfect place for a safe house.

"You'll be safe here until the operation is over. If you have to hold Harrington here for a few hours before we leave, nobody will know as long as you keep him inside the house."

Shaw took a key from his pocket and led Michael to the front door. Once inside, Michael looked around at the sparsely furnished house with the peeling wallpaper and damp spots over the walls.

"I never said it was The Ritz," Shaw said as he watched Michael's reaction to the rundown old house.

Michael ignored him as he looked around. The room contained a two-seater couch, a small table, and one chair.

"There's enough food in the pantry for three days, and the kettle works, so you can enjoy a cup of tea. Everything you need is here, so you won't need to venture outside at all if you don't want to."

"Is there a bed upstairs?" Michael asked.

Shaw shook his head. "The upstairs is empty. The couch over there will serve as your bed."

"What else should I know about?"

Shaw pointed to the threadbare rug covering the centre of the wooden floor. "A shortwave radio receiver is under the floorboards. Pull up the middle board and you'll see it. Colonel Z requested you have access to one in case they had any messages for you, and that's as good a place as any to hide it. We'll take it with us when we leave."

"Where exactly are we?" Michael asked.

He'd studied maps of Rotterdam during the build-up to this mission, but the exact location of the safe house and the place where Harrington was meeting his handler had been left out of the transmissions to avoid any possibility of interception.

"We're in Overschie," Shaw replied, "the Jewish quarter of the city. It's a good place for our kind of work. People tend to mind their own business here, and the canals and alleyways make it easy to move around unseen."

"Where is Harrington's meeting going to be?"

Shaw pulled a large envelope from underneath his coat. "It's all in here. Harrington is meeting his supposed business associates in an abandoned warehouse not far from here."

He tossed the envelope to Michael. "You won't see me again until after the operation. I'll be waiting for you outside the warehouse, and we'll go straight to the rendezvous point from there. Don't worry about the radio. I'll pick it up on my way."

The two men shook hands and Shaw turned to leave. At the doorway, he stopped and faced Michael. "If things go wrong, and God knows I've seen enough in my life to know that's always a possibility, get Harrington back here. I'll meet you, and we'll make our way to the rendezvous together."

Michael enjoyed the quiet for a few minutes after Shaw had left. He knew the dangers ahead, but he was as ready as he could be. Harrington was going back to England if it was the last thing he ever did.

After making himself a cup of tea, Michael made sure the blackout curtains were drawn tight, turned on the dim overhead light, and pulled back the worn rug.

He had three days before the operation, and he was going to make the most of them.

Chapter 31

After retrieving the shortwave radio and setting it up on the table, Michael opened the envelope Shaw had given him and emptied the contents, which weren't much: a page of typed instructions, a set of house keys, a hand-drawn map, and a business card with Shaw's contact details at the Embassy. On the back of the card, Shaw had handwritten a telephone number where he could be reached directly, even in the middle of the night.

It was only to be used in an emergency.

He picked up the typewritten piece of paper and settled back in his chair. With tea in one hand and the instructions in the other, Michael set about the document to see what, if anything, had changed.

GC&CS, along with MI6 operatives on the ground in the Netherlands, traced Harrington to Rotterdam. He was followed, and the operatives photographed him using a dead letter box in a park on the outskirts of the city.

A message was intercepted that ordered Harrington to meet with Compass and Anchor at an abandoned warehouse on the corner of Breevaartstraat. The warehouse is the second building down from the junction with Industrieweg that backs up to the Bornissehaven waterway.

The meeting is to take place at 11 pm.

We believe Compass and Anchor are codenames for Harrington's handlers. Further, we believe that one of them is SS Sturmbannführer Albert Kreise of the SD. We do not know who the other is.

The safe house is located on Burgemeester Konigssingel, and the operative should memorise his location in relation to the meeting place.

The memo was neither signed nor on headed paper. Michael knew from standard operating procedure that after committing it to memory, the memo should be destroyed, and no trace left behind.

Next, he studied the hand-drawn map provided by Alexander Shaw. It showed where the safe house was located in relation to the meeting place, and used arrows to show how to get there.

After carefully memorising the details, Michael struck a match and burned the memo and the map over the sink before washing the ashes down the drain.

He glanced at his watch. It was 5.30 pm, and with his empty stomach growling with hunger after the ordeal at sea, he opened the cupboards to see what delights MI6 had provided for him.

He wasn't surprised to see a loaf of bread alongside two tins of corned beef. A slab of hard cheese and a tin of pears rounded off the selection. This was the regular fare he'd found at all SIS locations, and it seemed to be standard-issue for everyone, regardless of rank or location.

After gulping down a thick sandwich and washing it down with his third cup of tea, Michael lay down for a couple of hours to rest his eyes. He'd been up all night and needed to sleep.

By nine o'clock, he was sitting at the table with a brew in his hand. He turned on the radio, and with a shiver running down his spine, he turned the dial from station to station, searching for her voice.

Most of the broadcasts were, unsurprisingly, Dutch. Some played music, but the majority sounded serious, no doubt a result of the dire situation the country, through no fault of their own, found themselves facing from the aggressor to their east.

He turned the dial for thirty minutes and was about to give up when the dial stopped on a German language broadcast. The airwaves hissed and crackled, but he caught a couple of words before it went silent.

He listened intently to see if the woman's voice would come back. After a few moments, the broadcast resumed and the hairs on his arms rose and crackled with electricity as he heard her voice once again.

Mina!

Michael was stunned when he heard her. Although he was sure it was her voice, she spoke her words in English! It may be broken, heavily accented English, but her words were clear and easily understandable.

Michael held his breath and listened as his heart beat in rhythm with her words. Every syllable touched a raw nerve in his body, and his shoulders twitched involuntarily as he absorbed her message.

To those who stand with us in the shadow of adversity, know this: the night may be dark, and the path perilous, but together, holding fast to what we cherish most, we will emerge into the light of a new day. Our resolve will be the dawn that banishes the night. Courage, my friends, and fortune favour the brave.

Our leader knows we are ready. He stands with us, ready to give his life for our righteous cause. Stand strong, for together we will send the Nazis back across the Rhine, where the people will rise and destroy them.

Be ready for further instructions, for they will be revealed as soon as the darkness begins. He stands with us and has vowed never to leave the Netherlands until the Nazis are defeated and removed from our soil.

This may be one of my final broadcasts, and it fills my heart with sadness to know that not all of you listening will live to see the light return to our lives.

My final wish is that those of us who sacrifice our lives know it is for something much greater than ourselves. Collectively, those of us that survive will rebuild Europe in our own image. We will create a world free of hatred and bigotry, where freedom and peace will reign forever.

If this is to be my last broadcast, then my final wish is for my love, who I hope is listening in a place safe from the peril of the Nazi war machine.

To you, I say that although my voice may be silenced, always know that neither my love for you nor my resistance to the evil that has consumed my homeland will ever be dimmed.

Should we both survive this war, you know where to find me. I will wait for you until my heart no longer beats in my body. Find me, my love, and we will rebuild our shattered lives together.

The radio fell silent, and Michael caught himself breathing hard and sweating. His heart beat as fast as it did after a long run, and he wiped his brow with his sleeve to remove the sweat dripping into his eyes.

"Mina!" he spoke aloud. "You're somewhere in Holland. Where are you? I'll find you and take you back with me on the Lysander."

He knew it was impossible, but hope filled his senses. *Where is she?*

Her words were spoken in English so the Dutch resistance, who she was clearly working for, would understand. She obviously couldn't speak Dutch, or she would have given her broadcast in the language native to the country she was fighting for.

German was obviously out, because nobody would listen to a German telling everyone to rise up and risk their lives for what they believed in.

It had to be English. Michael was so proud of her, and yet at the same time, he was frightened for her. Once the Nazi war machine rolled through Holland and the Low Countries, there would be nowhere else for her to go other than France, who would surely hold out against the Germans, or England.

Spain was another option, and he hoped she was aware of that as the hour of darkness approached.

Michael turned off the radio and looked at his watch. It was almost eleven pm. It was time for him to go out into the night and find the warehouse.

He had three days before the meeting, and he wanted to use the time wisely.

It made sense to do the reconnaissance under cover of night so he wouldn't be seen by prying eyes and followed back to the safe house. There were German spies everywhere, and there was less chance of him being spotted at night than there was during the daytime.

He made sure his false ID papers were in his pocket, and he grabbed his jacket and torch.

Chapter 32

Michael slipped out of the back door of the safe house, his heart pounding in a staccato rhythm against his ribs as he melted into the shadows of a narrow path.

The night air was cool and damp against his skin, the aroma of the nearby waterway mingling with the acrid tang of coal smoke and the sweet, cloying rot of garbage.

He moved silently, his footsteps muffled by the soft earth, his senses straining for any sign of movement, any whisper of sound that might betray a watcher in the darkness.

At the end of the path, he paused, pressing himself against the rough brick wall of a building as he scanned the deserted street. The moon played hide-and-seek behind a veil of scudding clouds, casting the world in an eerie, shifting, half-light.

He instinctively tugged his coat tighter around himself, his fingers brushing the reassuring weight of the Walther PPK nestled in his pocket.

Satisfied he was alone, he slipped out onto the street, hugging the shadows as he made his way towards the waterway. The buildings loomed over him like silent sentinels, their windows dark and shuttered, their facades worn and weathered by the relentless passage of time.

He could feel the history of this place, the weight of centuries pressing down on him, the ghosts of long-dead merchants and sailors and spies whispering in his ear.

At the end of the street, he turned right, following the curve of the waterway as it wound its way through the heart of the city. A bridge was just ahead, a narrow span of stone and iron that arched gracefully over the inky waters.

Michael quickened his pace, his eyes scanning the shadows for any sign of life, any flicker of movement that might signal danger.

And then he saw them.

A couple, wrapped in each other's arms, their faces inches apart as they whispered, giggled, and kissed beneath the gas lamp at the foot of the bridge.

Michael's heart fluttered in his chest, a sudden, irrational surge of fear and envy flooding through him. For a moment, he was paralysed, unable to look away, his mind filled with visions of Mina, of the feel of her in his arms, the taste of her lips against his.

Chiding himself, he shook his head to clear it of the treacherous thoughts. He couldn't afford to be distracted, not now, not when so much was at stake. He forced himself to move, to slip past the oblivious lovers and cross the bridge in a few swift, silent strides.

The luminous dial on his watch told him it was 11.30 pm. He needed to get a move on.

On the other side, he turned left, following the row of warehouses that lined the waterway like a row of rotting teeth sticking out on narrow strips of land across the water.

The air here was thick with the stench of fish and tar,

and the musty reek of damp wood, and Michael wrinkled his nose in disgust as he picked his way along the narrow strip of land between the buildings and the water.

Each of the strips of water between the rows of warehouses had a different name, and although he couldn't remember what they were, he used them as guides along the way.

At the third row of warehouses, he paused, his heart hammering as he studied the hulking structures. *Breevaartstraat.* This was the one street name he had memorised.

He'd found it.

The second building down was larger than the others, its walls of weathered brick and rusted metal looming up into the night sky like the bones of some long-dead leviathan.

He didn't dare use his torch, not even with the red filter, as it would stand out a mile in this environment.

Two large doors faced the road, with a small, pedestrian door close to the front on the right side of the warehouse that was almost invisible in the shadows.

They were the only doors, and other than a small window that would be a tight squeeze, there was no other way in or out that Michael could find.

Satisfied with his reconnaissance, he left the area. He didn't want to hang around too long and risk compromising the operation before it even began.

The main road that crossed the river was less than fifty yards past the warehouse. Although it was late, Michael could hear voices as a few late-night residents either walked or cycled past him.

Backtracking and crossing the river on the quieter road he'd used earlier, he used the same path by the river, but this time he turned up one of the narrow lanes leading to some apartment complexes and more narrow lanes.

Recognising a street from Shaw's rough map, he turned right. Lemkensstraat's two blocks of apartments had a path running between them that ended close to the safe house, and Michael intended to use it on the night of the operation.

Tonight, he just wanted to see it, and as he approached the lane, he could make out a shadowy figure walking towards him from the opposite side of Lemkensstraat.

He ran to the side of the apartment building and hid in the darkness, waiting for whoever it was to pass. The moon came out from behind the clouds to momentarily flood the lane with light, and Michael hugged the side of the building as whoever it was approached.

The person reached the lane between the apartment buildings. It was clearly a girl, because her long hair shone in the moonlight. She turned to look down the lane, and the moment her face came into view, Michael turned to stone.

He knew that walk, that shape, those curves that had haunted his dreams and tormented his waking hours for so long.

Her features, etched into his mind as deep as the Lord's Prayer, shone at him in the moonlight. Michael would recognise her anywhere, and he found himself unable to breathe.

His heart rattled against his ribs, drowning out every other sound, and although he couldn't see the colour of her eyes, everything about her shape and beauty screamed out to him, tugging on his heart like no one else ever could.

It was Mina!

She was here, in Rotterdam, walking alone through the deserted streets in the middle of the night. It defied reason, defied logic, defied every shred of common sense and caution that had been drilled into him during his training.

But there she was, as real and achingly beautiful as she had ever been.

But how? Why here, so late at night, in a tiny back-street in Rotterdam?

He wanted to run to her, to gather her in his arms and never let go, to tell her all the things he had never said, all the feelings he had kept locked away in the deepest, most secret corners of his heart.

But he couldn't. He couldn't risk everything, not now, not when the stakes were so high and the dangers so great.

He was hallucinating. His mind was playing tricks. Michael spurned the overwhelming urge to emerge from the shadows and call her name because if it wasn't her – and the odds were firmly against it – he would jeopardise the entire operation.

He stood there in the darkness, his mouth opening and closing like a goldfish out of water, not knowing what to do. All that training, all that work he'd put in to become an agent of Unit 317, the most elite unit in the British intelligence services, and here he was, flopping around like a fish on dry land, hopeless and helpless.

The girl turned, but before she walked away, she turned one more time, as if sensing someone was watching her in the darkness. Michael got a better look at her face as she turned, and was more convinced than ever that against everything that ever made sense in his life, the girl standing before him *was* Mina.

His Mina.

Still, he did nothing, said nothing, his body rigid with the effort of holding himself back, of keeping the desperate, longing cry that welled up in his throat from escaping his lips.

And then she was gone, disappearing down a narrow

lane between two apartment buildings, her footsteps fading into the night.

He couldn't allow the moment to pass, even if it meant compromising operational security.

Michael sprang into life and ran to the side of the apartment, peering around the side to see where she went. The girl looked behind her as if some sixth sense told her she was being followed.

Michael followed her with his eyes and observed her turning into a doorway of an apartment building at the end of the street. He hurried after her and followed her inside.

Her footsteps echoed on the second floor, and he listened as they stopped halfway down the hall and then ran to where he'd heard her stop on the floor above his head and made a mental note of where her apartment must be.

His legs wobbled as he made his way back to the safe house. *I'm going mad. It can't possibly be Mina. Not this far from home. It can't be.*

Yet he'd known she was in Holland. He just hadn't known where.

Now I do.

That night he tossed and turned, his head full of what-ifs and maybes. He argued against himself constantly, one minute berating himself for being so stupid as to think it was her.

The next minute he was shaking and sweating, worried that this might be the only chance he would ever get to see her again, to hold her again, and to kiss her again.

By daylight, he knew he couldn't let the moment go, not without knowing for sure. His dilemma now was how to do it without compromising his mission.

Sanders would be infuriated if he knew, so Michael

had to make sure Shaw didn't get wind of what he was doing. Although he wasn't supposed to see him again until the night of the operation, which was just two days away, MI6 had a knack of learning information people didn't want them to know.

To hell with them. This is my life, and as short as I'm sure it's going to be, I'm not letting her slip through my fingers again. If it's her, I'm going to find her.

Chapter 33

The dull overhead light in the makeshift living room cast a dim, morose shadow around the room, which mirrored Michael's mood perfectly. It may have been light outside, but the heavy blackout curtains he'd kept drawn were doing their job perfectly.

Michael had been awake all night, tossing and turning, arguing with himself. Almost delirious through lack of sleep, he'd made plans that were immediately considered ridiculous and cancelled.

He rubbed his eyes and got to his feet. Indecision wasn't something he was accustomed to, and if he didn't sort himself out, he knew he'd end up doing something stupid that would result in him being at the mercy of Albert Kreise.

Kreise! The mere thought of his name sent shivers running down his spine. *What if he knows the voice on the radio is Mina? Does he know where she is? Stop it!*

Michael rose to his feet, knocking the kitchen chair over as he got up. He had to do something, because just sitting there wondering was driving him up the wall.

He went upstairs to clean his teeth, and was dismayed when he looked at his reflection in the mirror. His hair was all over the place, but more noticeable were his eyes, that were bloodshot and heavy.

His face was pale, and he knew he needed rest if he was to be in top shape for what he was there for.

Sod it! I've got two more days to sleep. I've got to know if it's her.

Still not convinced about whether or not he was dreaming, he pulled himself together and made himself look presentable. Then he checked his watch. It was still early, so hopefully he could catch her if she left the apartment.

Checking the weather outside, he found the sun was shining, and it was a bright, pleasant morning.

He quickly retraced his steps from the previous evening, and was happy to find a small group of trees across the street from the entrance to the apartment block.

After making sure nobody was looking, he climbed one of the trees that gave him a good view of the entrance and waited.

In his rush to get there, he'd been lax about his needs. He'd done enough stakeouts to know he at least needed water, and he was annoyed at himself for being so unprofessional.

Usually meticulous in his planning, which made him so good at what he did, he wondered why it was that as soon as Mina was mentioned, all planning and preparation went out of the window, and he became a bumbling wreck?

Still chuntering at himself an hour later, he fell silent when a young blonde-haired girl walked out of the apartment. She was alone and carried a rucksack on her back. She stood for a moment, adjusting the straps before heading away from Michael in the general direction of the busier districts of Rotterdam.

It was Senta, Mina's younger sister. Although two years apart, the girls could pass as twins, especially from a distance. Michael immediately fell silent, his mind frozen in a mix of relief and disbelief.

A shiver raced down his spine, sending goosebumps cascading down his arms. *If Senta is here, then Mina must be here too. I wasn't dreaming! She is here.*

Resisting the urge to climb down the tree and approach her, Michael watched Senta vanish behind the apartment blocks as she went on her way.

Mina was in there somewhere, and he wasn't leaving until he found her, no matter how hungry or thirsty he was. If she didn't appear by nightfall, he decided he'd knock on her door. He knew roughly where her apartment was, so he wouldn't have to knock on too many doors to find her.

That was a last resort, as it would bring even more attention upon him, and that was the last thing he wanted. He was already breaking every protocol in Unit 317's handbook, and if this was to get out, Sanders would probably kick him out for being unprofessional and placing lives other than his own in danger.

Hours passed, and Michael became more and more agitated at himself for forgetting to bring water and sandwiches. But he wasn't moving, not until he found her.

In the late afternoon, his entire world burst open when he saw her exit the apartment. Her long golden hair shone in the late spring sunshine, and his heart turned cartwheels at the sight of her.

He was about to shout out her name when another girl of about nineteen, the same age as Mina, joined her. Her brown hair was cut short, and Michael thought she looked thin and pale.

Whoever she was, Mina was close to her. The girls

embraced and laughed as they strolled down Lemkensstraat together.

Michael waited until they turned down the street that went past his safe house before jumping down from the tree. His limbs were stiff from sitting for hours, and he was desperate to use the toilet, but he ignored the discomfort and ran after them, pausing first to make sure he wasn't being watched.

At the top of the street, they turned right, and Michael hurried so he wouldn't miss where they went. As much as he wanted to call out to her, he didn't dare in case he compromised not only his own mission, but Mina's as well. He knew she was broadcasting for the resistance, and God alone knew how much danger that put her in, especially with men like Kreise on the loose in Holland.

They stopped at a tram station a few hundred yards down. Michael joined a group of people, walking behind them to conceal himself from Mina, who constantly looked around, searching with her eyes for any signs that she was being followed.

Someone had trained her, and Michael was grateful for the extensive training he'd received that allowed him to counter her surveillance measures.

While they waited, Michael bought a cream-coloured straw hat with a wide brim from a street vendor next to the tram station. It was perfect for what he needed, and he tilted the brim as far as he dared, so she wouldn't recognise him.

He would bide his time until he got her alone. Then he would give her the biggest surprise of her life.

Hopefully, the best surprise of her life.

When the tram came, he watched as Mina and her friend boarded and found a seat near the front. He entered at the rear and sat on the opposite side several rows back, which gave him a clear view.

The tram jerked forward, and Michael stressed over his inability to speak Dutch. He obviously couldn't use German, and English might give him away to anyone listening for such things.

But he had no choice. When the conductor came around, he spoke as low as he could in his native English.

"Return ticket please to here from the city."

Hoping that was the right choice, the conductor looked at him for longer than he'd like before handing Michael his ticket.

"Enjoy your stay in Rotterdam, sir." He spoke too loud for Michael's liking.

Mina's friend got off at the next stop, along with many of the others on the tram. It was a busy junction, with tram lines heading in all different directions. Mina and her friend waved at each other, and then she was alone.

Michael considered sitting next to her, but it would have been too obvious to any observers, either German or Dutch. He needed to wait until the timing was right before making his move.

The wait was killing him. His heart screamed at him to join her, to sit with her, to touch her hand. But his training and instincts told him otherwise.

He had to wait.

Thirty minutes later, the tram stopped outside an old church called the Pilgrim Fathers Church. The name immediately piqued Michael's interest, and he made a mental note to research the connection the church had with the famed Pilgrim Fathers once his mission was over.

Mina exited the tram, and Michael followed, once again standing behind other passengers as they alighted.

He pretended to study the impressive drawings a street artist had made of the church as Mina looked around, then followed her from a safe distance as soon as she moved away from the tram stop

Canals sat either side of the narrowing strip of land, but Mina seemed to know where she was going. It appeared to Michael as though this was a place where strangers weren't welcome, and he did his best to blend in as he followed her.

Five minutes later, with the strip of land now only two houses wide, the swell of people thinned out and Mina walked alone. Michael closed the gap and was less than ten feet behind her when she abruptly stopped and turned off the narrow street into a cafe to her left.

Michael was too close to stop, so he carried on past, glancing inside as he went by. He saw Mina take a seat at the rear of the cafe. She was alone, but was clearly waiting for someone to join her.

With twangs of jealousy rising inside, he hurried back to the tram station and bought a different coloured hat from a street vendor. He placed the straw hat on a table outside a bookshop and hurried back to the cafe.

With his new hat firmly pulled down, Michael entered the cafe and immediately saw Mina leaning forward over the table in deep conversation with a man.

He felt his face flush with anger and resentment as he strode past them, heading for the toilet at the back of the cafe. By now, his eyes were watering, and it was painful to even walk, such was his desperation.

His mind ran at a thousand miles per hour as he relieved himself. Was it all a dream? A lie? Were the messages she sent not meant for him?

Resisting the urge to grab the man by the throat, he looked the opposite way as he walked by them, and occupied a table a couple of rows back on the opposite side where he could keep a close eye on them.

The man she was with was in his thirties and had a pock-marked face that spoke of a tough life. His hands, gesturing as he spoke, looked rough, as if they belonged to someone accustomed to hard manual labour.

His brown hair was cut short in an almost military fashion, and his dark eyes glanced around the cafe every few minutes like a searchlight in the darkness.

Michael ordered a glass of water and a coffee. He was thirsty, and they were a welcome relief. He pretended to read the newspapers, but in reality, he could barely understand a single word that was written.

The man with Mina locked onto Michael and stared at him for a moment too long. Michael knew he'd been spotted, so he waited a few more minutes before standing up to leave.

He'd seen enough, anyway. Whatever Mina was doing with this man, it wasn't a romantic tryst. Not one time did their hands touch over the table, and their body language didn't speak of two lovers meeting for a drink in a cafe.

It looked more to Michael's trained eye as though he was a resistance member giving Mina instructions for one of her broadcasts, and if this was the case, he didn't want to get in the way. As much as he loved Mina, there was a war to be won, and that was of far greater importance than his little love affair.

The man watched Michael intently, and he knew it was pointless leaving the cafe. He probably had men outside who would grab him the moment he left.

Not wanting to cause a scene, Michael sat down again and made eye contact with the tough-looking man. Their eyes locked, and Michael gestured for him to join his table.

The man said something to Mina, who turned her head to look at the stranger threatening their safety.

It was time.

With his heart thumping out of his chest, he removed his hat so she could see him.

Chapter 34

As Michael removed his hat, a simple yet deliberate gesture that cut through the murmur of the cafe, Mina's eyes widened in an instant of unguarded shock.

The colour drained from her face as if she'd seen a ghost from her past, her coffee cup hovering midway to her lips, now forgotten. Their eyes locked, and for a suspended moment, the world seemed to shrink to just the space between them.

Her hand visibly trembled, and she dropped her coffee cup on the table. Warm liquid splashed everywhere, but she didn't seem to notice. Her eyes remained fixed on the man staring back at her with so much love in her eyes that Michael felt as if the entire world belonged to just them.

For a moment, it did.

The breath caught in Michael's throat, and he found himself tearing up, unable to speak. He gawped as a tumult of emotions flickered across her features — relief, joy, and an overwhelming surge of disbelief.

He knew what was coursing through her veins because he was feeling it, too.

The man with her stared at both of them, and the hard features that moments ago threatened Michael's safety now looked on in stunned silence as realisation spread across his features.

Mina sat in rigid silence, unable to tear her eyes away from the sight in front of her. Michael was the same, but he was keeping an eye on everyone else in the cafe, all of whom were staring at the stranger in their midst.

In an instant, Michael realised that almost all of them were related in some way to the man with Mina, and he knew that her reaction had just saved his life.

The man touched Mina's arm, gently pulling at it to get her attention. He said something, and as he spoke, he rose to his feet. His eyes never left Michael, who sat still while the emotional theatre that Shakespeare himself would have been proud of, played out before him.

Mina rose unsteadily to her feet. Tears ran down her face, and she clasped her hand to her mouth. The man guided her out of her chair, and with the entire cast of what Michael presumed to be the Dutch resistance group watching, she stumbled on unsteady legs to the table where Michael waited for her.

He rose, his legs as unsteady as hers, and with the tension so dense that Michael could almost touch it, he reached out his arms.

"Mina." With that word, all the love, all the emotion he'd been holding inside for so long, came pouring out. Michael Fernsby, the star of Unit 317, became a blubbering wreck as the love of his life fell into his arms.

Everyone in the cafe stood up, and thunderous applause echoed around the room. Somewhere in the recesses of his mind, Michael noticed the owner had drawn the curtains and locked the door, keeping everyone and everything inside the cafe private.

Chapter 35

Michael's world exploded in a kaleidoscope of sensation, his heart pounding in an erratic rhythm against his ribs as Mina's hands found his, her touch electric and achingly familiar.

Their lips met, and he was lost, drowning in her taste, her scent, and the sheer, overwhelming reality of her presence. It was a kiss that seemed to last a lifetime, a kiss that said everything they couldn't put into words. It was a kiss that healed the shattered pieces of his soul and made him whole again.

After the longest, sweetest kiss of his entire life, Michael pulled away and looked into the eyes of the woman he loved with all his heart and soul.

"I thought I'd lost you." His voice trembled as he struggled to speak.

Mina's eyes shone with tears, her smile heart-melting and achingly beautiful. "I thought I'd never see you again," she mumbled, her English halting and accented, but still so perfect in every way.

"I listened for you every night." Michael's chest heaved

as he struggled to breathe. He felt himself sweating profusely, and he became acutely aware of the eyes gazing at him from around the crowded cafe.

"You heard my broadcasts?" Mina's eyes were wide open. "I sent you a message every night, hoping you would hear them and understand that they were for you. I wanted you to find me, Michael."

"I found you. I had to. Your broadcasts were the only thing keeping me going."

They kissed again, long and hard, and when they did, Michael felt the world falling away. The chatter of the cafe faded to a distant buzz, and the curious eyes of the onlookers melted into insignificance.

In that moment, there was only Mina, only the feel of her in his arms, the sound of her breathing, the steady thrum of her heartbeat against his chest.

A pointed cough shattered the spell, and Michael looked up to see the man with the pock-marked face watching them intently, his eyes hard and assessing.

Reluctantly, Michael loosened his hold on Mina, helping her to sit down before taking a seat beside her, their hands still entwined beneath the table.

Her thigh pressed against his, and Michael felt sensations running up the entire length of his body as the electricity surged. He could barely control the shaking in his limbs, and he grasped her hands to help ease the hopeless trembling.

The man sat opposite, his cold eyes locked firmly onto Michael's, making him feel as vulnerable as he'd ever felt. At this moment, there wasn't a single ounce of fight in him, and he hoped the man and the assembled group with him were friendly. Otherwise, he was powerless to resist.

"So, you are the famous Michael Fernsby." The man's voice was deep and accented, his English impeccable.

Michael glanced around, and every pair of eyes in the cafe were concentrated on him.

"I am, and I've been searching for Mina ever since she left Germany."

He was dying to ask her what had happened in Ryskamp, but now was not the time or place.

"Mina talks about you all the time, and she ends every one of her broadcasts with a personal message to you."

"I heard them, and I would have responded if I could."

"How did you know she was here?" The man's eyes narrowed as he got straight down to business.

Michael paused before answering. He didn't know if they were friendly, and even if they were, he still had to be cautious. Everyone stared at him, and he could have heard a pin drop.

"I didn't," he answered truthfully. "I honestly thought she was in France, and I was worried that I would never find her, at least not on this side of the war."

"Why are you here, Englishman?" The man's tone was harsh.

"Jeroen, please." Mina's voice was soft but insistent, her fingers tightening around Michael's in a gesture of solidarity. "Michael is not our enemy. He has done more to fight the Nazis than anyone I know. You can trust him, I swear it."

Jeroen's stare never left Michael. "I want to hear it from him. Why are you here?"

The fluttering inside his stomach that moments ago was filled with unicorns and rainbows, now became more ominous as the danger signs flashed before Michael's eyes.

Nobody could know why he was there, not even Mina, but he knew that if he lied, the Dutch resistance wouldn't treat him kindly. He berated himself for allowing his emotions to get the better of him. He'd learnt where Mina lived, and he should have waited until after the operation was over before finding her.

But then he knew that would have been impossible. The moment he snatched Harrington, Alexander Shaw would be waiting to whisk them all off to the waiting Lysander.

I should have never tried contacting her.

"Well? Why are you in Rotterdam?"

"Before I tell you anything, I want to know who I'm dealing with. Who are you, and who are all these people in the cafe?"

"Jeroen, you know who Michael is. I won't allow you to hurt him." Mina's face was serious. "By some miracle, I have found him again, and even if our moment is fleeting, I'm going to hold on to it for as long as I can. Please, Jeroen, let him go. You have my word that he is trustworthy."

"I don't doubt your word, Mina. But these are dangerous times, and trust is a luxury we cannot afford."

Jeroen stared at Michael, his eyes hard and uncompromising. Michael stared back with equal intensity. Whoever this man was, Michael would not be intimidated.

"Jeroen, perhaps more than most, I understand your predicament, but I assure you that I am not the enemy of the Dutch people. Quite the opposite, in fact." He was careful to pronounce his name exactly as Mina had done, which sounded more like Yeh-roon than Jeroen, but as he didn't speak Dutch, he hoped he'd said it right.

"Mina speaks highly of you, but it's quite the coincidence that you turn up right here, right now, in this cafe during one of our meetings."

"First, I don't even know who you are, and second, it is exactly that – a coincidence. I saw Mina this morning in Rotterdam, and by the time I caught her up, she was in this cafe. I still wasn't sure if my eyes were playing tricks on me, so I followed her in here to make sure I wasn't dreaming."

"While that may be true, it doesn't explain why you are in Rotterdam."

Michael leant forward, squeezing Mina's hand and enjoying the comfort it gave him.

"What has Mina told you about me?" he asked.

"Why are you here?" Jeroen wasn't about to be side-tracked.

Michael could feel the atmosphere in the cafe change from happiness and elation at their emotional reunion, to one of tension as Jeroen grilled Michael about why he was there.

"I came here to find Mina, but that is not the only reason. I have a mission, one that I cannot speak of, even to you. But know this… it is a mission that will strike a blow against the Nazis, that will bring us one step closer to victory and freedom. And I will see it through, no matter the cost, no matter the danger."

"That's not good enough, Englishman."

"I didn't even know if the woman I followed in here *was* Mina, and I had no idea that she was about to be involved in a meeting with the resistance, which I applaud and support, by the way. Any friend of Mina's is a friend of mine, and I would tell you more if I could. I'm sorry, and I don't mean to offend in any way, but be assured that we are fighting the same enemy."

"Jeroen, please," Mina pleaded. "You know what he is, and he can't tell you why he's here any more than you can tell him what you're planning. If you trust me with the broadcasts, then I insist you trust him. If you don't, then I refuse to do anything else for you."

A voice from the back of the cafe spoke in Dutch.

Jeroen replied, but Michael couldn't understand what they were saying. When it was over, Jeroen leant forward and grasped Michael's arm.

"I trust you, Michael Fernsby. From everything I have heard about you and your exploits against the Nazis, I have every reason to believe you are here to do what is necessary in our fight. I am the leader of our resistance group, and these are some of our people. Mina is an angel, and she has done a lot for us. We trust her, and we hope that in the coming days, we can work alongside the British and French to send the Nazis back where they belong."

Michael let go of Mina's hand and shook hands with the Dutch resistance leader. "I would help in any way I can, but I am here for a very important reason. Although I cannot say what it is, please believe me when I say that it benefits both our countries. The German invasion is imminent, and when it comes, we need people like you to carry the fight to them."

"Believe me, Michael Fernsby, we will. Of that, there is no doubt."

Jeroen looked at Mina and gave an indiscernible nod of his head, as if he was approving of her relationship. He turned his attention back to Michael.

"Is there anything we can do to help you?"

Michael shook his head. "Thank you, but we have it covered."

Jeroen rose from the table. "I'll leave you two to catch up. Enjoy your time in Rotterdam, Michael, and whatever you are doing here, I hope it is successful."

"The same to you too."

The two men shook hands and Michael watched as the owner of the cafe opened the curtains, unlocked the door, and stood aside as the resistance members filed out one by one. Jeroen was the last to leave, and as he did, he turned to Michael one more time.

"Mina knows how to get hold of me if you need anything."

With that, he was gone. Life returned to normal in the cafe, and Mina and Michael were left alone to reconnect with each other.

Chapter 36

The moment they were alone again, Mina threw her arms around Michael's neck and pulled him into her. Her warm breath on his neck sent shockwaves down his body, and for a moment he was back in the world where only the two of them existed.

It was a world where he could live forever.

Reluctantly, he pulled back, his hands resting on Mina's shoulders as he searched her face, trying to memorise every detail. Her eyes were wide and luminous, a stormy blue that seemed to hold all the secrets of the universe. He could drown in those eyes and lose himself forever in their depths.

"What happened?" he asked as they stared at each other in a manner that only long-lost lovers could.

"It's a long story," Mina answered. "I have so many questions, but I have to go. Senta and Anna are waiting for me at the radio station where I work. I'm already late, but I don't seem able to leave."

Michael smiled. "I feel the same. I really shouldn't be seen here, but I, too, seem unable to leave you."

He touched the back of her neck and enjoyed the electric sparks that flowed through his fingers. Her long blonde hair flowed down to her shoulders, and he gently ran his fingers down it as his shoulder blades twitched and juddered like an out-of-control tram.

"Is Jeroen the head of the resistance movement you work for?" he whispered in her ear, feeling the softness of her skin next to his mouth.

Mina nodded. "He tells me what to say in my broadcasts so everyone will be ready when the Nazis invade."

She pulled away and looked at Michael with fear in her eyes. "How long are you here for?" she asked.

"Not long. A day or so. Are you free after work?"

Electricity sparked between them as they touched hands. Mina's leg touched his, sending him into uncontrollable spasms of twitching muscles and nerves. He'd never felt anything like it in his entire life.

"You know where I live?" Mina shot him a look of surprise.

"It's a long story."

"Where do you work? I'll meet you there when you finish your broadcast."

Mina gave him the address of the radio station and then, with one last kiss and a touch of hands, she was gone. Michael gave her ten minutes and followed her out of the door.

He clocked a man watching for him as soon as he left the cafe. He berated himself for leaving the mission so exposed, but he knew what he had to do.

What was I thinking? I should have waited and caught her when she was alone.

He knew Jeroen would have instructed his men to follow him and find out what he was up to. A red mist descended over him, and he couldn't remember a time when he'd felt so angry with himself.

As much as he loved Mina, he was jeopardising the entire mission. Lives were at stake, and he was responsible for making sure he carried out his orders.

He had to lose his tail and find a way of seeing Mina without giving away the MI6 safe house.

He hurried back to the Pilgrim Fathers Church and stopped to look at the three arched windows that dominated the front of the building above his head. The centre window was the biggest, with the ones either side about half the size of the big one in the middle.

He craned his neck upwards to get a look at the white-painted bell tower perched on top of the church, and imagined a time in the future when it would ring to signify that peace had once again returned to Europe.

When he looked up, he quickly scanned his surroundings to see if his tail was still with him. He was, and as he glanced at him, he saw the man look imperceptibly to his right at someone else standing at the corner of the church.

Michael glanced over and saw another man wearing a brown sweater. He remembered seeing the sweater in the cafe, so he knew he was another member of the resistance.

Ignoring the tram station, he crossed the river, leaving the secretive cafe behind him.

After buying a map of the city, Michael headed towards a park that was about half a mile away. As he approached, he spotted a row of apartments in front of the park.

A woman helping a small child fumbled with the entrance to one of the apartment blocks. Michael held the door for her while he looked around for his interested friends.

They were sauntering down different sides of the

street. One stopped to tie his shoes while the other wandered past as if he hadn't a care in the world.

Whatever else they were, these men were not professionals, and they would end up dead if they followed the Nazis this way after the invasion.

Michael made a mental note to mention this to Mina and Jeroen if he got the chance to see him again before he left.

"Dank Je," the woman said as she herded her unwilling child into the apartments.

Michael smiled and waited until the last moment before the door closed on him. With the eyes of both his followers firmly fixed on him, Michael pushed the door open and hurried through, slamming it shut behind him.

He ran down the dark, damp corridor and out the other side into a thick copse of trees and bushes. Thinking it was his lucky day, Michael ran through the trees, being careful to avoid any hazards that could twist an ankle or a knee, effectively rendering his mission impossible.

He swore under his breath when he came out a minute later in another row of apartments. The realisation dawned on him that he was in the centre of two rows of apartments, and more than likely, the only way in or out was through the apartment complexes.

He tried two different doors about fifty feet apart, and both were locked. As he ran to the next one, he heard men shouting behind him. Jeroen's men must have found a way through the apartments.

A third door was locked, so he stopped to listen to his assailants as they pushed their way through the trees, trying to find him. Michael could clearly hear where they were, so he boxed around them and made his way back to the apartments on the other side.

One man was getting close, so he quickly climbed into

the branches and hid in the thick leaves above his head. The man passed underneath, and as soon as he was out of sight, Michael made his move.

The other resistance man was on the far side of the complex, so Michael jumped down and hurried as fast as he dared to the door he knew was open.

Once through, he locked it from the inside so the men couldn't follow. Then he backtracked to the door he'd entered from and hurried out to the busy streets.

Sighing with relief, Michael berated himself once again before making his way back to the Pilgrim Fathers Church, constantly watching for anyone else who might be tailing him, but the coast was clear.

Boarding a tram, he headed back to the safe house.

Chapter 37

Back at the safe house, Michael made sure all the doors were locked before checking the curtains. Satisfied nobody could see inside, he made himself a cup of tea and spread out the city map on the table.

It was two days before Harrington was due to meet Kreise and he needed time to think about how he was going to approach the warehouse and get himself ready to not only capture Harrington but also eliminate Kreise and anyone else who might be there.

Kreise! I'll concentrate on that tomorrow. Today is all about Mina, and as it's probably the last time I'll ever see her, I'm going to bloody well enjoy it. Sanders be damned.

He found the location of Mina's radio broadcasting station on the map, and was impressed with the care and attention that had gone into the resistance's decision to house it there.

Mina had warned him the administrative building where it was located was nondescript and displayed no identification of what was inside.

The first floor was, according to Mina, a normal

administrative office just like the row of other administration offices along the street. They serviced the busy port area, and Michael noted the proximity to the tram lines that gave good access to anyone coming and going from the area.

During normal working hours, the building was occupied by scores of port workers and transportation companies.

Some of the workers remained behind in the evening as it transformed into the hub of the Dutch resistance in Rotterdam. In the bowels of the building, the basement housed the radio transmitter that Mina and others used to broadcast their messages across Europe's borders to resistance groups and friendly nations allied against the Nazis.

The choice of location and the nondescript building provided the perfect cover for Jeroen and his resistance group.

It was getting dark by the time Michael completed his plans. He didn't have long if he was going to avoid Jeroen's men and enjoy his time with Mina.

He couldn't expose the whereabouts of the safe house, so bringing her back there was not an option. The house belonged to MI6, and God alone knew how many secrets it held between its walls. Exposing the house meant risking other operations MI6 might have planned, and Michael couldn't allow himself to be responsible for that.

Instead, he'd meet her at the radio station and walk her home. That would give them an hour or more together, and until the war was over, he would be happy with that.

There was little doubt that Jeroen would have someone watching the apartment building, but the resistance knew Michael wasn't their enemy. They would, however, be keen to see what the British intelligence services were up to.

They were itching to get back at the Nazis and would

relish the opportunity to help MI6 strike a blow against them but neither SIS nor Michael needed their help, not with this operation. The fewer people knew about it, the better, and Michael meant to keep it that way.

He ran up the stairs and gave himself a good wash all over with a small wash rag. Then he cleaned his teeth, combed his hair, and smiled at himself in the mirror.

Look at this, you handsome devil. Mina won't be able to resist you!

He smiled at his words. Of course she will. Who am I kidding? She probably had to get home to take care of Senta, but either way, he just wanted to be with her.

Michael relished the evening darkness as it gave him the cover he needed from prying eyes but he still doubled back, taking left and right turns before reaching a smaller tram stop farther down the street from the one he'd taken earlier.

He scrutinised the passengers, who all seemed to mind their own business. The tram crossed the Nieuwe Maas river, and he got off at the next stop.

He was still a half hour from the Waalhaven district where Mina's radio station was located, and he had a little time to kill before she finished her broadcast, so he wandered around and found a cafe situated down a side street well away from the hustle and bustle.

He took three more trams, doubling back and changing direction several times before ending up at the large conglomeration of train tracks at the southern end of the port.

Once again, he wandered around, taking last second turns to throw off any would-be followers, and after checking his watch, he stood in a darkened doorway of an administrative building on Hilgersweg.

The luminous dial on his watch told him it was almost

time for Mina to finish her broadcast, and he stood ready to greet her.

He'd done stakeouts more than enough times by now to know that the nervousness he was feeling was different to how he normally felt during operations. Even when his life was at risk, he could never remember feeling this nervous.

"Bloody hell, Michael. Pull yourself together," he muttered under his breath as he hopped from foot to foot, trying to get rid of the shaking in his legs.

At 10.00 pm, the doors swung open, and even in the half-light, her beauty cut through him like a spear. His heart banged so hard he thought it was going to explode, and he found himself breathing as hard as he would if he'd just returned from a long, hilly run.

He resisted the powerful urge to run to her, and instead watched as she scanned the street, hopefully looking for him.

Nobody approached her, but Michael still didn't reveal himself. Instead, he disappeared down a dark alley and ran to cut her off before she reached the tram stop.

As she approached the end of the street, Michael stepped out of the shadows, taking her by surprise. She was about to scream before she realised who it was.

"Michael," she yelled. "You almost gave me a heart attack." Her broken English immediately set his heart racing as he threw his arms around her, kissing her long and hard.

As they kissed, Michael watched the man tailing them emerge from the shadows, so he manoeuvred Mina around, whispering in her ear.

"Don't stare, but do you know that man? He was hanging around outside the radio station and now he's following us."

Mina stiffened, but played along with Michael. "I've seen him before at the cafe. He works for Jeroen."

Michael's suspicions were confirmed. As long as he kept his distance, he wasn't a danger to them.

"Did you find the radio station from my directions?" Mina whispered as they walked slowly together towards the tram station, hand in hand.

"You gave excellent directions, Mina. I couldn't have missed it if I'd tried."

They made small talk on the packed tram as it took them back to the Overschie area and home. Mina's leg pressed against his, the heat of her skin seeping through the thin fabric of her dress. It sent his emotions into overdrive. Strong, tingling sensations coursed through his body, and he fought to control himself as the tram bounced rhythmically along its tracks.

Twenty minutes later, the tram came to a halt at the stop near the safe house. To Michael, it felt like only seconds had passed, and he wasn't ready for it to be over. Not ever.

Peacefulness had spread throughout his body, and he wanted it to last forever. In Mina's presence, he felt different. Calm, and yet excited at the same time. He couldn't explain it, but he hoped she felt it too.

They climbed off the tram, with their shadow not far behind and Michael cheekily turned and waved at him, letting him know he'd been seen.

As Mina quickened her pace, a flicker of disappointment crossed Michael's mind. They hurried past the safe house, and he cast a fleeting glance to confirm it was just as he had left it. But that concern evaporated almost instantly. Her fragrance enveloped him, her very presence a mesmerising force, drawing him in until he was entirely lost in her aura.

Outside her apartment building, Michael hesitated and pulled her close. If this was to be the end, he wanted one more moment alone with her. He kissed her and was about to say something when she placed her finger over his mouth to shush him.

"Come with me," she whispered. "Be quiet."

Assuming she was taking him to see Senta, whom he'd only spoken to one time at Ryskamp when Alwyn Lutz lay dead at their feet, Michael passively followed her.

Their tail stopped at the apartment's entrance and didn't follow them up the steps, but Michael knew he'd hang around until he left and then try to tail him back to wherever he was staying.

Mina led him to the second floor where she stopped, turned around, and kissed him hard on the lips. A dull light flickered down the hallway, but other than that, it was dark and full of shadows, though light enough for Michael to see the fire and passion in her eyes.

"My friend works nights at the hospital, and she won't be home until the morning. I told her about you, and she gave me the key to her apartment. Do you want to come with me?"

Her hand playfully ran down his chest, sending a tsunami of shockwaves through his body. Michael shook, unable to stay still and his face burst into a wide smile.

"Lead the way."

Without another word, Mina took him by the hand and led him down the corridor to an apartment at the opposite end. He stood, frozen in time, as she fumbled with the lock.

As the door swung open, she turned and placed her arms around his waist, leading him into the darkness, her eyes never leaving his. He kicked the door shut behind them, and Mina momentarily broke away to make sure it was locked and secured.

Without turning on the light, she led him to the bedroom, and when she closed the door behind them, Michael's body convulsed with desire.

The love he'd held for her ever since he'd first clapped eyes on her at Ryskamp all those months ago poured out in a burst of passion he never knew he possessed.

It was obvious she felt the same, and their bodies came together with a frenzied tenderness that Michael knew would live in his heart and mind forever.

Chapter 38

"Spending time with you today has made it the most wonderful birthday I've ever had." Mina snuggled next to Michael in the afterglow of the greatest night of his life.

"Today is your birthday?" Guilt immediately set in. "I wish you'd told me earlier because I would have got you something nice."

"Oh, Michael. You already have. Being with you like this is the best gift I could ever have, and if the war means that we never meet again, I'll cherish this night for the rest of my life."

"I feel the same, except that I hope it isn't the last time we're together."

He reached over and tickled Mina on the side of her ribs. She laughed and squirmed before she broke away and pushed him off.

"How old are you today?" Michael asked. "Twenty?"

Mina nodded. "Yes, I'm an old woman now."

"Well, I'm glad you like younger men."

Mina playfully punched Michael in the chest. "I want to spend the rest of my life with you." Her expression was serious. "I love you, Michael Fernsby. I've loved you since the day you walked into my life in the barn at Ryskamp."

Michael reached over and kissed her long and hard. "I love you too, Mina. When this is over, will you marry me?"

"Yes! Yes! You know I will."

"I'll hold you to that. Promise you won't do anything dangerous with the resistance. I couldn't bear it if something was to happen to you."

"I could ask the same of you, but I know you wouldn't listen. There's a war to be won, and we all have to do our part."

"I can't argue with that, but I want you to be safe and away from any danger."

"Nowhere is safe from the Nazis. Hitler won't stop until he takes over the entire world. Even that won't be enough for him, because then he'll hunt down every innocent Jew he can find until none are left. Nobody is safe, Michael. Not me, not you, not anyone."

Michael looked long and hard into Mina's eyes. "I'm so proud of you for standing up to the Nazis. You've already paid a high price, and I understand your need to get back at them. I just want you to be safe, that's all."

"I have to do what I can, Michael. You understand that. Senta is working with the resistance as well as me, as is Anna, my friend from Germany who we're staying with. We're all doing what we can. I have to, after what they did to Mama and Papa."

Mina's eyes filled with tears as she recounted what had happened at their farm in Bavaria.

"The Gestapo came when we were helping a Jewish family escape Germany. Someone betrayed us, and if it wasn't for Herr Stummer and his wife, we would all have been arrested."

"I heard you talking about it on one of your broadcasts." Michael pulled her close again. "I'm glad you and Senta got away, but I'm sorry about your parents. Do you know what happened to your mother?"

Tears dripped onto Michael's chest as she spoke. "No. They arrested her and took her for questioning. We think she's in a concentration camp, but we don't know where."

"I'm so sorry, Mina." The words were not enough, but Michael didn't know what else to say.

"Dieter Lutz, Alwin and Carl's father, shot Papa right in front of us. He blamed us for Alwin and Carl's deaths."

"None of that was your fault. It was mine and mine alone."

"It doesn't matter whose fault it was. They're dead, and I hope they rot in hell along with every other Nazi who dies in this war."

"When it's over, we'll work together to find your mother." Michael knew his words would never heal her soul, but he had to try, nonetheless.

"What happened to your brother?" Mina asked, bringing back painful memories from the depths of Michael's brain. "You never told me, and as far as I know, the Nazis never found him, because if they had, it would have been all over the news."

"David died in Munich before I got to Ryskamp." Now it was Michael's turn to fight back the emotions of severe loss.

"I didn't tell you at Ryskamp because I hardly knew you and wasn't sure which side you were on."

Mina stroked Michael's chest with her fingertips, sending comforting chills down his spine. "I know how you must feel about that. Now it is my turn to be sorry."

"Don't be sorry, Mina. Collectively, Britain and her allies will defeat the Nazis and restore order to Germany and the world. Their regime will end, and when it does, we will find our loved ones who are still alive and bury those who didn't survive. We will move on and make a new life together, you and I."

"I hope so, Michael. It's what keeps me going, and it's what helps me sleep at night. I worry about you every day, and I won't want to live if they were to kill you."

"You have to take care of Senta. I plan on surviving this war, and I plan on raising our children together with you in the future."

Mina looked up and smiled. "That's what I want too. Do you think it will happen?"

"I do," Michael nodded. "It has to."

A moment of silence ensued as they held each other tight.

"Who are you living with here? I saw you with another girl about your age this morning."

Mina laughed. "That's Anna Rosenberg. She was my best friend. We grew up together in Germany, and I helped at her father's general store at the weekends in Glatten whenever I could."

"What happened to them? Are they Jewish?"

Mina nodded. "Yes. The Brownshirts painted terrible slogans and signs on the outside of their store, and then they destroyed it on Kristallnacht. We helped them leave Germany before the Nazis could find them, and now here we are, living together in Rotterdam."

"What happened to Ryskamp after you left?" Michael asked.

Mina shrugged. "I don't know. Dieter Lutz probably took it over and lives there for all I know. Whatever else happens, I'm reclaiming it when this is over. Ryskamp is ours, and has been for generations."

"You'll get it back. Ryskamp belongs to you and Senta."

"It's almost morning. Esther will be back soon, and we don't want her to find us in her bed together."

She rolled out of the bed and dressed herself. Michael watched, already feeling the loneliness of their separation bearing down on him.

"Will we see each other again?" she asked, sensing that this was it, their last moments together. "I have to meet with Jeroen at the cafe tomorrow, and then I have to help Senta with something she is doing for them. We can meet after my broadcast tomorrow night?"

Michael bowed his head, trying to ignore the emptiness clawing at his soul. "I have to leave tomorrow. I have a job to do, and then I have to leave."

Mina turned and placed her hands on his shoulders. "The Nazis will be here soon, and we will have to leave as well. I don't know where we will go, but I'm guessing France might be the only safe place for us."

"Don't forget Spain and Portugal. If France falls, they might be the only places you can go where the Nazis won't be able to get to you. Unless..." he trailed off mid sentence.

"I can't come to England with you, if that's what you're thinking. As much as I'd love to, my place is here with Senta and Anna. We will win, my love, but until then, we must fight apart from each other and hope that we survive the war."

"How will I know where you are?" Michael asked.

"I'm a radio operator, remember? I'll find a radio wherever I end up, and I'll broadcast to you every night, just as I have always done. I won't be able to tell you where I am, but you know where I'll be when it's over. I will wait for you there, no matter if I wait for the rest of my life."

"I'll be there." Michael held her hand. "As long as I survive, I promise I will be there."

Michael dressed in silence. Before she reached the door, Michael stopped her. She turned and held him close one last time. "I love you, Michael Fernsby."

"I love you too. Is there a back door to this place? I need to avoid our friend out there waiting for me."

Mina grinned. "You really are a spy, aren't you? I'll show you the way."

Mina led Michael by the hand through the dark, narrow corridors that smelled of stale tobacco and mould. She went down a set of stairs at the opposite end of the corridor from where they entered and stopped at a locked metal door.

"This is as far as I can take you. Please remember this night, Michael. It is the best birthday of my life, and I love you with all my heart and soul."

They kissed passionately one more time, and with his voice catching in his throat, Michael looked longingly into her eyes one last time.

"I love you too, Mina. This has been the best night of my life, too, and I want many more of them. Please take care of yourself and Senta, and I promise I will find you. Somewhere, somehow, I *will* find you."

The door creaked open, and Michael held it, so it didn't swing too far. The noise of the rusty hinges made him cringe, but there was nothing he could do about it.

He glanced around, but it was pitch black and impossible to see anything. He pulled back and kissed Mina one more time before disappearing into the darkness.

"I love you," he said as Mina faded into the abyss.

They were the truest words he'd ever spoken, and he vowed to himself that this would not be the last time he saw her.

At the edge of the apartment building, Michael stopped to listen and allow his eyes time to adjust to the darkness. There was no sign of the resistance man who had followed him all day, but he knew he would be there somewhere.

He ran to the next apartment block one street over and stopped again, listening and straining his eyes for any sign of movement.

The night was still, so he ran to the next apartment block, and then the next, until he reached the last one. There was still no sign of the resistance, so he kept to the shadows until he reached the rear of the safe house.

Once again, he paused. Nothing. The night was quiet and calm. Nobody was out there watching him, so he slipped through the rear door and locked it behind him.

Turning on the kettle and the overhead light in the only room that had any furniture, he slumped onto the couch. For a while, he allowed his mind to immerse itself in the memories of his time with Mina, and then forced himself to push it to the recesses of his brain, where it would be stored for the rest of his life.

Now it was time to prepare himself for the real reason he was in Rotterdam: Edward Harrington, and more importantly, for himself at least, Albert Kreise.

The mere thought of Kreise made his blood boil, and if he was there tomorrow night, Michael would have the element of surprise against his archenemy.

The following evening, one of them would die, and he would do all he could to make sure it was Albert Kreise.

Chapter 39

Michael lay awake on the lumpy settee, staring into the gloom. After hours of tossing and turning, he had to accept that sleep would not come. His mind churned relentlessly, thoughts of Mina bleeding into his anxieties about the mission ahead.

Try as he may, he could not get her out of his mind. Her beauty, her gentle touch, her fragrance, everything about her that drove him crazy flooded his mind, blocking him from hardening his heart for what was about to come.

With the rising of the sun, Michael was up and about. The kettle was on, and he helped himself to bread and hard cheese. The next thing he did was to set up the short-wave radio on the table.

He went over and over his plan for the evening's action, hoping Shaw was as good as his word and would be waiting for him with the vehicle that would take him and the captured businessman to the waiting Lysander.

In the afternoon, he forced himself to lie down and rest. He didn't know when the next opportunity would arise, and he didn't want to make any mistakes because he was fatigued.

By dusk, he was ready. The radio, that had revealed no messages from either London or Mina, was hidden under the floorboards, and any trace of Michael's presence was gone from the safe house.

Complying with Shaw's instructions, he left the keys in a drawer in the kitchen and checked his rucksack for the twentieth time.

He ruefully told himself that Unit 317's motto should be 'He who prepares, wins'.

The Walther PPK was freshly oiled and fully loaded, and the spare ammo was in his jacket pockets, ready if needed. Which he hoped he didn't. If Kreise was there, he would deal with him personally, hand to hand.

At nine o'clock, he was ready. He had two hours before the meeting, and he wanted to get there early so he could find a suitable place to set up the ambush.

Retracing his steps from his previous reconnaissance, Michael quickly found himself close to Mina's apartment block. Memories of their shared moments the previous night threatened to overwhelm him, but he pushed them away, berating himself for the hundredth time for allowing his emotions to interfere with his mission.

The night was clear, which wasn't ideal. He moved slowly, keeping to the shadows as much as possible, crossed the river, and cautiously made his way to Breevaartsraat, where the third row of warehouses dominated the narrow strip of land jutting out across the waterway.

Using the clear night sky to his advantage, Michael ran across the street, stopping in the shadows of the smaller warehouse directly opposite the one where Harrington would be meeting with Kreise in less than two hours.

He watched for any signs of movement, but everything was still and quiet. If the SD were involved in this operation, Michael knew they would be much more professional than Jeroen's men, who had followed him the previous couple of days.

He was early on purpose, and as the SD had no reason to believe the British intelligence services were onto them, there was no reason for them to get there any earlier than they had to.

Still, Michael knew they were thorough and professional. They would arrive in plenty of time to scope out the area just in case anything was out of place or irregular.

He'd just got there first.

A row of thick, prickly bushes at the rear of the warehouse was the perfect place for his rucksack, so Michael took a mental note of where he'd hid it, and climbed a drainpipe to the roof. On the top, he lay flat on his stomach and inched his way towards the edge facing the target.

The evening wasn't cold, but it was cool enough for him to be grateful for his jacket and he pulled it tight around his neck and settled down for a long wait.

In previous stakeouts, he'd always been able to shut down his active mind and focus on the task ahead. But tonight was different. No matter how much he tried, he couldn't get Mina out of his head.

The events of the past twenty-four hours would forever be remembered as the greatest day, and night, of his life. They would only be bettered by more of the same, and his mind tormented him with thoughts that he might never see her again.

He cursed himself under his breath. As much as he would cherish the memory, he should have stayed away from her. Not only had he made the mission harder for himself, but what was Mina going through?

The thought stuck in his gut like a knife. He hadn't considered the repercussions for Mina, and now he was mad at himself all over again for being so thoughtless.

As he berated himself, he remembered the tender moments they'd shared and the love in her eyes that told him everything he'd ever wanted to know about her.

As much as he longed to see her again, to lose himself in her embrace and shut out the world, he knew it was nothing but fantasy. Mina had her role to play, just as he had his. Anything more was a dangerous indulgence they couldn't afford.

No, I did the right thing. If I die tonight, at least she will have a memory of me that nobody can ever take from her.

The possibility of dying conjured an image of Albert Kreise. The thin lips and the cruel eyes burned in his mind, sending shivers all the way to his feet.

Kreise! That one image snapped Michael back into reality. In an instant, the spark that made him so good at what he did was switched on. Fire burned in his chest as other memories, evil deeds committed in the name of Adolf Hitler by Kreise, the former Kriminaldirektor of the Gestapo, and now a ranking officer in the SD.

David appeared, as he so often did in times of emotional strife. If anyone ever knew Michael held imaginary, full-blown conversations with his dead brother, he would be certified insane.

Perhaps they were right, and yet David always knew how to cut to the heart of things. His loss ached like an old wound in bad weather. And the daydreams where they argued were a cold comfort compared to the empty world without him in it.

"Remember what that monster did to us, brother.

What he did to me, and to Heinrich Adler. You need to prepare yourself and stop pandering to your thoughts about Mina. If you ever want to win this war and see her again, then Kreise has to die. It's either you or him, and if you don't buck up, you'll be joining me under the ground tonight. Is that what you want? How do you think Mum and Dad would feel if you just rolled over and gave up because of a girl?"

Michael groaned. He didn't need reminding of Kreise's inhumanity. His dreams were filled with nightmares about SS Oberführer Gustav Adler and his young nephew, Heinrich Adler.

Michael had thought he'd managed to get Heinrich safely out of Germany, but had later learnt that the Gestapo had caught him crossing the border into Switzerland and taken him to a eugenics facility called Alderauge on the outskirts of Munich where the Nazis killed adults and children who were deemed unworthy of life.

Heinrich was deaf and, because of complications at birth depriving his brain of oxygen, he was considered slow, and fell under the category of 'unworthy of life'.

Although Michael had killed the doctor responsible for many of the gruesome deaths, there was no doubt that he'd been replaced quickly. Young Heinrich hadn't stood a chance.

'I don't need reminding about Adler or his nephew. Nor do I need reminding about what Kreise has done to us. Stop this and leave me alone,' he thought.

David's voice faded from his mind, and what was left behind was the cold, battle-hardened operative of Unit 317. The thought of Kreise galvanised him, and Michael clenched his fists as if to acknowledge the change in his emotional state.

Once again, David had come to his rescue, like a

ghostly protector overseeing his wellbeing. Michael shelved the thoughts and memories of Mina to a place where he could find them later, and focused on the real reason he was there: Edward Harrington.

It was time to get to work.

Chapter 40

Now focused, Michael looked at his watch. It was 9.45 pm. He scanned the warehouse district, taking in the eerie silence and the looming shadows of the buildings against the night sky. Everything was quiet, and not a single person was in sight.

He shifted position on the roof, trying to find a more comfortable spot that didn't put his legs in imminent danger of going to sleep. Stakeouts were always a test of endurance, both mental and physical, and despite the adrenaline fizzing through his veins, Michael could feel the telltale heaviness creeping in at the edges of his awareness.

To keep himself sharp, he started counting the scraggy bushes and spindly trees ringing the perimeter of the target warehouse. There weren't many, but it gave his mind something to focus on beyond the endless waiting.

He considered trying the door on the side of the warehouse and entering if it wasn't locked. He could find somewhere to hide and ambush Kreise when he arrived.

But the SD were smarter than that. Kreise wouldn't just walk into a trap. What would happen if the meeting took place on the outside of the warehouse, or even worse, at the rear where he couldn't see?

Kreise would come and go, and Harrington would more than likely get his defection. Michael had to be better than that.

As his eyes scanned the bushes around the perimeter of the warehouse, he spotted movement in the darkness. One, no, two men appeared from the rear of the building, where there was nothing but water.

Then he remembered a narrow path behind the warehouses from his previous reconnaissance. The two men must have approached from the road and slipped behind the warehouses.

He'd missed them, and Michael furiously admonished himself. Slips like that were the difference between life and death, and he was never usually this lax. This was his final wake-up call, and he heeded its warning.

He pressed his body as low as he could get it on the roof and watched as the two men across the street took up positions on either side of the warehouse near the front.

One of them unlocked the side door and stepped back, hiding in the darkness on the rear side wall. These were either SD or Dutchmen working with them, and Michael knew he had to eliminate them if he was going to take Harrington alive.

He wondered where Alexander Shaw was at that moment, hoping he was doing his job and was close. Once Harrington arrived, everything would move rapidly, and Michael needed Shaw to be on the ball to get him out of there quickly, before more SD or Dutch Nazis arrived.

He slithered to the rear of the warehouse and shinned down the drainpipe, making as little noise as possible. He jumped up and down to make sure nothing rattled when he moved, and checked his weapons for the umpteenth time.

His Walther PPK was in his waistband, and the custom made, multi-purpose dagger with a seven-inch blade was attached to his belt. He took a deep breath and made the sign of the cross on his head and shoulders.

Keeping to the narrow path behind the buildings, he hurried to the last building on the narrow strip of land jutting into the Bornissehaven waterway. Now he was out of sight, he sprinted over the road and threw himself to the ground on the other side.

Happy he hadn't raised any alarms, Michael crept towards the target, keeping to the narrow path and pausing at each building to listen for any signs of movement.

Two minutes later, he was at the rear corner of the warehouse. The first target was fifty feet down the side of the wall, hidden in the bushes. The second was unsighted on the other side.

Now he was glad he'd counted the bushes, because he knew exactly which bush the enemy combatant was hiding behind, and exactly how many there were between them: Six.

Any movement now would be easily seen, so he hid inside the second bush from the end as it was the thickest and waited, hoping the men would patrol their areas.

Wishing he'd asked for an old-fashioned bow and arrow, he waited patiently. His watch told him it was 10.15 pm.

Harrington would be there within the hour.

By ten thirty, neither man had moved. He was going to have to come up with a Plan B. If he stayed where he was, he'd miss Harrington completely, and if he tried getting to either man, he'd be spotted before he got anywhere close.

Without going loud, there was no way to eliminate

them, so Michael backtracked and retraced his steps to the warehouse across the street. He climbed back to the roof and hugged it as close as he could.

Although it was dark, he could make out the shadows against the silhouettes around the warehouse.

At precisely eleven o'clock, a vehicle turned onto the road and stopped outside the warehouse.

From his vantage point, Michael watched as a figure that was almost definitely Edward Harrington emerged from the vehicle. All he needed now was Kreise to make an appearance, and then he'd make his move.

The time for stealth was over. There was no chance of Michael being able to take out Kreise and his two henchmen as well as subduing Harrington without going loud, as he called it.

His mission was to take Harrington, alive if possible, but dead if he had to. Until now, he'd never entertained the thought of ending Harrington's life, but the situation he was facing gave him no other choice.

Michael closed his eyes and took a deep breath. This would be one more face to add to his nightmares.

Harrington approached the side of the warehouse, and as he swung the door open, the man hiding nearby leapt from the shadows and shoved Harrington roughly into the darkness inside.

His accomplice sprinted from the other side, and within seconds, he, too, was inside the warehouse.

Michael's heart raced as he realised what was happening. Harrington was no longer useful to the SD. Kreise must have got wind of MI6's interest in him and decided he was too much of a risk.

Kreise must have set up this meeting to kill him!

Realising there was nothing he could do but watch to make sure Harrington was finished, Michael remained where he was. Shouts and screams could be heard coming from the warehouse.

"Where's Zobart?" A man shouted in German at the top of his lungs. "I was supposed to meet him here with Kreise. I demand to see them now."

Zobart! Michael's mind zoned in on the file related to the Dutch Minister of Defence and Maritime Affairs. Dansey had suspected him all along of being a double agent, but later changed his mind.

Was he the one responsible for Jamie Hawke's death? Although there was little doubt that Kreise was instrumental in pulling the trigger, was Zobart the man who'd set it all up?

The questions raced through Michael's mind as he watched the fight from his perch on top of the roof opposite the warehouse. Harrington staggered out of the door, clutching his stomach.

An attacker followed and grabbed him by the hair. His partner joined in, and as one stabbed Harrington repeatedly in the chest and stomach, the other slit his throat from the rear.

Harrington fought valiantly, but as his life drained away, he slumped to the ground and writhed around for a few moments before falling still.

Michael almost felt sorry for him, and he would have if it wasn't for the images of the tortured civil servant, Sir James Baker, that came to his mind.

As the men lifted Harrington's limp body off the floor, a car screeched around the corner and skidded to a halt in front of them. Michael assumed it was Kreise, arriving to claim the prize and oversee the disposal of the body.

He pulled the Walther PPK from his waistline and readied it, hoping to get a clear aim at Kreise as he exited the vehicle.

It wasn't Kreise. It was Alexander Shaw.

Shaw! What was he doing here?

At this point, it was obvious that Kreise wasn't coming. He'd sent his hatchet men to dispose of Harrington. What he hadn't accounted for was the intervention of MI6, and certainly not of Unit 317, or he would have been here himself with a small army of men.

Michael cursed as he slid backwards towards the drainpipe. A minute ago, he was happy to witness the SD doing the dirty work for the SIS, but now he had to intervene.

Alexander Shaw had ruined everything. He was supposed to be waiting for Michael to bring Harrington to him, not drive into the middle of a fight. Even if Michael was losing, his orders were to not get involved.

Chapter 41

Michael shinned down the drainpipe as fast as he could. At the bottom, he ran to the edge of the warehouse and threw himself to the ground so Harrington's attackers wouldn't see him.

Shaw was bent over Harrington's dead body, and before he could react, one of the attackers approached from behind and plunged a knife into the base of his neck.

Shaw collapsed on top of Harrington and Michael could only watch as a pool of dark liquid spread out from the two men, forming a large puddle around them.

The other attacker joined in, and they grabbed one body each and dragged them towards the waterway at the back of the warehouse.

Michael sprinted over the road and ran down the opposite side, trying to cut them off before they got there. At the far end, he waited behind the warehouse wall.

He didn't want to use his gun in case Kreise was somewhere close with more men. Whatever he had to do, it had to be done as silently as possible.

The noise they made dragging two heavy bodies

covered any sound Michael might have made, and as the first attacker reached the corner of the warehouse, he sprang into action.

Michael lunged, low and savage, taking the SD operative by surprise. By the time he'd dropped Harrington's body, it was too late. Michael's dagger had pierced his heart, killing him instantly.

His comrade reacted swiftly and was on Michael before he could react. His knife slashed downwards towards Michael's chest, but he missed when Michael shifted his body moments before the impact.

Michael yelped as the knife cut into his left bicep. Warm blood ran down his arm, but he didn't have time to worry about it.

Michael knocked the knife out of his attacker's hand, but the frenzied attack didn't stop. It didn't even slow down.

The man was on top of him, and he was bigger and stronger than Michael. He crashed his fists into Michael's head, making everything momentarily go black and out of focus.

Michael reached out with his left hand, frantically searching for something to hit back with before it was too late.

The attack slowed, and the heavy-breathing man smirked as he raised his arm in the air. Michael saw the gleam of metal in the moonlight and realised he was about to be killed with his own knife.

He reached up, grabbing the stronger man's arm, and with his right hand, he jammed his fingers as hard as he could into his left eye. The SD agent gave a bloodcurdling scream and loosened his grip.

Michael didn't miss a beat, rising and pushing the man off him in one movement. He kicked him under the chin as hard as he could, and as the man fell back, he saw the knife fall from his grasp.

He grabbed his knife and slammed it down into the man's chest, the agony sending him into waves of shock as he bucked and writhed on the ground.

"Where's Kreise?" Michael knew he only had a few moments before the man died, and he wasn't wasting it with remorse.

"SS Sturmbannführer Kreise is going to kill you all, Englander." The man's last words were delivered with a hatred Michael had rarely heard, and he was glad when his eyes closed and his heart stopped beating.

After checking to make sure both men were dead, he ran to Alexander Shaw, who had rolled away from Harrington and now lay on the ground staring up at the stars.

Dark liquid oozed from the wound on the back of his neck, and as Michael cradled his head in his hands, fresh blood ran out of the corner of his mouth.

"Hold on, and I'll get you to a hospital."

"I thought they'd killed you." Shaw coughed up more blood, struggling to speak. "I thought it was you. I was coming to help."

"You're a very brave man." Michael's eyes misted as he cradled the dying man in his arms.

"Make sure Dansey knows I didn't leave you, and that I came to help."

"You can tell him yourself when we get back to London. I'm taking you to a hospital, and when you're strong enough to move, Dansey will see that you are taken back to London. I'll tell him myself what you did here tonight, and he'll be waiting for you."

A smile formed on Shaw's lips as he gripped Michael's arm and pulled him close. "Listen. This is important. The

Germans are on the move. London called off the Lysander pick up. Go back to the safe house and listen to the radio for further instructions, but make sure you get out before they get here, because they'll kill you if they find you."

Michael looked up at the heavens. Why now?

He looked down to say something, but he was too late. Shaw's grip on his arm loosened, and Michael watched as his eyes closed and he fell limp in his arms.

Alexander Shaw was dead.

Chapter 42

Michael knelt on the blood-slicked cobblestones, cradling Alexander Shaw's lifeless body in his arms. The night's chill seeped through his clothes, mingling with the icy hollowness in his gut, because Shaw shouldn't have been anywhere near the action.

He was supposed to have been safe in the vehicle, waiting for Michael and Harrington.

Now he was dead, and Michael blamed himself. He knew Shaw's final moments would be added to the growing list of others that haunted him in his dreams.

He didn't have time to worry about it now, but he knew that in the quieter moments in the middle of the night, Shaw's death would haunt him to the edge of insanity.

If the Germans were on the move, Rotterdam would be swarming with Wehrmacht and SS troops within days, if not hours. And he'd be right at the top of their hit list.

He had to get out before they arrived, but before he did, he had to warn Mina and make sure she was safe. A wild idea of taking her and Senta back to England with him formed in his mind, but whatever she did, she wasn't staying in Rotterdam, and that was final.

He knew he didn't have long before the Dutch authorities arrived, or even worse, Kreise with a posse of armed men, so he quickly dragged the two dead enemy agents to the door on the side of the warehouse.

He briefly considered throwing them into the water but decided against it.

Then he did the same to Harrington's body, but not before searching him for any documents. He was clean, so he piled him up alongside his two dead comrades.

He ran back to Shaw and searched his pockets for the keys to the vehicle, which he retrieved along with the keys to the safe house. Finding them, he opened the rear door and gently carried Shaw's body to the back seat.

Then he ran to retrieve his backpack. He took his torch and entered the warehouse, just in case there was something of interest to the SIS.

The warehouse was completely empty, so Michael dragged the three dead bodies inside, locked the door with the keys he'd retrieved from the SD operative's pocket, and threw them into the Bornissehaven waterway.

With his nerves on fire, he drove towards the safe house, fighting the urge to put his foot down and speed. He knew he couldn't leave a vehicle outside with a dead body in the back seat, so he grabbed his map and searched for the nearest hospital.

The Coolsingel Hospital was about fifteen minutes away by vehicle, close to the Nieuwe Maas river, so he carried on past the safe house and made his way there.

Once there, he pulled up by the side of a building and gently laid Shaw's body on a grassy bank. He knew he'd be found soon, and although the body carried no identification, Michael would make sure London knew what he'd done with him. That way, at least his family would have some closure.

He drove back to the safe house as quickly as he dared. If the Germans were on the move, it would be all over the radio, and he had to know what his orders were before panic and chaos hit the streets.

His left arm stung, and blood dripped into the sink. Michael grabbed the first aid kit that every MI6 safe house supplied and patched it up as best he could.

His arm needed stitches, but for now, a good cleaning and a bandage would have to do.

He quickly set up the shortwave radio and turned it on. While he waited for the kettle to boil, he turned the dial, listening to the crackling of the radio as he scanned the airwaves.

His watch told him it was 2.15 am.

With a cup of refreshing hot tea in his hand, Michael got to work, scanning the frequencies for any messages from London. He also listened for Mina, but it was too late for her broadcast.

None of the English or German-speaking stations mentioned anything about the Wehrmacht moving over the western borders, so Michael assumed that MI6 had been privy to information not yet released to the public.

Thirty minutes later, he found a station where he heard the familiar chimes of Big Ben ringing out. A male broadcaster with a crisp Oxford accent began speaking.

Michael turned up the volume and grabbed a pen and paper.

This is London calling in the overseas service of the British Broadcasting Corporation.

Before I read the news, we are broadcasting important messages to our friends and allies in Western Europe, particularly those who follow our weekly gardening tips on a Sunday afternoon.

Good evening, this is the BBC from London. As the twilight embraces our serene landscapes, we invite you to unwind with our evening selection of classical compositions, interspersed with insights on timely garden cultivation.

Roses are reaching their zenith, and the night air softens, signalling the moment our dedicated gardeners have long awaited. At the second location, the most discerning horticulturists are poised to harvest only the choicest blooms, those that reach perfection under the light of the full moon.

To these valiant cultivators, we say – equip yourselves lightly and make haste, leaving behind the remnants of yesteryear's toil. The midnight blue orchids, once your pride, must now be allowed to blend seamlessly back into the garden's tapestry, untouched and unacknowledged.

You have a mere five nights to complete your task, culminating under the watchful lunar gaze on the eve when the spring tide reaches its peak. Should you find the garden paths obstructed, seek out the northern shores, where a Seagull's Nest or a Lantern's Light may offer discreet passage by sea. And if the storm clouds gather too quickly, take shelter with our allied cultivators until the tempest passes.

May your nocturnal endeavours be crowned with success, and may you find your way guided by our gentle melodies. Stay tuned for more peaceful interludes, as we continue to bridge the tranquil expanse from Britain's shores to your secret gardens.

This is the BBC, wishing you a pleasant evening.

Michael threw down his pen and reached for the one-time codebook hidden in one of the secret compartments in his rucksack.

His codebook contained sufficient codes for six days, which was more than enough for the duration of his mission. As the codes changed daily, any more than that would have been too bulky for him to carry around.

As each day passed, he'd diligently destroyed the code words for that particular day by burning them. All he had left were the code words for this day, which was now May 10, and the next day.

After that, he would be back to dead letter boxes, and the less secure, but more flexible method of coding that was taught at Ravenscourt Manor to all members of Unit 317. This consisted of a half dozen one-time codes specifically designed for him that could be used in direct communications with London in an emergency.

Today's codes were embedded in the middle of a programme about gardening. Michael knew from his training that important messages would be broadcast every hour during the day, so he knew as he heard it repeated over the airwaves that it carried vital information for his survival.

Using his finger, he found the corresponding entries of the message in the codebook. The fact that it was about Sunday afternoon gardening tips confirmed the message was for operatives of Unit 317.

Roses are reaching their zenith, and the night air softens.

The Wehrmacht is crossing the border. The war for Western Europe has begun.

At the second location, the most discerning horticulturists are poised to harvest only the choicest blooms, those that reach perfection under the light of the full moon.

The second location was Le Touquet airfield in northern France. The full moon was next projected to be May 15.

To these valiant cultivators, we say – equip yourselves lightly and make haste, leaving behind the remnants of yesteryear's toil. The midnight blue orchids, once your pride, must now be allowed to blend seamlessly back into the garden's tapestry, untouched and unacknowledged.

This told operatives of Unit 317 that they were to leave

behind whatever they were doing and leave it in a state where the enemy couldn't benefit.

You have a mere five nights to complete your task, culminating under the watchful lunar gaze on the eve when the spring tide reaches its peak. Should you find the garden paths obstructed, seek out the northern shores, where a Seagull's Nest or a Lantern's Light may offer discreet passage by sea. And if the storm clouds gather too quickly, take shelter with our allied cultivators until the tempest passes.

This told Michael he had five nights to reach Le Touquet airfield. Seagull's Nest and Lantern's Light referred to Calais and Dunkirk, respectively.

The allied cultivators referred to the British Expeditionary Force, the BEF, who were opposing the Germans in France and the Low Countries.

Michael read his now deciphered orders:

All Unit 317 operatives in Western Europe were to make their way to Le Touquet airfield in northern France.

They had five days to get there, or the Westland Lysander attached to Unit 317 would leave without them.

Edward Harrington, the focus of his mission, was to be executed and left behind.

The transport aircraft would leave on the evening of May 15, five nights from now.

If any operatives couldn't make the rendezvous, they were to make their way to either Calais or Dunkirk, and find a boat to take them across the English Channel.

If that failed, the last resort was to find the nearest fighting unit of the BEF and attach themselves to them until safe passage could be arranged to get them back to London.

Spreading out his map of Europe, he found Le Touquet located on the coast about forty miles south of Calais.

At a rough guess, Le Touquet was around two hundred

and fifty miles from Rotterdam, which was easily doable in Shaw's vehicle.

At least it was if the German advance didn't block his path.

The biggest takeaway Michael got from the message was that the situation was urgent, and he had to get out of Rotterdam now, before it was too late.

He glanced at his watch, which now told him it was 3.15 am.

Chapter 43

Although his eyes burned from lack of sleep, Michael had no time to waste. Mina had to know what was coming, so he left everything at the safe house and ran to her apartment on Lemkensstraat, his injured arm throbbing in time with his footsteps.

Keeping to the shadows, he used the pathways between the apartment blocks so he wouldn't be seen. Knowing which apartment was hers, he bounded up the stairs to the second floor three at a time.

Outside her apartment, he hesitated before knocking. The last thing he wanted was to wake up the entire complex, but this couldn't wait.

He knocked gently. When nobody came, he knocked louder. A neighbour in the apartment next door opened her door to see what the commotion was all about.

"What are you doing here at this ungodly time of the night?" the older lady asked grumpily in German. "Don't you know that some of us have to work in the morning?"

Michael immediately felt sympathy for her. Like many

others, she was probably Jewish and had fled Germany to escape the Nazis.

Now they were invading the western nations, and soon there would be no place left for them to hide.

"I'm sorry. I have urgent news for the lady who lives here."

The angry woman shook her head before stepping back inside her apartment.

Michael heard the lock turning. A middle-aged man with a balding head peered from behind the door wearing a pair of striped pyjamas. His eyes, struggling to focus from the fog of sleep, stared at Michael through a pair of oversized glasses that made him look like an owl.

"Yes?" he asked.

"I'm sorry to bother you, Herr Rosenberg," Michael spoke in German, but the man cut him off.

"Who are you, and how do you know my name? What do you want at this time of night?"

Michael was about to reply when the girl with the short brown hair he'd seen with Mina three days earlier pulled the door open from behind the old man.

"Who are you?" she demanded, staring at Michael as if he were the SS coming to take them away.

"My name is Michael Fernsby, and I'm here to see Mina. I apologise fo—"

A shriek from behind the door stopped Michael mid sentence. Mina appeared, her hair wild and uncombed. To Michael, it was the most beautiful sight he'd ever seen.

"Michael!" she yelled, forcing her way past the old man and the girl.

Other apartment doors were opening, so Mina grabbed his arm and pulled him inside. Once the door closed, she threw her arms around him and gave him a long, passionate kiss.

"Yuck." Another voice from behind Mina spoke up. "Put him down, Mina, for goodness sake."

"You're hurt." Mina's eyes clouded as she looked at his battered face. "What happened?"

"I'm alright," Michael answered. "It's not as bad as the first time we met."

Mina half smiled, but she dabbed at his face with her pyjama top. "Why is your arm covered in blood?"

"I covered it as best I could. You are too important, Mina and I had to come here first."

Mina pulled away and stepped aside. Senta stood beside the old man and the brown-haired girl Michael took to be her friend, Anna.

"Senta, it's good to see you again." He didn't know what else to say with all of them staring at him.

"You'd better have a good explanation for this," the old man said angrily.

"I do, and once again, I apologise for the lateness of the hour. The news I bring is of vital importance and could not wait."

"Please, sit." The old man waved his hand towards a worn couch in the cramped apartment.

Michael sat, and Mina immediately sat next to him. He held her hand, and the familiar feeling of calm seasickness washed over him again. His stomach gurgled, and he felt the same as he did on a rollercoaster ride as her hand sparked electricity throughout his body.

Senta scowled. She didn't look as thrilled to see him as Mina did, but she sat on the threadbare arm of a chair alongside Anna, who stared at Michael with more interest than disdain.

"Well?" Herr Rosenberg, the old man, asked.

Michael looked at Mina one last time before turning towards the faces staring at him.

"I don't know what you know about me," he started.

"Too much," Senta interrupted. "If it wasn't for you, we'd still be on our farm at Ryskamp. My father would still be alive if you hadn't shown up."

"Senta, that's enough," Mina snapped at her younger sister.

"It's alright," Michael held up his hand. "I understand your anger, and I am very sorry about your parents. Believe me, Senta, I would do anything to get them back for you."

Senta scowled, but the look from Mina warned her to remain silent.

"I work for the British government," Michael continued.

"We know. You're a spy." Senta couldn't help herself.

Now it was Michael's turn to scowl. "I understand your anger, but you must listen to me. We don't have much time."

He glanced at Mina, and even in the hostile environment he faced, all he wanted to do was reach over and kiss her. Instead, he pursed his lips and continued speaking.

"We received notification from London that the Germans are on the move. They're about to cross the border and invade. It isn't safe for you here anymore. You have to leave, and you have to do it now, before it's too late."

Silence fell over the room as they absorbed Michael's words. Although the invasion had been imminent, now that it was here, it was different.

"Are you sure about this?" Herr Rosenberg asked. "We've had several false alarms these last few months."

"This has come from MI6," Michael said. "So, I'd believe it if I were you."

"We have nowhere to go," Herr Rosenberg said flatly.

"We've already lost everything we had because of the Nazis."

"Papa." Anna grabbed her father's arm. "We can go to your cousin in the South of France. We'd be safe there."

"And how would we get there? We have no transportation, no money, and not enough food to get us there." Her father's eyes welled up. "I've failed you. I've failed all of you."

Senta glared at Michael before turning her defiance towards Mina. "I'm not going anywhere. Those Nazi pigs killed Papa. With the resistance, it's our turn to kill them."

"Herr Rosenberg." Michael addressed Anna's father, who had shouldered all the responsibility for their plight. "None of this is your fault. You haven't failed anyone. You have already done more than most, and it isn't over yet."

Senta jumped up and opened a cupboard door. "If it's true, it'll be on the radio."

"Not yet, it won't." Michael stopped her. "My guess is the Western governments are waiting until they actually invade before telling everyone so as not to scare them."

"You mean to make sure if it's true or not," Senta snapped.

"If you want to see it that way." Michael didn't have time to argue about it.

"Herr Rosenberg, I have a vehicle and we can travel to France together. You can drop me off and then take it to wherever your cousin lives. I have enough money to get you there, and we can buy food along the way."

"I can't possibly take anything from you," Herr Rosenberg answered. "I don't know you."

Michael turned to Mina. "Please, Mina, tell them who I work for. Tell them how serious this is. You must leave, now."

Mina held his gaze and shook her head slowly. "Anna

and her father should leave with you now. You can trust him, Anna. If he says he'll get you there, then he'll get you there."

"What about you?" Michael asked, panic rising in his chest.

Mina shook her head again. "As Senta said, the Nazis killed our father, and probably our mother as well, by now. We are staying here and fighting back."

Michael groaned. This wasn't going the way he wanted. "Mina, I can't leave you here. They'll kill you, and I can't allow that to happen."

"What are you going to do?" Senta asked. "Kidnap us and drag us to France?"

Michael sighed. "No. I just want you to live, that's all."

Mina moved forward and held Michael's hands in hers. "I love you, Michael, but my place is here with Senta. We can't keep running from them. Sooner or later, we are going to have to make a stand, and here we have a strong resistance movement that hates the Nazis as much as we do. Please, you must understand why we can't go with you."

"Then I stay too." Anna stood up. "I'm not going without you."

"I'm not going either," her father said. "I'm not running away while these brave women risk their lives. I can't."

Michael rose to his feet. Helpless and lost, he took Mina's hand in his. "I understand, and in your position, I would do the same. I love you, Mina, and I am very proud of you."

They hugged for a long moment. Michael never wanted it to end, because he knew he would never see her again. But eventually, she pulled away and looked into his eyes one last time.

"Remember our promise."

She backed away, tears rolling gently down her face.

Michael, forcing back the emotion, turned and opened the door. As he stepped into the darkness, he was shoved roughly back inside by an unseen assailant.

By the time he'd recovered and got to his feet, three men were inside the apartment and the door was closed behind them.

Chapter 44

Three pistols pointed at Michael, giving him no chance to respond. He held his arms in the air in a gesture of surrender.

"Jeroen!" Mina yelled in her broken English. "It's Michael. You met him at the cafe. Put your guns down before someone gets hurt."

"What are you doing here?" Jeroen asked in a gruff voice.

Michael lowered his arms and watched as the men holstered their weapons. "I could ask you the same question," he said.

"We don't have time for this." Jeroen turned to Mina and Senta, who stood together beside Michael. "I have it on good authority that the Wehrmacht is on the move and will cross the border at first light. Our leader wants us to be ready. Senta, do you have that drawing for me?"

A previous conversation with Mina flashed through Michael's mind as Senta disappeared into her bedroom. Mina had told him about Senta's legendary ability to recreate incredibly detailed drawings after only seeing her subject one time.

He suspected she had an eidetic memory, and now it seemed she was putting it to good use recreating images of targets for the Dutch resistance.

Senta reappeared with a pencil drawing in her hand. From what Michael could make out, it was of a bridge crossing a large river.

"This is good," Jeroen said. "Are you sure the location of the artillery guns is correct?"

"They are drawn exactly where they are located," Senta said proudly.

"Good," Jeroen said. "Mina, I need you to spread the word to our people that the moment has arrived."

"When?" she asked.

"Now."

"What are you doing here, Fernsby?" Jeroen asked. His tone had softened from when they first entered the apartment.

"I came here to tell everyone the same thing you just did, that the invasion begins today."

"He was trying to get us to leave with him," Senta sneered. "But we refused."

Jeroen raised his eyebrows. "You're leaving right as the Nazis attack us?"

"My mission is complete," Michael answered. "I'm needed back in London."

"I was going to ask why you look so beaten up. I take it your mission was successful?"

Michael shrugged.

"Don't worry." Jeroen's lips curled into a wry smile. "The warehouse will be empty when the police search it in daylight."

Michael was stunned. "What? How?"

"You might think we are amateurs, Mr Fernsby, but I assure you we are not."

"You were there?" Michael asked, trying to use the time to work out in his mind what had happened.

"We've had our eyes on Edward Harrington for some time, and when he was spotted in Rotterdam, we followed him, hoping he'd meet with his Nazi handlers. We were about to accost them when you showed up and dealt with them. Most impressive, if I may compliment you. I see now why everyone speaks so highly of you."

Michael stared at Jeroen with his mouth wide open and cursed himself for thinking the resistance unit were amateurs. Clearly, he'd been wrong, and they were as professional as it could get.

"You're hurt." Jeroen signalled with his hand at the blood dripping onto the floor from Michael's wounded arm. "That needs stitching."

"I'll see to it when I get the chance." Michael was still stunned at being outfoxed by Jeroen and his resistance group. He had a newfound respect for them, and now he understood why Mina worked for them.

"We can see to it now. Mina, is that friend of yours still in the apartment down the hallway? The one you two occupied the other night?"

Mina blushed. Senta bent forward and pretended to vomit, while Anna burst into a wide smile. Even her father raised his eyebrows at Mina and broke into a half smile.

"I clearly underestimated you." That was all Michael could think to say.

"Don't chide yourself too much. Most people do."

"I'll go get her." Mina, still blushing, cast Michael a cheeky smile before scurrying out of the door and closing it behind her.

"Where are you headed?" Jeroen asked Michael. "We

heard the radio broadcast earlier this evening. It was clearly a coded message that I assume was meant for you?"

At that moment, Michael felt completely unworthy of his position as an operative for the SIS. "You'd make an excellent agent for the Dutch government," he said, avoiding the question.

Jeroen smiled. "Where do you think I learnt all this?"

"Fair enough. They were my orders to leave Rotterdam and head for home."

"Whatever your orders, it clearly stated that you had five days to carry them out. I was sceptical when I first saw you because you looked too young to have the kind of reputation your name carries. However, after seeing you in action tonight, I am left in no doubt as to your capabilities."

"What are you saying?" Michael asked, confused.

Before Jeroen could answer, the door burst open and Mina ran through, followed by a tired-looking woman in her late twenties with collar-length dark hair and eyes that betrayed a lack of sleep.

"Mina tells me you are hurt?" she asked in good English.

"It's nothing." Michael didn't want any fuss.

"Michael, this is Esther. She's the nurse I was telling you about."

"You're dripping blood all over the floor," Esther said. "Sit down and let me look at it."

"I'm sorry to drag you down here at this ungodly hour," Michael said as he sat on the couch and removed his jacket. "I know you work late."

"Take off your shirt," Esther ordered as she pulled a dark brown glass bottle of liquid from her medical bag. "Don't be shy."

Michael looked, but the bottle contained no markings

or brand names, though as soon as she opened it, he knew what it was. It was the Dutch equivalent of Dettol, the strong disinfectant smell that all hospitals and doctors' surgeries throughout Britain were known for.

He was immediately taken back to the times when his mother would treat the cuts and scrapes he and David picked up when they were young boys. The first thing she would do was clean the wound with Dettol.

Esther used a rag to clean Michael's wounded arm, and he had to grit his teeth to stop himself from calling out at the cold liquid as it stung and penetrated both the wound and his nostrils.

"The wound is deep," Esther said, continuing to wipe away the blood. "It looks like a knife wound." She looked at him disapprovingly.

Without waiting for an answer, she reached back into her bag and pulled out a curved needle and a roll of silk thread.

"This may hurt."

Michael thought she sounded unsympathetic, as though the pain from suturing his arm was the price to pay for waking her up so early.

Esther got to work on his wound, and ten minutes later, she was done.

"Take care of it and, if possible, get the stitches removed in a couple of weeks."

"Thank you," Michael said. "I appreciate you taking care of me."

"You're welcome. Now go and win this war for us."

Esther hugged Mina and Senta and left the apartment, no doubt heading back to her bed.

"Should we have told her?" Senta asked Jeroen.

"The hospital will call for her soon enough," Jeroen answered. "Let her rest. She's going to need it."

Mina reappeared wearing her jacket and squeezed Michael's arm. "Well, my love. This is it. Remember our promise."

"I'll take you to the radio station," Michael said, stepping forward.

Jeroen blocked his path. "My men will take her. You and I need to talk."

Michael objected, but the look on Mina's face told him not to. Instead, he leant forward and kissed her one last time.

"I'll be there. Stay safe, my love, and don't do anything stupid or dangerous."

Mina snorted. "*You're* telling me that?"

"Read this word for word." Jeroen passed Mina a handwritten note with the message that would mobilise the Dutch resistance.

Mina touched Michael's hand one more time, and then she was gone. One of Jeroen's men followed her out of the door, leaving Michael feeling hopelessly lost without her.

Chapter 45

Jeroen sat next to Michael on the couch and studied the drawing Senta had made for him. He looked at Anna Rosenberg and her father.

"Unless we stop them, the Germans will be here in a few days. If there is anywhere else you can go, I'd advise you to leave now before it's too late."

Anna shook her head and stared at Jeroen defiantly. "I'm not going anywhere. The Nazis have taken everything from us, and it's time to fight back."

Jeroen shook his head. "You're very brave, Anna, but I don't recommend it. You and your father need to leave now while you still have a chance."

"He said the same thing," Anna pointed to Michael. "And I gave him the same answer. I'm not leaving Mina and Senta. If they're fighting, then so am I."

Jeroen shrugged. "It's your choice, but make sure you know what you're getting into before you begin."

"We have nothing left to lose," Anna said. "The Nazis have taken everything from us."

"What about your father?" Michael asked. "You need

to consider him before you do anything dangerous and rash."

"I'm very proud of my girls," Herr Rosenberg said. "We've already had this conversation and we're not going over it again. We stay and fight."

Michael sighed and turned to Jeroen. "What do you want from me?"

Jeroen's pock-marked face softened, and even saddened, as he gazed at Michael. He handed Senta's drawing to him.

"This is the Willemsbrug Bridge. It's one of the main traffic bridges into Rotterdam. The army is going to try to hold it, but if they lose control, there is nothing to stop the Wehrmacht from rolling into the city unimpeded."

Michael could hear the heartbreak in his voice as the country and the city he so desperately loved faced ruination from the Nazis, and he wished he could do something to help.

Jeroen continued. "Our worry is that the Dutch forces won't be able to hold the Germans back. If the bridge falls, defending the city is as good as over."

Michael sighed. "I understand, but what do you think I can do against the might of the Wehrmacht?"

"If the bridge falls to the Germans, we want to have the ability to blow it up before the tanks roll over it. Until last night, we had that capability."

"What happened?" Realisation was slowly dawning on Michael as to what Jeroen was asking of him.

"Three of my men failed to report in last night. They were supposed to meet the rest of our group at the cafe where you and I first met as soon as we got the word from our leader, the Dutch Minister of Defence and Maritime Affairs, that the invasion was underway."

Zobart! Harrington was supposed to meet him at the warehouse.

"I'm sorry to hear that," Michael replied, ignoring Zobart for the time being. "Do you have any idea what happened to them?"

"Actually, I do. I have good reason to believe the two SD operatives you killed last night were responsible for their disappearance. They were seen tracking Micha, who was the explosives expert for our organisation. That is why we followed them last night, hoping they would lead us to Micha and the others. We were about to question them when you stepped in and killed them."

"So, you weren't following Harrington then!" Michael raised his voice, angry with the story Jeroen had told him earlier. "You were following the SD operatives and just happened to run into Harrington at the warehouse."

"That's not quite true." Jeroen looked uncomfortable. "We had been monitoring Harrington, but with the invasion about to happen and the disappearance of Micha and the others, we focused our attention on finding them, as I'm sure you can understand."

Michael calmed down. He understood perfectly and would have done the same himself. "Have you found your men?"

"Yes." Jeroen's face told Michael the bad news. "They were all shot in an abandoned warehouse near the Nieuwe Maas river late last night."

"No!" Senta yelled out. "Are they dead?"

Jeroen bowed his head.

"I'm glad Michael killed the Nazi scum," Senta shouted, her face deep red.

"While I agree, Senta, it doesn't solve our immediate problem." Jeroen was all business, which Michael appreciated.

"Let me guess, you want to know if I am trained in explosives?" Michael asked.

Jeroen nodded. "It would be a massive favour to the Dutch people if you were able to place explosives and a detonator at the bridge so we could blow it up if it falls."

"What about the other bridges?" Michael asked. "Even if you are successful and manage to blow up this bridge, there are several others the Germans could use to get into the city."

"That is true, but none can take heavy traffic like the Willemsbrug Bridge. If we take that out, it will seriously hamper the invasion force and give us a chance to at least hold them off until reinforcements arrive to help defend the city."

"I see." Michael sat back and considered his options.

"Are you trained in such things?" Jeroen asked. "From what I hear, operatives from Unit 317 are trained in several different methods of clandestine warfare, including explosives and detonations, if I am not mistaken."

Michael stared at Jeroen, once again surprised at the extent of his knowledge of both himself and Unit 317.

"You look surprised, but you shouldn't be. I was a member of GS III, the Dutch intelligence service, until about a year ago when I left to build the resistance groups we would need in the event of invasion. I know all about Unit 317 and how you operate."

"That explains a lot," Michael shot back at him. "I was beginning to think you'd been bugging mine and Mina's conversations."

Jeroen laughed. "Even I'm not that devious."

"Do you have the material needed for such a device?" Michael asked.

"We do."

"Take me to it, and I'll do my best to rig up what you need, which is an explosive device with a remote detonator, if I heard you correctly."

"That's what we need. We are in your debt, Michael Fernsby. Mina was right when she told me you could be trusted."

"I don't have long, so let's get going. As you already know, I have to be somewhere else in less than five days."

Jeroen stood up and offered his hand to Michael.

As they shook hands, Michael wondered if Zobart was the reason why Jeroen's men had suddenly turned up dead.

Chapter 46

SS Sturmbannführer Albert Kreise stopped his Renault Primastella behind a dark, empty warehouse close to the mass of railway tracks in the Waalhaven district.

He killed the engine and sat for a moment, listening to the tick of the cooling motor. He'd just received word from Berlin that the invasion of France and the Low Countries was underway at last. Even now, German troops were massing on the borders, poised to sweep across the continent like a steel tide.

German troops would be in the streets of Rotterdam in just a few hours, and for Kreise, it couldn't come soon enough.

He waited impatiently for the arrival of the man he'd bought off several months earlier. Wilhelm Zobart, the Dutch Minister of Defence and Maritime Affairs, had proven to be an excellent source of information, and it was he who was instrumental in bringing down the English shipping magnate, Robert Stourcliffe, at the back end of the previous year.

Five minutes later, headlights pierced the darkness, and

a vehicle pulled into the space beside Kreise. Even in the dim light of the moon, Zobart's thick, bushy eyebrows gave him away at first glance.

"You really need to shave off those ridiculous eyebrows, Zobart." Kreise got straight down to business. "They make you stand out a mile away."

Zobart ignored the insult and glared angrily at Kreise.

"I'm sure you know by now the Wehrmacht is on the move," Kreise said casually, as if they were preparing for a family picnic on a lazy Sunday afternoon.

"I heard," Zobart snapped.

"You look angry, Wilhelm. You've known it was coming for months, so why the long face now?"

"We had an agreement, Kreise. You were supposed to leave the resistance for me to deal with. You had no right killing those men."

"Ah, so that's why you're angry." Kreise's eyes narrowed. "The agreement was that you kept the resistance away from us and from what we were doing. They followed my men on an important mission. Their actions left my men with no options other than to eliminate them."

Kreise glared at Zobart. "Their deaths are on you, Zobart. You should have controlled them better."

"The resistance is off limits. That was our agreement."

"Not anymore." Kreise got to the point of the meeting. "The Wehrmacht will be in Rotterdam within days, if not hours. I need you to give me the names of the men and women in the resistance so they can be arrested before the army arrives."

"Impossible! I cannot, in good conscience, betray my men like that."

"You dare talk to me about betrayal?" Kreise thundered. "Your government would hang you from the nearest lamppost if they knew what you've done."

Zobart scowled but remained quiet.

"I also need to know the whereabouts of Queen Wilhelmina and the Dutch government so they can be apprehended and prevented from leaving the country. You have my word that they will not be harmed."

"I have your word?" Zobart laughed. "You would sell your mother's soul if it helped your precious Führer. Your word counts for nothing."

"One more comment like that and I'll kill you here and now." Kreise's face turned deep red as the anger raged through his body. "You will do as I say, or you, your family, and everyone you've ever held dear will die. Do I make myself clear?"

Zobart remained silent.

"You have benefited more than anyone these last few months, and it's only the beginning. Once we have control of the country, you can have whatever you desire. All we ask in return is your continued cooperation."

"Cooperate or die. Is that it?" Zobart's voice was hoarse and strained.

"It's always been that way. You've known that from the start."

"What do you need from me?" Zobart squirmed in the car seat. It was obvious to Kreise that he'd rather be anywhere than meeting with him at that moment.

"Well?" Zobart snapped. "We have a crisis on our hands, and I'm expected to be with the rest of the government, not sitting outside an abandoned warehouse talking to the enemy."

"You know what I want. I want the names of the resistance, and I need to know what they are planning. I also want to know the whereabouts and the movements of your queen and her government, as well as the names of key figures and leaders in the city. You know who they are, because we discussed them at length before."

Zobart sat still for a few moments before answering. "Our agreement remains the same after the occupation?"

"Whether you want to believe it or not, Zobart, I am a man of my word. You'll be a very rich man after this."

Zobart sighed. "Here is what I am prepared to give you, and it will have to suffice. I don't know the whereabouts of Queen Wilhelmina. None of us do. As for the rest of the government, they are in The Hague, where I should be right now. By my absence, they will know I have double-crossed them."

"None of that will matter. Your country will be in our hands in a matter of hours, and your government will no longer exist."

"As for the resistance," Zobart continued. "I don't know what you think I am, but I'm not privy to what their plans are. They purposely work in the shadows so men like me can't betray them."

"Don't lie to me, Zobart!" Kreise thundered. "If you value the new home you are about to move into and the riches placed into your bank accounts, I suggest you lose the amnesia right now before it's too late."

"I don't know all the names. I'll have to get them for you."

Kreise leant out of the window of his vehicle. "I want those names today, Zobart."

Zobart frowned and gently nodded his head in acknowledgement.

"There is something else I need, and I need it with no delays."

Zobart sighed. "What?"

"The name and location of the girl who broadcasts every night to the resistance. Don't think I haven't heard her sending instructions and messages over the airways. She's clearly German. I need her name and location."

"I don't know who she is."

"You're lying, Zobart. We both know the resistance answers to you. The men your resistance tried to follow are tracking her down as we speak, so make it easier for her by giving me her name."

"I don't know her name. But I know where she broadcasts from."

"That will do."

"May God forgive me," Zobart muttered before handing a piece of paper through the car windows. "This is all I know, I swear. I don't have all their names, but I do know they are planning to blow up the main bridge over the Nieuwe Maas river before your heavy vehicles get here. The location of the radio station and their meeting places are on the list as well."

Zobart paused.

"Was there anything else?" Kreise asked.

"You said your men were tracking down the girl from the radio broadcasts?"

"So?"

"Are these the same men who killed the three resistance men?"

"I already told you they were."

Zobart sighed. "Then I guess you haven't yet heard."

"Heard what?"

"The British businessman, Harrington. That's who they were meeting, I presume?"

Kreise's eyes narrowed. "What do you know of that?"

"Not much. Just that Harrington and two unidentified men are lying dead in an abandoned warehouse next to the Bornissehaven waterway."

Kreise's eyes shot open. "How do you know this?"

"I heard from a trusted source right before coming to this meeting. I'm presuming they are your men?"

"Who killed them? Your resistance?"

Zobart shook his head. "No. From what I can gather, it was a young English spy called Fernsby. I assume it's the same Michael Fernsby who caused you so much embarrassment in Germany last year."

Kreise froze at the mention of Fernsby's name and took a few moments to calm down and gather his thoughts.

"Fernsby? Are you sure?"

Zobart shrugged. "I'm merely relaying what I heard."

"I'll be in touch, Zobart. Get somewhere safe for the next few hours and don't go out on the streets. I'll be in touch, and you'd better have what I need. Remember, we're in total control now."

Kreise started the vehicle and jammed his foot on the pedal. He almost missed the sharp turn as he sped out of the parking space behind the warehouse. His mind raced at a thousand miles per hour.

Fernsby! What is he doing here? Was he sent by the British to eliminate Harrington? Probably. The city will be sealed off soon, so if he's here, he'll be trapped in Rotterdam with no way out.

Not this time, Fernsby!

Albert Kreise temporarily cast his archenemy to the back of his mind. He had more important tasks to take care of.

Chapter 47

The pre-dawn darkness enveloped the battered army truck as it trundled through the deserted, pre-dawn streets of Rotterdam as it made its way towards the Nieuwe Maas river and the Willemsbrug Bridge.

Every bump and pothole jostled Michael against the unyielding bench seat in the back of the truck. His ill-fitting Dutch army uniform chafed at his neck, and the woollen jacket felt more like a straitjacket than a uniform.

Somewhere high above, the drone of Luftwaffe bombers could be heard delivering their payloads of death and destruction.

Behind them, the staccato thunder of explosions echoed through the streets, each concussive blast lighting up the sky like Bonfire Night on a cold November evening.

The ground trembled beneath the truck's tyres as the shockwaves rolled out from the port district, and the acrid stench of smoke and cordite stung Michael's eyes as it hung thick in the air.

And yet, despite the chaos erupting all around them, the streets remained eerily quiet, with the citizens of

Rotterdam huddled behind shuttered windows and bolted doors in the hope they wouldn't be targeted. Michael could sense the change in the atmosphere.

"It's really happening," Jeroen murmured, his voice barely audible over the rattle of the engine. "Everything we've feared, everything we've been preparing for. It's here, now."

A ragged chorus of agonised yells greeted his words, the men's voices raw with adrenaline and barely leashed aggression. Michael felt a surge of admiration for Jeroen's ability to rally his troops, to kindle the flame of hope and defiance in the darkest of moments.

But beneath the bravado and bluster, he could sense the undercurrent of fear, the knowledge that they were about to face an enemy far superior in both numbers and firepower. These men would be lucky to survive the coming onslaught, let alone emerge victorious.

And yet here they were, ready and willing to lay down their lives for a cause greater than themselves. It humbled Michael, even as it tore at his heart.

As the truck lurched around a corner, the thought of Mina rose in his mind, a bright flare of panic amidst the swirling darkness. Was she safe? Had she managed to get out of the radio basement before the bombs began to fall? The idea of her alone and vulnerable in the midst of the chaos was like a knife twisting in his gut.

"Did you send word for Mina to get out safely?" he shouted to Jeroen over the engine's roar.

"She's safe, for now. They're bombing the port, so she has time to send the messages and get out before the fighting begins."

Conversation ceased as they drove in the pre-dawn morning towards the river. At the first checkpoint, Jeroen jumped out of the truck and stood beside it, deep in conversation with a soldier.

Michael couldn't understand what they were saying, but he could hear the urgency in Jeroen's voice that obviously got through to the soldier, because moments later he was back in the truck as it took off on the last leg of its journey.

Michael raised his eyebrows at Jeroen.

"We're through," he announced, pounding the side of the cab with his fist. "Kolonel Janssen's orders. They'll let us pass."

Silence fell again as the truck rumbled along. A few minutes later, the driver stopped and turned off the engine.

"Looks like we're here," Jeroen announced. "Leave the talking to me."

As the eight men jumped out of the back of the truck, they found themselves surrounded by a group of about twenty nervous-looking soldiers pointing their rifles at them.

Jeroen raised his arms in the air and stepped forward.

"Stop." A roar from the centre of the group commanded.

Jeroen shouted something in Dutch and pointed towards his jacket pocket.

Hands grabbed Michael, pushing him to the rear of the group so he wouldn't be asked any questions as the heated conversation unfolded. Eventually, the officer shouted something to his men, and they backed away.

"We don't have long," Jeroen said to Michael after the men were out of earshot. "From what the officer told me, the Wehrmacht have crossed the border and are coming straight for us."

"Who is this Kolonel Janssen?" Michael asked. "He seems to have a lot of clout, whoever he is."

"He's the military commander for the defence of the city. He's a bitter old dog who should have been a general long ago, but his constant battles with the government about the readiness of our forces put a stop to that. Kolonel Janssen is a man of action, and he saw what was happening as early as 1936. He begged our government to mobilise and strengthen, but they refused. Now they know he was right, but it's too late and they won't admit it."

Michael pursed his lips. "He sounds like Churchill in England. A lone voice in the wilderness."

"At least they listened to Churchill. Nobody ever listened to Janssen. I'm surprised he isn't here to greet us. He's usually here, there, and everywhere, and he lives for action."

"He's not here?" Michael asked.

"Not according to the officer who just stopped us. He couldn't find him either."

Michael wanted to ask how Jeroen knew him, but now wasn't the time. The Luftwaffe was already bombing the ports, and it wouldn't be long before they turned their attention to the bridges and other military installations. All they were waiting for was daylight.

According to Jeroen, Micha had already placed TNT at strategic points on the bridge. He'd wired the explosives in parallel a few nights earlier and got as far as connecting them to a junction point underneath one of the bridge's main stanchions.

All that remained be done was running a length of detonator cord to a remote location to make it ready to blow.

"There's a maintenance access, just under the northern pylon." Jeroen gestured downstream, towards a narrow stone stairway cut into the embankment. "It should give us a clear line of sight to the roadway, and enough cover to stay hidden until the crucial moment."

"That's where you want the detonator cord run to?" Michael asked, making sure he understood what the resistance leader wanted.

"Yes."

He grabbed the reel of cord and ran alongside Jeroen to the junction point. The other men dispersed and went about doing whatever they were tasked with.

Jeroen held a torch while Michael connected the line to the junction point, and then he stepped backwards, unrolling the cord as he moved.

Jeroen followed behind, covering the cord with debris from the side of the road. Michael would have liked to have been able to conceal and protect the cord better, but there wasn't enough time.

It would have to do.

Ten minutes later, the two men reached the maintenance access. Stone walls shielded them from prying eyes as they crouched low and connected the cord to a plunger.

Jeroen had a man on standby who would remain behind, hidden in the tall grass. At the first sight of the Wehrmacht taking the bridge, and hopefully, with as many soldiers and vehicles on it as possible, he would push the plunger and blow up the Willemsbrug Bridge.

It wouldn't stop the German advance, but it would hold them up long enough for the Dutch army to regroup and organise their defences.

At least, that was the hope.

By the time he'd finished, silvery trails in the fading darkness signalled that dawn was breaking. The sound of the Luftwaffe's engines was now accompanied by shadows streaking across the sky.

The bombs could be clearly heard as they pounded

military installations, known communication centres, railway lines, industrial hubs, and the airfields on the outskirts of the city.

And, of course, the port, which is where Michael had heard the first bombs drop an hour earlier.

The city itself was largely untouched, and it was clear that the Germans were going after the infrastructures that aided the home war effort.

Except for the operative remaining behind, the rest of the men stood by the truck waiting for Jeroen and Michael to return. As they were about to jump in the back, one of them looked up and let out a sharp yell.

"Look!" he shouted loudly.

In the breaking dawn, what seemed like hundreds of specks in the sky fell towards the earth on both sides of the river. From a distance, they looked almost peaceful, like dandelions drifting in the breeze.

Michael immediately recognised them as paratroopers, the elite vanguard of the Wehrmacht, and he knew exactly what they were doing.

"They're coming for the bridge, so they can hold it for the main force when it arrives," he yelled at Jeroen, who was watching the sky intently.

The specks got larger as the men dropped closer to the ground. Their open parachutes guided them down in a well-rehearsed drill. German warplanes flew overhead, and the roar of Dutch anti-aircraft guns was deafening as they blasted the sky, hoping to shoot down as many enemy planes as possible.

"Go!" Jeroen shouted at the driver as the last man clambered aboard the truck.

The truck lurched forward as it left the scene. Behind them, the first paratroopers were landing. Michael watched as the Dutch army immediately engaged them in a fierce firefight. From what he could see, the Dutch were giving as good as they got, and for now, at least, they were holding the Germans off.

The truck pulled into an empty warehouse in the city, and as soon as the doors closed, the men stripped off their army uniforms and changed into civilian clothes.

"You know where to go," Jeroen said to his gathered resistance fighters. "Wait in the safe house and don't leave. I'll be there shortly with new orders."

"What if we're bombed?" one of them asked, looking nervously at the roof.

"Then go to the cafe and wait for me there. You know what to do."

The men dispersed, leaving Michael and Jeroen alone.

"I guess this is where we say goodbye." Jeroen offered his hand. "I can't thank you enough for what you have done for us. I wish you a safe passage back to England, and I hope that together, we can send the Nazis back to hell, where they belong."

Michael shook Jeroen's hand. "I'm not leaving until I know Mina is safe."

Jeroen let out a half smile. "Which is exactly what I thought you would say. Come, I will take you to her."

"There's something else." Michael hesitated.

"What do you need? We owe you one, so ask away, Englander."

"I need access to a radio. I have to send an important message to London."

"Follow me."

Jeroen pointed to two bicycles propped up against the wall.

Chapter 48

A loud knock on the door stirred Kolonel Maarten Janssen from a deep, exhausted sleep. Another loud knock woke him up, and a third told him that whatever it was, it must be important.

It'd better be.

He leapt out of bed, still half dressed from the night before. Rapidly throwing his trousers on, Janssen stumbled to the door as the loud knocks continued.

"Yes, yes, I heard you. This had better be important." Janssen wiped the sleep from his eyes and threw the door open.

A nervous-looking guard stood before him. "I'm s-s-s sorry to wake you, sir," he stammered. "But General Winkelman is on the telephone, and he says it's important."

"Thank you, Soldaat," Janssen's harsh tone immediately softened. "I'll be right there."

The soldier threw a salute and marched away, back to his post.

Janssen grabbed his jacket and ran to his office.

General Henri Winkelman was the commander-in-chief of the Dutch armed forces, and if he was calling in the middle of the night, then it must be important, especially as he'd met with him just a few hours before, in a tense and acrimonious briefing at The Hague.

His stomach growled, and the grizzled old career officer took a deep breath to control the anxiety that was making it hard to breathe. Not one for showing any emotion, Kolonel Janssen closed his eyes and braced himself for the news he expected to hear.

The Germans are coming.

Janssen glanced at his watch as he scurried into his office and picked up the telephone. It was four am.

"General Winkelman, how can I help you?" Kolonel Janssen, or Frontline Maarten as he was better known by the men he commanded, was a man of few words.

"It's nice to talk to you again so soon, Maarten. I trust you had a safe trip back to Rotterdam?"

"Yes, sir, I did." Janssen hated small talk.

"Believe me when I say this, and I hate to say you were right all along, but we just received word that the Luftwaffe has crossed into Dutch airspace. Waves of bombers are headed our way, probably to The Hague, but also to Rotterdam as well. The invasion has begun, Maarten, and I hope you're ready for what's coming."

A silent scream tore through Janssen's head. He wanted nothing more than to tell the general that he'd been warning of this day for years, but nobody had listened to him. The government was too focused on remaining neutral, and they refused to pay attention when he'd warned them years earlier of the need to rearm so they could defend themselves.

Now it was too late. The Nazis were coming, and there was little they could do to stop them.

"Where are the queen and the government?" Janssen asked, keeping what he really wanted to say bottled inside, which wasn't always the case for him.

It was common knowledge that he'd been repeatedly overlooked for promotion because of his outbursts. He should have been a general years ago, but his constant fights with authority about the state of the Dutch defences made him very unpopular with the top echelons of the Dutch government, so they sent him out of the way, to defend Rotterdam where he couldn't cause any trouble.

"The queen and her government are safe, and their whereabouts are no concern of yours," General Winkelman said in a prickly voice. Janssen knew he hated admitting he was wrong, but now the Germans were on the move, he didn't have a choice.

"What are your orders, General?" Janssen knew this wasn't the time to ruffle the general even more than he'd done the day before when he'd raged at them for not listening to him all those years ago.

"Defend Rotterdam and hold on to her for as long as you can. I hate to say this, but you're our best field commander, and if anyone can get the best out of our troops, it's you."

If the situation wasn't so dire, Janssen would have milked that comment, because it was the first compliment the general had ever given him.

But the time for mind games was long gone. This was now a battle for the survival of the Netherlands herself, and nobody was more patriotic than Kolonel Maarten Janssen.

"I'll hold the city for as long as I can, sir. On that, you have my word."

"We'll hold The Hague for as long as we can as well. May God help us, Maarten."

Janssen replaced the receiver. Holland was beyond saving. At this point, nothing could stop the Nazis from taking over the country. But that wouldn't stop him from giving everything, including his life, to defend it as long as he could.

Janssen reached for the telephone.

"Wake up all the senior officers on your list and tell them to be in the conference room in ten minutes."

"Yes, sir."

Janssen slammed the receiver down and stormed out of his office. The fury he'd held in check for years flooded out. With his face, deep red and angry, he kicked open the door to the outside world, and stepped out to look at the night sky, listening for the telltale sound of enemy warplanes.

The Wehrmacht would be right behind the Luftwaffe, and he vowed to take as many of the Nazi bastards down with him before the city fell.

The skies were dark and silent, and Janssen knew he was witnessing the last moments of peace before the Second World War broke out over Western Europe.

He stomped towards the building that housed the conference room within the headquarters of the army group that was responsible for the defence of Rotterdam.

Janssen had chosen the Katendrecht peninsula on the south side of the Nieuwe Maas river because of its proximity to the Willemsbrug Bridge that was key to the Germans gaining control of the city.

Although better known for its seedy establishments, the Katendrecht peninsula was the perfect place for his forward headquarters.

He was surprised to find one of his senior commanders, Luitenant-Kolonel van der Meer, already seated in the conference room, dressed and waiting, and looking for all the world as though he'd been up and awake for hours.

"I couldn't sleep, Maarten. I tried, but I've been tossing and turning all night. Eventually, I gave up, and when one of the guards ran by me outside, he told me you wanted everyone in here. I'm assuming something is happening?"

Janssen grimaced as he slumped in his seat at the head of the table. "The invasion is happening. The Luftwaffe will be here soon, and no doubt the Wehrmacht will be right behind them."

"You always said it would happen, and now it has. I bet the government wishes they'd listened to you now."

"It's too late for that," Janssen said, standing up as six pale and sleep-deprived senior officers stumbled into the conference room looking as worried as Janssen had ever seen them.

"Gentlemen, waves of German bombers have crossed our borders and will be here in the next few minutes. The Wehrmacht are on the move and will be here by daylight. The war has begun, and we will defend this city until the last Nazi has been sent to hell."

Silence fell on the small gathering before it erupted in shouts and yells. Janssen held up his hand, and the room fell silent again.

"You know what to do, so report to your posts and don't let your men see any fear or hesitation. Lead from the front and show them what it means to be a proud Dutchman."

"Here, here!" came back the shouts. The officers had gone over their plans on multiple occasions, and they knew what to do in their sleep.

As the room fell silent, explosions could be heard in the distance.

"It begins," Kolonel Janssen proclaimed.

He started for the door when, out of nowhere, bursts of gunfire opened up close by. Before anyone could react, an explosion blew open the door to the conference room, knocking Janssen and his fellow senior officers to the ground.

Everything went dark, leaving men and equipment strewn across the conference room floor. Janssen watched as a group of men wearing Dutch army uniforms ran towards them.

Then everything went dark.

Chapter 49

SS Sturmbannführer Albert Kreise rubbed his eyes and stifled a yawn as he waited in his vehicle in the darkness for the others to join him. Although exhausted from lack of sleep, he'd looked forward to this day for a long time.

He was parked inside an empty warehouse on the edge of the Katendrecht district of Rotterdam, which was as well known for its seedy establishments as it was for its dockyards.

Several times during the early hours, Kreise had heard drunken men muttering to themselves while they took a leak at the side of the warehouse. It was a relief when they moved on, because if any of them had ventured inside, it would have been a death sentence.

The Katendrecht district was also the headquarters of the army group that controlled and defended the city, and although small compared to the barracks that housed the soldiers and their equipment, the vast majority of the city's top brass were assembled in the Katendrecht headquarters that evening.

Including Kolonel Maarten Janssen, the military head

of the defence forces. As long as he was actively engaged in the city's defence, his men would continue fighting for him, and that was the reason he was Kreise's first target.

While he waited for the small, but frighteningly well-trained group of men to arrive, he kept himself awake by congratulating himself on how he'd got to where he was this evening.

It wasn't that long ago he'd been sent into exile by Heydrich for the humiliation in Denmark. His cheeks burned at the thought of Michael Fernsby, but if Zobart had been right in his intelligence, Fernsby was in Rotterdam, and if he was still here in the next twenty-four hours, he would be trapped with no way out.

Then, and only then, he would turn his attention to finding Fernsby and ending him once and for all.

And Kreise couldn't wait.

He'd spent the last three months working undercover as a businessman specialising in import/export. This gave him the all-important access to the port areas without arousing any suspicion, but more importantly, it granted him access to the city's leaders and the influential people who ran and defended Rotterdam.

The first man he'd cultivated was Wilhelm Zobart, the Dutch Minister of Defence and Maritime Affairs. As the most important man in the city, with ties to just about everyone who mattered, Zobart was the perfect target for Kreise to blackmail.

After that, it had been a simple job collecting the names of those who needed to be rounded up and removed when the invasion started.

Today was that day, and it was beginning with the loudest and most vocal voice in the entire city, Kolonel Maarten Janssen.

The sound of a large truck pulling up outside the warehouse brought Kreise's thoughts back to the here and now. He jumped out of his vehicle and opened the main doors, standing back to allow the Dutch army truck to reverse in before closing the doors behind it.

Once inside, Kreise turned on the lights and stood back as a dozen men dressed in Dutch uniforms jumped out of the back of the truck.

They lined up and stood quietly to attention, their weapons shouldered, as their officer jumped down from the front passenger seat.

These were men from the feared Brandenburg unit, named after the location of their headquarters in Germany.

The Brandenburgers were men highly trained by the Abwehr for special operations behind enemy lines. They were experts in covert entry, explosives, hand-to-hand combat, and had a working knowledge of weaponry from all across Europe.

The vast majority were fluent in foreign languages, and they had proven to be highly successful in the Polish campaign the previous September.

They were perfect for what Kreise had in mind for them.

Entering Rotterdam under the guise of Dutch barge crews, the men, all fluent in Dutch, had disseminated into the general populace a few days earlier. Then they laid low and waited for the invasion to begin.

Their commander, Major von Lohr, had picked up the truck during the night from a drop off point arranged between Zobart and Kreise.

Now they were here, and Kreise could hardly contain his excitement at what was about to transpire, the fruition of months of careful planning and scheming.

"Sturmbannführer." Major Lohr nodded curtly.

"Major," Kreise replied, eyeing the Abwehr officer carefully. In his mid-thirties, Major Lohr had piercing black eyes and short, jet-black hair. Although he was clean shaven, Kreise could easily see how he could be mistaken for Hitler himself if he had a moustache.

"The men are ready," Major Lohr announced.

"Good. I'll listen for your signal, and I'll meet you in there. Heil Hitler!"

Kreise shouted the last sentence as loud as he dared. In unison, the men raised their right arms and shouted the same words back at him.

Major Lohr opened the side door of the warehouse and stepped outside. His men grabbed bags of equipment and followed him out of the door.

Kreise stood at the doorway and watched as the men disappeared into the darkness. Timing was everything with this operation, and the Brandenburgers were the best at what they did.

Kreise followed a safe distance behind, keeping a sharp eye out for any military patrols. Hiding behind one of the district's red-light pubs, he watched as Major Lohr and his men took up their positions.

Right on time, Kreise heard the security fence rattle as someone unlocked the chain that secured one of the gates in the rear corner of the military compound from the inside.

Lohr's men ran inside, weapons at the ready. Fifteen minutes later, all hell broke loose.

Gunfire burst out from all around the compound as Lohr's men took out the guards. In the background, the sound of Luftwaffe bombers pounding the port area was music to his ears.

A loud explosion close by made him jump, and this was the signal for him to act. He emerged from the shadows and pushed through the open gate. The path to the conference room was strewn with dead bodies, all of them Dutch, from what he could tell.

The conference room door was blown off and Kreise used his torch because the explosion had blown the lights. Six men sat on their knees, facing the far wall with their hands on their heads. Half a dozen of Lohr's men guarded them, their rifles aimed and ready.

Kolonel Maarten Janssen sat on a chair on the opposite side of the room, his face a twisted mask of hatred and anger. Two of the Brandenburgers watched him like a hawk, and it was obvious to everyone that one false move would result in a quick death for the famed military commander.

Lohr stood in the centre of the room with another man who Kreise immediately recognised as Luitenant-Kolonel van der Meer, the Dutch officer he'd turned during several covert meetings.

"Luitenant-Kolonel van der Meer, I'm glad you saw this through. You will be well rewarded for your efforts."

"I don't want any rewards," van der Meer stared at Janssen, who glared at his compatriot as if he was the devil himself. "I just want to save Dutch lives, and if this is the only way of guaranteeing it, then so be it."

He stared at Janssen. "I'm not a traitor when all I'm doing is saving lives. Thousands of lives, perhaps even more. You are the traitor by continuing to fight, knowing full well we cannot win. Our people will die for nothing other than your overinflated ego, Maarten, and I couldn't allow you to do that."

"So, you betrayed us and handed the keys of Rotterdam to the enemy." Janssen spat the words out. "You are a traitor, van der Meer, and you will pay for what you have done."

"The only people paying are the ones who resist us." Kreise stepped forward. "You have done a good job, Major Lohr."

He stepped in front of Luitenant-Kolonel van der Meer. "You have done the right thing and saved countless lives. The Reich will stay true to our word, and as many of your countrymen as possible will be spared."

"We don't have long," Major Lohr intervened. "Do what you're here for so we can get out of here."

"Indeed." Kreise was enjoying himself, but he knew Lohr was right.

He stepped in front of the men lined up against the wall, checking all their faces against the ones he'd memorised so perfectly from the photographs proved by van der Meer.

"It's them," he announced, stepping aside.

The Brandenburgers opened fire in unison, shooting all six officers in the backs of their heads. When the noise settled, all lay dead on the floor, blood oozing from their head wounds.

Janssen leapt to his feet and charged, but was immediately taken down by the butts of two rifles. Once down, another heavy blow sent him into silence.

Luitenant-Kolonel van der Meer looked away, no doubt ashamed of what he'd facilitated.

"You know it was the right thing to do," Kreise assured him. "By removing the military heads, the defence of the city will crumble, and the surrender of your forces will save many lives."

Van der Meer nodded, his face pale in the torchlight.

"Go to your men and tell them about the tragic events that happened here. Insist they lay down their arms, and when they do, you will be rewarded for your loyalty to the Reich."

Van der Meer scowled and hurried away from the carnage. Kreise knew his time would come, but for now he was useful, so he'd keep him alive.

Two of the Brandenburgers picked up Maarten Janssen's limp body and carried him away.

"Take him to the safe house," Kreise shouted. "Hold him there until the Wehrmacht arrives to relieve you."

"What will become of him?" Major Lohr asked as they made their way back to the warehouse and their vehicles.

"Once the Wehrmacht is here, he'll be paraded on the streets of Rotterdam in a demonstration of our power and the futility of resistance. Then he'll be sent to a prison camp in Germany where he'll live out the rest of his life as a failure."

Lohr shrugged his shoulders. His part of the mission was over, and his mind was already on what his unit had lined up next.

Kreise started his vehicle and watched as the truck disappeared down the street to the safe house. Dawn was breaking, and as he looked up at the sound of aircraft overhead, he saw wave after wave of paratroopers leaping out of their aircraft on their way to securing bridges and other vital infrastructure in advance of the main military thrust.

The Luftwaffe continued to pound the ports and their other targets relentlessly, and at that moment, he had never been more proud of being an SS officer in the Sicherheitsdienst. His moment had arrived, and nobody, especially Michael Fernsby, could stop him.

Rotterdam would soon be his, and he would rule it with an iron fist. Heydrich would have no choice other than to promote him and make him chief of the SD in Holland.

Chapter 50

Memories of saddle sores and a screaming backside filled Michael with dread as he stared at the bicycles. The agony of his legendary bike ride through Germany to Denmark was still fresh in his mind, and he'd vowed to never to punish himself like that again.

Now here he was, having to ride once more. He shrugged and shook his head.

Jeroen smirked, but remained silent.

Does he know? How could he? Michael shelved the questions until a more appropriate moment and grabbed the handlebars. "Lead the way."

Chaos greeted the two men as Michael followed Jeroen in the early morning daylight towards Mina's apartment in the Overschie district. Gunshots and fighting to their south could be clearly heard as the Dutch army fought valiantly to keep control of the city.

Overhead, the Luftwaffe pounded strategic targets, and the earth shook as eardrum-shattering bursts of anti-aircraft guns hammered the sky in defiance.

Michael thought of the innocents who would lose their

homes, their possessions, even their lives in the relentless onslaught for control of the city, and he wondered how much longer the Dutch could hold on before the Nazis claimed victory.

Rotterdam would fall, of that he had no doubt. Regardless of the bravery shown by Jeroen and countless others, the outcome was inevitable. The Germans were too strong, and as they rode their bikes, he was grateful for the narrow sea that separated Britain from the European mainland, as it might yet prove to be the best line of defence Britain had against the seemingly invincible Germans.

They rode for forty-five minutes in silence, each consumed by their own thoughts. Michael pushed the carnage to the back of his mind and concentrated on the hope that Mina had made it home safely.

His chest pumped at a furious rate as they reached Lemkensstraat and Mina's apartment block. They pushed the bicycles into the entryway and carried them up the stairs.

Outside Mina's apartment, Michael hesitated before knocking loudly. It might be early in the morning, but the cacophony of destruction ensured no one in Rotterdam was sleeping.

Although they'd been expecting it for some time, it was a shock to the system when it finally happened. Michael was feeling it almost as much as the residents were, and his heart broke for what the future held for them.

Especially the Jews who lived in the area.

The door burst open, and a frantic looking Mina flew into the corridor. She grabbed Michael and threw her arms around his neck. "Thank God you are safe. We were worried the Nazis had caught you."

"We thought the same about you." Michael panted as

he held her, struggling for breath, more in relief than anything else. "I was worried you'd be caught in the bombing."

"They were bombing the docks, so I was safe." Mina replied, holding his arm as they went inside the tiny apartment.

Anna and her father were huddled around a radio on the kitchen table. Senta sat on the couch, her face as pale as her blonde hair.

"We can't escape them," she said to nobody in particular. "Even when we run away to another country, they follow us over the border. Nowhere is safe, and if they aren't stopped, Hitler will take over the entire world."

"Britain and France will stop them," Michael reassured her. "And you should see the brave Dutch soldiers at the Willemsbrug Bridge. They're fighting for their lives, and from what we saw, they are giving as good as they're getting. We should all be very proud of them."

"Nevertheless." Jeroen joined the conversation. "Rotterdam will fall. It's only a matter of time, and that's when we become more important. We do what the army cannot, and that is to make the Germans regret the day they ever set foot in the Netherlands."

Silence fell as they listened to the radio broadcasting in English so they could all understand it. Fierce fighting was reported in both Belgium and Holland, which was where the major thrust of the invasion was expected to come from. Then it would be France's turn.

Luxembourg would probably fall on the first day, but the others were expected to provide stiff resistance, especially as Britain and France had positioned most of their forces in Belgium to meet them head-on.

Mina poked Michael in the ribs to get his attention. "I'm glad you're here. I thought you'd be gone by now."

"I'll probably leave tonight. There's something I need to do before I go." He glanced at Jeroen, who was listening intently to the radio.

"Jeroen, I need access to a radio," Michael reminded him.

"Yes." Jeroen pulled himself away from the terrible news. "I'm sorry, I forgot. Mina has a radio you can use."

Michael stood up. "This can't wait. I need to send an urgent message to London."

He looked at Mina. "And then I need to get some rest before I have to leave."

Mina stared at the floor for a moment before fixing her eyes on Michael. Something was different between them. He could feel it. It wasn't the closeness they had, or the love they shared. That still felt the same.

What had changed was the situation around their relationship. They knew the war was bigger than either of them, and whatever they shared would have to wait until, one way or the other, the war was over.

People were dying by the thousands, and this was just the beginning. What gave them the right to find happiness when families were being torn apart by Nazi bombs and bullets at this very moment?

Michael felt it, and he could tell that Mina felt it too. They may be able to steal a few moments of happiness before he left, but that was all it would be. They both understood the futility of promises.

And yet, that was all they had.

Whatever happened next, Michael felt great relief that they had finally, in a unique twist of fate, found the time to join together a few nights earlier. Their eyes, that had locked onto each other for the last few minutes, conveyed everything words could never do. Michael knew the love he felt was being returned in kind, and that made him complete.

He looked away and took a deep breath. It was time to step up and get to work. His feelings would have to wait.

Jeroen rose from the chair. "Mina, would you come with us and send Michael's message?"

Mina opened her mouth to speak, but Michael cut her off. "It's safer for her here. If you show me where it is, I can send the message myself."

"It takes a lot of training to get the frequencies right," Jeroen answered. "I understand you are trained in such things, but Mina is an expert, and she knows our radio setup like the back of her hand. If you want to be sure your message reaches its destination, you would be advised to take advantage of her expertise."

"I know all that," Michael said. He looked at Mina and somehow fell in love with her all over again. "But she is safer here. I know enough to transmit, and then I'll be on my way."

"It's my radio, and I'm sending your message." Mina's face hardened. "And that's the end of it. I have the key to the room, and I'm not giving it to you."

She looked so indignant that Michael wanted to laugh. He would have if the situation wasn't so serious.

"That's settled then," Jeroen said. "All three of us are going."

"I'm coming too," Senta shouted.

"No!" Five voices all shouted in unison.

"You're staying here, and that's an order." Jeroen tapped her on the shoulder. "You'll be needed soon enough, but for now, stay here and stay safe."

Senta's face dropped, but she didn't argue.

"Let's go." Michael headed for the door.

Chapter 51

Once outside the door, Jeroen grabbed Mina's arm and pulled her close. "Did you do it?"

Mina nodded. "Yes."

Michael headed towards the staircase, but Mina stopped him. She leant into him, whispering in his ear. "The radio's here."

Michael shot her a confused look, but he didn't say anything. He knew the corridor wasn't the safest place to talk. Memories of another corridor in Munich a lifetime ago flashed through his mind when Gerda Yung had taken him and David to her friend's apartment, where they'd been involved in a shootout with the Gestapo.

He shook his shoulders and forced the grizzly memories from his mind.

Mina beckoned for him to follow, and she led the way to the end of the corridor where Esther lived. He was even more surprised when she knocked three times on her door.

The door cracked open, and Esther stood aside while Mina, Jeroen, and Michael entered her apartment. As soon as the door closed, Michael pulled Mina to him.

"The radio is here?" he asked.

"Jeroen's men helped me move it during the night. The previous place is on the south side of the river, and it's too dangerous to cross now the Nazis are here."

"But why here? Why Esther's apartment? Don't you realise how dangerous it is?"

"Of course we do," Jeroen answered. "We're going to move it around from place to place. This is just the first stop."

"Does Senta know it's here?" Michael asked.

Mina shook her head. "Esther isn't only a nurse," she said changing the subject. "She's the one who trained me to use the radio."

Michael stared at Esther with a newfound respect and shook his head. The bravery of these people never failed to surprise him.

"Alright, let's get this done with."

"What are we doing?" Esther asked, already dressed in her nurse's uniform. "I have to go to the hospital. The casualties…" Her voice dropped off, her message understood by all.

"You go," Jeroen said. "We'll get the radio out of here as soon as we can."

Esther left, locking the door behind her.

The radio was on a lace-draped table in Esther's bedroom. Michael exchanged a knowing glance with Mina when they stood by the bed together, and he squeezed her hand, allowing the memories of their shared night to fill his senses.

The wire antenna ran out of the window and was attached to the branches of a tree. It wasn't the most discreet setup Michael had ever seen, and it worried him that someone would notice it.

"It's not secure enough," he said to Jeroen. "It's a security risk, and I expect you to take Mina's safety seriously."

"We're preparing a more secure location. This is just for a few days until the bombing stops and it's safer to move around the city. Then we'll move it."

Michael gave Mina the frequency range that Alison Turnberry, Unit 317's secretary and radio operator, monitored. He knew this was manned twenty-four hours a day, so even if Alison wasn't at her desk, the radio operator would get the message and pass it onto Sanders and Dansey.

While Mina prepared the radio, Michael sat down with a pencil and paper to write out his message. He grabbed the codebook from a concealed pocket in his ever-present rucksack and thought about how he wanted to word his message to Tony Sanders, and, no doubt, Colonel Z, and whoever else would read it in the higher echelons of British intelligence.

The one-time code pad was still good for today and tomorrow, so he wrote out his message in clear English, making sure that neither Jeroen nor Mina could see what he was writing:

Harrington dead. Killed by two SD, now also dead. Have proof Zobart double agent. Shaw dead. Leaving tonight for RV. Fernsby.

He double-checked to make sure he'd got the salient points across. With Morse Code, it was important to be as succinct as possible for several reasons, not least of which was security. The longer a message transmitted, the more risk there was of it being intercepted, which could be, and often was, fatal for the radio operator.

Another reason was accuracy. Because each character was transmitted as a series of dots and dashes, there was always a potential for errors, even by the very best operators.

Happy that his message was as short as he could make it, he turned to his codebook and, using the code of the day, set about breaking it down into a series of unintelligible letters.

By the time he'd finished, his message was a string of nonsensical letters that began with the following:

NVJGH YXKWU OPLZA ... ZXYVA OPLQW XZNVZ ...

The message was impossible to crack without the codebook, which only he and 317's headquarters possessed.

At least in Rotterdam, anyway. Other operatives of the unit would have the same codebook, but they were elsewhere in Europe, hopefully on their way to the coast and the safety of the British Isles.

Satisfied with his message, he triple-checked it and passed it to Mina. Without saying a word, he went to the toilet and burned the original, uncoded message, over the bowl. Then he flushed the ashes down the toilet.

On his return, he sat on the bed while Mina donned the headphones and turned the radio dial. She picked up the coded message, looked at it, and stared up at Michael, who was trying to speak to her.

She removed the headphones and looked up so she could hear what he was saying.

"Are you sure you don't want me to do it?" he asked. "We only have one go at this, and it needs to be accurate."

"I'm very familiar with Morse Code." Mina's face flushed.

"Very good. I was just making sure. I'm not doubting you, Mina."

Mina pulled a face and replaced the headphones. Then she began transmitting the message in Morse Code, tapping it out one letter at a time. When she finished,

Michael took the message and burned it over the toilet bowl.

Ten minutes later, Mina held up her hand to stop any chatter. London was responding with a message of their own. She wrote down a series of letters, and when she'd finished, she handed it to Michael, who went back into the bathroom to decode it.

Orders forthcoming. Standby.

"Standby for a further message," Michael told Mina. He hurried back into the bathroom to destroy the message.

Thirty minutes later, the radio burst into life. Mina scribbled down the message as she received it, and when it was over, she handed it to Michael.

As before, he sat on the toilet seat to decode the orders that had no doubt come directly from Dansey himself.

Eliminate Zobart. Then head for the coast.

He'd expected this, which was why he'd sent the message in the first place. Half of him was angry that London was ordering him to remain in Rotterdam when they knew better than anyone how dangerous it was with the invasion underway.

The other half was glad because he could spend more time with Mina and try to convince her to leave with him when it was over.

At the end of the day, he worked for a unit that specialised in operations behind enemy lines. This wasn't the first time he'd done it, and if he survived, he'd no doubt do it again. Staying in Rotterdam wasn't at all unusual, not for someone like him.

A dispensable asset. That's all he was.

He burned the message and rejoined Mina and Jeroen, who waited patiently for his instructions.

"I'm staying for now. For a few days at least."

Mina looked as though she was going to say something,

but the serious look on Michael's face told her otherwise. Instead, she turned the radio off and joined the two men sitting on the edge of the bed in silence.

Each of them was lost in their own thoughts and for ten long minutes, the morbid silence sucked the atmosphere out of the room as thoughts of war, death, and defeat consumed the occupants.

"It's time to rest." Jeroen finally broke the silence. "This is going to be a long and arduous fight, and we're no good to anybody if we aren't rested."

He rose to his feet. "I'll be back later with instructions for your next broadcast. Until then, get some sleep."

Jeroen gave a half-hearted smile and let himself out of Esther's apartment. Mina locked the door behind him and raised her eyebrows at Michael. "We have the place to ourselves for a few hours."

"It'd be a shame to waste it," Michael answered, standing up and sweeping Mina into his arms.

They fell onto the bed, all thoughts of bombs and war momentarily blocked from their minds. Whatever time they had left together, they would not waste it on Adolf Hitler and his Nazi war machine.

They knew hard times were coming, and they both knew their stolen moments together might be all they ever had.

"So be it," Michael murmured as he pulled Mina closer to him.

Chapter 52

Hours later, Michael woke with a start. The front door of the apartment slammed, jolting him from a deep sleep. Mina leapt up beside him, instinctively reaching for her clothes.

More banging from outside the bedroom made it obvious that someone was there. Michael threw on his underwear and grabbed the Walther PPK from his rucksack on the floor close to the bed, where he could reach it in an emergency.

He ran to the wall beside the door, his weapon at the ready, caught Mina's eye and pointed towards the bed. She nodded, and sliding to the floor, she rolled into the shadows beneath the bed frame.

Michael placed his hand on the door handle and yanked it open.

He threw himself to the ground and rolled out of the way, expecting a hail of bullets to follow him. Instead, the welcome, if not sarcastic, voice of Esther broke the tension.

"I hope you didn't break my bed springs! Now get out, because I'm tired, and I need to sleep."

Tension turned to embarrassment, and Michael felt his cheeks burning. He stood up and watched as Mina rolled out from under the bed, her face equally as red as his own.

They stood side by side, wearing nothing but their underwear, as Esther walked into her bedroom with an amused, almost stern look on her face.

"You look tired," was all Michael could think of to say.

"You look content," Esther came back at him.

All three burst into fits of laughter, and Esther shook her head as they dressed and left the bedroom.

"I'll be back later to use the radio," Mina said sheepishly.

"How was the hospital?" Michael changed the subject.

"Horrible." Esther's face turned serious. "There are so many casualties from the bombs. Many are burned beyond recognition from the fires, and I lost count of the number of blast victims. We ran out of beds and had to set up an emergency ward outside the main hospital. It was that bad."

Esther sighed, deep creases on her face revealing the fatigue she must be feeling.

"We don't have enough doctors or nurses. I'm not supposed to go back until tonight, but I'll grab a couple of hours and then I'll report back for duty. I've never seen anything like this before."

"I thought the Germans weren't bombing the city," Mina said. "Only the ports, bridges, and other areas that are important for them to damage and destroy."

"They are, but they're not very precise, are they?" Esther answered. "The bombs are landing all over the place, and even when they hit their targets, the fires spread, and debris flies everywhere. Homes are being turned to rubble, families are being torn apart, and for what?"

"For what indeed?" Michael said. "And this is just the beginning. This is what war does, and it's only going to get worse. Come, Mina, let's get out of her way so she can get some rest."

"I'm sorry," Mina said, holding Esther's hands in hers. "Is there anything we can do to help?"

Esther shook her head. "Not right now, although we might need more people to help if the casualty rate keeps rising."

Michael closed the door to the apartment behind them and waited until he heard Esther turn the lock. As much as it pained him to think of the growing casualties, he had to make sure the transmitter was safe.

Hating himself for being so heartless and cold, he held Mina's hand as they reached her apartment. Close contact with her made him feel vulnerable and emotional. Most of all, it allowed him to feel human, and that is what he wanted more than anything else.

He kissed her on her lips, feeling the familiar tingling running up and down his spine and the goosebumps on his skin at her touch.

"I have to go. Go inside, and whatever you do, don't venture out onto the streets. I'll be back later to see if there's any more orders from London."

"What are they making you do?" Mina clung onto Michael's arms in a vicelike grip. He didn't struggle, because he never wanted to let her go.

"I can't talk about it, but I have to leave as soon as it's over. I'm serious, Mina, I want you and Senta to come with me. Rotterdam will be crawling with Nazis soon, and there will be nowhere for you to hide."

He left out the part where, as a radio operator for the resistance, she would be top of the Nazi hit list.

Mina shook her head. "What kind of person would I be if I left them now, with all of this going on? What about Anna and her father? Esther, Jeroen, and all the others who will be left at the mercy of the Nazis?"

Michael bowed his head. He knew she was right, and he loved her even more for it.

"My love for you grows stronger every moment. You are brave and kind, and yet the sweetest girl I have ever met."

"Remember that when you're gone. I love you, Michael Fernsby."

They kissed passionately, and then Michael watched as Mina disappeared into her apartment. He stood for a moment to calm his raging emotions, and then turned on his heels and headed to the safe house.

Whatever else he felt, he was here for one purpose, and one purpose only: to win the war for the Allies. Beginning with the traitor with Allied blood on his hands, Wilhelm Zobart.

Chapter 53

Heavy fighting in and around the city continued into the night. The Dutch defenders fought valiantly, defying overwhelming odds to keep the Wehrmacht at bay.

The battle for the Willemsbrug Bridge was lost, and the Nazi war machines were crossing in force. Hour by hour, minute by minute, the situation in Rotterdam was worsening. The blitzkrieg methods adopted by the German military were overwhelming not only the Dutch forces, but Belgium's as well.

News of Luxembourg's surrender was all over the radio, and Jeroen feared Holland wouldn't be far behind. All they had left were pockets of resistance, and that wouldn't last much longer.

Jeroen's plan was to disrupt the Nazis as much as possible, especially after the occupation was complete. One of the first operations his band of resistance fighters had been tasked with was the destruction of the Willemsbrug Bridge, and by now, that should have been destroyed.

Except it wasn't.

Michael Fernsby had run the line from the explosives

set by Micha, and all that Lars had to do was push the plunger, and the bridge should have collapsed into the river, taking hundreds of the invaders with it.

Either Lars was dead, or the detonators failed. As Lars never returned to the safe house, Jeroen assumed the worst and accepted that he was dead.

With the Wehrmacht not far away, Jeroen and two of his most trusted men pushed their rubber dinghy into the still waters of the Nieuwe Maas river and paddled gently towards the Waalhaven district on the other side.

They kept their heads down and hoped the searchlights wouldn't pick them up as they silently glided across the dark, inky coloured river. Shouts in German shot across the water, and Jeroen could feel the nervous tension around him.

Although this was a dangerous mission, neither of the men with him had uttered a word of dissent. Both knew the risks, but they would die for their country, and Jeroen knew his men would follow him to the gates of hell if necessary.

They reached the riverbank on the other side without incident and dragged the boat out of the water, hid it behind a larger fishing boat, and gathered their rucksacks. Jeroen pulled them together in a huddle by the side of the boat.

He let out a sigh. At least they'd made it across the river.

"We all know what we have to do. If any of us fall, the mission comes first, do you understand? We have to get the quartz crystals that Mina left behind."

Hendrik Visser, Jeroen's second in command and most trusted resistance fighter, and Ruben Voss, the young but fearless fighter he'd trust with his life, nodded in agreement.

"Let's go."

Jeroen led the way through the shattered remains of Waalhaven to the administrative building on Hilgersweg. Beyond, the twisted, blackened ruins of the busy train lines could be seen in the pale moonlight, still smouldering from the bombs that destroyed them.

Jeroen's anxiety level went up more notches when they reached the administrative building that had housed their radio broadcasting equipment before Mina removed most of it two nights earlier.

The building was all but destroyed, and there was no way anything in the basement could have survived the onslaught. Still, he had to check.

Somewhere in that rubble were the quartz crystals Mina had been forced to leave behind, and he had to at least try to find them.

Leaving Hendrik and Ruben on watch, Jeroen ran to the rubble and hid behind a massive piece of concrete lying on what used to be the pavement in front of the building.

Satisfied that he wasn't being watched, he crawled over the rubble in an attempt to find a way in to where the basement used to be.

Smoke drifted amongst the ruins, and dirt swirled in the aftermath of the destruction. Jeroen's nostrils filled with the acrid smell of smoke and cordite, making it hard to either breathe or see.

The remnants of a wall collapsed a few feet from where he stood, reminding him of the precariousness of the situation. In front of him, sticking up from the shattered concrete, was a blue chair, the same blue chair that Esther had sat on. More recently, Mina had used it when she transmitted her messages to other resistance groups in the city.

The sight of the chair caught Jeroen off guard, and for a moment, he lost focus and allowed his mind to wander to better times when Rotterdam wasn't under attack.

Esther trained Mina in that very chair, and Jeroen closed his eyes as the memories flooded into his mind. His heart ached, and all he wanted at that moment was to sweep her into his arms and tell her that everything would be alright, and that no more innocent citizens would die at the hands of the Nazis.

He scowled, forcing the thoughts of her from his mind. He had a job to do that required his full attention, and thinking of Esther was a distraction that could get him killed.

But still, his eyes lingered on the blue chair. Images of Esther sitting in it, laughing at his stupid jokes refused to budge, and he snarled inwardly at his momentary weakness.

He'd always vowed to never get involved with anyone he worked with because it made both of them vulnerable, and it weakened his resolve when it came to the difficult decisions.

But with Esther, he couldn't help himself. The pull on his heartstrings was too much, and he'd fallen for her hook, line, and sinker. So far, they'd kept their relationship secret, but Jeroen worried what would happen if either were captured by the Nazis.

He would do anything to protect her, and that was his biggest weakness.

Her work at the hospital was dangerous enough, but it wasn't as dangerous as being a radio operator, especially when the Nazis had control of the country.

As much as he liked Mina, and he would do everything in his power to protect her, he was secretly relieved that Esther was no longer doing it. Although he'd never admit it, he was much more comfortable with a German being targeted than his beloved Esther.

Not that he'd ever tell Esther that, because she'd leave him in a heartbeat if it ever came out. But he couldn't help how he felt, and somehow the sight of the blue chair amongst the rubble made it all so clear in his mind.

He shook his head, ridding himself of the distracting thoughts.

Sifting through the rubble, he choked back the dirt that clogged his throat. It was difficult to see, but he persevered in an ever-more frantic search.

Chapter 54

Ten minutes later – or was it thirty? – Jeroen lost track of time in the ruins – he uncovered the desk they used for the radio transmitter. Like everything else in the rubble, it was smashed and broken, but Jeroen looked beyond that and pulled out the bottom drawer that was covered with stones and silt.

The bag of crystals was miraculously intact, protected from the destruction by the concrete pillar that leant over the desk. He grabbed the bag of quartz crystals that allowed the radio to transmit on different frequencies and placed them in his rucksack. Without them, they'd be stuck with the ones they had at the apartment, which weren't many. Then he began making his way back to his comrades.

The hackles on his arms and neck rose as his sixth sense kicked in. He'd learnt to rely on his instincts over many years of dangerous operations, and he never disregarded them when they warned him something wasn't right.

After throwing himself onto a piece of rough concrete,

cutting his arms and legs in the process, he looked for hand signals from Hendrik or Ruben to confirm or deny his senses, but nothing was forthcoming.

Movement to his left caught his eye, and he watched as a shadow emerged from behind Ruben. He couldn't shout, and nor could he fire his weapon. Doing either would surely bring a unit of armed Wehrmacht upon them in minutes, so he was forced to watch in horror as Ruben was taken unawares.

The shadowy figure grabbed Ruben from behind, and Jeroen's heart sank as he watched his friend's neck break from a single, violent twist from behind.

Hendrik was next. He was as tough as nails, but when Ruben's killer joined the fight, he had no chance.

He fell, silently taken down by the best-trained men Jeroen had ever seen.

His chest was tight as a drum. He wasn't scared. After a lifetime of intelligence work, and after what he'd witnessed recently, he was way beyond that point.

He was angry. Furious. Incensed. All he wanted to do was jump out of his hiding place and attack the men who'd killed Ruben and Hendrik so easily.

But he wasn't stupid, he knew he'd be killed in an instant. Maybe that was what he wanted? An image of Esther flashed into his mind, and he forced it out quickly.

He fought his instincts, knowing that more was riding on the success of this mission than his or any others' lives. The quartz crystals were vital if the resistance were going to be a functional unit in the future, and as much as he hated to admit it to himself, the entire resistance structure in Rotterdam relied on him as their leader, especially after the death of Pieter De Jong at Cafe Verhaal.

If he sacrificed himself tonight, everything they'd ever fought for, everything Ruben, Hendrik, and probably Lars had died for, was for nothing. He couldn't allow that. He had to get out of there and live to fight another day.

Hendrick, Ruben, and Lars would be avenged.

He slipped away from the ruined administrative building, stopping frequently to look and listen for the quiet assassins who were surely searching for him.

Emerging from the rubble on the opposite side of the building from where the assassins attacked Ruben and Hendrik, Jeroen ran towards what used to be busy rail and tram lines.

Now, like everything else in this area, it was destroyed. Bent, twisted pieces of track rose from the ground, torn from their couplings with brutal force from the air attack.

He weaved his way around them, and almost made it to the other side, where tall grass grew in the fields.

A man emerged from behind a rail carriage laying on its side.

The two men stood around fifty feet from each other, staring, weighing each other up from a distance. Recognition dawned on Jeroen as the man's face came into view in the pale moonlight.

He knew who he was!

"I'm sorry about your men." SS Sturmbannführer Albert Kreise's voice was flat and unemotional. "I was hoping for someone else to show up."

"Who were you expecting, Kreise?" Jeroen asked, frantically searching for the two assassins who were no doubt closing in. Kreise was stalling, trying to get his attention while they snuck up on him.

"No matter." Kreise ignored his question. "You're high on my list of targets. I would advise you not to resist or my men will have no choice other than to kill you right here."

Jeroen threw caution to the wind. At this point, it didn't matter if the entire German army descended upon him.

He wasn't getting out of this alive, so there was no need for him to be quiet any longer.

He knew the standoff was designed to distract him, so he threw himself to the ground and pulled his pistol from his pocket. Kreise had vanished, but one of the assassins was on the rail tracks, around twenty feet behind him.

He raised his weapon, but before he could fire, a burst of gunfire from behind the assassin caught Jeroen by surprise. The bullets missed, but they gave Jeroen enough time to fire off some of his own.

The assassin, caught in the open, dropped to the ground. Kreise, ever the opportunist, emerged from his vantage point behind the rail carriage, his gun out before him.

Jeroen let off a bullet, sending him scurrying back for cover.

Who's firing? Jeroen was confused. *Who else is out there?*

Another burst of gunfire revealed who it was. The second assassin emerged and ran to the rubble at the edge of the railway lines, firing all the way.

The mystery man rose from his hiding place, and even in the pale light of the moon, Jeroen could see the deep, dark-coloured liquid oozing from a wound in his head.

It was Hendrik! He wasn't dead. Instead, limping badly, and with his left arm hanging uselessly by his side, he'd come to save his comrade's life, and Jeroen wasn't going to let that pass.

Hendrik fell under a hail of bullets from the assassin.

Using the noise to cover his tracks, Jeroen ran for the fields and the cover of the tall grass. Kreise appeared from the side of the rail carriage, but he was too far away for his bullets to have any accuracy.

Kreise ran after Jeroen, firing all the way, but his bullets fell short. Jeroen darted into the long grass and crouched down, hidden from view.

Kreise shouted orders to the assassin, but Jeroen knew this area like the back of his hand, and he melted away before the Germans could find him.

An hour later, he found himself back at the Nieuwe Maas river, wading into the freezing water to launch the boat. Ignoring the biting cold that threatened to overwhelm him, Jeroen pulled himself into the small dinghy and rowed as fast as he dared to the other side.

There weren't as many Germans on the opposite side of the river, so he hurried to his safe house with the quartz crystals, shaking his fists with rage at the Nazis. He hated everything they stood for, and with the time he had left on this earth, he vowed to avenge the men who had given their lives both for him and for the Netherlands.

How did Kreise know exactly which building to target? How could he know this? Someone has betrayed us. Who?

These and other questions burned into Jeroen's mind, punishing him, and making him suspicious of everybody.

Especially the German girls, Mina and Senta. Were they truly as loyal as they seemed?

Whoever it was, they would regret the day they ever crossed the Dutch resistance.

Chapter 55

Michael spent the next two days scouring the airwaves for clues to the whereabouts of Wilhelm Zobart. He had to be in Holland somewhere, and it probably wasn't The Hague, because members of his own government would be searching for him after realising the man entrusted with the defence of the country had betrayed them.

Movement was difficult anywhere in Holland, so Michael was sure he'd gone to ground until the occupation was complete and his government had surrendered.

He was probably somewhere in Rotterdam, but where was anyone's guess. Michael had already searched his primary home in the city, but that was empty, with no signs that anyone was living there.

Wherever he was, he'd eventually surface, and when he did, Michael would be ready.

Despite the risks, Michael kept the shortwave radio turned on to keep up with the occupation. He left it on German-speaking broadcasts, because they were more likely to carry news of Zobart, especially if he was to be installed as the interim leader of a puppet government, which Michael suspected might happen.

But there was nothing. Just the grating, guttural voices of the German announcers, their words a twisted mockery of the truth.

The big news coming out of London was that Neville Chamberlain had been replaced as Prime Minister by Winston Churchill. This was good news as far as Michael was concerned, because Churchill represented the bulldog, never-say-die spirit Britain needed, and the speeches he delivered were the single most inspiring thing Michael had ever heard.

He couldn't wait to get back home and listen to his voice on the radio, stirring up the British public like no other could ever do.

After dark he packed away the radio and left to gather whatever supplies he could as his food supply had run out. He knew the shops were devoid of goods, and in any case, he didn't possess a ration card, so no shop would sell him anything.

His best option was to find Jeroen and seek supplies from him, so he made his way to Mina's apartment, hoping to find him there, which was doubtful, because nobody had seen him for the last two days.

Mina wasn't home, so he tried Esther's apartment. He knocked, and Esther opened the door a few inches to see who it was. When she saw Michael, she quickly opened the door and allowed him to enter.

Michael was dismayed to find Mina sitting at the desk in Esther's bedroom with her headphones on, working the radio transmitter. It was only a matter of time before Kreise, or whoever else was in charge, located the signal and raided the apartment.

He was about to wave at her to let her know he was there when Jeroen appeared from behind the door.

"Jeroen, I'm glad you're here. I haven't seen you since you left to get the crystals for the radio. Did you get them?"

Jeroen gestured to the couch and closed the door to Esther's bedroom. Esther sat next to him, and Michael noted the familiarity and comfort level between them as they sat with their legs and arms touching.

He noted it, but didn't say anything. That was their business and had nothing to do with anyone else.

"I got them," Jeroen said, his voice flat, his mind elsewhere.

"What happened?" Michael asked. "I know something did by the way you're acting."

"They were waiting for us." Jeroen looked into Michael's eyes, revealing the pain he was feeling inside. "They knew the radio station was there, and they knew we would go to it."

He stared at Michael.

"They killed two of my best men. They knew we were going to be there," Jeroen repeated, his voice trailing off into a whisper.

His face was pale, and his eyes looked heavy. It was obvious he hadn't had much sleep since the incident. Michael understood, because he knew that feeling better than most.

"Kreise was there," Jeroen continued. "He told me he was expecting somebody else, but I was high on his list, so he would arrest me instead."

He paused, staring at Michael. "I think he was waiting for you to show up, not me."

Kreise! The mere mention of his name sent Michael's body into involuntary spasms. His fists clenched, and he felt his face and neck reddening.

"Why would he think you'd be there?" Jeroen asked.

"I don't know," Michael answered truthfully. "Maybe he knows I'm here, and he thinks I'm working with the resistance. He isn't why I remain here, but if I get the chance, believe me, I'll happily kill him."

The room fell silent, and Michael could feel the tension rising.

"Someone betrayed us." Jeroen broke the silence. "And when I find who it is, they will regret crossing me."

Michael bowed his head. "I know how you feel, and if there is a mole in the resistance, you need to find and stop them before the entire network is taken down."

"Which is what I will do," Jeroen said, his jaw clenched tight. "Whoever it is."

"I'm worried that the radio is going to be compromised." Michael changed the subject. "It's been here too long already, and it's only a matter of time before Kreise finds it. Then you'll all be in serious trouble."

"I'm working on it," Jeroen answered. "It's time we turned it off until after the bombs stop falling on us. Then we'll move it every few days and keep Mina out of the way."

Jeroen shot Michael a dark glance. "Don't worry, Michael. As long as she isn't the traitor, we'll look after her."

Michael's head shot up. "Mina is not your traitor. She may be German, but she hates the Nazis just as much as you do. Perhaps more, because of what they've done to her family."

"Perhaps. I'm not ruling anybody out at this stage."

"It's not Mina, and nothing had better happen to her." Michael felt the anger rising in the pit of his stomach. "She risks everything for you every day, and her broadcasts are heard all over Europe. You know she isn't transmitting anything except what you tell her to."

Jeroen sighed and set his face in a grimace. "You are right, of course. Please excuse my suspicious nature. I can't help it after a lifetime of working in the shadows."

"Just make sure you look in the right direction and aren't sidetracked because she's German. Mina is as loyal to you as all your men are."

"Not all," Jeroen corrected him.

Michael shrugged before changing the subject. "I need your help, Jeroen. I'm sorry to put this on you after losing your men, but I'm out of provisions and I need enough food to last at least another week. Can you get it for me?"

Jeroen nodded his head. "I'll have what you need tomorrow evening. Meet me here."

He got to his feet. "Now, if you'll excuse me. Esther has to go to the hospital, and I'm escorting her there."

The two men shook hands, and Michael stared at the door long after they'd left. Not only was he worried that Kreise would find Mina, but now he was worried that Jeroen might do the dirty work for him.

She had to leave with him, whether she wanted to or not. Both she and Senta were in danger, and he couldn't walk away knowing they were going to die.

He was pulled from his thoughts by Mina bursting through the door. She ran to Michael, and for a long moment, they held each other, both lost in their own thoughts.

"Jeroen lost two men," Michael said finally, pulling away from her.

"I know. He told me. He said we're all under suspicion, even Senta. I'm worried, Michael. He thinks that because we're German, we must be the traitors. We're not, but I don't know how to prove it to him."

"No harm will come to you or Senta," Michael said, his heart hardened by his thoughts. "Not while I'm here."

"How can you protect us?"

"I know who the traitor is, and I'm going to kill him."

Mina's eyes widened. "You know who it is? How? Who is it?"

Michael shook his head. "It's part of why I'm here, Mina. I can't talk about it, but please believe me, I will rid the resistance of their traitor."

A steely determination fell over Michael, a familiar feeling he'd become accustomed to over the last year. His mission had just taken on even more importance than it had an hour earlier.

Before, it was business. Now it was personal.

Chapter 56

Albert Kreise followed the Dutch army truck as it turned off the main road in the Bergschenhoek district. Somewhere behind the dense woods lay the Lage Bergse Bos, a small park area with a lake and hiking trails for the citizens of Rotterdam to enjoy.

The narrow lane in the woods was just about wide enough for the truck to pass through, and Kreise followed its lead by killing his headlights the moment he turned onto it.

The truck pulled to a stop while the driver's eyes adjusted to the moonlight, which was a relief to Kreise because he was driving blind and feared he'd crash into a tree at any moment.

Slowly, his eyes adjusted, and he was glad of the clear night skies. The truck lurched forward, and Kreise followed, keeping a safe distance from the mud and dirt kicked up by the truck's tyres.

Several twists and turns later, the truck stopped, and seven heavily armed men jumped out of the back. They immediately dispersed through the thick woods towards the secluded lake house that was now serving as a safe haven for Jeroen's resistance.

Major Lohr waited by the truck for Kreise to join him. "Wait until I step outside. That will be your signal that it is clear to enter."

"Remember, I want them alive," Kreise replied.

"We'll do our best."

According to Zobart, Jeroen jealously guarded the location of his safe house, and only the active members of his resistance group knew of its existence. He felt safe there, away from prying eyes, and if it wasn't for Zobart giving them up, Kreise doubted they'd ever find him.

As an added bonus, because of its quiet, remote location, Kreise hoped Fernsby was there too. Capturing him, as well as the troublesome resistance leader, would make it a perfect night's work.

Major Lohr vanished into the woods, leaving Kreise to find his own way to the house. He walked a short way until he reached a clearing, where he turned sharp left and headed towards the lake, making sure to stay inside the tree line so he wouldn't be seen by whoever was on guard.

The night was clear, and Kreise could make out the outline of the house from his vantage point in the trees. He watched as a Brandenburger expertly took out the resistance man patrolling around the perimeter.

Then all hell broke loose. Shattering glass preceded loud explosions as Lohr's commandos hurled hand grenades through the windows. Shouts and screams, mixed with gunshots and loud bangs, came from within, and Kreise listened with ever-increasing respect for the Brandenburgers and their leader, Major Lohr.

Kreise closed in, waiting near the front entrance for Lohr's appearance which would signal the all-clear.

A man ran out of the door and jumped down the

porch steps. He sprinted towards Kreise, his head turned towards the house and the soldier in pursuit of him.

Kreise stepped out of the cover of the trees and shot the startled man in the midriff, dropping him instantly. The soldier, seeing what was happening, turned around and ran back to the house.

Kreise stepped over the wounded man and kicked his gun out of his hand, then reached down, grabbed him by the jaw, and turned his head, using his torch to flash a bright light into the man's face. Disappointed, he realised it was neither Fernsby or Jeroen, so he kicked the man hard in the groin, enjoying the cries of pain from the bleeding, wounded resistance fighter.

Kreise dragged him to the nearest tree, used a piece of the rope he'd brought, and secured him until the operation was finished. This man would answer a lot of questions before his wounds got the better of him.

By the time he'd finished, Lohr was standing on the deck of the porch and Kreise hurried towards him, eager to see Fernsby begging for mercy under his boot.

Lohr's Brandenburgers had eight men on their knees in the front room of the lake house. Kreise smiled to himself at the sight of doors blown off their hinges, and walls demolished by the grenades.

"They're all here," Lohr announced.

Kreise heard the truck pulling up outside as he walked up and down the line of captured men. Each looked towards the ground, and Kreise smacked them around the head to make them look up at him.

He studied each man intently, but neither Jeroen nor Fernsby were amongst them.

"Where's your leader?" he roared at the man on the far right of the group.

Silence.

Kreise kicked him hard in the face, knocking him backwards with a sickening thud as bone and sinew broke under the onslaught. Kreise wiped the blood from his boot on the man's jacket and grabbed him by the hair.

"I'll ask you again. Where is Jeroen?"

"He's not here," the man replied. "We don't know where he is."

"Lies!" Kreise screamed. "Tell me where he is, or your men die, here and now."

"I swear, I don't know where he is. He never tells us where he's going."

Kreise let go of the man's jaw and stood upright. He went to the man on the far left of the row and aimed his pistol at his head.

He looked at the anguished face of the man he'd just accosted. "Last chance. Where is Jeroen?"

"I swear, I don't know!" the resistance man shouted, pleading, but Kreise didn't care.

He pulled the trigger, and in an instant, the man fell back, blood splattering all over Kreise's hand and jacket.

He stepped to the next in line and looked at the man on the far side.

"How many more do I have to kill before you tell me where Jeroen is?"

"I don't know," the man whimpered, crying out loud. "Please believe me. I don't know where he is."

Kreise shot the second man in line. Like before, he collapsed backwards with blood pouring from the gaping wound in his head.

As he raised his gun to the head of the third man, he looked up at Kreise. "Please don't kill me. I have a wife and three children."

Kreise didn't care. He looked over at the sobbing man at the end of the row. "Where is Jeroen?"

"I don't know," he sobbed. "I'd tell you if I knew. Please stop this madness."

Kreise fired. And stepped to his right.

"He's at the hospital," the man kneeling next to the one at the end said.

"Tell me again," Kreise ordered. He was enjoying this.

"He's at the hospital," the man said louder. "He goes there most nights to see his lover, who is a nurse."

"Finally, someone has sense. What is her name?"

The man hesitated. "I don't know her name. All I know is that Jeroen goes there to see her, and sometimes stays at her apartment."

Kreise fired, and a fourth man fell.

"All right, stop!" the man yelled. "Stop killing us and I'll tell you everything I know."

"Take him," Kreise ordered Major Lohr.

Immediately, two Brandenburgers grabbed the man and dragged him to the waiting truck outside.

Kreise stepped past the remaining men to the one who refused to comply. He raised his weapon and fired, dropping him in a pool of blood along with the rest.

The two remaining men knelt with their heads bowed and Kreise hovered over the next one, his weapon aimed at his head.

"This is a very important question, and your answer will determine whether you live or die. Where is the English spy you're working with?"

"The Englishman?" the man seemed confused.

"You obviously know who I'm talking about." Kreise's eyes narrowed. "Where is he?"

"I don't know. I saw him once at the cafe where he met the girl. Other than that, I have never seen him."

"What girl?"

"The one who transmits the radio messages."

Kreise stepped back, stunned. Realisation hit him like a sledgehammer.

The German radio operator! It's the girl from the farm in Bavaria. She's been helping him all along.

Her name escaped him, but he'd check his files and find out who she was. Kreise's jaw set in stone as he turned to Lohr.

"Take this one too."

Lohr's men grabbed him and dragged him outside. Kreise turned to the last remaining man and shot him in the head without uttering a single word.

Although neither Fernsby nor Jeroen were there, he was more than happy with what he'd discovered. The two men in custody would reveal a lot more, and the result would be both Jeroen and Fernsby in his custody.

The resistance in Rotterdam would be crushed, and the female traitor would be returned to Germany to face trial for her crimes. Heydrich would be pleased, and he, Albert Kreise, would be honoured and promoted as a result.

Kreise marched out of the house and looked at the man tied to the tree. He'd already succumbed to his injuries, so Kreise left him where he was. He marched back to his vehicle and drove back to his headquarters to question his new best friends.

Chapter 57

The Dutch army truck stopped outside the Pilgrim Fathers Church on the strip of land between two canals not far from the north shore of the Nieuwe Mass river.

Normally at this time, the streets would be full of commuters making their way to work, but this morning, the streets were full of Wehrmacht soldiers setting up road-blocks and taking control of the city.

Major Lohr was glad Kreise chose to stay behind at his temporary headquarters on the south side of the river to question the men they'd arrested at the lake house.

This time, he was free to do it his way, and although Kreise ordered him to bring anyone left alive back to him, Lohr didn't intend for anyone to survive. He was tired of playing soldiers with the Dutch resistance, and wanted to get him and his men back to proper work, infiltrating ahead of the main military thrust to cause mayhem and confusion within the enemy ranks.

His men streamed out of the truck, weapons at the ready. They were still wearing the same Dutch army uniforms they'd worn the previous night, and although the men were fatigued and needed rest, Lohr knew they were as deadly and efficient as any soldier fresh from a good night's sleep.

In his opinion, the Brandenburgers were the best-trained unit of any army in the world, and his were the best of the Brandenburgers. He loved his men, and in return, they were as loyal to him as any man could be.

The strip of land narrowed as the men ran silently towards the cafe at the far end. The normally busy streets were deserted, and Lohr knew the remaining resistance fighters holed up inside the cafe would have the advantage if his men were seen approaching.

The one thing Lohr had was the element of surprise, and mirroring the Wehrmacht's blitzkrieg tactic of striking fast and hard, his men would attack without mercy and hopefully take them by surprise.

Lohr had done his homework the previous night. One of his men had visited the area and drawn a map of the layout for Lohr to study before the attack. All his men knew the exact location of the cafe.

They were ready.

As they'd done at the safe house, the Brandenburgers wasted no time in carrying out their operation. Led by their fanatical leader, they lobbed grenades through the windows on both floors of the cafe.

The dust hadn't settled when they charged through the shattered door, shooting anything that moved. With a primal scream, Major Lohr led his men into the killing zone, intent on wiping out the resistance in Rotterdam.

Most of the group had been killed or captured at the safe house, so Lohr wasn't expecting fierce resistance at the cafe. What he found was a small group of determined men and women taken by surprise at the sheer speed and violence of the Brandenburger attack.

Rapid gunfire and the smell of cordite filled the cramped cafe, shattering the wooden tables that moments earlier had been full of breakfast plates and coffee cups.

Pictures on the wall exploded, their fragments joining the rest of the debris as the cafe was systematically destroyed by the rampant Nazis.

Adrenalin coursed through Lohr's body as he watched men fall to the ground, their bodies shattered by the MP-40 submachine guns that had recently replaced their older MP-38s.

Lohr emptied his thirty-two-round magazine in seconds and dropped behind the shattered remains of a table to reload. Rising to his feet, he led the charge up the stairs.

He fired through the wooden doors of the bedrooms before kicking them open. In the second one, a woman in her early thirties huddled over a young girl in the corner. Lohr raised his weapon, but hesitated when she held out her arm as if it would stop the bullets.

"Please, sir. We only came here for some food. Please don't kill my daughter."

Lohr wavered before lowering his weapon and indicated for them to get out. The woman grabbed the girl by the hand and ran out of the door.

There was a line that even he wouldn't cross, and he realised that was the difference between his unit and the SS, who wouldn't think twice about murdering women and children if it suited their purpose.

Feeling morally superior, Lohr continued clearing out the upstairs rooms. The entire operation lasted less than ten minutes, and by the end of it, ten Dutch resistance fighters lay dead, scattered amongst the debris of the ruined cafe.

Lohr winced when he saw two women amongst the

dead, but he didn't say anything to his men. In the heat of battle, they would have fired at anything that remotely represented any danger, and if some of them were women, then it was justified, and he and his men would be able to sleep well at night knowing they were carrying out their duty as soldiers of the Reich.

With no prisoners, Lohr and his weary men retreated to their temporary headquarters on the opposite side of the river to await the next task set for them by the SS officer.

Chapter 58

Lotte van Houten ran from the carnage, clutching seven-year-old Sofie Meijer's hand as she dragged her behind. Her mother, Hanneke, was dead, shot to pieces in the massacre. Lotte hoped Sofie didn't see her mother as they ran past, and she tried her best to shield her from the gruesome sight.

Fear gripped Lotte's body as she ran. Her primary concern was getting away from the murdering Nazis rampaging through the cafe, killing everything that moved. She was under no illusions that she, too, would be dead if she hadn't grabbed Sofie from her hiding place in the wardrobe and tried to shield her with her own body.

Lotte had told Hanneke countless times to find somewhere safer to leave Sofie during their meetings, or better still, to stop coming at all. As she'd just discovered all too well, being associated with Jeroen was far too dangerous for a woman with a young child.

Now Sofie was motherless, and Lotte hoped her father would see sense and take her somewhere safe for the rest of the war.

He was at the safe house by the lake with Jeroen, and as that was over twenty miles away, Lotte had no way of getting there. The roads were full of German soldiers, and travel anywhere was fraught with danger. But even if they weren't, Lotte had never driven a vehicle in her life. She would have to find somewhere else to take refuge with Sofie.

Sofie was unusually quiet. Normally she was loud and playful, always laughing and lifting everyone's spirits in the cafe where Lotte had been living for the last few months.

But not now. She had seen and heard things no child should ever witness, and heaven help her if she'd seen her mother's bullet-ridden body on the way out.

Lotte ran past the Pilgrim Fathers Church, and as she was about to run inside, she noticed a Dutch army truck parked outside. It was guarded by two men dressed in the same uniforms as the murdering Nazis, and she realised they were from the same unit.

The two men watched as Lotte slowed down and calmly walked past, talking softly to what they must have assumed was her daughter. One of them even tried to smile at Lotte as she passed, and it took everything she had not to scream.

Instead, she smiled back, forcing the bile in her throat to stay down.

He's lucky I don't have a gun right now, or they'd both be dead.

Lotte's thoughts were brave, but inside she was fighting back the terror that urged her to run as fast as she could. Her hands trembled, and her legs felt like jelly as she tried acting like it was just another day in Rotterdam.

Another day of watching the roof of her world cave in.

With nowhere else to go, Lotte sat on a bench outside a tram stop near the church. All the emotion she'd been holding back since the attack, all the fear, relief, and anger, poured out of her as she rocked back and forth, sobbing uncontrollably, hardly able to breathe or see through the veil of tears that ran from her eyes.

Sofie laid her head on her shoulder, which made her feel even worse. Wasn't she supposed to be comforting Sofie? It certainly wasn't supposed to be the other way around, and feeling like a terrible human being, Lotte forced herself to calm down and act like the adult she was supposed to be.

A thought struck her, and she turned to Sofie, speaking to her softly while stroking her hair that still smelled of cordite.

"I think I know where Jeroen might be. Did your mother ever take you to Esther's apartment?"

Sofie looked up, and for the first time since the attack, she spoke. Although she couldn't make out what she said, for some reason, this comforted Lotte more than she could ever say, and the tears flowed freely once again.

Sofie reached up and wiped Lotte's eyes, which made her cry even harder. Then she handed Lotte the stuffed doll she'd been carrying, and that opened the floodgates to Lotte's soul.

She grabbed Sofie and held her to her, cuddling her as tightly as she'd ever held anyone in her entire life.

"I'm so sorry, Sofie. I'll take care of you, I promise."

"It's okay, Lotte. Mamma and Papa will take care of both of us."

With great relief, Lotte realised that Sofie hadn't seen her mother's corpse, and she held her tight to her chest. She tried pulling herself together again and relaxed her grip.

"Have you ever been to Esther's apartment?" she repeated.

Sofie shook her head. "No. Mamma never took me there."

"Well, Esther is a nurse, and she's really kind and funny. I'm sure she's got a big soft bed for you to sleep in. Do you want to go and see her?"

"Will Papa be there?" Sofie asked, her eyes wide and innocent.

It broke Lotte's heart, but she held herself together. "Maybe," she said. "We can wait for him there."

Sofie nodded and jumped off the bench.

Lotte noticed people were staring at her. There was a huge commotion coming from the direction of the cafe. Smoke billowed high in the air, and Lotte choked when she realised the soldiers had set it on fire before they left.

Police and firemen were rushing to the scene, and German soldiers herded people away from it. Several stared at her and Sofie, as if realising they were part of the carnage.

Lotte rose to her feet and grabbed Sofie's hand. She'd had a meltdown, but now was the time to step up and take control of the situation before she found herself arrested and probably blamed for killing everyone and starting the fire.

Hand in hand, Lotte and Sofie hurried away from the scene and walked the three kilometres to Overschie and the nurse's apartment. More than anything else, she hoped Jeroen was there because he would know what to do.

Jeroen always knew what to do.

Chapter 59

Heavy banging on the apartment door stirred Jeroen from the deep sleep he'd just fallen into after a busy night at the hospital helping Esther, who was sitting up in bed beside him, rubbing the sleep from her eyes.

The knocking became even louder and more urgent as Jeroen threw on his clothes and stumbled to the door. He grabbed his pistol in case it was the Germans, and unlocked the door as the pounding got louder still.

"Jeroen." Casper Groen, one of the original members of the group, pushed past him. He'd been at the hospital where he worked as a night porter.

"Casper, I saw you just a couple of hours ago. What's wrong? You look terrible." Jeroen forced the fatigue from his mind.

Casper looked as white as a ghost, and from the look of anguish on his face, Jeroen knew something was wrong. Esther joined them and placed her hand on Jeroen's shoulder as they sat on the couch.

"The lake house." Casper choked on his words, unable

to speak. He threw his hands in the air in a gesture to Jeroen that something awful had happened. "It's terrible."

"What happened?" Jeroen asked. His back straightened, and his mind sharpened as he tried calming Casper down long enough for him to get his story out.

"They're all dead."

"All of them?" Jeroen looked at Esther, his eyes wide in disbelief.

"All of them." Casper bent forward and clasped his knees. "All lined up with their hands tied behind their back. They were executed, Jeroen, all of them."

Jeroen leapt to his feet. "Tell me everything you saw."

"I went to the lake house after work, and when I got there, Ferre was tied to a tree outside. He was dead, so I went inside, and that's where I found them. There was blood everywhere. All of them were executed."

Casper burst into tears, and he clasped his hands to his knees even tighter. Jeroen placed his hands on his shoulders.

"I know this is hard, Casper, but I need you to think. How many of our men were there? You said all of them, but are you sure? How many?"

"Six. I counted six of them. Plus Ferre outside."

Jeroen collapsed in the chair, wringing his hands together as the terrible news sank in. "Seven of them? How?" he asked of nobody in particular.

Casper shook his head. "Someone must have told them, because otherwise, how would they have known they were there?"

"It must have been Kreise." Jeroen's fist crashed into the cushion of the couch next to him. "But how did he know? Who told him?"

"Who else besides us here knew about the lake house?" Esther asked.

"Everyone there, obviously. Us here, and the rest of them at the cafe. That's all."

Jeroen's head snapped up. "The German girls know about it. That's the second time we've been ambushed in as many days. Kreise is one step ahead of us, and there's no way he could do that if someone wasn't telling him."

Before anyone could say anything, another loud knock rattled the apartment door.

Esther gestured for Jeroen to remain seated. With the chain firmly attached and Jeroen's weapon at the ready, she cracked the door open.

A second later, she removed the chain and stood aside as a distraught Lotte van Houten stepped inside holding the hand of an equally forlorn Sofie Meijer.

Chapter 60

Michael decided to stop at Mina's apartment before heading to the safe house to sleep. He'd been cycling around the city most of the night, dodging German patrols to check out three homes he knew Zobart possessed in Rotterdam.

All three were in total darkness, and he'd broken into all of them. Although luxuriously furnished well beyond the means of a normal minister's salary level, the houses were empty. Wherever Zobart was, he wasn't at any of his own properties.

Michael was beginning to think he wasn't in Rotterdam at all. Perhaps he was in The Hague, because after all, that was the seat of the government.

He'd already decided to stay in Rotterdam a few more days until he'd exhausted every possible avenue in his search for Zobart, but he was increasingly becoming more and more convinced that he was somewhere else.

Nobody answered the door at Mina's apartment, so he went down the hallway to try Esther's. He knocked gently and stood back, hoping Mina was there.

The door cracked open, and Michael saw Esther's face as she peered through the tiny gap. Recognising Michael, she closed the door, removed the chain, and opened it wide enough for him to enter.

As soon as he did, he could tell something was amiss. For one, the atmosphere was so tense he could cut through it with a knife.

For another, the apartment was full. Some he knew, others he didn't, and all their faces were tear-stained and full of sadness.

Jeroen sat on the couch next to a woman who looked to be in her thirties. A young girl around seven or eight sat between them, clutching a stuffed doll while the woman stroked the girl's matted hair.

Another man sat on the floor under the window, clutching his knees to his chest, looking broken and defeated. Even the ever-positive Esther looked as if she'd been crying.

Senta sat in an armchair staring at Jeroen with a mixture of sadness and anger on her face, and Mina, who normally ran to Michael when she saw him, just stood in the doorway to the bedroom staring at him as though her world was ending.

Michael focused his attention on Jeroen, as he was the leader of this group of resistance men and women. He looked in equal parts sad and angry, mirroring Senta's features.

"What's happened?" he asked.

Nobody spoke. Michael assumed they were showing deference to Jeroen, who looked up at Michael with pain in his eyes.

Out of respect, Michael softened his stare and cocked his head to the side. He remained silent, waiting for Jeroen to tell him what had happened.

Finally, after a long, awkward silence, Jeroen closed his eyes and sighed. "It's over. The war has only just begun, and we're defeated."

"Why?" Michael asked. "What happened?"

"Kreise. That's what happened. Somehow, he knows exactly where we are and what we're doing. He's several steps ahead of us, and we're broken."

"What did he do?" Michael pressed. The very mention of SS Sturmbannführer Albert Kreise's name made the hairs on the back of his neck and arms rise.

His hatred for Kreise went far beyond the meaning of the word. Before his war was over, above anything else he did, Albert Kreise had to die. And he wanted to be the one who killed him.

Jeroen tried to speak, but he choked up and stopped, lowering his head to stare at the floor. Michael closed his eyes. Whatever Kreise had done, it had to have been terrible for Jeroen to act like this.

"What did he do?" he asked again, gently prompting the gathered resistance group for answers.

"He attacked the safe house where the men were hiding." Esther spoke for Jeroen. "He lined them up and executed them all."

Mina shuffled across the room and stood next to Michael. She grasped his hand and pressed her mouth to his ear. "The little girl's father was one of them. He was tied up outside and shot."

Michael crunched his face, screwed his eyes together, and took a deep breath and exhaled. War was horrible, and the personal stories it created broke his heart. Especially when it involved innocent children.

Jeroen whispered something to the woman sat next to him. She prodded the little girl in the ribs. "Your hair is filthy, Sofie. Let's give you a bath and get you cleaned up."

The young girl said nothing. She just nodded. Her little face looked completely devastated, and Michael felt a well of sympathy tinged with sadness and anger rising in his chest.

He shook his head as he watched the woman lead her to the bathroom, all the while clutching the rag doll she was carrying.

"It gets worse." Jeroen looked up. "He kept two of them alive, and he's no doubt interrogating them right now. The SS are depraved individuals. That man will do anything to destroy us."

Silence fell until the woman and the girl left the room.

"After he attacked the lake house, he sent his men to the cafe. They threw grenades into a cafe full of women and children." Jeroen broke off, choking on his words.

He paused for a moment to regroup. "They stormed in and shot everyone. Lotte was allowed to leave because she was sheltering a child, but nobody else was shown any mercy."

Jeroen looked at the floor, his eyes full.

Michael gritted his teeth, choking back the emotion. "I'm so sorry. Kreise is a monster." That was all he could think of to say.

"What about him?" Michael indicated with his head at the man sat on the floor clutching his knees. "Was he there, too?"

"No." Jeroen shook his head. "Casper worked at the hospital last night and found the carnage at the lake house this morning. He came here to tell me."

Casper didn't look up.

"The worst of it is that Lotte isn't Sofie's mother." Jeroen said. "That's Hanneke, and she was killed in the cafe."

"Both her parents were killed?" Michael asked, stunned.

Jeroen nodded.

"Does she know?"

"Not yet. We didn't have the heart to tell her."

"My God!" Michael clutched Mina's hand tightly. "How do you tell a child that her parents are both dead?"

"I don't know," Jeroen admitted. "Sofie doesn't have any other family as far as I know, so Lotte is going to leave the resistance and raise her far from us, where it's safer."

Michael nodded. "That's the least you can do for her."

"Sofie won't be the only child to get orphaned in this war." Jeroen's tone hardened. "When the Nazis have taken everything from us, life has no meaning anymore. All we can do is lay down our lives in the fight for justice and revenge."

"And freedom," Esther added.

"Yes, and freedom." Jeroen agreed.

"Someone betrayed us." Jeroen stared straight ahead, his face contorted with pain and anguish. "There's no other way Kreise could have known about either the lake house or the cafe. Not to mention the ambush when I went to get the quartz crystals from the building in Waalhaven."

"And he keeps blaming us for it." Senta, who had remained silent up to this point, shouted, "Because we're German, he thinks me and Mina did it. We hate the Nazis for what they did to Mamma and Papa!"

Her face flushed, and Michael could see she was angry and hurt by Jeroen's accusations.

"Why does he think we left Germany in the first place?" Senta continued. "Because we wanted to help the SS kill innocent Dutch women and children?" she shouted again.

"Keep your voice down, Senta," Mina said. "They'll hear us outside."

"I don't care," Senta shouted. "He wants to blame us because he doesn't want to believe it could be one of his precious Dutch men or women betraying him. We're the easy target."

"I'm not blaming you," Jeroen snapped. "I said it's a possibility. Believe me, if I truly thought you'd betrayed me, you would be dead by now."

Jeroen glowered at Senta, but she didn't back down, staring back at him, defiant and proud.

"Mina and I are doing everything we can to help you. We're as upset as you are at what happened. I just wish you'd believe that."

Jeroen opened his mouth to respond, but Michael waved his hand and cut him off.

"This isn't getting us anywhere. All it will do is get us killed if you keep shouting at each other like that. Listen to me, Jeroen, because what I have to say is important."

All heads turned to Michael.

"Kreise knew where your safe house was. He knew about the cafe, and he was waiting for you in Waalhaven. Now he has two of your men, so it's only going to be a matter of time before he finds out about this apartment."

He paused for breath. "The radio transmitter is here, and it won't take him long to work out that Mina is the German girl who helped me escape from Bavaria when I was injured. He'll be here before the day is out, and if anyone is still here, you'll be arrested and probably killed."

Everyone fell silent as they processed what Michael was saying. Jeroen looked up, nodding his head. "He's right. We have to clear this place and get out of here."

"What about Anna and her father?" Mina asked.

"They'll be arrested for harbouring us. Not to mention the fact that they are Jews."

"They need to be moved as well," Jeroen said. "Leave it with me, and I'll have a new place for us before the afternoon is through."

"There's no need for that," Michael said. "I have a safe house that is owned by British intelligence. You will be safe there, at least until you can find somewhere more suitable."

"Where is it?" Jeroen asked.

"Close to here. I'll take you there now, but the radio needs to be moved somewhere else. I can't allow Kreise to track it and find us."

"Fair enough. I'll find a new location for the radio transmitter," Jeroen said. "In the meantime, get everyone to Michael's safe house and away from here."

"There's one more thing." Michael locked eyes with Jeroen.

"What?"

"Who owns the lake house you were using as a safe house?"

"Our leader, why? Are you suggesting the Minister of Defence and Maritime Affairs betrayed us?"

"Wilhelm Zobart is the reason I am still here in Rotterdam. He is working with Kreise, and he has betrayed not only you but both Britain and Holland. And before you ask, I have proof of what I say."

Jeroen's face was a picture of disbelief and shock.

"What proof? How do you know this? Why didn't you tell me earlier? I could have stopped the attacks and saved my men and women. Their blood is on your hands, Fernsby!"

Jeroen rose to confront Michael, but both Esther and Casper stopped him. Casper jumped to his feet and stood in front of Jeroen as Esther grabbed him from behind.

"It isn't the Englishman's fault, Jeroen. I told you of my suspicions, as did several others. You wouldn't listen to us. I'm not blaming you for what happened, and you're not blaming him. Zobart is the traitor, and we have to deal with him. We're not blaming Fernsby for confirming what we already knew and tried telling you."

Casper pushed Jeroen back into his seat and stood in front of him. Michael remained where he was, hoping Jeroen would see sense, but quite prepared to defend himself if he had to. Jeroen was done blaming Mina and Senta, and he would not stand around while he convicted them without proof.

He didn't dare to think what the consequences would be, but he wasn't standing idly by and allowing that to happen. Jeroen was a good man who loved his country dearly, but he needed to see who his true enemies were, and not create them in his own ranks.

"Jeroen, I'm telling you that Zobart is our enemy," Casper said. "You need to believe me before anyone else gets killed."

"Who?" Jeroen asked. "There's nobody left to kill."

"There are a lot of you left." Michael jumped into the conversation. "As bad as this is, you need to snap out of it, Jeroen, and lead the people you have left. You have a roomful of loyal men and women right here who will follow you to the very end, but you have to step up and lead them."

Jeroen stared at the floor and said nothing. Michael could almost see the cogs of his brain whirling around, trying to process what had happened.

"How many others are there?" Michael asked. "Were all of your men and women in the lake house and the cafe?"

"No." Jeroen looked up. "Beside us here, there's one

more, Kees, who was doing something else last night. Unless Kreise got to him, he should be alive."

"What about the man on the bridge I ran the detonator cord for? Have you heard from him?" Michael asked.

Jeroen shook his head. "The Germans have control of the bridge and Lars didn't blow it. I can only assume the worst and that he is dead."

"So, you have a smaller group. Recruit more, and fight back," Michael said. "This is going to be a long war, and your country is going to be under German occupation for a long time. You'll have many opportunities to hit them where it hurts, so use this moment, and remember it when times get hard. We will prevail, Jeroen, and when we do, that will be the time to honour those who lost their lives in the struggle. Not now. Now is the time to fight back for all we are worth."

"A noble speech, Englishman," Jeroen said. "You are right, of course. If it is Zobart then show me your proof and I will believe you. And tell me, what are you going to do to him when you find him?"

Michael stared at Jeroen. "That's between me and Zobart. Right now, everyone needs to get out of here. And move that radio transmitter somewhere else."

"I have to go to the hospital," Esther said. "Tell me where your safe house is, and I'll meet you there later."

Michael told them the address.

Jeroen leapt to his feet, the colour returning to his face. "Mina, dismantle the radio and have it ready to move in the next thirty minutes. Senta, I have a list of provisions for you to collect, and when you do, observe the enemy and see if you can spot any SS activity."

"I will, but I'll wait for Lotte and Sofie, and I'll take them to Michael's safe house before getting the supplies," Senta said.

Michael was glad to see Jeroen recovering from the shock and taking control of the situation.

"Casper, you and I are going to find what's left of our group, and we'll meet at Michael's safe house later. Then we regroup and decide what our next step will be."

Michael pulled Mina aside and gave her a long kiss before pulling away. "Be careful out there, and whatever you do, don't be seen with the radio."

"I know, Michael. I love you, and I'll see you later."

"I love you too." They kissed, and then Michael was gone.

As much as he sympathised with Jeroen and his group, he was here for one reason only, and he couldn't allow himself to be drawn into helping the Dutch resistance wage war on the Nazis.

Chapter 61

Michael spent the next hour cleaning the safe house so his new guests would be as comfortable as possible. He'd forgotten to mention that he didn't have any furniture, but he was sure Jeroen could find what they needed.

He cleared the kitchen table of his scribbled notes about Zobart and secured them in one of the secret compartments in his rucksack, and he burned anything he no longer needed, such as the list of Zobart's properties that he'd already searched.

With the shortwave radio safely hidden underneath the floorboards, Michael stretched out on the couch and closed his eyes. He'd been awake all night, and it was going to be a long day.

Jeroen and his group moving in didn't change anything regarding his mission. He was still focused on finding Zobart, and now he'd told Jeroen about it, he was hoping he'd stop blaming Mina and Senta and instead help him find the man so he could eliminate him and get out of Rotterdam.

As much as he wanted to stay with Mina and protect

her, he knew the longer he remained in the city, the more likely it was that Kreise would find him. And he knew what awaited if that happened.

With the blackout curtains firmly closed, Michael's eyelids closed and he slipped into a restless sleep. He drifted in and out of sleep, and in that moment, between light and dark, the faces of the dead came to life before him.

Visions, or were they dreams? In his semi-conscious state, he couldn't determine either way; the brave German woman he'd known by her codename of Mother appeared holding the rucksack he now possessed in front of her.

The image switched to the railway station in Ravensburg, Germany, where she gave her life so he could live. In his mind, he was kneeling on the ground, cradling her dying body in his arms as Albert Kreise stood over them, sneering and telling Michael that he was responsible for her death.

The image faded, to be replaced by Martin Heinze, the former Abwehr officer he'd met in Hamburg lying in a barn on the outskirts of Berlin. Except, in his dreams, Mother was next to him, holding his hand and telling him to let go of the grenade and join her in death.

Michael tossed and turned, sweat forming on his forehead. He opened his eyes, and before him stood the familiar hazy figure of his dead brother, David.

Michael sat up, sleep no longer an option. "I was waiting for you to appear."

David's pale face was serious, unlike his normal appearance when he was either complaining about being dead, or forcing Michael to man up, encouraging him to do what he didn't think he was capable of doing.

This time, he didn't say a word. He just stood there, shaking his head as if to tell him something was wrong. An eerie feeling came over him, and as he rubbed his eyes and sat up, David abruptly disappeared, leaving him alone with his thoughts.

Michael hated moments like this, because they forced him to appraise his guilt for the growing number of people who had died, either by his hand, or for him so he could survive.

He knew he would have to live with the guilt for the rest of his life, and he knew the dreams were his subconscious mind reminding him, indeed forcing him, to never forget what he'd done.

He rose to his feet and padded to the sink to grab a glass of water. As he poured, the drone of approaching aircraft filled his ears and senses, and the house shook from the vibrations of what seemed like hundreds of warplanes directly overhead.

He ran to the window and pulled back the blackout curtains, flooding the room with light. He squinted as his eyes adjusted, and looked up at the sky, watching in awe as it darkened with the sheer number of warplanes threatening everyone's safety.

The Dutch army was fighting hard in the city, and although they were fighting a losing battle, they hadn't given up. As a result, the Wehrmacht didn't have full control, and from what Michael heard on the radio, the same was happening in Amsterdam and other cities across Holland.

He assumed this was the German response.

Before he could move, the earth shook as thunder struck from the skies. Wave after wave of bombers dropped their loads on the helpless city below, and Michael felt the ground shake as they exploded in the centre of the medieval city.

He shuddered at the thought of innocent women and

children dying by the hundreds, but there was nothing he could do about it.

More bombers flew directly overhead, and Michael could hear the whistling from the bombs as they dropped towards the earth. He didn't move; there was nowhere to go, nowhere to escape the death raining down from above.

Heavy explosions just a few streets away blew him off his feet, and the windows shattered, showering him with shards of sharp glass that cut into his skin like a hot knife through butter.

Luckily, none of the cuts were deep, and he shook the glass off his body as he staggered to his feet.

Smoke and fire billowed high in the air as far as he could see, and the smell of burning rubber filled his nostrils. More explosions blasted the lunchtime air as vehicles blew up in front of demolished buildings, leaving Michael in no doubt as to the catastrophe being unleashed on the city of Rotterdam.

If this was the German High Command showing what would happen if they didn't surrender, then they were demonstrating their power in the most brutally effective way possible.

Another massive explosion close by almost shattered his eardrums as the blast threw him off his feet once more. This was really close, and for the first time, his mind turned to Mina and the rest of the resistance crew, who should have been at his safe house by now.

For fifteen minutes, terror rained down from the skies. The Luftwaffe dropped what must have been a hundred tonnes of bombs on the beleaguered city centre, bringing Rotterdam and its citizens to their knees.

The safe house rattled and shook, and although he took shelter underneath the overturned couch, he knew it was a futile gesture. If he took a direct hit, his life was over in the blink of an eye, and there wasn't a damned thing he could do about it.

It ended as suddenly as it had begun. The waves of Luftwaffe bombers turned around in the air and flew back to their bases, their crews no doubt congratulating themselves on a job well done.

Explosions continued long after the bombers were gone. Burst water pipes spurted water in the air, flooding basements and streets, and hampering rescue efforts that were like catching a tidal wave with a fishing net, such was the scale of the devastation.

Michael ran from the house, desperate to see Mina's apartment block unscathed. The apartment block to the right of hers looked intact, and his hopes began to rise that the area had been spared.

Turning the corner onto Lemkensstraat, he stopped in his tracks. Men, women and children stumbled around, covered in blood and dust, shouting helplessly for their loved ones.

Half of the apartment block closest to Mina's was gone, destroyed by a German bomb. These must have been the bombs that shattered his windows.

Concrete and debris were scattered everywhere, and Michael was forced to step around it. People begged for his help, but he ignored them as he fought his way to Mina's apartment block.

Clouds of dust and dirt made it hard to see, and he felt helpless as he pushed past the throngs of survivors searching through the rubble for missing family. It broke his heart, and he felt lousy, but he shut his mind off to their cries.

Mina! She's all that matters to me now.

Chapter 62

Shock and distress lined people's faces as Michael pushed past them. Mina's block came into view, and Michael fell to his knees when he saw what had happened to it.

The whole centre of the apartment block was missing. This must have been a direct hit, and the middle of the apartment block was now a gigantic crater where thirty minutes ago families lived and played.

Mina's apartment was right in the middle of the crater, and anyone who had been anywhere near her apartment would have had no chance of survival.

On his knees, Michael stared at the carnage. His brain couldn't take in what he was seeing, and he fought an internal battle for his sanity. Mina couldn't be gone. She was his world. His rock. His reason for living.

He couldn't go on without her.

With his heart on the verge of exploding, he spotted a hint of blonde hair in the distance. Either that or his mind was playing tricks on him.

He ran towards it, tripping over dead bodies and

debris, but never taking his eyes off the girl with blonde hair who had her back to him.

The girl was on her knees, holding something in her arms. From the rear, Michael couldn't see who it was, but as he got to her, he shuddered to a halt and threw himself to the ground.

"Mina! Thank God you're not hurt!" Michael screamed out and grabbed her shoulders.

Her face turned, and to Michael's horror, he saw it wasn't Mina. It was Senta, and her face was streaked with dirt and tears. Michael looked at who she was cradling, and time stood still when he saw who it was.

"Oh, no." He closed his eyes, but was unable to hold back the tears that blurred his vision.

In her arms lay Sofie, the little girl he'd seen in Esther's apartment. She was streaked with dirt and blood, and her eyes were closed, never to open again.

Michael stroked her hair, as if that would bring her back. Then he saw the stuffed doll still clutched in her right hand, and that sent him over the edge.

He leant back and roared to the heavens. "No!" he screamed at the top of his lungs.

Senta never moved. Nor did she look away from Sofie, lying in her arms. Michael knelt next to her, unmoving, for at least fifteen minutes, his brain shut down, unable to take in the horror of what he was witnessing.

Finally, he reached over and tugged at Senta's arm. "Mina?" he asked, not wanting to hear the answer.

Senta shook her head. "I don't know. She left right before the bombs fell to take the radio somewhere."

"Do you think she survived?" Michael asked, realising it was a stupid question even before he spoke.

"I don't know. I don't know how any of us could have survived it."

"Where's Lotte and the others?" Michael asked.

Senta pointed to a large clump of concrete roughly twenty feet away. Michael rose to his feet and saw Lotte's torso sticking out from underneath the concrete, which must have weighed a tonne or more.

Delirious, he shouted at Senta. "What about Anna and her father?"

Senta shook her head and pointed at the concrete slab. Michael walked around the other side and saw Anna's dead body underneath her father's, who even in death tried to shield and protect her.

This was too much, and Michael collapsed to the ground. Hopelessness gripped him like a vice, and he felt lost, defeated, and completely alone and defenceless.

The Germans had won.

After what seemed an age, he came to his senses. He rose to his feet and went back to Senta, who was still holding Sofie in her arms.

"What about Jeroen, Esther, and Casper?"

"Esther went to the hospital, and the other two went to find their friends. Other than that, I don't know."

More people had arrived from the local area. Michael mourned for them because the devastation in the city centre meant that anyone on the outskirts like Overschie would have to wait.

He turned to Senta. "Are you hurt?"

Senta shook her head. "No. I was waiting outside for Lotte and Sofie when the bombs came."

"We can help by placing the victims on the grass for the authorities to collect when they have the time to get here. Come on, Senta, help me, please."

Like himself, Senta was in shock. He was trying to bring her back around, and the only way he knew how was for her to get busy and fill her mind with something useful.

He helped her to her feet and pried Sofie from her arms, then carried the little girl to the grass bank in front of the river and gently placed her down.

His vision blurred when he tucked the stuffed doll in her arms. Kneeling beside her, he clasped his hands together and Senta joined him and bowed her head as he said a prayer over her.

"My Lord, I lay Sofie before You, this innocent child whose life was taken so tragically. Her light was a beacon of hope and joy, and in her short time, she brought love and laughter to all who knew her. I ask You to embrace her soul with Your eternal peace and grant her the comfort she deserves in Your heavenly kingdom."

"Forgive us, Lord, for the world in which we exist has failed to protect her. Forgive me for the moments I was not there to keep her safe. May her spirit find the serenity that eluded her in her short life, and may we carry her memory as a guiding light in our continued struggle for justice and peace. Amen."

"Amen." Senta echoed Michael's last word.

They rose to their feet, and with one final, forlorn look at Sofie, they joined the countless others who had survived the bombs, and got busy finding the victims, laying them out on the riverbank.

It was dusk by the time Michael got Senta back to his safe house. His mind screamed at him, hoping to find Mina waiting for him, but she wasn't there.

Jeroen and Casper were there, along with one other man. This, Michael assumed, was all that was left of the resistance group after Kreise's murderous attacks.

Michael raised his eyebrows at Jeroen and pointed at the man sitting next to Casper.

"That's Kees. He's the one I told you about before."

Senta hugged Jeroen before going upstairs to wash the dirt and blood from her body. Michael turned to the three men, who sat on the couch in complete silence.

"Lotte and Sofie are dead, and Mina is missing. I'm going back out to find her. Where did she take the radio, Jeroen?"

"The hospital took a direct hit." Jeroen ignored Michael's question. "Esther is dead."

Michael's head dropped. He couldn't take much more of this. Anger replaced much of his sorrow, and he felt a surge of hatred, the likes of which he'd never felt before, coursing through his veins.

"Where did Mina take the radio transmitter?" he asked again, this time more firmly.

"There's a vehicle repair garage a few kilometres from here. We helped her carry it there, and we left her setting it up."

"Tell me where it is," Michael demanded.

Jeroen told him. "I'm coming with you. The Nazis are not getting away with this."

Parched, Michael gulped down several glasses of water. Then he made Senta, who sat on the stairs in complete, dumbfounded shock, drink as well.

While she drank, Michael took the radio from under the floorboards and tuned it to a radio station transmitting in Dutch. The men listened in silence, and when the voice stopped, Michael turned it off.

"Well? Did they bomb other cities? What are they saying about it?"

"Only Rotterdam," Jeroen said. "The Nazis gave us an ultimatum, telling us that if we don't surrender, this is what will happen to the rest of our cities."

"What did the Dutch government say?" Michael asked, frustrated that he couldn't speak the language.

"The government escaped to your country along with the queen," Jeroen said. "So far, they have said nothing."

Michael turned the radio back on, leaving it tuned to

the Dutch station. "Keep listening for news," he ordered Jeroen's men. "The government will have to respond to this, and we need to know what they say."

The Nazis may have defeated the western nation, but they hadn't taken the fighting spirit out of them. The reckless bombing they had just carried out would only fuel the resistance to fight back, and Michael was right there with them, shoulder to shoulder.

He would remain there until Zobart was dead, and he would carry these memories into the future as a reminder of what he was facing.

The Germans may have won the battle, but they had not won the war.

Michael grabbed his trusty Walther PPK along with several spare magazines and headed for the door. Jeroen paused, turning to his men.

"Stay here and listen to the radio. Don't go anywhere. That's an order."

"Yes, sir."

Senta jumped down the stairs. "Mina is my sister and I'm going with you."

"You're staying here," Jeroen ordered.

"You'll have to shoot me to stop me." Senta meant it.

Jeroen shook his head. "Stay with us and don't do anything stupid. We'll strike back, but we have to do it on our terms and not through anger. Do you hear me?"

"I hear you. I'm finding my sister."

Senta and Jeroen headed out after Michael.

Chapter 63

It took the bedraggled group almost two hours to walk the four kilometres to the repair garage where Mina had set up the radio transmitter.

The garage was to the northeast of the city centre, and from the damage and debris, it was obvious that the Luftwaffe had concentrated their bombers on the heart of Rotterdam.

Just like at Mina's apartment block, the bombing wasn't very accurate, and several stray bombs had destroyed buildings and lives along their route.

Fires raged from the direction of the city centre, and the stench of the burning city was everywhere. Many citizens helped with the fires, others searched the debris for missing loved ones, and more still just wandered around, lost and aimless after losing everything in the Rotterdam Blitz, as it was being called.

Surprisingly, the Wehrmacht were assisting the Dutch emergency services with the fires, and Michael saw at least two units moving debris and sifting through the wreckage, searching for survivors.

Michael watched in dismay as the orchestrators of the carnage helped the locals clear it up. The tension between them was palpable, and it was a strange dynamic to see the perpetrators now working with the very people they'd ruthlessly attacked to clear up the carnage they'd created.

Michael loathed them, but he also realised that the average Wehrmacht soldier wasn't much older than he was, and they'd likely been given no choice in the matter.

Still, he had little sympathy for them. None, after he thought of little Sofie clutching her rag doll.

His stomach clenched, and he found himself covered in sweat as Jeroen led them to a nondescript road called Noordmolenstraat. Michael memorised the route from his safe house in case he had to come here again on his own, but all the way there, he fought his emotions, and the urge to sprint away to find her was foremost in his mind.

Images of Mina lying crushed underneath a collapsed building haunted his mind, and his internal battle raged as they turned the corner onto Noordmolenstraat.

His turmoil consumed him, and he didn't even see the Wehrmacht soldiers blocking their path. A dozen or more heavily armed soldiers stood in their way, and Michael would have walked right into them if Jeroen hadn't stopped him.

"Papers!" one of the soldiers barked in German.

Jeroen acted as if he was frightened. His hands shook as he fumbled inside his jacket pockets for his papers. Senta stared straight ahead, refusing to look at the men she held responsible for all the evil in her world.

Michael didn't blame her. The panic raging inside him over the fate of his beloved Mina consumed his every thought and action, and he impatiently produced the false papers London had provided in what seemed a lifetime ago.

"Name?" a soldier barked at him as he snatched the identification papers from his hand.

"Julien Mercer."

"Why are you here? Are you missing someone from the bombing raid?" The soldier spoke in German, a great relief to Michael.

"My wife. We can't find her," he replied in German, grateful the soldier couldn't speak Dutch.

It felt remarkably satisfying to refer to Mina as his wife, and amid all the chaos and heartache, he found a crumb of comfort in the brief thought of one day marrying her and making it a reality.

If she's alive!

Reality struck, and the familiar feeling of panic hit him in the solar plexus. He hopped around in front of the soldier, impatient to move past him and find Mina and the repair garage.

"You can't go down this road. Look for her somewhere else." The soldier offered no explanation as to why they couldn't use Noordmolenstraat, but now wasn't the time to argue.

"Good luck." The soldier shoved the papers into Michael's midriff.

Jeroen and Michael exchanged glances as they waited for the soldier to return Senta's papers that Jeroen's men had forged. For some reason, the soldier looked Senta up and down several times, and Michael began to suspect something was wrong.

He gripped the Walther PPK in his coat pocket, more than ready to use it against the enemy if he had to. After what they had done to the people of Rotterdam and the resistance group, he relished the idea of hurting them back, no matter how minuscule it would be in the bigger picture.

Finally, the soldier handed Senta her papers back. Taking Michael completely by surprise, shockingly, he smiled at her. "You speak good German. And you're a very pretty girl."

"Danke." Senta looked as surprised as Michael, but she remained calm and composed.

Michael forced the rising bile back down his throat and remained silent as the soldier flirted with Senta, who handled it well.

"I hope you find your missing loved one," the young soldier said. "But you can't go down this street. It's out of bounds."

Senta was about to say something, but she changed her mind at the last moment. Instead, she forced a smile and said nothing.

Michael breathed a sigh of relief as they walked away from the soldiers.

"That was too close," Jeroen muttered as they put distance between them.

They walked back the way they had come until they reached the next street that ran parallel to Noordmolenstraat. They turned right, and as soon as they were out of sight of the soldiers, Jeroen pulled them into the shadows of the buildings.

"I don't know why that street is blocked, but it probably explains why Mina can't get out. The garage is down there."

"We'll get to her from the back," Michael said.

The others agreed, and Jeroen led the way, stopping halfway down to make sure they weren't watched.

Michael was relieved when he saw the buildings on this street appeared to be unscathed.

Jeroen calmed his grated nerves when he pointed towards a gap between two buildings.

"It's down there," he whispered.

Michael's stomach churned as Jeroen led the way into the darkness. At the other end of the buildings, they emerged into a courtyard of some description, and Jeroen, who had obviously been there before, led them across the courtyard to a small building with a flat roof.

"There." He pointed at the smallest building on the block.

"There's a door on the side that's difficult to see from the road," Jeroen whispered. "Watch out for any soldiers."

Michael had been watching, and nobody had seen them enter the courtyard.

Jeroen grabbed a set of keys from his pocket and led the way to a door on the side of the garage. All the windows were covered from the inside with newspapers, making it impossible to see in or out.

The lock turned with a squeak, which made Michael cringe, and Jeroen pulled the door outwards.

He went first, followed by Senta and then Michael. It was pitch black inside, and Michael couldn't see anything. Jeroen closed the door behind them, sealing them inside the darkness.

Lighting his torch, Jeroen flashed it at a dark-coloured motor vehicle in the middle of the garage floor. Crouching behind it, he flashed his torch on and off three times.

They waited in the silence for a response from Mina.

If she was there.

Clearly, this was a rehearsed set of actions, and Michael's innards churned like a raging storm. His mind refused to calm down, and he was moments away from a full-blown panic attack.

Senta shook and trembled by his side, and he could tell that she, too, was moments away from erupting.

A series of three flashes came back at them from the

other side of the garage, and Jeroen answered it with two more flashes.

Two more from the other side, and Jeroen stood up. "Mina, where are you?"

Mina emerged from the far side of the garage, and when she saw Senta and Michael, she burst into tears and hugged them both as she reached them.

"I'm so glad you're alive," she said between sobs. "The bombs. They were terrible. I thought you were…"

She broke off, unable to finish her sentence.

Mina and Senta hugged and cried. Senta, who had held everything together until now, let it all out in her sister's arms, sobbing her heart out, trying, and failing, to tell Mina what had happened.

Michael stood back alongside Jeroen, the emotion of the moment making it hard for either of them to utter a word in case they, too, lost it.

Senta finally calmed down and told Mina what had happened to Anna and her father. She saved the news of Sofie until last, and when she told her, Mina collapsed into her arms, and they cried together for several more minutes.

Finally, Mina let go of Senta and threw her arms around Michael. "I thought I'd lost you."

Unable to speak, Michael held her tight, savouring her touch and fragrance, although the latter was overwhelmed by the fires and the smell of discarded oil inside the garage.

After a long pause, he composed himself enough to speak. "I thought I'd lost you too. Everyone that's left is at my safe house. We can't stay here because the soldiers have closed this road off."

"Where's the radio?" Jeroen broke in. "Is it working?"

"Yes, but I haven't been able to run the antenna wire because of all the soldiers outside. They came right after the bombing stopped and I haven't been able to get out."

"We need to leave." Michael was insistent. "It isn't safe here."

As they spoke, a commotion erupted on the blocked road outside. Jeroen placed his finger to his lips to silence everyone and pointed at the door on the side of the garage.

"Is the radio hidden?" he whispered to Mina.

She nodded. "Yes. I hid it underneath a pile of sacks in the corner."

Jeroen opened the door and peered outside. Almost immediately, he jumped back inside and locked the door.

"They're everywhere. Soldiers are in the courtyard, running towards that road." He pointed to the blocked-off road.

Michael pulled a newspaper from the bottom corner of the window facing Noordmolenstraat. All four crouched down and watched what was happening in the melee outside the garage.

Michael and Jeroen exchanged glances. Both knew the consequences if they were captured, and both had an unspoken agreement that none of them would be taken alive. If the Wehrmacht were searching for them, then this was where it would end.

Michael had his weapon ready as he watched through the window. At least fifty soldiers now lined the street outside, their weapons in their hands.

They faced the building opposite the garage, so whatever was going on, it didn't appear as if they were the target. The soldiers parted, and a vehicle came to a halt on the side of the road a short way from the garage on the opposite side of the street.

Michael's fist clenched, and his mouth set in a snarl when he saw who emerged from the vehicle.

Kreise!

Chapter 64

SS Sturmbannführer Kreise stood back while the Wehrmacht did his dirty work. On his order, a squad of soldiers shot the lock off the front door of the house opposite the repair garage.

Michael and the others watched through the windowpane as they burst into the house. Nothing was heard for several minutes, until the soldiers reappeared, pushing and shoving a middle-aged man with a bald head in front of them.

The man had his hands raised in the air, and Jeroen let out a sharp, sudden yelp when he got a good view of his face.

Two soldiers crossed the street to stand outside the garage window. The man they'd arrested stood in the middle of the road while the soldiers aimed their weapons at him. Kreise stepped forward, taking command of the situation.

"Karel de Graaf, you are under arrest for aiding the resistance in the city. I suggest you tell me where Jeroen and the rest of his group are hiding, because otherwise, things will get very painful for you."

"I don't know where Jeroen is."

De Graaf sounded and looked calm, but Michael knew that on the inside, he'd be terrified.

"You know exactly where Jeroen is hiding, and you'll tell me one way or the other. It would be better for you to tell me now." Kreise's last sentence dripped with malice, and Michael's knuckles turned white as he clenched them tightly.

"Take him," Kreise ordered the soldiers.

Jeroen ground his teeth next to Michael. It was obvious he knew this man, and they'd watched with morbid fascination as Kreise put the fear of God into him before having him whisked away for questioning.

Torture, more like, Michael thought as the soldiers grabbed de Graaf and dragged him to a waiting truck. De Graaf protested his innocence all the way, and when he reached the truck, he turned his head and faced Kreise one last time.

"How?" de Graaf asked.

Realisation dawned on him, as he guessed who had given him away. "You never asked me where Zobart is hiding." He glared at Kreise. "The real traitor lives like a lord in the Englishman's home he always coveted. He's the one who betrayed me, and he'll betray you when he gets the chance. Jeroen will discover who betrayed me, and he will kill you all. Zo—"

Kreise stepped forward and struck de Graaf hard in the face. De Graaf collapsed in a heap, silent and bloody.

The Wehrmacht soldiers picked him up and threw him into the rear of the waiting truck. Michael's heart was heavy as he watched helplessly as the truck disappeared out of sight.

"Search the house from top to bottom." Kreise barked his orders at the soldiers. "I'll be at my headquarters questioning de Graaf. Remain on standby for when he tells us where Jeroen and Fernsby are hiding."

The Wehrmacht officer sent a group of his soldiers into the house, and the rest he dismissed. The street fell silent again as Kreise followed the truck to the police cells where he was holding the political prisoners.

When the soldiers had gone, Jeroen let out a loud sigh and turned around, slumping against the wall underneath the window. Michael replaced the newspaper so nobody could see inside and faced Jeroen.

"You clearly knew who he was," Michael said. "Who is he?"

In the dim light of Mina's torch, Jeroen's face twisted into a mask of utter hatred. "His name is Karel de Graaf."

"He's in charge of the housing committee on the city council. He provided the safe houses we needed to operate in case of a German invasion."

Jeroen paused before adding. "He was also the liaison between myself and Wilhelm Zobart."

"Who knew about this, other than yourself and Zobart?" Michael asked.

"That's the thing. Nobody knew. Zobart must be the traitor, and if it's the last thing I ever do, he'll pay for what he's done. Karel de Graaf is a good man, with a wife and two children."

"What does this mean to us?" Senta asked. "Will Kreise be able to find us now?"

"Not while you're in my safe house," Michael said. "But you can't go anywhere near any of the places you stayed at before. Kreise will know where they are before the night is through, and he'll have soldiers searching for you at every known location."

"What do we do now?" Mina whispered.

"We stay hidden, out of sight," Jeroen said, his jaw set. "Then we find Zobart, and we kill him."

A thought suddenly struck Michael, and he grabbed Jeroen's arm.

"I know where Zobart is."

"I heard his words," Jeroen answered. "But I don't know what he meant."

"I do. He said that Zobart is living in the Englishman's home he always coveted. Sir Robert Stourcliffe did a lot of business in Rotterdam, and he had a very expensive home here. Zobart was a known associate of Sir Robert, and I bet if we can find his home, we'll find Zobart."

"You said his name is Stourcliffe?" Jeroen asked, his eyes wide in the torchlight. "Isn't he the one who betrayed your country to the Nazis?"

"The one and only."

"Then I know where he lives."

Jeroen led the way back to the safe house in Overschie. All the way back, Michael was consumed by thoughts of finding Stourcliffe's house and taking out Zobart.

That was his mission, and then he was ordered to make his way back to England. For him, though, one vital piece was missing from Dansey's orders.

Kreise!

Chapter 65

After a few hours of sleep, Michael awoke to see what was left of Jeroen's resistance group.

The radio was tuned to a Dutch station, and the broadcaster was speaking rapidly in a serious tone.

Mina pushed a steaming cup of coffee into Michael's grateful hands and kissed him gently as they came together.

"What's the latest?" he asked.

"The news channels report that Holland is surrendering to the Germans." Jeroen looked up from the kitchen table. "General Henri Winkelman, the commander-in-chief of the Dutch armed forces, is meeting with the Germans right now, and an announcement is expected shortly."

Jeroen's eyes filled with unshed tears. Michael's heart tightened, and he placed a comforting hand on the Dutchman's shoulder. He knew how he would feel if Britain fell, and his heart ached for all the Dutch men and women who would now be subjugated to Nazi rule.

"They think they've won." Jeroen's voice was tinged

with a mixture of sadness and anger. "But they have another think coming. We will never surrender to them, and we will strike back from the shadows until every last one of them is dead and that madman Hitler is forced to surrender."

"The French and the British will beat them," Michael said reassuringly. "They'll be back over the Rhine before you know it."

"I wouldn't be so sure," Jeroen said. "So far, they've looked to be pretty unbeatable."

"Nobody is unbeatable," Michael said harshly. "It might be difficult, but we will prevail. We have to, or the entire European continent will be under Nazi rule."

Jeroen stared defiantly at Michael, nodding his head in agreement.

"I need to find Robert Stourcliffe's house," Michael changed the subject. "That's where the man Kreise arrested last night said Zobart was hiding. Zobart has done a lot of damage to both Holland and Britain, and he needs to be stopped."

"Wilhelm Zobart's treachery has cost the lives of countless brave Dutch men and women," Jeroen said. "He will pay the price, and his head will be mine to take."

"I don't care who does it," Michael said. "All I want is to see him dead and then I have to leave."

He glanced over at Mina, who looked back with a defiant sadness in her eyes.

"When this is over, I want you and Senta to come with me to England. We'll be together, and you will be safe there."

Mina's lips trembled as she looked at Michael, her eyes resolute. "I love you, Michael," she whispered, her voice catching. "But this is bigger than us."

Her gaze drifted to the resistance fighters huddled over

the map. "I can't abandon them to the Nazis. My place is here, fighting for our future."

"There's no time for sentiment," Jeroen cut in. "The Englishman owned the most prestigious home in Rotterdam, and I know where it is."

Michael took a long, loving look into Mina's eyes before tearing himself away to focus on Jeroen's words.

"Show me," he said.

Jeroen pointed at a circled mark on the map. "The house is here, by the side of the Kralingse Plas, or lake, as you'd say in English. It's on the north shore of the lake, and is isolated and gated."

Michael bent forward to see where Jeroen was pointing. He gave a low whistle when he realised what he was looking at. Images of a similar home in the suburbs of Berlin flooded his mind as he remembered Admiral Ludsecke's home from his last mission, where he successfully captured the Kriegsmarine's U-boat plans from the aristocratic admiral.

"You look like you've been there before," the ever-astute Jeroen said.

Michael shook his head. "Not this one. I've been to a similar one somewhere else. What do we know about it?" He changed the subject.

"It's big and sits at the edge of the lake." Jeroen blew out his cheeks. "There are no other houses anywhere near it, and it sits at the end of a long driveway in the woods."

"Security?" Michael asked.

"We don't know. None of us has ever been there. It's the most exclusive part of the city, reserved for only the wealthiest of people."

"Stourcliffe certainly fitted that description," Michael said. "I need to go out there so I can see what I'm up against."

Jeroen grabbed Michael's wrist. "We're doing this together. Zobart has betrayed us in the worst possible way. Whatever he has done to your country, he has done to us many times worse."

Michael sighed. Jeroen was correct, and although he didn't want to drag Mina or Senta into it, he knew he had no other choice.

"You're right," he said. "We do this together. But let's get one thing straight right from the start. I'm in charge of this mission, and if you *are* going to be involved, you'll all follow my orders. Is that understood?"

Jeroen looked at Michael and their eyes locked for more than was normally comfortable. Neither shifted their gaze, and the tension in the small kitchen rose as they stared at each other.

"I trust you, Englishman." Jeroen finally broke away. "You will lead the operation, but know that we will go our own way if the situation demands it."

"Fair enough."

The two men shook hands.

"Now let's get to work."

Chapter 66

Five days later, Senta adjusted her cap to make sure that every strand of her newly-dyed dark hair was tucked away. Kreise would, by now, know all about Mina and Senta, and he would be on the lookout for the telltale blonde hair both girls possessed.

Jeroen's men had spent the last three days hidden in the deep woods that overlooked the secluded mansion on the north shore of Kralingse Plas.

They'd observed the daily routines around the mansion, taking particular notice of when deliveries were made, who was making them, and what they were delivering.

They also noted the comings and goings of staff members, such as cleaners and gardeners, and they carefully observed the guard tower to see when and how they changed shifts, and how observantly Zobart's private guards performed their duties.

Armed with everything they needed, Jeroen worked with a local bakery that supplied the mansion. The owner was a fiercely proud former soldier, and after the formal surrender of Holland to Germany, he readily agreed to work with the resistance without asking questions.

Now, with the basket on the front of her bicycle, Senta cycled the seven kilometres to the grandiose, aristocratic area known as Kralingse Plas.

The basket was full of freshly baked bread, and to the devastated city and its German occupiers, she looked just like any other ordinary Dutch girl going about her everyday business.

The biggest issue was her lack of Dutch, but as most Germans didn't speak the language, Jeroen considered her safe in that regard. Just in case, he'd spent several hours going over the words she'd need to carry out her mission. If the conversation became deeper, she'd just act dumb and pretend she was hard of hearing.

Nobody stopped her along the way, and Senta sighed in relief as she left the ruins of the city behind her. She hit the lake on the west shore, and as she cycled around the edges of the water, she marvelled at the opulence of the houses that spread out close to the shoreline.

From what she could see, most of the development was on the south shore, where several large houses lined the road. The east shore looked almost as bereft as the north, although she did see a couple of large properties along the bank.

A marina was to her immediate right, so she turned left and followed the road around the lake until it turned sharp right into the north shore.

Here, the trees and woodland were much thicker, and the narrow lane took her into the woods away from the water. A short while later, the lane rejoined the lake, and Senta got her first view of the massive mansion that Zobart now called home.

Her grip tightened on the handlebars as nausea

churned in her stomach and she swallowed hard, fighting to keep her composure. She was here to strike a blow at the heart of the Nazi machine, and she would happily die for the cause if it ultimately helped rid Europe of Hitler and his evil regime.

The lane ended at the high walls of the mansion where she turned left along an even narrower lane and re-entered the woods. Following the wall for what seemed like an eternity, she turned right and rode a short way until she reached the wrought-iron gates set in tall stone pillars that informed any visitors of the affluence and importance of the occupants.

Senta sighed and took a deep breath, stopping momentarily to look into the deep woods, feeling comfort knowing that Jeroen and his men were in there somewhere, ready to come to her aid if needed.

Approaching the gates cautiously, she noted the stern faces of the two guards dressed in German army uniforms. Their presence, now everywhere in the city, was a stark reminder of the occupation and the dangers that came with it.

"Delivery for Herr Zobart," she said in German.

She handed over her forged papers, her internal organs reacting as if she'd been poisoned. The guards scrutinised the papers, and Senta struggled to control her hands, gripping the handlebars to stop them shaking.

After the longest pause, the guard passed her papers back to her and stepped aside. His comrade opened the gate and waved her through. She passed with purpose, a front for the turmoil that she felt inside.

Once inside the grounds of the mansion, she cycled around slowly, observing every detail, no matter how small.

The expansive grounds included massive gardens at the rear of the house, replete with a swimming pool and tennis courts. The landscaped gardens had flowerbeds displaying an array of colours that looked as pretty as anything she had ever seen. A central fountain topped off the magnificent display of opulence.

At the front, more expansive gardens led to a private boathouse that no doubt housed more than one boat for Zobart to use for recreation on the lake.

Senta turned her attention to the front of the house, with its tall, ornate windows, and noted it had eight steps leading up to the grand entrance.

The kitchen entrance was around the back, so she pushed her cycle around the house, taking the time to notice as much detail as she could for later.

Several men wearing the black uniform of the dreaded SS roamed the grounds. They were heavily armed, and Senta assumed they were Zobart's personal protection detail.

Five more, no doubt Dutch Nazi sympathisers, stood near the side of the house.

One of the SS men ran to her, yelling at her to stop. His face was red, and Senta's heart skipped a beat. She was on her own inside the grounds, and if they discovered she was spying, her life would be in grave danger.

"What are you doing?" the guard yelled.

"I'm sorry," Senta replied in her native German. "I've never been here before, and I'm lost. I'm trying to find the kitchens for this delivery."

The guard yanked back the cloth covering the loaves of bread and demanded to see her papers. Senta's breath caught in her chest as he scrutinised them for far too long.

He thrust the papers back at her, and when he spoke, his tone had softened. "This is a big place, and it's easy to get lost. The kitchen entrance is over there." He pointed to a door that was far less elaborate than the others she had seen around the property.

"Thank you," she said.

Senta blew out her cheeks and approached the kitchen doors. She took a good look around the entrance because it was surrounded by thick bushes and shrubs. The door itself only had a single lock from what she could see, so this could be a good place to gain entry.

The hard part would be getting to this point, past the guards, who seemed to be very attentive and alert.

She knocked, and a short while later, the door opened. A woman in her mid-forties spoke to her in rapid-fire Dutch, which Senta didn't understand a single word of.

Realising she wasn't Dutch, the woman became suspicious and rummaged through her basket carefully. When she found nothing out of place, she calmed down and waved her away.

Senta got a good look at the inside of the kitchen, taking careful notice of the inside locks. As she'd suspected, the door only had one lock. There wasn't a bolt on the inside, so this was probably the place for Michael and Jeroen to gain entry.

She waved at the guards watching her every move and pushed her bicycle to the gates, where the two men on guard searched her basket, presumably to make sure she hadn't stolen anything from inside the kitchen.

Satisfied, they waved her out, and with a sigh of relief, Senta cycled as calmly as she could away from the traitor's home.

Chapter 67

For security reasons, Senta took a different route back to the safe house. She looked in the woods for Jeroen, but try as she may, she couldn't see anything.

She pedalled through the bombed-out ruins of the city centre so she could see the devastation with her own eyes, and when she got there, she immediately regretted her decision. The sight of people's faces etched with desperation as they searched through the debris for missing loved ones broke her heart.

As she approached a junction with a town square, a gathered crowd stopped her in her tracks. A group of Nazis stood at attention at the top of the steps leading to a grand building that Senta had never seen before.

More and more joined the crowds, forcing Senta farther and farther forward until she was almost at the front. Feeling uncomfortable, she began wriggling her way towards the side so she could get out and make her way back to her new temporary home.

The crowd went quiet as a group of men sharply dressed in Dutch army uniforms were marched out in front of the crowd. Their leader was not manhandled or mistreated, but instead, walked with his head held high in a show of dignity and resistance.

He stopped in the centre of the steps and turned to face the crowds. Another group appeared, and they looked to be senior German officers.

Senta almost choked when she saw another man appear and approach the microphone at the top of the steps.

It was Albert Kreise! The sight of his familiar, despised face sent an icy shiver down her spine.

Kreise cleared his throat and pointed at the Dutch officer.

"My name is SS Sturmbannführer Kreise, and I am responsible for the security of Rotterdam and The Hague. The man before you is Kolonel Maarten Janssen, the beloved leader of the Dutch forces in Rotterdam."

Kreise fell silent for a moment while he waited for the murmurs to calm down.

"Kolonel Janssen means a lot to you. I know that, and that is why he is being paraded before you today, to show you we are not the evil, cruel invaders many of you believe us to be. The kolonel is being well treated, as is befitting an officer of his rank and stature."

Kreise again paused for effect before continuing.

"He is here to show you how we treat your leaders. If you respect our authority, you will be treated with the same respect. If you defy us, or work with the resistance, you will face the consequences, which will be harsh and immediate."

Senta had seen enough. Janssen's face painted a picture of quiet fury, and Senta knew he would never surrender, no matter how many times they paraded him in front of the citizens of the city.

Jeroen would never surrender either, and Senta would stand alongside him to the bitter end.

Edging her way out of the melee, she broke free of the crowds and caught the eye of Kolonel Janssen as she walked away. He gave her a brief nod of his head as if to tell her to continue fighting, no matter the cost.

A wave of patriotism washed over her. Though she wasn't Dutch, the shared struggle and suffering of the people had woven a deep connection into her heart.

More than most, she knew what the Nazis were capable of, and she would never surrender as long as she had breath in her body.

She nodded back at Janssen and shuffled away from the crowd. Kreise was still rattling on in German about how great and lenient the occupiers were, and how they would make Holland a great country again.

She ignored his rhetoric, and while everyone was fixated on his words, she made her escape to the safe house, where she would reveal her findings to Michael and Jeroen.

It was time to put Senta's gift, or superpower, as she called it, to good use. Her eidetic memory combined with her talent as an artist would enable her to create several drawings portraying Zobart's mansion in vivid detail. What Michael Fernsby would do with it was up to him.

As Senta navigated the war-torn streets, her thoughts drifted to the Englishman. She had resented him at first for the chaos he'd brought to her family. But now, after seeing his genuine love for her sister and his relentless fight against the Nazis, her feelings had softened.

Fernsby hated the Nazis, and he was highly skilled at what he did. Senta realised as she rode her bicycle down the bumpy cobbled streets that she'd changed her mind about the English spy.

I actually like him. I never thought I would think that, but I do. So, I hope he stays alive, because I actually care for him.

She smiled to herself at how the war was changing her attitude towards people she'd decided to hate long ago.

Now she would do everything in her power to help the English spy, and she would stand by his side through thick and thin, no matter how dangerous the mission was going to be.

She dismounted outside the bombed-out apartment complex that was formerly her home, and pushed the bicycle through the rubble to the rear of the safe house, making sure nobody was following her.

Once inside, she half ignored the relieved faces as they greeted her like a long-lost friend, and locked herself in the bedroom she shared with Mina. Well, at least some of the time. Most of the time, Mina was with the Englishman.

She grabbed some paper and a pencil and concentrated as her hands moved swiftly on the paper. She sketched the mansion's layout from memory. Each line and detail, especially the kitchen door and its surroundings, emerged with meticulous precision.

She also drew Kolonel Janssen standing proudly against the aggressor, and she added Kreise in the foreground, knowing his face would provide the motivation Jeroen and Fernsby would require if they were to pull this mission off successfully.

An hour later, Senta proudly presented her artwork to Michael and Jeroen, who waited patiently alongside everyone else in the cramped safe house.

Chapter 68

Michael spread the drawings out on the kitchen table and turned towards Senta, who was being smothered in Mina's relieved embrace.

"These are incredible, Senta. Truly," he said, his voice filled with genuine awe.

Senta disentangled herself from Mina's hug, meeting Michael's gaze with a modest smile. "Thank you. I just want to do my part."

"You're sure they're accurate?" Michael asked.

"They are accurate," Mina cut in. "Senta has a perfect memory. She's the best asset any resistance group could ever have."

"Yes, she is," Michael agreed. "These are better than anything I've ever seen from London. We could do with you over there."

Senta smiled. "My place is here, but I'd be willing to help whenever I can."

Mina pulled Senta towards the bathroom to help dye her hair back to its natural colour, leaving Michael, Jeroen and the rest of the resistance men in the kitchen.

"She really has an eidetic memory?" Michael asked.

"I know it's hard to believe, but she does. All she has to do is see something once and she can recreate it with incredible accuracy," Jeroen said.

"That's a gift that makes her even more of a target for the Nazis," Michael lowered his voice. "You need to take good care of her, as she's the greatest asset you've got."

"I know," Jeroen answered. "And that's why I use her sparingly. If the Nazis ever find out about her, they'll move heaven and earth to take her from us."

"We could use her in London," Michael repeated his earlier statement. "She could do wonders for the war effort."

"That's up to her," Jeroen said. "As great as she is, I do worry about keeping her safe. Every organisation on both sides would covet her if it ever got out."

"You say that now." Michael glared at Jeroen. "Yet a few days ago, you were accusing her and Mina of betraying you."

Jeroen's face turned deep red. "I didn't accuse them of anything," he snapped. "Someone was betraying us, and they were the obvious candidates."

"And yet it wasn't them. It was Zobart all along." Casper, who'd stood quietly studying the drawings, chimed in. "I told you that, Jeroen, but you refused to listen to me."

"I was wrong." Jeroen looked his friend in the eyes. "I was wrong, and you were right. I won't make that mistake again. Both Senta and Mina are vital assets."

"Especially Senta." Michael drove the point home. "She has a special gift. It's so rare that every intelligence organisation on earth would covet her, so please be careful with her, Jeroen."

Jeroen didn't answer. Instead, he closed his eyes and

bowed his head. It was obvious to Michael the enormous responsibility of protecting such a precious and rare talent weighed heavily on his mind.

Someone as special as Senta could change the course of the war, but that was a conversation for another time, Michael decided. Right now, he was grateful for her unique abilities as it would help him complete the gruesome task he'd been set by his masters in London.

He turned to the drawings and set about making his plans with Jeroen.

Chapter 69

Three days later, they were ready.

Michael and Jeroen waited beside an empty warehouse in the darkness by the side of the blown-up railroad tracks close to downtown Rotterdam.

The luminous dial on Michael's watch told him it was 10.42 pm. From their earlier reconnaissance runs, the Wehrmacht patrol should pass by in the next thirty minutes, and when they did, he was ready.

Casper was hidden by the side of the road less than one hundred feet from them, and Kees was on the opposite side of the road.

Neither Michael nor Jeroen were talkative, and the men waited in silence as the tension mounted. Everything they'd planned relied on the success of this operation, and as dangerous as it was, they had to succeed.

Michael felt the familiar pangs of terror banging away at his ribs, and he welcomed them like an old friend. The fear heightened his senses, and he needed the adrenaline to flow to be at his ruthless best.

Jeroen stepped from foot to foot in a nervous display

that told Michael that he, too, was experiencing the same feelings and reactions.

Twenty minutes later, the sound of an approaching vehicle made Michael shudder and shiver involuntarily.

It was time.

Casper rose from his hiding place as Kees ran into the middle of the road. The approaching vehicle slowed down as it caught Kees in its headlights.

From his vantage point behind the warehouse, Michael watched as the vehicle's searchlight cast its powerful beams on Kees, who stood rooted in apparent fear in the middle of the road.

A split second later, Kees bolted across the road and joined Casper, who fired a shot at the vehicle as they ran towards the darkness of the warehouses.

The vehicle slammed into gear and went after them, their searchlights probing the shadows for the two men.

Casper and Kees skidded around the corner of the warehouse where Michael and Jeroen waited. The Wehrmacht patrol, possibly sensing a trap, came to a halt before reaching the end of the warehouse.

Sweat trickled down Michael's forehead as the familiar growl of the German engine reached his ears. The sight of the Kübelwagen, or the bathtub as he'd always called it, sent a shiver down his spine.

He shuddered as he remembered the last time he'd encountered one of the bathtub-shaped vehicles. The memory of driving it into a swollen river near Hamburg with the bodies of two dead soldiers in the back made him feel sick, and he pushed the thoughts from his mind and focused on the threat that now confronted him.

Shouts in German accompanied the sound of slamming doors and boots thumping onto the ground. Michael and the others spread out and slunk farther into the shadows behind the warehouse.

Casper quickly scaled the drainpipe to the roof and disappeared, leaving Michael alone.

The sound of German boots on gravel grew louder. Michael crouched in the bushes, his muscles tense, ready to spring into action. Two German soldiers came into view with their rifles at the ready.

A commotion erupted from the other side of the warehouse. The two German soldiers stopped and ran back to aid their comrades.

Michael threw his knife from the bushes, catching one of the soldiers square in the back. He yelled out and fell to the ground. His companion skidded to a halt and turned around, but he was too late.

A sudden explosion shook the windows of the warehouse, and it was quickly followed by a second one as Casper and Jeroen took out the bathtub at the front of the warehouse.

As Michael approached at speed, the remaining soldier spun around. He raised his weapon to fire, but he was too late. Michael's Walther PPK roared into action, firing two bullets into the young soldier's chest.

He was dead before he hit the ground.

Michael turned around and ran back to the injured soldier trying to get to his feet. One more bullet to the temple dropped him like a stone.

Casper joined him, and they quickly stripped the uniforms from the dead soldiers. Michael's heart felt heavy at the sight of two young men not much older than he was lying dead before them. He hated war, and he felt a wave of self-loathing for the part he was playing in this brutal conflict.

Casting the dark thoughts from his mind, Michael

helped Casper drag the bodies into the empty warehouse, and they dumped them alongside the others, who Jeroen and Kees had killed.

The bathtub was destroyed by the grenades that Casper had thrown down, and the four men made sure the driver was dead before pushing it inside the warehouse.

Taking the MP-40 submachine guns from the dead soldiers, they shouldered the weapons.

Jeroen closed the doors to the warehouse, and the four men quickly vanished into the night before more Wehrmacht patrols arrived at the scene. Michael hoped the carnage wouldn't be discovered for a few days, which would give them time to carry out their mission before the city was locked down and the inevitable reprisals began.

Chapter 70

The four men walked through the night for over two hours to Kralingse Plas and the woodlands at the rear of Stourcliffe's old home.

Jeroen led the way through the back streets and dark alleyways to avoid the German patrols, and they laid low when they did come across them.

The men silently took their positions in the dark woodlands on the north shore where they could keep their eyes trained on the house.

They changed into the German uniforms, an act that always made Michael want to vomit. Knowing that its former owner was dead made his skin crawl, but he quietened his emotions and changed in silence.

After refreshments from the rucksack he carried everywhere with him, the four men took it in turn to do thirty-minute stag duty while the others slept.

At four am, Michael woke Jeroen, who sidled next to him in their vantage point.

"The men know what they're doing?" Michael asked.

Jeroen nodded. "We all do."

"Shift change is at seven thirty. We have to be in and out by then." Michael relayed his orders to Jeroen.

"We know. But I'm not leaving until I know Zobart is dead."

"None of us will leave if we're still there at shift change," Michael reminded him. "They'll know they're under attack and there will be too many of them."

Jeroen nodded again. Michael knew he wouldn't risk his men's lives for the sake of his own vanity. Whatever else he was, Jeroen was a skilled fighter who loved his men, and Michael respected him for it.

Jeroen woke Casper and Kees, and together they checked their weapons. Michael hid his rucksack and turned to the three men staring at him.

He checked his watch. It was four thirty.

"Zobart will be waking up soon. It's time."

Without waiting for a response, he led the way out of the trees, and in a well-planned movement, the men broke into two separate groups.

Michael and Jeroen approached the gatehouse while Kees and Casper scaled the wall at the rear.

The two guards at the gatehouse lowered their weapons when they saw two Wehrmacht soldiers approaching them.

"What are you doing here?" one of the guards asked.

Without hesitation, Michael threw his knife at the one who spoke, catching him in the neck. Jeroen pounced on the other, silencing him immediately and giving him no chance to raise the alarm.

Michael retrieved his knife and wiped the blade on the dead guard's uniform. Then he made sure the gate was closed so nobody could enter or leave.

They ran to the rear of the house and quickly located the kitchen door where Casper and Kees were waiting for them. Three dead Dutch collaborators were slumped over a flowerbed near the doorway.

Michael slammed the butt of his MP-40 on the handle of the door and stood back as Jeroen kicked it open.

A startled cook, presumably preparing breakfast for the Nazi guards, threw his hands in the air as the four men ran inside. Another ran away before he could be stopped.

Jeroen spoke to the cook in Dutch, assuring him he wouldn't be harmed. He ordered him to stay put and keep out of the way.

He grabbed the cook by the arm and pulled him towards him. "Where is Zobart's bedroom?" he asked.

The man, wide-eyed and terrified, stammered as he replied in Dutch.

"What did he say?" Michael asked.

"Third floor. All of that floor is the private rooms of the owner, which is Zobart now that the Englishman is dead."

Michael raced out of the kitchen towards the stairway. The kitchen worker who'd run away was shouting at an SS officer, who was yelling down the telephone line, reporting the attack to his superiors.

With all surprise now gone, Michael went loud. He raised his Walther PPK and shot the SS man. Then he grabbed the telephone receiver and slammed it down, ending the call.

Michael and Jeroen raced up the stairs, leaving Casper and Kees to take care of whoever was on the ground floor. They were working on the assumption that Zobart's security detail would be limited during the night, and that most of them would be asleep.

Bursts of gunfire from MP-40 submachine guns ripped through the silence, and Michael heard Casper yelling at someone before another burst of gunfire erupted.

Once the ground floor was cleared, Casper's job was to cut the telephone lines, and as Jeroen had complete faith in his men, Michael believed he would carry out his duties diligently.

The upstairs floors were in complete darkness, so Jeroen shone his torch while Michael followed with his weapon at the ready.

A door to their right burst open, and at least two men ran into the narrow corridor. Jeroen continued up the stairs to the third floor, leaving Michael alone to face the threat.

Michael threw himself to the ground and lay still, listening for any movement from the darkness. A creaking floorboard not ten feet from where he lay gave someone away, and he opened fire.

A groan, and then a thud as whoever Michael had shot collapsed to the floor. Luckily, the corridors were narrow, and it was virtually impossible for anyone to open fire while they were standing behind someone else.

As soon as he'd fired, Michael leapt to his feet and jumped into the open stairway leading to the third floor. Seconds later a burst of gunfire peppered the area where he'd lain just moments earlier.

Michael listened intently, and when the footsteps reached the stairwell, he leapt out, landing on top of his assailant, and as they fell to the floor in a tangled mess, Michael's hand felt the cold steel of the man's pistol pressed against his chest.

Michael pushed hard against the gun, and a split second later it went off, firing into the wall and grazing Michael's side. His own weapon had been knocked out of his hands, so he reached for the man's hand, pinning it down underneath his weight.

The assailant was strong, and his hot breath brushed against Michael's cheek. As they struggled and fought,

Michael lost his grip on the man's wrists, and the next thing he knew, he was knocked aside by the heavy blow of the pistol crashing into his temple.

For a moment, everything went black, and Michael's body went limp. The assailant pushed Michael off him and rolled over. He was almost on top of Michael, and his hand with the weapon was free.

Michael's senses flooded back, and he knew he was in serious trouble. Instinctively, he grabbed the man's hair and pulled his head towards him as hard as he could.

The man yelped, and as their heads clashed, Michael sank his teeth as hard as he could into the assailant's cheek. Hot liquid splashed all over his face, but he ignored it and bit even harder.

The man screamed, and Michael, still biting hard, rolled over. In intense pain, the man yielded and rolled with Michael. Now on top, Michael let go, sat up, and crashed his fists as hard as he could into the assailant's face.

The enemy underneath him groaned, and his body fell limp. Michael grabbed the pistol from his hand, turned it towards him, and fired.

The man jerked and made a strange sound. Hot blood splattered over Michael, but he didn't care. He forced himself off his assailant and rose to his knees. The man beneath him groaned, and then fell silent.

Michael didn't have time to reflect on what he'd just done. There were other SS soldiers in the house, and they had to be dealt with before they could get to Zobart. Michael would pay a heavy emotional toll later, but right now, he didn't have time to dwell on it.

He rose to his feet and ran up the stairs to find Jeroen.

At the top of the stairs, he stepped over a dead body. The lights were turned on, so he could see what was going on. Another body lay halfway out of a room into the corridor, and farther along, another sat against the wall covered in blood, groaning and talking to himself.

The door at the end of the corridor was open, so Michael stepped inside to find Jeroen standing in front of a large wardrobe, speaking to someone in Dutch.

"Jeroen, it's me, Michael," he said, hoping Jeroen wouldn't mistake him for an enemy combatant.

He joined him at the wardrobe and saw who he was talking to. Zobart's unmistakable bushy eyebrows gave him away as he cowered inside the wardrobe, still wearing his pyjamas. Someone else was behind him, but Michael couldn't tell who it was.

He stepped away, leaving Jeroen with Zobart while he swept the rest of the third floor for more enemy guards. Satisfied that Jeroen had killed them all, he rejoined him and closed the bedroom door.

He prised Jeroen away from Zobart, who looked at Michael, terrified, and backed farther into the deep closet, forcing whoever was behind him to gasp for air.

Michael dragged Zobart out of the closet and forced him to his knees and Michael's heart dropped as the second person emerged. He may have disliked Zobart before, but now he completely despised him.

It was a young girl, no older than ten or eleven. She was half dressed, and from the look on Jeroen's face, he was about to kill Zobart, not for what he'd done to the resistance, but for what he'd done to this defenceless little girl.

The girl screamed when she saw Michael, and she tried running for the door. Jeroen stopped her and gathered her up in his arms. "It's alright, little one. He's a friend and I promise, nobody is going to hurt you."

Jeroen turned to Michael. "Are you hurt?"

Michael shook his head. "A few cuts and bruises, but that's all."

"You might want to look in a mirror." Jeroen waved his head at the young girl. "I've got this. Go look at yourself."

Michael remembered the blood splatter from the fight, ran to the bathroom, and saw his reflection in the mirror. He was covered from head to chest in blood, his face a grotesque picture of someone who'd been savagely attacked, and although it wasn't his blood, he could see why the young girl was so frightened of him.

He washed his face quickly in the sink and watched as the water turned bright red as he washed the blood of his enemy off his body. Looking more human, he wiped himself down with a towel and rejoined Jeroen, who was holding Zobart in a vicelike grip by the throat.

Michael got a good look at the girl. She had shoulder-length brown hair and stood about chest height. She was thin, almost frail, and had freckles all over her face.

The fear in her eyes broke Michael's heart, and he resisted the urge to comfort her, as it would probably frighten her even more.

"Do you speak English or German?" Michael asked the young girl.

She shook her head, her eyes as wide as dinner plates.

"Her name is Margriet, and she's eleven years old." Jeroen spat the words out, his eyes never leaving Wilhelm Zobart. "She's from the orphanage downtown that was destroyed by the bombs."

"So, she has nobody left to care for her?" Michael asked, his anger at bursting point.

Jeroen shook his head. "There are plenty of people who will care for her. I gave her my personal guarantee that a loving family would take her in and look after her."

The respect Michael had for Jeroen shot up another ten notches. "Thank you," was all he could think of to say.

Turning to Zobart, who was on his knees staring at the window, Michael grabbed his jaw and turned his face towards his. "You have betrayed your country, and you have betrayed the brave men and women of the resistance who relied on you for their protection."

Zobart stared straight ahead, his face a mask of hatred.

"You also betrayed my country, but above all else, you have betrayed the laws of decency. I was sent here to kill you for your betrayal, but instead, you will die for the crimes you have committed against this young girl and God knows how many others like her."

Zobart closed his eyes. "You can't kill me. I know too much about the Nazis and what they are planning to do in Europe. You need me, or they will walk all over you, just as they have done to the rest of Europe."

Michael looked up and nodded at Jeroen, who understood what he was trying to say. Jeroen took Margriet's hand and led her out of the bedroom, whispering to her in Dutch, and although he couldn't understand the words, Michael knew exactly what he was saying.

He was telling her to look straight ahead and not to look at the dead bodies strewn across the floors.

Michael turned his attention back to Zobart, who he still held by the jaw.

"Take me to Dansey. He knows how valuable I am to your country. I will tell him everything, and only then will British intelligence have an advantage over the Nazis."

"That's not happening."

Michael raised his Walther PPK and ended Zobart's life.

He'd seen enough.

Chapter 71

SS Sturmbannführer Albert Kreise glanced at the luminous dial on his watch. The loud, heavy knock on his door had better be important. At five twenty in the morning, it had better be life or death.

Or Reinhard Heydrich. He'd been known to call at all hours of the night.

The heavy thuds continued, and Kreise threw on some trousers before grumpily opening the door to see who was disturbing him. A young, night-duty SS officer stood before him, his face pale and his eyes wide as he faced his commanding officer.

"Well?" Kreise snapped. "It'd better be important."

"It is, Sturmbannführer. SS Scharführer Keller called from Herr Zobart's home. He was cut off mid call, but he told us the house was under attack."

"Under attack?" Kreise thundered. "From whom?"

"He didn't say, sir."

"When did this happen?"

"Just now. I came to inform you right away."

Kreise slammed the door in the young officer's face

and paced around his cramped bedroom in his temporary headquarters.

Who would attack Zobart? And why?

Then it hit him. Any thought of sleep immediately dispelled, Kreise grabbed his shirt and jacket and raced from his room. The only ones who would be audacious enough to attack the Dutch Minister of Defence and Maritime Affairs would be Fernsby and Jeroen.

They were the only people who had good reason to despise Zobart, and they were the only ones who had the means to do it.

Kreise ran to the sleeping quarters of Major Lohr, the head of the Brandenburgers. He was annoyed to find his bed empty, so he ran to the quarters where his men slept.

"Where is Major Lohr?" he shouted, turning on the lights and waking up everyone in the room.

All four of them.

"Where are the rest of your men?" Kreise asked, his voice less aggressive.

"The major took them on a mission. We were relieved of duty as we were up for the previous seventy-two hours on another job," one of the men said as they all leapt out of their beds.

"Well, we have an emergency. The Dutch Minister of Defence and Maritime Affairs is under attack from the resistance, and we believe they've already killed the SS men guarding him. He's important to us, and we need to rescue him."

"Isn't this a job for the Wehrmacht?" the Brandenburger asked.

"No," Kreise snapped. "This one's personal. We have to do it."

"Did you get permission from Major Lohr?"

Kreise's nostrils flared. "Zobart will be dead by the

time we find him. He'll be filled in when he gets back here. This is an emergency, and I am ordering you to assist me. Now move!"

"Yes, sir!" the man seemingly in charge shouted.

Kreise ran outside and commandeered the first vehicle big enough to carry himself and the four Brandenburgers. He drove the VW Kübelwagen to the front of the building, cursing at the gears as they crashed and ground as he struggled to tame the beast.

The four Brandenburgers ran outside, heavily armed and ready for action.

"You drive," Kreise ordered the man in charge. "I'll give directions along the way."

"What are we facing?" the lead Brandenburger asked.

"There can't be many resistance members left," Kreise said. "We killed most of them at the lake and the cafe. So, only half a dozen or so."

"That's all?" the Brandenburger was clearly expecting to face greater odds.

"Then there's the English spy, Fernsby. He is to be left to me. Capture him, but do not kill him. Do you understand?"

"How will we know what he looks like?"

"He's the youngest of them all, and he's the only one that can't speak Dutch."

"That's enough. We'll get him for you, sir."

Kreise gave directions to the mansion on the north shore of Kralingse Plas. They were stopped three times by Wehrmacht roadblocks, and each time Kreise angrily told them to step aside, as it was a matter of great urgency.

By the time they reached the front gates, it was five fifty. Kreise hoped they weren't too late.

The two young Wehrmacht soldiers at the front gate lay dead inside the gatehouse. Kreise's neck turned deep red in fury as he opened the gate to allow the Kübelwagen passage to the house.

The lights inside the house blazed brightly, and the Brandenburgers lined up outside, checking their weapons one last time.

"Go inside and find Zobart," Kreise ordered. "Kill any man that opposes you, but not Fernsby. I want him alive."

"We'll do our best, sir," the lead Brandenburger answered.

The men spread out and ran inside. Kreise remained outside, waiting for the all-clear from the highly trained soldiers who were experts in this type of warfare.

Bursts of gunfire erupted from inside the house and Kreise let out a deep sigh, relieved they'd got there in time.

Finally, after all this time. Fernsby is mine.

Chapter 72

Michael stopped dead in his tracks at the sound of gunfire from the floor below. He, Jeroen, and Margriet were on the second floor, stepping over the bodies of the men Michael had killed earlier.

Casper and Kees were below, waiting in silence for them before they headed back to the safe house in Overschie. There hadn't been any gunfire for a while, so either they'd found more Nazis or collaborators hiding somewhere, or there was a new attack.

Michael wasn't going to take a risk, not with Margriet in tow. He led the way into one of the bedrooms at the far end of the corridor and pulled open the door to the large wooden wardrobe in the corner of the room.

"Wait in here and don't make a sound," he whispered to Margriet. "Don't come out under any circumstances. We'll find you once we know it's safe."

Margriet's frail body shivered under the glow of the bedroom light. Although she didn't understand what he was saying, she knew what he meant. Michael felt pity for her, but now wasn't the time to show it. He took his torch from his pocket and passed it to her.

Margriet gave a watery smile as Michael pushed her into the recesses of the wardrobe. As he closed the door, he held his finger to his lips and smiled at her.

The brave little girl gave him the thumbs up sign.

Jeroen killed the light, and the two men crept towards the stairs. The commotion on the ground floor had reached fever pitch. Casper was screaming at someone, and in the middle of it, Michael heard the one voice that made his blood boil.

Kreise!

Armed with a renewed resilience, he looked at Jeroen, who must have heard it too. His jaw was set in granite, and he snarled at Michael as he pointed for them to go downstairs.

As they approached the top stair, a figure emerged on the bottom step that was lit by the bright lights of the ground floor. Kees stood below them, clutching his stomach. "Kreise," he yelled, before another bullet smashed into his skull, killing him on the spot.

Michael and Jeroen leapt back up the stairs and stood on either side of the stairwell. Michael pointed to the ceiling, indicating they should try to find another way out. Jeroen nodded in agreement.

"We have your friend down here. What's his name? Casper?" The familiar voice of Albert Kreise drifted up the stairs like a creeping fog.

He spoke in English, telling Michael that he knew he was there.

"Come on down and we'll spare his life. You are surrounded, and you have nowhere to go. I want Fernsby, and I want Jeroen. The rest of you will be left alone. I give you my word."

Michael's lips curled into a sneer. Kreise's word meant nothing, and he didn't believe a single word. Casper was going to die, and there was nothing they could do to help him. He didn't know how many men were with Kreise, but he had no doubt there were more than enough.

Michael once again pointed upstairs. Jeroen flinched, but gave the thumbs up. Michael pointed for Jeroen to go, and indicated he would go get Margriet.

"This is your last chance," Kreise shouted up the stairs. "Give up now, or Casper dies."

Neither Michael nor Jeroen answered, because it would give away any advantage they may or may not have.

A few seconds later, Kreise shouted up again. "Have it your own way."

Casper was shoved to the bottom of the stairwell. He raised his hands as if to protect himself, and a second later, he collapsed from a single bullet.

Jeroen's chest heaved, and Michael clenched his fists. He hated Kreise more than any man alive, but right now there was nothing he could do about it.

A burst of gunfire up the stairs forced the two men back from the edge of the stairwell. Heavy footsteps pounded the stairs, and Michael knew whoever had killed Casper and Kees was now coming for them.

Jeroen ran down the corridor towards the rooms at the far end. Michael did the same on the other side, and by the time the men reached the top of the stairs, the corridor was empty.

Michael killed the lights, so the men had no way of knowing how many rooms there were, or how many men were up there.

He hid in the room opposite where Margriet was. If his last breath was saving her, then it was a worthy death. He just hoped it didn't come to that.

He pushed everything out of his mind and listened as door after door was kicked open. He lay underneath the bed with the MP-40 aimed at the door.

The doors next to him smashed open. He listened to see if more than one at a time was being kicked in, but they weren't. The corridors were narrow, and that was one thing that served in his favour, no matter how many men were out there.

Finally, only two bedrooms remained. Michael tensed his muscles and forced the fear from his mind. Calmness washed over him, comforting, like a hot water bottle on a frosty night. Everything seemed to slow down, and his mind felt empty and at peace.

The door flew inwards, its hinges shattered. The barrel of a rifle appeared, but Michael held his ground and waited. Someone on his knees crouched near the doorway, his feet giving him away in the light of the corridor; the men must have turned them back on.

Michael fired two bullets at the area between the wall and the doorframe. A groan, followed by a thud as a soldier fell into the doorway. Michael immediately fired again, making sure it wasn't a ploy to flush him out.

Another soldier leapt over his dead comrade and opened fire in the room. Michael, from underneath the bed and beneath the soldier's arc of fire, couldn't miss, and he didn't.

The soldier fell over his dead comrade, and everything went quiet. Michael waited in case it was a trap, but after what felt like an age, he realised it wasn't. There had been two soldiers on his side of the second floor, and he'd killed them both.

Cautiously, he rolled out from under the bed and ran to the wall near the door. He changed his magazine and once again fell to the floor. He rolled over the dead soldiers, ready to fire at anything that moved.

Gunfire came from the opposite end of the corridor, followed by shouts. First one burst, and then another, as Jeroen and the soldiers exchanged fire.

Michael lay on the floor and took aim at the shadows at the other end of the corridor that was lighted by a single bulb. He squeezed once, and then again, releasing a burst of six rounds. Two men fell silent.

He ran to the stairwell and peered around the edge. All he could see were the dead bodies of Casper and Kees. No other sounds could be heard.

He jumped past the gap in the stairs and ran towards Jeroen. When he reached the last door on the right, he checked the two men for signs of life. One was dead, but the other groaned when he shook his body.

Michael moved his weapon and grabbed him by the hair, yanking his head up in a painful arc.

"Jeroen," he whispered. "It's me, Michael. Are you alive in there?"

"I'm alive."

Michael turned his attention to the wounded soldier. "How many of you are there?" he whispered in German.

The soldier didn't answer, so Michael yanked his head even farther up, forcing more grunts from beneath him.

"I'll ask one more time. How many of you are there?"

"Four." The soldier's voice was hoarse and pained.

Jeroen stepped over the two men and knelt by the stairwell, in case more were on their way.

"Where is Kreise?" Michael asked.

"Downstairs."

Believing him to be telling the truth, Michael let go of the man's head. He searched him thoroughly, removing several pistols and knives from his body. He took the weapons and stood up.

"Make a move towards us and you're dead. Do you understand me?" Michael kicked the soldier in the ribs.

"Ja. I understand." The soldier lay prone.

Michael stepped towards Jeroen, who had joined him in the hallway.

"He says there were only four of them," he whispered in Jeroen's ear. "Kreise is alone down there if he's telling the truth."

Jeroen stepped softly down the stairs, taking each one slowly. Michael remained behind, his weapon ready to fire at the slightest sign of movement.

Jeroen reached the bottom and lay on the ground with his feet facing the stairs. Michael followed, being careful to make as little noise as possible.

The two men searched the ground floor, but there were no signs of any more soldiers. Finally, Michael stopped, lay on the ground, and indicated for Jeroen to follow suit.

"Kreise! We know you're here. Your soldiers are dead and we're coming for you." For many reasons, that statement felt good, and he waited for the inevitable retort from Kreise.

What he wasn't expecting was for Kreise to run off like a coward, but the sound of a bathtub engine firing confirmed that was exactly what he was doing.

Michael and Jeroen ran after him, but by the time they reached the courtyard, the Kübelwagen was at the front gate and out of range.

"He's a coward," Jeroen said.

Michael kicked the wall in frustration. "I never had him down as a coward."

"We need to get out of here before the Wehrmacht arrives," Jeroen said, turning back inside the house.

Michael ran after him and caught him up at the wardrobe where Margriet had remained hidden throughout the entire ordeal. Michael helped her out, and he held her hand as the frightened little girl stepped over dead bodies on the way out.

Jeroen stopped and said a silent prayer over Casper and Kees, and then they both helped Margriet into the woods. Michael retrieved his rucksack, and together, they made their way back to the safe house and Mina.

Chapter 73

Mina rushed to the door when the bedraggled group reached the safe house mid morning. She was about to throw herself on Michael when she stopped in her tracks.

"Who's this?" she asked, staring at the pale-faced young girl hiding between Michael and Jeroen.

"Mina, this is Margriet," Michael answered. "She's from the orphanage that was destroyed in the bomb blitz."

Mina held out her arms and smiled at the girl with the freckled face. Margriet smiled, and for the first time since they'd met, Michael saw happiness, or perhaps it was relief, in her eyes. Whatever it was, it cheered him to see her less tense and scared.

"Come on in." Mina held Margriet's hand. "Are you hungry?"

Margriet nodded.

Michael knew they had little food to share, but nobody would mind giving their rations to her, especially once they knew the circumstances of how Michael and Jeroen had found her.

Senta ran down the stairs at the sound of Margriet's

voice, and the sisters set about making her feel welcome. After polishing off a bowl of porridge, sweetened with the last spoonful of honey Senta had been saving for days, Margriet went upstairs with Senta to clean herself up and rest.

Mina turned to Michael. "What happened?" she asked. "Where's Casper and Kees? And where did you find Margriet?"

"That's a lot of questions." Michael slumped wearily on the couch. Jeroen, who had remained quiet all the way back from Zobart's house, sat next to him.

"They didn't make it." Jeroen's eyes filled with unshed tears. "Kreise found out about us being there and attacked us with a squad of soldiers."

He looked at the floor. "They killed Casper and Kees."

"We were lucky to escape with our lives," Michael took over.

"What about Margriet?" Mina asked.

Mina cried as Michael explained how they had found her in the wardrobe behind Zobart.

"What kind of man can do such a thing?" she asked, her eyes red from anger and sadness.

"A monster who deserved to die, that's who," Michael answered.

"What are we going to do with her?" Mina asked. "That was the last of our porridge. We don't have enough food to feed us, never mind a young girl."

"She needs a good home, and I know just the place," Jeroen said. "Please ask Senta to come down here."

Senta rejoined the group downstairs, her eyes red and puffy from the tears that stained her face.

"She cried herself to sleep, but not before she told me what that monster had done to her. I hope you killed him."

"He's dead," Jeroen said flatly. "It's too dangerous for

her to be with us. Senta, I need you to take her to the bakers where you got the bread from the other day. Tell him I sent you and explain what happened to Margriet. He's a good man who will take care of her for us."

"You trust this man?" Senta asked.

"With my life."

"Alright. I'll take her as soon as she wakes up."

"Now that we've struck a blow to the Nazis, they'll step up their search for us," Michael said. "Mina and Senta will stand out like a sore thumb with their blonde hair and thick German accents. It isn't safe for them to be out on the streets."

"I'll dye my hair again," Senta said. "And Mina's too. That'll make us less obvious."

"Fair enough," Michael said. "But we need to find somewhere else to stay. This house is too exposed, and we're too easy a target here."

He turned to Jeroen. "Can you think of anywhere?"

"We can use the garage where Mina stored the radio," he replied. "It's not ideal, but it will do for now. It's more protected than we are here, and it will do until we can find somewhere else outside the city."

Michael looked at Mina, the sadness in his eyes telling her everything she needed to know.

Mina's eyes clouded, and she reached for Michael's hands.

"It's called war, Michael." Jeroen intervened. "What gives you, me, or anyone else here, the right to a happy life when the world is falling apart? There's so much evil in the world today, and we owe it to everyone that's already lost their lives to fight for what is right."

Michael nodded. He knew they were correct. Hell, he even felt the same way, and yet when it came to Mina, he was a bumbling wreck who would do anything to protect her.

"I know. I just can't help but want to protect her, that's all."

"It's called love." Jeroen's tone softened. "It's the one thing the Nazis can't destroy. We'll win this war, and then, God willing, you two will survive and make a life together. But for now, you need to use your skills to defeat Hitler and his Nazis."

Michael and Mina locked eyes. Jeroen was correct, and there was nothing else either of them could add.

Chapter 74

The courtyard between the two buildings was quiet in the early morning sunshine. Jeroen led the way, with Michael and Mina close behind. Senta had taken Margriet to the bakers with a note from Jeroen.

The garage with the flat roof came into view, and Jeroen unlocked the side door with a set of keys from his pocket. All the while, Michael stayed vigilant in case they were being watched, but everything appeared serene and calm.

The windows were still covered in newspaper, and the inside was dark and smelled of oil. Jeroen turned on the light, which barely lit the interior of the forty foot by twenty foot garage.

Michael remained outside to make sure nobody could see in with the lights on, and happy they couldn't, he entered and locked the door behind him.

The dark-coloured vehicle sat in the middle of the garage, and Jeroen patted the roof as he walked past. "This is our last resort escape vehicle," he said. "It belongs to my father, but it's there in case of emergencies."

Michael glanced at Mina, still struggling to get used to her new look. Her hair, now dark brown, had been cut to the neckline, and she looked completely different from how she'd been just twenty-four hours earlier.

Mina caught him staring at her. "What? You don't like my new look?" she flirted with him, flashing her eyes and tilting her head to the side.

"You'd look beautiful even if you were bald."

Mina punched him. "No, I wouldn't," she said.

Mina pulled a pile of sacks away from the corner, revealing the radio transmitter and the coiled antenna wire she'd hidden the last time she'd been there during the bomb blitz.

"Nobody has been here." Jeroen let out a sigh of relief. "It's far from perfect, but the courtyard gives us protection when coming and going, and Noordmolenstraat is normally a quiet road."

"It wasn't the last time we were here," Michael reminded him, remembering Kreise and the squads of soldiers lining the street when they arrested the housing officer.

"That was then. I chose this place because of its seclusion," Jeroen answered. "They won't be back. You two wait here. I'm going to get some supplies and I'll be back. Remember, it's two knocks followed by four."

Michael locked the door behind him, and when he turned, Mina was laying the sacks along the floor.

"What are you doing?" he asked.

"When are you leaving?" she replied.

Michael felt a crushing weight settle in his chest, and each breath was a struggle. He leant against the vehicle, the cool metal a steadying presence as he fought against the tide of despair.

"Jeroen and Senta won't be back for a while." Mina's eyes glinted in the dim light. "Come here, Michael."

The oppressive weight immediately lifted, and Michael rushed into Mina's outstretched arms.

"I love you," he said as they fell to the floor.

Chapter 75

Later that afternoon, Jeroen and Senta returned, Jeroen with a bag full of supplies, and Senta with a heavy heart after leaving Margriet with the baker.

"She clung onto my arm and wouldn't let go." Senta's voice broke as she told her story to Mina. "The baker was kind, and assured her he would take care of her until they found her a family, but she wanted to stay with me."

Senta wiped her eyes. Michael, still trying to get used to Mina's new look, now had to contend with Senta looking the same.

"I told her she wasn't safe with us, and that the Nazis were searching for us, but she didn't care. She was so brave, Mina. She wanted to join the resistance, so I told her that in a couple of years when she was older, I'd find her, and she could join us. That made her happy."

"I thought you were gone a long time," Mina said, holding her sister's hand. "I was worried about you."

"I didn't come straight back here. There was something else I wanted to do first."

"What?" Jeroen snapped. "We agreed you'd come

straight here. You know how dangerous it is out there for us."

Senta looked at Mina, ignoring Jeroen's harsh words. "You look different. Your cheeks are flushed. What were you up to while we were gone?"

Mina blushed and looked at Michael. Both grinned and said nothing.

"You're disgusting." Senta hit Mina playfully. Even Jeroen smiled, which was something he'd rarely done since Michael had first met him.

"Well?" Mina asked. "Where did you go?"

Senta's face turned serious and she pulled a rolled-up piece of paper from her pocket and held it out to Michael.

"I know you're leaving tonight, so I walked the route you need to take, at least some of the way. I was stopped three times, but it w—"

"They stopped you three times?" Jeroen cut in angrily. "What were you thinking?"

"I wanted to check my new papers now I look different. Now we know they work. Anyway, I was on a very important mission."

"What was so important that you had to risk everything for it?" Jeroen asked.

"This." Senta passed the paper to Michael. "It's your route out of Rotterdam tonight. You need to go inland to avoid the bigger waterways before turning west towards France."

Michael stared at Senta, stunned that she would do this for him.

"You can't use the bridges over the Nieuwe Maas because they're heavily manned, so you need to go east until you clear the city. Then you cross the river and head around Rotterdam."

"You did this for me?" Michael asked, unrolling the map over the car bonnet.

"Well, I didn't go all the way to France, if that's what you're asking."

Everyone laughed, and the tension fell from the room as Senta explained Michael's escape route out of Rotterdam.

"I've drawn a line where you should go. Obviously, if the way is blocked, you'll have to find a different route, but that's where you should strive to end up."

"I don't know what to say," Michael said, poring over the hand-drawn map.

"Just say you'll stay alive so you can take care of my lovelorn sister over here." Senta bumped her shoulder into Mina, who giggled in response.

"I can't promise I'll survive the war, but if I do…" Michael broke off and took Mina's hands in his. "If we both survive, I promise I'll take care of her for the rest of my life."

"You're going to make me cry," Mina said. "Stop it."

They kissed, and then Michael took the map to the rear of the vehicle so he could study it in silence. Mina and Senta stayed together, sorting out the supplies and making sure the radio was ready for the message Michael had to send to London. Jeroen sat alone, lost in his own thoughts.

Michael worried what would happen with the small, ragtag group of resistance fighters. He knew Jeroen would recruit new members, but he couldn't stop the deep ache in his bones that kept him awake at night worrying about Mina and Senta, the only remaining members of the group.

This was going to be a long war, and he doubted they would be able to stay ahead of men like Kreise for the duration of it. The ramifications of them being captured drove him crazy, and he refused to allow the thoughts to enter his mind.

Mina set the antenna wire up through the small window at the rear of the garage that overlooked the tree-lined courtyard. When it was ready, she turned the radio on and set it to the frequencies Alison Turnberry monitored in Unit 317's headquarters beneath the streets of London.

Michael coded his final message that, when decoded, read:

Target dead. Mission accomplished. Headed west. Fernsby.

Simple, effective, to the point.

Mina sent the coded message and waited for a response. Every second the radio was turned on, Michael sweated more and more. He knew the Nazis scanned for radio transmitters, and he was terrified they would discover her before she'd completed her transmissions.

Ten minutes later, Mina wrote the response from London. After it was done, she turned the radio off, removed the headphones, and passed the coded message to Michael.

Decoded, he read the message to himself before burying it in one of the hidden compartments in his rucksack.

Mission accomplished. Apt 204, 37 Av de Sceaux, Versailles. Marcel Bertrand. Avoid BEF and Wehrmacht. Over.

Now he knew where he was headed, he wondered why he had to avoid the British forces in France. From the brief radio reports he'd heard, the Wehrmacht was pushing deep into France with their blitzkrieg tactics, but the radio made it sound as though the Allies were holding their own.

The tone of the message told him otherwise. It appeared the Germans were winning rapidly, and if he was to avoid contact with the BEF, that could only mean that

Sanders didn't want him anywhere near the army if, and when, it was defeated in northern France.

Michael bit his lip and frowned. The future of Europe looked bleak, and he felt helpless as he looked across at the people he loved dearly. If France fell, Britain would stand alone against the might of Nazi Germany.

The future of Europe looked very bleak indeed.

Chapter 76

Jeroen and Senta left Michael alone with Mina for the rest of the day. They lay on the sacks together, their arms and legs intertwined. Mainly they slept, but in between they whispered to each other, making promises both knew they couldn't keep.

They tried keeping their emotions in check, but now and then Mina would sob quietly in Michael's arms, breaking his heart and making him want to disobey his orders and remain by her side.

As nightfall came, the four of them sat solemnly on the cold floor, eating the meagre supplies Jeroen had scrounged from sympathetic shop owners.

Mina held Michael's hand in hers, savouring the feel of her touch. He tried to commit the feelings to memory, though he knew it would never be enough. His eyes filled as they locked onto hers, and for the millionth time that day, he was lost in the deep blue ocean of beauty that stared back at him.

Jeroen, who had barely spoken a word all day, broke the gloomy silence. "You have been a great friend to us,

Michael. None of us here today would be alive if it wasn't for you, and I will be forever grateful for your help. It's people like you that will turn the tide against the Nazis, and I am proud to have known you."

Already filled with more emotion than he could handle, Michael dropped his head as he felt warm tears run down the side of his face.

"I'm sorry you lost so many men. I wanted to kill Kreise, but even if I did, all they'd do is send someone else in his place who might be even worse."

Michael paused and took a deep breath. "I pray for your continued survival, my friend, and I will be sure to tell the authorities in Britain all about you, in the hope that more help can be offered."

Jeroen shook his head. "That won't happen. If France falls, Britain will stand alone as the only country not yet under their control. They will need every man and woman they can muster to continue the fight."

"That may be true," Michael answered. "But helping the resistance fight from within is important, and I'm going to stress that to them after seeing it so many times with my own eyes."

"Something else has been bothering you, Jeroen," Senta said.

Michael watched her, full of admiration at the way she had stepped up since the bombing. And the gift she had was a blessing to the Allied cause.

"What is it?" she asked Jeroen. "We are all that's left, and if we are to survive, there can be no secrets between us."

Jeroen shook his head. "There are no secrets. We are defeated, and unless I can rebuild and trust new men and women, we are as vulnerable as a butterfly in a tempest."

Mina gripped Michael's hand so hard he could see his

fingers turning white, but he didn't care; every moment was precious, and he never wanted it to end.

"Michael was right all along," Jeroen said softly. "Once the dust settles on the occupation, two blonde German girls who can't speak Dutch will stand out a mile. You'll be captured as sure as I am sitting here this evening, and there is nothing I can do to protect you."

"We're not leaving, if that's what you're saying," Senta said, her voice rising in pitch. "And anyway, we're no longer blonde."

"You are brave, Senta." Jeroen touched her arm. "You both are. But your presence here makes it more dangerous for me, because you stand out too much. You need to be somewhere where you are safer, where a bigger group can better protect you. Especially you, Senta, because you have a special gift that every nation, both friend and foe, will covet once word gets out."

"And it will," he added.

"What are you saying?" Mina asked. "That you don't want us here anymore?"

"That's not what I am saying at all. I cherish both of you, and that is why I must insist that you leave with Michael. I would never forgive myself if I kept you here for selfish reasons, and then something happened to you."

The garage fell silent while Jeroen's words sank in.

"You must leave and go to England. Or at least get to France, where you can find a resistance group that can take care of you and use your special gifts to help us win this war and kick the Nazis out."

Mina and Senta exchanged a deep look that only sisters who had endured terrible times together could understand. Michael remained silent, keeping Mina's hand pressed in his.

After a long pause, Mina broke the awkward silence.

"We've had this discussion between us many times, Jeroen. I would give anything to go with Michael, because watching him walk away from me is the hardest thing I will ever have to do."

She stifled a sob and gripped Michael's hand even tighter.

"The Nazis have taken everything from us. They took our farm, our parents, and even forced us out of our own country. We have lost friends, and now I'm going to lose Mi—" Mina's voice broke.

"We're staying here to fight." Senta finished the sentence for her. "Even if it costs our lives, we're staying. And if you think we're putting you in danger, then leave us. We will fight alone, without you."

"I would never do that to you," Jeroen said. "That is not what I meant. What I'm saying is that you need to leave. Tonight, with Michael, who will get you safely out of Holland."

"And then what?" Senta asked. "We hide in England where we will be hated by everyone for being German? Especially when the Luftwaffe drop their bombs on London and Britain's other cities. We can't leave, Jeroen. We can't."

"It's time." Michael rose to his feet. "I want nothing more than to take Mina and Senta with me, but I cannot and will not force them. You are one of the bravest men I have ever met, Jeroen, and I know you will do everything you can to protect them."

Jeroen, Mina, and Senta rose to stand with Michael one last time.

"You are right." Jeroen clasped Michael's arm. "I will rebuild the resistance in Rotterdam and make the Nazis regret the day they ever set foot in my city. As for these two stubborn mules…" He broke off to prod Mina in the ribs.

"I'm proud and honoured to have them fight by my side. With their skills, we will strike back and do our best to disrupt them at every turn."

Michael held Jeroen's gaze. They shook hands, and then Jeroen grabbed him by the shoulders and gave him a bear hug that almost took the breath out of his body.

"I see now why Mina loves you so much. She believed in you long before any of us ever knew you, and it has been a privilege. Take care, Englishman. I wish you all the best of luck. The way to France will be paved with danger, and you must be very careful. But you are the most resourceful man I have ever met, and I know you will make it back to England safely."

"The same goes for me, Jeroen. You are a true giant in the resistance, and you will rebuild and bring chaos to the Nazis. Be careful, my friend. And please take care of my precious Mina until I can find her again."

The two shook hands once more, and Jeroen melted into the gloomy darkness of the garage now the light had been turned off after dark.

Senta gave Michael a kiss on the cheek. "My sister needs you, so be careful out there. When the war is over, I look forward to being your chief bridesmaid."

Michael smiled and hugged Senta tightly. Out of anyone he had ever met, Senta was the one who impressed him the most. Her maturity and skill set were unmatched, and that worried him and reassured him in equal measures.

"Thank you for the map. I wouldn't have known where to go without it."

"It's not much, but it will get you out of Rotterdam, at least. Remember, head for Dordrecht, and then east until you reach Gorinchem. From there, find Antwerp. After that, you're on your own."

"Thank you. I couldn't do this without you."

One more kiss on the cheek, and Senta vanished into the recess with Jeroen. This left Mina, and with tears streaming down her face, she threw her arms around his neck.

"I will never forget our time here, my love. If this is all we ever have, I shall cherish it for the rest of my life." Her tears fell onto Michael's collar, soaking it through.

"This is only the beginning," he replied. "I love you, Mina Postner, and I will be back for you. Remember, once the war is over, wait for me at Ryskamp. As long as I am alive, I will find you there."

"I will wait for you for the rest of my life. If I am not there, it is because I didn't survive the war. Never doubt my love, Michael. I am yours and you are mine. Forever."

"Forever," Michael repeated.

Their lips met one final time, and with the scent of her body lingering in his nostrils, he pulled away and unlocked the door.

"Remember that I love you. Forever."

"Forever." Her words drifted through the dark as Michael stepped into the night.

Chapter 77

The courtyard was dark and silent, which is exactly what Michael wanted. He checked his rucksack for the hundredth time and felt its weight after Mina had stuffed it with hard cheese, bread, and even an apple. A bottle of water topped it all off, and with everything he needed, he set off for France.

The luminous dial on his watch told him it was ten thirty, so he had at least seven hours of darkness before he had to find somewhere to hole up for the day.

Senta's directions would get him to the edge of the city, but after that he'd go his own way. It was a little less direct than Senta's directions, but from the map he'd been studying, there was less likelihood of running into a garrison of German soldiers.

At least, that's what he hoped.

With his heart heavy, the first thing he did was retrace his steps to Kralingse Plas where Zobart had lived in Robert Stourcliffe's lakeside mansion. He didn't need Senta's map for this because he'd memorised the way before the Zobart mission.

The walk took him forty-five minutes, and he was grateful he didn't run into any patrols along the way. Every few minutes, he stopped and told himself he had to keep going. Every fibre of his body screamed at him to turn around and go back to Mina, but he knew he couldn't.

Why did we have to live in these times? Why couldn't we have met in the inter-war years when we could have been together without any problems?

But then he remembered that if it hadn't been for Kristallnacht, he would never have met Mina at all, and he took comfort that at least something good had come out of the chaos and heartache caused by the Nazis.

For him and Mina, at least.

At Kralingse Plas, he rested in the woods on the east side of the water. For some reason, he felt safe in the forests and woodlands. The trees gave him protection, and he enjoyed the solitude they provided.

He sat against a tree trunk and took a sip of water. All the time, his mind raced with thoughts of Mina alone in the middle of war-torn Rotterdam, surrounded by men like Albert Kreise. It was the hardest thing he'd ever done to walk away from her, and he vowed to never do it again should they be lucky enough to meet in the future.

Wiping his eyes, he stood up and carried on. He had a lot of ground to cover if he was to get clear of the city by daybreak.

Using the alleyways and avoiding the roads as much as he could, he headed east towards the flat farmlands and his way out of Rotterdam.

As the night wore on, clouds rolled in, blocking the moon from lighting the way. The stars disappeared, and it wasn't long before raindrops fell, drenching Michael to the skin.

Ignoring the cold rain that stung his face, Michael

pushed on, and an hour later, he took another small break in some shrubbery. He wasn't too far from the edge of the city, and so far, he'd avoided the patrols he'd seen. One more push and he'd be safe.

After a drink of water, he got to his feet and entered the side of the road on the edge of the shrubs. His mind, full of the memories of Mina's sighs and touch, never noticed the roadblock at the junction waiting in the darkness.

As he approached the four-way stop, a light from a vehicle was turned on, blinding him in its wake.

"Halt!" The command he'd been dreading pierced the silence. He thought about running back to the shrubs but didn't have time. The soldiers were already pointing their weapons at him.

He held his hands in the air, his chest pounding so hard he could barely hear the soldier barking at him. An all too familiar tingle ran down his spine, turning his legs to jelly.

With no other choice, he slowly approached the bright light.

"Halt!" The command came again, this time more forceful.

Michael stopped, noting there were two soldiers at the roadblock. One stayed where he was, all the time training his weapon on Michael. The other stepped towards him, cautiously, indicating with his rifle that he was to keep his hands in the air.

The soldier aimed his rifle at the ground, telling him to drop to his knees. Michael complied, all the while keeping an eye on the two men. He mentally kicked himself for not paying attention.

This is how you get yourself killed.

"Papers!" the soldier barked. Michael got a good look

at him. He appeared to be in his early twenties, not much older than he was himself.

The vehicle shone a single light, which told Michael that it was a motorcycle. A sidecar was attached, but as he was blinded from the headlight, he couldn't tell much more from where he knelt.

The rain, which had been falling heavily, subsided to a drizzle, which could be seen in the headlight as it floated to the ground, soaking everything in its path.

Michael pointed to his rucksack on his back. He'd decided not to let the soldiers know he spoke German, and hoping they didn't speak Dutch, he chose to communicate through sign language.

The soldier indicated he could remove the rucksack to get his papers.

"What are you doing out after curfew?" the soldier barked in German. Michael held his hands in the air as if he didn't understand what he was saying.

"Papers!" the soldier shouted even louder.

The second soldier stood to the side of the headlight, and Michael could see a metal box by his feet. He recognised it immediately from his training at Ravenscourt Manor as the Feldfernsprecher 33 field telephone the Wehrmacht used to communicate with their headquarters.

The receiver was hung over the top of the box, indicating that it was assembled and ready to use. Michael sighed. He was in trouble, and he knew it.

He lowered his arms and slid the rucksack from his shoulders.

"The idiot doesn't understand German." The soldier looked over his shoulder at his companion and laughed.

"He's probably drunk," his comrade replied.

With the two men looking at each other, Michael used

the moment to act. He grabbed his knife from his belt and lunged at the soldier stood near him.

He knocked the rifle barrel to the side and smashed the handle of the knife into the soldier's temple. The weapon fell from his hand, and he slumped limply into Michael's body.

Michael caught him and used him as a shield to protect him from the other soldier. He spun him around and held the knife to the soldier's throat.

"Throw your gun down, or I'll kill him," Michael yelled in German.

The second soldier, stunned at what was happening, hesitated.

"I won't ask again."

A plan was forming in Michael's mind, but he needed to get past the soldiers first.

The soldier bent forward to lower his weapon, and as he dropped it, he grabbed the field telephone and ran behind the motorcycle where Michael couldn't see him because of the headlight.

He heard the soldier screaming down the line that they were under attack, and as the soldier yelled, the one he held came around.

Struggling, the soldier burst into life. He was much stronger than Michael anticipated, and he burst from his grip with relative ease.

As he broke free, he turned to face his enemy, and with a wild look in his eyes, he pulled a pistol from his belt and went to aim it at Michael.

He never managed it. In a flash, Michael closed the gap and buried his knife in the soldier's chest. As he heard the air expel from his mouth, Michael once again hated himself for what he was doing.

Every person he killed was another nightmare to be

added to all the rest as the body count piled up in his consciousness.

I don't have time for this right now.

Forcing the thoughts of what he'd done from his mind, Michael concentrated on the second soldier, who was still yelling into the field telephone. Michael ran around the motorcycle and threw himself onto the ground as he passed the headlight.

The soldier gripped the handset of the telephone as though he was a deer caught in a set of headlights. But Michael knew better. These were well-trained soldiers who had seen action in Holland and probably Poland before it. The man was no coward.

He was right because while the man gibbered as though terrified, he produced a pistol from underneath his leg and pointed it towards Michael.

He was too late. Michael shot the soldier in his torso, and as he fell, he let out a bloodcurdling scream.

Michael ran to the wounded soldier and knelt over him. He removed his jacket and patted him down for weapons, but he didn't have any more.

"Stay where you are while I get away and I won't kill you."

The soldier nodded.

Relieved, Michael rose to his feet and threw the soldier's jacket into the sidecar. Then he rammed the motorcycle into gear, glad of the extensive training he'd received at Ravenscourt Manor, and sped away from the scene.

He knew the Wehrmacht would soon arrive on the scene, and he had to get as far away as possible before they got there.

~

MAJOR LOHR of the Brandenburgers slammed open the door to the canteen where Albert Kreise was having a late dinner.

"There's been an incident to the east of Zobart's lake house. A soldier called on a field telephone requesting help as they were under attack from a single assailant. One of my men was monitoring the operators and confirmed the details."

"It's got to be Fernsby." Kreise jumped up and grabbed his jacket. "Where and when did this happen?"

"A minute ago. Two at the most. He stole the motorcycle and rode east."

"He's trying to get out of Rotterdam," Kreise said.

The two men ran to the Brandenburgers' truck where four more waited inside with the engine already running.

"We've got him," Kreise said with a wild look in his eyes. "He's heading east out of the city."

The Brandenburgers raced out of the Wehrmacht compound at full speed.

Chapter 78

The motorcycle and sidecar picked up speed as Michael opened up the throttle on the straight road he identified as Dorpstraat as he flew past a road sign.

His heart pounded in his chest, each beat echoing in his ears as he tightened his grip on the handlebars. He took a deep breath, easing off the throttle, forcing himself to focus and control the roaring beast beneath him.

After a couple of miles, his breathing steadied, and he got better control of the motorcycle.

From his training, he knew he was on a BMW R75, 750cc motorcycle. These rugged motorcycles were ideal for navigating the war-torn streets of Rotterdam with their powerful engines and firm, yet precise, handling.

Twenty minutes later, with the carnage behind him and the open fields not far ahead, Michael slowed to a pedestrian pace and breathed a sigh of relief.

He was almost there, wherever that was. He'd long since strayed from Senta's directions, and since the roadblock incident, he'd raced off at breakneck speed into the unknown.

All he knew was that he was headed east, which is what he wanted if he was to get out of the city and avoid the deep waters of the estuaries heading out to sea.

Unable to tell exactly where he was, Michael was relieved to see fewer and fewer buildings. The landscape seemed to be opening up into the countryside, and he knew that sooner or later he would be free of the city so he could turn south and head towards Antwerp.

From out of nowhere, a truck with no lights on blocked the road at a junction. It was dark, and Michael didn't see it until it was too late. He swerved, but the sidecar smashed into the rear of the vehicle.

The BMW spun around, throwing Michael off the seat. He crashed into the road, the gravel scraping his arms and legs as he slid to a halt in the grass at the side of the road.

Before he could regain his senses, shouts and groans came from the vehicle. It was another roadblock, and Michael hoped he'd hurt at least some of the soldiers in the pileup.

Footsteps running towards him brought him to his senses. He rolled into the tall grass on the side of the road and pulled the Walther PPK from his belt. Ignoring the searing pain from the road burn, he held his breath and listened.

Four torches came on simultaneously, each one aiming their light into the long grass. Shouts in German left him in no doubt as to who had set up the roadblock, so he fired.

And rolled.

Fired and rolled.

He did this three times, and at least twice dropped whoever was behind the torchlight. The torches went dark, and he heard shuffling on the ground as his enemies threw themselves down.

Michael rolled farther into the grass, noticing the ground beneath him getting wetter and wetter the more he rolled away from the road.

A river must be close!

A few feet farther, he rolled out into a narrow gravel lane. The instant he did, a heavy boot crashed into his midriff, knocking all the air out of his body.

Winded, Michael could hardly breathe. He curled into a ball, gasping for air and his weapon fell from his hand, lost somewhere in the pain and confusion.

More blows rained into him as whoever it was kicked as hard as he could. Michael protected his head, and although a few kicks got through, splitting a gash over his left eye, he managed to keep control of his senses.

The man screamed in German as he kicked. "Major Lohr! He's here. I've got him."

Men running towards him told Michael he had mere moments to live.

I'm not dying like this, curled up in a ball like a cowering animal.

He caught the boot as it crashed into his chest and twisted, bringing his assailant to the ground. Grabbing a handful of gravel, he leapt up and smashed it into the man's face, rubbing it into his eyes as he forced his body weight on top of the soldier.

The soldier screamed, and Michael, aware that his comrades were mere feet away, dived over the narrow lane back into the wet marshland, which it had now become.

Moments later, several voices shouted at the soldier as hands reached down to drag him out of the way. Without his weapon, Michael didn't have any way of killing them, so he rolled in the mud, getting closer and closer to the river.

If he could make it to the other side, he might make it, but he had to get there first.

More than one man ran into the marshland, but the thick mud sucked their feet into the ground, making their progress slow and difficult.

Michael, with his weight spread evenly across the mud, rolled more easily, and he could hear his assailants struggling in the marshes.

There were three men, although he was sure he heard at least one more at the roadside. That was too many for him to handle without his weapon. He had another in his rucksack, but it was no use there, where he couldn't get at it.

One of the men got close. Michael stopped and held his breath, glad of the blanket of darkness and heavy clouds. He pulled his knife and waited.

The soldier stood so close Michael could hear him breathing. He lowered his hands, listening intently for signs of Michael crawling in the mud.

Michael simultaneously crashed his knife into the man's foot while grabbing his MP-40 submachine gun with the other hand.

The man screamed and fell to the ground, holding his foot in agony. Michael thrust the knife as hard as he could under the man's chin, and as warm liquid splashed all over his hand, the soldier fell silent.

His comrades were clearly well trained, because they never shouted to him, nor otherwise made a noise. All Michael heard was the sound of them thrashing through the soggy mud towards the melee.

Michael, clinging on to the MP-40, rolled away as far and as fast as he could.

The marsh got wetter and wetter, and he realised he

was at the water's edge. He slid down a small bank and held his breath, waiting and listening.

The mud made gurgling sounds as the soldier's legs sank deeper and deeper. Michael waited until the nearest soldier was about ten feet away, and he let loose with the MP-40.

Three rounds smashed into the soldier, dropping him instantly.

Gunfire to his right thudded into the tiny bank, so Michael slid farther down until his body lay in the freezing water, which took his breath away as he allowed it to cover him up to his shoulders.

He shivered and tried ignoring the freezing numbness gripping his body. Instead, he concentrated his thoughts on the area where the gunfire came from.

But it was silent. The soldier had obviously followed Michael's lead and was close to the ground, making his passage along the riverbank easier and quieter.

The next thing Michael knew, a hand grabbed him and forced his head underwater. He bucked and fought, but his hands sank in the mud, not allowing him any traction to push himself upwards towards the life-giving oxygen just inches away.

He struggled, and then slowly but surely, the air in his lungs was gone. He felt bubbles rising from his mouth brush past the side of his face, and as his lungs seared, he thought of his beloved Mina before images of his mother and father flashed through his mind.

Suddenly, the grip on his head relaxed, and the soldier yanked him up from the water by the hair. Gasping and choking, Michael struggled for air while a torch was shining in his face, blinding him.

He couldn't see the face on the other side of the torch,

but as the panic of nearly drowning subsided, he calmed his mind enough to hear what the man was screaming.

"It's him. It's Fernsby."

Through bloodshot eyes, Michael saw his captor had short, dark hair, and looked to be in his mid-thirties. His eyes looked as dark as his hair, and whatever else he might be, Michael knew he was a highly trained soldier used to killing people.

"Bring him to me." A voice rang out from the darkness.

Kreise! Michael would recognise his voice anywhere. *What was he doing here? How has he found me so quickly?*

He didn't have time to dwell on it because the soldier snatched Michael out of the water by his hair, making him wince with pain.

As his hands rose from the thick, clinging mud that had entrapped them, Michael gripped the handle of his knife. As soon as it was free, he sliced up, out of the water, catching the soldier on the side of his face by his right eye.

The soldier yelled out and stumbled backwards, falling into the water. Michael was on him in a flash, forcing him down, thrusting for all he was worth, over and over. Warm liquid floated by his hand before the cold water took it away downriver, never to be seen again.

Michael threw himself on top of the soldier, forcing him deeper into the river, not allowing him to surface. Eventually, the struggling stopped, and the body went limp beneath him.

Michael let go, and the body of the dead soldier slowly rose to the surface and drifted off downstream.

"Lohr, where are you?" Kreise yelled. "Have you got him? Remember, I want him alive."

"Coming," Michael yelled, trying to keep his voice deep and guttural to match Lohr's tone.

He staggered out of the water, forcing his legs one at a time through the thick, deep mud that clung to his body.

He grabbed the MP-40 that was still on the riverbank and rolled out of the water.

Now it was just him and Kreise.

Chapter 79

SS Sturmbannführer Albert Kreise stood by the side of the truck, shining his torch towards where he thought Major Lohr would appear, dragging Michael Fernsby with him.

"Lohr, where are you?" Kreise's voice was tense, sensing something was amiss.

The truck and the wreckage of the BMW motorcycle blocked the junction in the middle of the road. Michael crossed the narrow gravel lane and stayed low in the grass.

Kreise must have known by now that Lohr wasn't coming, and once again, he made a move to clear the area and get out of harm's way. He turned off his torch and opened the door to the truck.

Michael lay in the grass no more than fifteen feet from his hated enemy, and in the gloomy, drizzly darkness, he could just about make out the shape of the truck.

The door opened, and he knew Kreise was once again showing what a coward he was. He fired, shooting one bullet at the open door.

A grunt, followed by a thud as Kreise fell to the ground.

Michael threw down the MP-40 and rose to his feet. He ran to Kreise, who was using the truck to get to his feet. Michael crashed into him, knocking him down again.

"Finally, it's just you and me," Michael snarled as he grabbed the SS officer.

Kreise's eyes were wide with shock and fear. Michael was so close he could see it, even in the dim light. Then they flashed with anger as he realised what was happening.

Quick as a flash, Kreise pulled a knife out of his shoe and tried to thrust it into Michael's side. Michael threw himself sideways, narrowly avoiding the blade as it sliced through his jacket.

He grabbed Kreise's hand and twisted, making him drop the knife to the ground. Then he stood up and dragged Kreise to his feet.

"Using a weapon on you is too easy," he said, shoving the wounded SS officer towards the river.

Michael's vision blurred with rage, and memories of Kreise's atrocities flashed through his mind like a relentless storm. His hands trembled with the force of his anger, each breath a battle to stay in control.

"You think by killing me you will be safe?" Kreise asked as he stumbled and fell towards the river.

Realising what he was about to do, Kreise pushed back, talking rapidly as Michael shoved him closer and harder with each touch.

"I can get you out of here," Kreise pleaded. "Nobody but us needs to know. Go, and I'll say I never saw you."

Michael knew Kreise was stalling for time.

"Take off your coat," he ordered, wanting to make sure he wasn't concealing any more weapons.

"Why? It's cold and wet."

"Now!"

Kreise started to remove his jacket, but as he did, he produced a small calibre gun. Michael saw it and grabbed Kreise's hand. He twisted hard until bone cracked and Kreise screamed in agony.

Michael didn't stop. He continued to twist, forcing Kreise to his knees.

"This is for every man, woman, and child you've ever harmed. It's for my brother, for Heinrich Adler, and the countless others you've murdered in the name of your mad Führer."

"You don't need to do this," Kreise pleaded, holding his broken wrist by his side as Michael shoved him to the water's edge.

"Nobody deserves to die more than you, Kreise. I've dreamt of this day for a long time."

"You're not a murderer, Fernsby. Unit 317 doesn't murder people."

"You're right," Michael shouted as he dragged Kreise deeper into the muddy, freezing water. "We only kill people who deserve it."

Kreise formed a fist and threw it at Michael's face, but Michael didn't even flinch when it caught him on his cheek. Instead, he grabbed Kreise by the throat and thrust him under the water.

Kreise kicked and fought, but Michael didn't stop. He held him there for a long time, waiting for the evil Nazi to stop struggling and succumb to the water, waiting to end his life.

Finally, after a long struggle, Kreise stopped fighting. Still, Michael didn't let go. He held him underwater for several minutes longer, until there was absolutely no possibility of him still being alive.

He stood rigid in the water as he released his grip and

watched as Kreise's body rose to the surface and slowly floated off down the river.

Albert Kreise, his sworn enemy and the biggest danger to the lives of Mina, Senta, and Jeroen, was dead. For now, at least, they were safe.

Chapter 80

The Wehrmacht would no doubt soon be at the scene of the carnage, and Michael had to get away as fast as he could. He scanned the scene, his eyes darting between the crumpled BMW and the hulking truck. He knew he needed a less obvious way out.

Removing the cleaner clothes from one of the dead soldiers, he crammed them into the top of his rucksack. He made sure his spare Walther PPK was inside a rubber waterproof container, and then, without hesitation, he plunged into the freezing river.

He swam for at least fifteen minutes and finally emerged, drenched and freezing cold on the other side.

Shivering uncontrollably, Michael forced himself to his feet and ran, each step shaking off the icy grip of the river as he pushed forward, desperate to put as much distance as possible between himself and the scene of the slaughter.

Thirty minutes later, Rotterdam and the woman he loved were behind him. He had around three hours before daylight, so he used it to put as much distance between himself and the city as possible.

It was a long way to Paris, and he knew it would be fraught with terrible danger. With the Wehrmacht driving forward on the Western Front, Michael didn't know if he would even beat them there. All he could do was hope, but if all else failed, he would find a fishing boat on the Atlantic coast and sail it back to England himself if he had to.

He reached another river, which he gleaned was the De Lek from the map of Holland he'd brought with him from London. Not wanting to swim again if he could help it, he found a bridge a few miles upriver that was manned by a German patrol, but not too heavily.

He lay in the wet grass, watching their movements, waiting for the ideal time to get across without being seen. He waited for over an hour, and the dawn was breaking across the night sky.

At least the rain had stopped, but if he didn't get across soon, he'd be stuck until the next night, which was the last thing he wanted.

The three soldiers took it in turns to guard the bridge, with two at any given time watching the road. As dawn broke, their replacements arrived, and the two groups stood in a circle, presumably discussing the handover.

Michael dashed to the side of the newly arrived truck, which blocked the view from the other one, and dashed past as quietly as he could.

On the other side, he threw himself to the ground and turned around to make sure he hadn't been seen. He hadn't, and his heart rate dropped to where he could breathe again.

As the morning sun rose, he reached a farmhouse on the edge of a village. He ran to the barn and hid in the corner with the chickens and the horses.

He took off the German uniform and put his own

soaked but mud-free clothes back on again, deciding he would have a better chance of getting help from the locals if he wasn't wearing an invader's uniform.

He buried the uniform in the dirt in the rear corner of the barn and closed his eyes to get some much-needed rest.

As soon as he'd drifted off, he was prodded awake by someone kicking his feet. He awoke, immediately wide awake and fearing the soldiers had already found him.

Did the guards on the bridge see me after all?

A farmer and his young son stood over him, the father pointing a rifle at his chest.

He asked him something in Dutch, which he didn't understand, so he took a chance and answered in English.

"I'm sorry, I don't understand. I'm English, and I'm trying to escape. Can you understand me?"

The farmer glared at Michael for far too long. Michael felt the familiar surge in his stomach, and he closed his eyes in fear of what he might have to do.

The last thing he ever wanted was to hurt innocent citizens, but he couldn't allow the Dutch farmer to hand him over to the Gestapo or the SS.

No, he would do as little damage as possible, but he wasn't going back to Rotterdam as a prisoner.

"Why you here?" the farmer asked in broken English.

"I was helping the Dutch resistance in Rotterdam, but we were defeated," he said truthfully.

Maybe there's hope after all.

"Where you going?"

"I'm trying to get to France. To the coast. If you let me go, I promise I'll leave right away."

The farmer and his son had a conversation in Dutch. After a few moments, the farmer turned back to Michael.

"Come." He lowered the gun and pointed towards the farmhouse in the distance.

Michael grabbed his rucksack and followed the farmer. The young son ran ahead and reappeared with a kindly-looking woman with a worried look on her face.

After being shown into the kitchen, the farmer and his wife had a heated conversation that Michael couldn't understand. In the end, he rose from the wooden chair and held up his hands.

"I'm sorry. I didn't mean you any harm, and I certainly don't want to put you in any danger. If you let me leave, the Germans will never know I've been here."

He went to leave, but the farmer's wife stopped him.

"No. You stay for breakfast. Any enemy of the Nazis is a friend of ours."

The woman set to and provided Michael with two boiled eggs and three slices of bread. Times were hard and the farmers needed the eggs for themselves, but their kindness was overwhelming, and his heart glowed from their generosity, which he did not deserve.

"Thank you," he said, wolfing down the breakfast. He hadn't realised how hungry he was, and he felt much better with a full stomach.

The food was washed down with a glass of milk, which tasted as sweet as honey.

At the end, he looked at the farmer's wife, who sat opposite, watching his every move like a hawk. "I don't know if you understand me, but I am very grateful for your help this morning."

He reached into his rucksack and pulled out a wad of Dutch Guilders. "Please, let me repay you for your kindness."

The woman pushed the money back at him. "No," she said in good English. "We don't want money. Our eldest son has been captured by them, and we don't know where he is. We hope the British and French beat them and get them out of our country."

Her eyes filled up, and she grabbed Michael's hand. "Please, Mister Englishman, we are glad to help you."

The farmer came back into the kitchen and said something to his wife.

"My husband wants to know where you are going?" she asked.

"I told him before, but he probably didn't understand me. I am trying to get to Paris so I can rejoin my unit."

The woman spoke to her husband, who gestured outside with his index finger.

"He says he can't take you to Paris, but he can take you as far as Dordrecht."

"I am very grateful." He meant it. "You have been very kind to me."

The woman said something else to her husband and turned back to Michael. "Wait here."

She vanished, and when she came back, she was carrying a clean set of clothes in her hands. "Our son is about your age, and these are his clothes. Wear them so you won't stand out if the Nazis see you."

"How can I repay you if you won't take any money?" Michael asked, completely humbled by their kindness.

If they knew what I did last night, they wouldn't be so kind.

"Win the war, that is how you repay us."

Michael went to the outside toilet to change into the fresh clothes that fit fairly well with all things considered. He took the time to retrieve the weapon from his rucksack and add the spare rounds to his pockets. He didn't know when he'd need them again, but he was sure it wouldn't be long.

Looking more like a local Dutchman, he followed the

farmer out to the barn, where he pointed at a cart full of potatoes. "In there. I take you to Dordrecht."

The woman gave Michael a hug, and her eyes filled up again.

"I hope you find your son," he said, which was completely inadequate for what they were doing for him.

The woman hugged Michael.

"Thank you," he said, climbing into the back of the potato cart and covering himself with straw.

The farmer hooked the cart to the horse, and along with his son, they set off to the markets in nearby Dordrecht.

It was going to be a long and dangerous journey, but as always, it starts with the first steps. The cart rumbled down the road, and Michael drifted off to sleep with the rocking and rolling of the cart as it bounced along the bumpy roads.

Chapter 81

SS Obergruppenführer Heydrich slammed the telephone down on the desk in his office at the RSHA building on Prinz-Albrecht-Strasse 8 in the heart of Berlin.

He glared at the wall for several minutes, his already hard, emotionless features casting a terrifying look at the secretary he'd summoned to his office.

His eyes were a window to his black soul that was incapable of emotion or empathy, and Marlene's hands trembled while she waited for his instructions.

Finally, with an icy stare that bored right through her, he spoke in a deadpan voice that was one of the most feared in the whole of Nazi Germany.

"I want the heads of the SS, Gestapo, and the SD in my office first thing tomorrow morning."

"Yes, sir. What shall I tell them is the agenda?" Marlene's voice shook as she spoke. Nobody wanted to be near the Blond Beast when he was angry, and this was the angriest she had ever seen him.

"The agenda?" Heydrich's fist slammed onto the desk, his face contorted in a snarl as he glared at Marlene.

He paused, and the secretary didn't dare utter a sound.

"The agenda is Unit 317."

"Unit 317?" Marlene blinked. She didn't have a clue what he was talking about.

"Yes, Unit 317. Do you remember Albert Kreise, Marlene?" his eyes bored through her once again.

Albert Kreise. Yes, she remembered him. He was the ambitious SS officer Heydrich had sent to Rotterdam to round up the resistance. Marlene had never liked him, but why was Heydrich mad at him now?

"Yes, sir. I remember Herr Kreise."

"He may have had his faults, but Kreise was a good man."

"Was?"

"Yes, Marlene. *Was*. Unit 317, that damned British intelligence unit killed him a few days ago, along with several Brandenburgers. They also killed our Dutchman in Rotterdam, who took care of business for us, and kept us updated with the resistance."

Marlene squirmed. She was only a lowly secretary, and she didn't know what to say when one of the most powerful men in the Reich talked to her like this.

"I'll let them know, sir."

"Let them know what, Marlene? That they killed Sturmbannführer Kreise? Most of them don't even know who Kreise was."

Marlene remained silent.

"The Führer already ordered that any member of that unit be killed on first contact, but I'm taking it further. I'm ordering that we go after them, find out who they are, and then we strike them down in their own backyard."

Heydrich's eyes bored deeper into Marlene's soul.

"I want them to bring me a plan to exterminate Britain's Unit 317. Every single one of them."

"I'll let them know, sir."

Marlene hurried out of Heydrich's office and sat in front of her typewriter. As she pressed the keys, she felt sorry for whatever this Unit 317 was. They had incurred the wrath of the most feared man in Germany, and Marlene knew he would never rest until they had been destroyed.

SS Obergruppenführer Reinhard Heydrich was furious, and that meant only one thing:

Death.

The End…

Get a FREE Book!

Before John Howard found sanctuary on the streets of Henry VIII's London, Andrew Cullane formed a small band of outlawed survivors called the Underlings. Discover their fight for life for free when you join J.C. Jarvis's newsletter at jcjarvis.com/cullane

Please Leave A Review

If you loved Ludsecke and have a moment to spare, I would really appreciate a short review.

Your help in spreading the word is gratefully appreciated and reviews make a huge difference to helping new readers find the series.

Thank You!

More Books by JC Jarvis

Fernsby's War Series

Ryskamp

Alderauge

Ludsecke

Rotterdam

Evasion Coming Soon!

The John Howard Tudor Series

John Howard and the Underlings

John Howard and the Tudor Legacy

John Howard and the Tudor Deception

About the Author

J.C. Jarvis is the author of the breakout Fernsby's War series.

He makes his home at www.jcjarvis.com

Email: jc@jcjarvis.com

Printed in Great Britain
by Amazon